At the study, the   low fire glowed
around the room. *Good, someone already lit the fire.*
Brielle slipped into the dim room, crossed to the
fireplace, and set the candle on the mantel. A flash of
lightning illuminated the room, drawing her gaze to the
shelves beside the fireplace.

She perused the shelving, trying to find the perfect
book. She realized the one she wanted was three
shelves up, and she couldn't reach that high. Climbing
to her knees on the lower cabinet, she stood and
reached to the shelving above. Her fingertips barely
touched the book she wanted. She stretched a bit more,
and just as she was about to reach the spine marked
Love Poems and Sonnets, a crack of thunder startled
her, and she fell backward off the bookcase. Her cry
was cut short when she hit something solid. A warm,
muscular chest shifted along her back, and strong arms
cradled her. Mortified, she kept her eyes shut. *How
much worse could it get?*

Then the chest shook with a chuckle. The voice
that belonged to it said, "Careful what ye seek, lassie.
Ye might find something ye aren't looking for." In utter
embarrassment, she kept her eyes shut. It was Colin.

"Ye can open your eyes, Brielle." She turned her
head farther into his chest. That was a mistake. He was
shirtless and smelled too damn good.

Stone of Love

by

Margaret Izard

Stones of Iona

Stone of Love

Cover Art by *Lisa Dawn MacDonald*

The Wild Rose Press, Inc.
PO Box 708
Adams Basin, NY 14410-0708
Visit us at www.thewildrosepress.com

Publishing History
First Edition, 2024
Trade Paperback ISBN 978-1-5092-5336-4
Digital ISBN 978-1-5092-5337-1

Stones of Iona
Published in the United States of America

Dedication

To my husband and my true love, who believed in me, told me never to give up, and showed me that anything is possible. To my kids for encouraging me to chase my dreams. Thank you for your love and support. I dedicate this book to you.

Chapter 1

The Fae believed true love was powerful enough to reach between the realms of the world, even powerful enough to save a human soul.

Brielle turned, taking in the castle grounds as the breeze ruffled the trees. Her name came light on the wind. She moved toward the sound, and the chapel ruin peeked through the woods as dusk settled on the cliff.

Standing still, Brielle stared for a moment. The ruined shell sat in the fading sunset, its black and gray shadows rising to the sky. Some buildings spoke to her, an energy she could not describe yet understood. At times it was a chill, other times a sensation of someone near her, a lightness for goodness, and a heaviness for evil.

She could swear a person stood next to her, but when she checked, no one was there.

Taking a deep breath, she released it slowly as the wind came up, carrying her name again. An awareness of something ethereal overcame her.

The broken skeleton of a once-grand chapel spoke a warning, as a chill spread up her spine. The sun shifted, casting the side of the chapel in menacing crimson. When the rays shone against the walls, the structure glowed like a beacon—a sign of hope for the future.

"Come on. John's waitin' for ye."

Startled, she turned to Ronnie as he strolled around the car, popped the trunk, and grabbed her luggage. He'd pulled the car under the *porte cochere*. Standing inside, she got a good look at the archway. The machine-made bricks showed they'd added it more recently, and from her studies she knew it wasn't part of the original castle layout.

Rounding the front corner, Brielle made her way up the castle's stone steps. The pull of the chapel's energy was intense, making it difficult not to glance over her shoulder. Unable to resist, she twisted, and the sun moved, casting the chapel back into the shadows surrounded by darkened woods, a silent sentinel for the spirits long gone.

Shaking off the sensation, she proceeded up the castle stairs. John MacArthur stood at the top to greet her. Studying him as she climbed the steps, Brielle found him younger than she had imagined from their conversations. He stood tall, with light-brown hair and a strong nose.

As she drew closer, John smiled. "Greetings, dear—I hope the drive was nice." He took her luggage from Ronnie. "We'll need the men to start the chapel renovation bright and early tomorrow morning."

Ronnie reached into his pocket, pulled out a business card, and handed it to Brielle. "Ronnie MacTavish, driver, handyman, yer foreman for the renovation project ye came halfway around the world for." She took the card as he smiled at her. It had a cartoon Scotsman in a kilt holding various tools. She glanced at him, and he winked. "Anything ye be needin' ye call on Ronnie."

She pocketed the card. "Thanks. I'll see you tomorrow. We can go over the plans for the chapel."

Ronnie waved and headed down the steps to the car.

After finishing graduate school, Brielle's next adventure was her dream job: renovating a Scottish chapel ruin.

John tilted his head for her to follow him into the long foyer. She skipped, keeping pace with John's long strides. Thankful to stretch her legs after the long flight "across the pond," Brielle skipped again as she met John's steps.

"Thank you for arranging everything for my trip. Ronnie was very informative during our stunning drive around the loch."

John shifted her luggage and continued. "Aye, everyone knows the Road Eighty-Nine has the most stunning views of Loch Etive."

They emerged into a vast room with a blazing fire in the immense hearth, large enough to roast two deer, with the mantel rising two stories to the vaulted ceiling. Her gaze roamed over the sitting area, then the entrance to what must be the kitchen. As they continued through the great hall toward the main stairs, it amazed Brielle how well-preserved the historic hall was after a complete modernization.

As John climbed the stairs, he glanced over his shoulder, smiling. "We'll get you settled in the west wing. Ye will have a view of the loch and marina that's most stunning at sunset. Mrs. Abernathy will bring ye up a plate for dinner. Ye likely want to rest. Burn off some of that jet lag. Ronnie and the guys from the wharf will clear the rubble tomorrow morning, so if ye sleep late, don't worry. Work will start anyway."

She followed John down a long hallway, passing portrait after portrait of past lairds. Gazing at the history in each frame, it seemed like she stepped back in time. One image at the end of the hall was so dramatic Brielle stopped to admire it.

The man in the portrait was close to her age. Tall and dressed in a kilt, a white shirt with the plaid draped over his shoulder, his knee-high boots laced up. He stood outside the castle where the rock foundation rose from the grass. She figured seventeenth, maybe eighteenth century. He appeared very muscular, standing with his left foot resting on a rock, the artist having captured him so well that he looked lifelike.

Brielle squinted, stepping forward to peer more closely. He might be breathing. He had jet-black hair and a strong jawline and piercing sky-blue eyes. Brielle stared into those eyes. They seared her in place, seeing into her heart. Her blood drummed in her ears, and her focus narrowed to the man only. He breathed, and his hand rose as his head tilted. His hand reached out, and his fingers brushed her, caressing her cheek.

John cleared his throat. "Laird Alexander Roderick MacDougall—twenty-third laird of the MacDougalls."

Brielle jumped back, blinking. The portrait hadn't moved. She blinked to check her vision; the picture didn't change.

"D-Did—"

"The resemblance is uncanny, you know," John said.

Brielle glanced at him, touching her warm cheek. "The resemblance?"

"The current laird. They are practically identical."

John turned back to the portrait. "I hadn't seen him in years, till the funeral. He hasn't been to Dunstaffnage since his childhood."

She recalled the funeral, the passing of Emily and Ronald MacDougall. "I am so sorry to hear of their passing…Emily was someone I wanted to work with. I am sorry I couldn't make the funeral."

John sighed, staring at the portrait. "Yes, many will miss them." He lowered his head and continued down the hall.

Brielle followed him. Her back tingled as if someone watched her as she stepped away from the portrait. Her eyes drifted over her shoulder to the laird in the painting, and his eyes seemed to follow her. Time slowed. The laird's head tilted down. His eyes stared at her as if he saw into her heart. He grinned and winked at her. Her pulse sped up as heat crawled through her like a lover's caress. Time sped up, and Brielle whipped her head back around. *Too much travel and jet lag. Now I'm seeing things.*

John led her to a bedroom in the west tower of the castle. There was a solid oak bed with red coverings and a folded red fabric with patterns of green and blue she recognized as the MacDougall plaid.

Brielle stepped into the room. She turned in a circle and stopped at a recessed window with a built-in sitting area and a stone bench on each side. The benches held rich, red velvet cushions. The window opened like French doors. Brielle shifted to the enclosure and peeked out. She viewed a sunset over the castle's grounds, the marina, and the entire landscape of Glen Etive in the distance. The scenery swept her away into a dream of Scottish Fae and magic, a welcome escape.

John spoke from behind her. "Breathtaking, isn't it?"

Brielle glanced at him over her shoulder. "Good Lord, yes, it is."

John pointed to the window. "The doors open, but there's no screen. And remember to close them—the weather here can be unpredictable. A rainstorm can blow in off the ocean and catch ye unaware, knock the power out."

John turned to leave. "I'll leave ye to it. The bath is just beyond this door. And in case of a storm, candles and something to light them are within each room. Yers is on the table." He opened a door perpendicular to the window seat, showing her the bath.

A heavyset woman elbowed her way into the room, balancing a tray. She wore a typical day dress with supportive shoes and an apron. Her salt-and-pepper hair piled high in a messy bun. Wiry tendrils escaped, adding a touch of whimsy. Her bright smile reminded Brielle of her mother, giving her a sense of home.

"Oh, there she is now. Glad ye made it, Ms. DeVolt. I've got yer tray just here, dearie." She set the tray of cheese, crackers, meat, and a couple of cookies on a small round table, then turned to face Brielle. She threw her arms wide and wrapped her in a bear hug, squeezing her a bit at the end. Brielle became nostalgic; the woman smelled of vanilla, like her grandmother.

"I am Mrs. Abernathy, and anything ye need yer to let me know. I'm here daily to make meals and tend to things." Mrs. Abernathy held Brielle's shoulders and studied her face. She gushed, "Ye be a beautiful thing, ye are." Brielle blushed as Mrs. Abernathy turned to the table and waved at the tray of food.

"I've got ye a pile of food for any hunger ye may have. There's some soothing chamomile tea so ye can try to get some sleep to rid ye of that nasty jet lag from yer trip. We'll have ye used to our land in no time."

The woman's sweetness and care threw Brielle off guard. Only her mother or Professor MacGregor had gone to such trouble to comfort her. She was usually the one caring for everyone else.

"Thank you so much Mrs. Abernathy. I am certain"—she stifled a yawn—"it's more than enough." Mrs. Abernathy waved her hands and headed to the door.

"Look at me, keeping ye up. Ye get yourself something to eat and some rest. Tomorrow will be a bright new day, you'll see." Mrs. Abernathy closed the door on her way out.

Unable to resist the window seat, Brielle grabbed a cup of tea and a cookie. She settled onto the bench, so her view was of the marina and the glen just beyond. As Brielle stared out the window, the colors of the mountains shifted as her gaze traveled farther up the hills. The landscape moved, calling to her. She wished her mom were still alive so she could tell her the magic was there. *Mom, I've made it. I've made it to Scotland, and it seems like coming home.*

Her mom's voice came clear in her mind, her highland lilt soft: *"It's as if magic was born there."*

Magic. Earlier, as they drove their way farther up the castle's cliff, the view of the marina and village had caught her eye.

Her gaze roamed over the town. Areas showed some modernization, but other places were almost like something from a historical movie.

Her mom's voice came to her again: *"Parts of Scotland are so old it's almost as if it was untouched by modern man."*

History was Brielle's passion, and she would spend the summer immersed in Scottish history. She had prepared for this with years of undergraduate work in history and graduate work as an anthropologist. She was ready to put her skills and knowledge to the test on her own project to manage, overseeing the thirteenth-century chapel renovation and recording it for the Historic Environment Scotland.

As she took a sip of tea, her cell phone rang. There couldn't be too many people calling her. Before leaving the States, she had ditched her old cell number. She grabbed the phone from her pocket, smiled at the number, and answered.

"Hello, Professor MacGregor."

"Hello, Brielle," came his booming Scots voice, "I just wanted to make sure ye arrived, and all is just fine."

Brielle replied, "Yes, sir, here in the castle and settling in. How are things at the university?"

"Good, good, right, ye are. Things are good here, good." He sounded a bit preoccupied. "Well, better today. Just giving ye a heads-up, dear. I know ye told me not to give this number out. But I had to give it up to the police."

Brielle sat up, spilling her tea. "What? The police? You just said everything was good. What's happened?" Brielle jumped up from the window seat, spilling hot tea on her shirt, as she kept the phone to her ear.

"Aw, nothing much, and it's all fixed now. The construction people are repairing the damage. But the police may call ye. I already told them ye were gone, but they said they may need a statement from ye, anyway."

"Professor, what happened?" Brielle leaned against the window seat enclosure, worried, as she rubbed her forehead. She knew what would come next. *Damn.*

"Well, it's that boyfriend of yers. Well, ex, that is."

Brielle rolled her eyes. She thought she had left her troubles behind in the States.

"Tony came by looking for ye. Well, demanding is more like it. He didn't like it when I told him ye was gone. I wouldn't tell him where ye went to either. He got mad and tore up the classroom for antiquities. He made a good mess of things. Made a hole in the wall before anyone could come."

She sighed, trying not to cry.

"I just ran, hollering to get help. I've never seen someone get so mad—like he got some berserker in him."

She sensed the pressure building into an enormous headache, and it snaked down her neck, gripping the muscles along the way. "Oh God, Professor Mac, I am so sorry. I hope he didn't hurt anyone." It would be awful if he hurt anyone else. "I hope there was nothing of true value to the university lost. He is just crazy. But now that he knows I am gone, he'll leave you all alone," Brielle said as she grabbed a napkin from the tray, blotting the spilled tea. She wished she could wipe that part of her life away, too.

"Well, I didn't give in and tell him where ye had gone. And he does not have this number, so ye are all good. Police hauled him away, anyway. Let us hope he'll stay locked up for a while, eh? Just enjoy yourself.

Do some good work for the MacDougalls." He sighed. "Sad thing that Emily won't be there to work with ye. God rest her soul. I'll miss her, I will. Ye keep track of yer progress and document everything. The university and Scotland's Historic Environment will want a full accounting of the chapel renovation. Hopefully, it will end in a museum tour for ye, eh?" He laughed.

She laughed too, missing him already. After she had first lost her father, then a year later, her mother, he'd been like a dad to her. "Yes, I will get it all documented, but a tour? That's getting too far ahead of us. I've got to get through the renovation first. Say hi to your wife, and I miss you all." She sighed. "Bye."

Brielle hung up, then turned her phone off, wanting to shut off her past. She set it on the table, poured herself another tea, and settled back on the seat.

"Tony…he can't leave well enough alone. It's not enough for him." She said that aloud, like she usually did. She needed to get away from his dominating possessiveness. It was too much for her to handle.

The chapel renovation project had come at the perfect time in her life. She was so glad Emily turned to her longtime friend, Professor Mac, to help find someone to lead the project. For Brielle, it wasn't just an opportunity to work on an actual historical renovation but also a new start. A reset on life.

When she shifted, a paper crinkled. Her backpack had fallen over as she'd stood up, and a travel brochure on Scotland sat beside her. She sighed and picked up the booklet, staring at the beautiful picture on the cover. An embracing couple gazed at each other in front of a loch with a mountain landscape at sunset. It seemed perfect.

They said true love showed a woman she was wanted and adored and would take every opportunity to ensure her safety. She knew fake love brought women down, making them believe they were ugly and worthless. As tears gathered in her eyes, the picture blurred. The couple shifted into a blob.

Blinking her tears away, she gazed out the window at the setting sun over Loch Etive, the mountains framing the view in amethyst and lapis hues. The kind of love her ex had shown her chipped away at a woman's personality little by little, persuading her she was less deserving. After a while, the woman would believe it. She hoped that being in her mom's homeland was enough to save her.

****

"The Fae fables are our bedtime stories. Some tales haunt, and some make ye laugh. Ye'll never understand them until ye are full grown, and then, my son, they will become yer sole existence."

It was how his ma had always put him to bed—a bedtime story from the *Fae Fable Book* and her advice for the telling. Being back in Dunstaffnage Castle after so many years was more challenging than Colin MacDougall had imagined. Now that his family's title and lands—Dunstaffnage and Dunollie castles—were his concern, he found himself sitting across from the captain of the castle, having to face the duty of being laird. Colin thought he would have more time to develop his law career before diving into the responsibilities of being a laird. He didn't realize he would have to do this so soon, that his parents would not be here.

"I am truly sorry about yer parents' death. Ye

realize everyone loved and admired them," John said as he sat on a chair in front of the desk.

"Thanks, I'll miss them more than you know." Colin had just arrived that evening, at John's urgent summons, from the law firm he was a solicitor for in Edinburgh.

"Want a dram? Toast them both." Colin rose and walked to a table behind the desk filled with crystal glasses and decanters of assorted liquor ready for any guest his da had entertained. He picked up two glasses and poured a generous measure into each. His da's whisky scent permeated the room and reminded him of happier times when he and his da used to sit and discuss things, helping him with life's challenges.

"He never skimped on much. This whisky is the best I've had." Offering the other glass to John, Colin sat at the desk and took a generous sip, sighing. He had known that one day he would become laird to the clan, but figured his father would be well into his nineties before that would happen.

He turned to John. "The MacArthur, hereditary Captain of the Castle. Slàinte." He toasted John as John leaned over the desk so the glasses would clink.

"Slàinte," John said as he sat back and sipped his drink.

Colin rested against the chair. "So, you called me away from the law firm for a reason? My parents spent a good amount of time here."

John took another sip of whisky and replied, "Yes, that's part of it. There is more you need to hear."

Colin nodded, encouraging John to continue, thinking he would complain about the aging castle. There was also the chapel that his ma got a grant from

Scotland's Historic Environment to refurbish, as they investigate, care for, and promote Scotland's historic environment. The chapel renovation was his mother's personal endeavor, now his to oversee after her death.

John leaned forward, set his glass on a side table, and sighed. "So, how much information about this property did yer parents share with ye? Specifically, your father?"

Colin shrugged. "Nothing more than they liked to spend time here. Not very much." His gaze fell on the *Fae Fable Book* in a glass case by a window, and he recalled being tucked into bed by his mother. "There was a folklore story my mother told me at bedtime as a child. One story from the *Fae Fable Book* they keep here. Three stones, fairies, fight for good and evil, typical Scottish lore."

John sipped his whisky, took a breath, and said soberly, "The castle sits in the original location of Dun Monaidh, home of Duncan MacDougall, Lord of Lorne. His son became known as the King of the Isles. The people have rumored for centuries that this land holds special spiritual power."

Colin rolled his eyes and set his elbows on the desk. "John, I know my family history."

John set his glass on the desk, got up, and paced in front of the fireplace. "Well, it's about those stones."

Colin laughed. "Ye mean my mother's bedtime story? It's just a silly fable made to make her children mind themselves. Faith, hope, and love come together to protect mankind. The evil Fae will come to get ye if ye are not good. There's no truth to it."

John sighed and ran his hands through his hair. "This lore is part of the responsibility of my ancestors to your family. As told by my father and generations before him, it is my duty to inform the laird of the legend of the Stones of Iona if his father failed to tell it to him. It's yer duty to the stones ye need to know about."

Colin sat back. "Yer duty? My father never mentioned a duty to any stones."

John returned to his seat and squared his shoulders. "It dates back to when the stones first came to the MacDougalls in the eleventh century, and they gave the *Fae Fable Book* to the family as part of the duty to the Stones of Iona."

He took a deep breath and continued: "The Fae entrusted the magical stones to yer ancestors. The Fae, known as Tuatha Dé Danann, asked the family to keep the stones safe for all mankind. There are three stones—well, four. Yer family kept the Stone of Love, the Stone of Hope, and the Stone of Faith for the Fae. The three stones combined make the Stone of Destiny appear, which is the stone that holds the highest power. Yer family and the Fae must protect the stones from falling into the hands of evil."

Colin barked a short laugh. "My bedtime story is now part of your duty. The Fae are nothing but folklore, and the stones are nothing but a myth." He leaned forward. "John, have you seen the stones, ever?"

John set his glass on the table. "No. For generations, my family has accepted this as part of the keeping of the castle. Part of our obligation to the MacDougall clan." John dropped his hand to his side. "This has never been up for debate. It's what we do as our duty."

Colin pinched the bridge of his nose—he felt a

headache coming on. "So, you haven't seen them, but you believe they are here. Do you know, or were you ever told, where the Fae hid them?"

Sighing, John placed his head in his palms and rubbed his face. "No, as the laird, you become entrusted with the stones, but I suspect your father never had the chance to pass along more information before his death. The legend of the stones is important. Things have changed since your parents' death, leading me to consider that this is more than a tale." He paused. "The legend of the stones, the magic, is real."

Colin froze and peered at him. "You believe this is real?"

John rose and crossed to the window. "Well, plausible, I'd dare to guess." He glanced back over his shoulder. "Before your parents' death, the Green Lady MacDougall ghost materialized crying on the wall walk. The ghost disturbed Mrs. Abernathy so badly that she left for the day. Your parents were worried, since her spirit heralded the fate of your family members. If she is laughing, it's good news to befall the family, but if she's crying, it's an omen of evil. She showed the day before your parents' death." John sighed. "Colin, she was crying."

Colin abandoned his drink. "The castle's green spirit that I've never seen, yet another story told to us to keep us in line." He tapped his finger on his chin. "Wait, Mrs. Abernathy, isn't she the housekeeper who is into the spirits and ghosts of the castle, claiming every creak this old place makes is a ghost? And now you're linking my parents' accident to the castle ghost?" He held his head in his hands, took a deep breath, and released it. "The authorities suspected foul play. The cause of the car crash was never determined in the investigation. They ended up dismissing the case as an accident. But to link it to the resident ghost?"

John crossed the room, rubbing his neck. "Well, these events started before yer parents' accident. The first event was when the wall walk facing the chapel fell. I'd had it repaired a few months ago. It was solid." He ticked off the events on his fingers. "The next day was when the ghost surfaced." He made a fist. "Somehow, I believe it tied these events to yer parents' accident, but I can't put it together. The stones hold power, but what that is and how it works seems yer da never passed down. I think it's all linked. I don't know how."

John stood there a moment. Then his head snapped up. "I'd guess that was when your cousin discovered the crypt under the chapel."

Now, this was getting interesting. Colin grabbed his glass, gulped down all its contents, and asked, "There's a crypt under the chapel? When was this discovered?"

John paced before the desk. "Well, just before your mother had the Scotland Historic Environment out. They dated the chapel back to the thirteenth century, but earlier use of the crypt was clear before they sealed it after the Jacobite uprising. Because of the crypt, the Scotland Historic Environment became more interested in the chapel's renovation." John nodded. "Aye, all the issues began when yer cousin found the crypt."

Colin got up and filled his glass with whisky again. "Cousin? Which one? There are so many."

"Yer first cousin from the Ross side, Sarah. We haven't seen her in years. She showed up one day after hearing yer ma was interested in renovating the chapel. Sarah was the one who found the sealed opening to the crypt and insisted yer ma have it opened before anyone from the Scotland Historical Environment could examine it. The accident claiming yer parents' life occurred the day after. After yer parents' death, Sarah just up and left"—John waved his hand around the ceiling—"claiming this depressed her too much. She even missed the funeral."

John rubbed his hand down his chest. "For generations, my family has cared for this castle, and nothing has gone awry till now."

Colin picked up his glass and took a good gulp.

John leveled his eyes with Colin's and then said, "The chapel renovation was something both yer parents thought important. Perhaps when ye meet the Scotland Historic Environment's project manager tomorrow, she can explain it to ye."

Colin slammed his glass on the desk. "Wait, what? We just buried my parents. Can't they wait?"

John spread his arms wide. "No, yer ma scheduled this project months ago. The project manager arrived from America earlier today. The church historian, Marie Murray, the one for the mosaic flooring, will arrive tomorrow. They will ramp up work quickly to take advantage of the summer weather."

Colin stepped to the fireplace. "America? The best expert the Scotland Historic Environment sends on a *Scottish historical renovation* is an *American*? This is my ma's special project, the renovation. My parents planned to renew their wedding vows when it was complete."

John shrugged and sipped his drink. "She's a

scholar, an anthropologist, handpicked by yer ma. The society recommended others over her, but yer mother insisted on this one to oversee the restoration." John went over to Colin and put his hand on his shoulder. "Colin, this is a great deal to take in. Things may become clearer tomorrow."

Colin finished his drink. He needed to be alone to go over this in his mind: Fae, stones and lore, the castle, the chapel. There was a crypt, and John thought these events were all linked to his parents' death. It was too much.

"Sure, we'll go over the rest of this tomorrow. I need things set here so I can return to Edinburgh. My caseload at the law firm is heavy. I even declined my bereavement leave for my parents' death. I can't spend time here dealing with some bedtime stories."

John glanced up at Colin. "Ye won't be staying on to oversee the chapel renovations?"

Colin set his glass on the desk. "Nope, this is what ye are here for, captain of the castle. I've got to head back. You've got the gist of my ma's renovation project. I'm sure you'll have it in hand."

Colin clapped John on the back. He strode to the door and said over his shoulder, "Ye can deal with the American."

Chapter 2

"I can't go down there again. I've come all this way, but I just can't."

"Aw, now, ye shouldn't be so hard on yourself, Brielle. Once ye take a flashlight, it's not that bad," Ronnie said.

Brielle sighed—she had done it again. You would think she would have learned to keep her mouth shut by now.

"Nope, I'm gonna do this," Brielle said. Taking a deep breath, she flicked on her flashlight and descended into the square opening of the crypt. *A history expert, scared of dark places. How stupid.* She'd hidden it this long, but not anymore. She would overcome her fear of dark, closed-in spaces.

Focus. She took one step down. On previous trips, she'd taken measurements and mapped the tomb for comprehensive reports on the renovation.

Her foot found the next step, and it grew darker. *Think of history.* This trip down into what she considered "the hole into hell" would allow her to examine the sarcophagus lid of Lady Katherine MacDougall, interred here after they built the chapel. She would take a few pics, get measurements, and get out before passing out.

Deep breaths. Think history. Stepping off the ladder, Brielle approached the lady's casket and shined

19

her flashlight on the top. The design was so beautiful. Her face looked so serene. The lady's arms lay folded across her chest, holding something. Brielle glanced again. It was a heart she held. For a moment, Brielle got caught up in her thoughts, processing what she saw.

Her mind shifted as she considered the meaning of the heart shape in the vault. She recalled from her studies that, in theory, the heart shape first became associated with sex, and eventually with love, and was usually shown upside down. They made hearts with two humps to represent the different shapes of the body, the buttocks, or breasts.

She examined the sarcophagus again. The heart shape the lady clutched to her breast sat right side up, the two humps facing her chin. This likely meant she had her heart, or another's heart, taken with her to the otherworld in death.

Brielle took a few pics, the flash bringing much-needed light to the darker corners of the room. *Be brave. Remember, history.* She tried to stay down to take a measurement, then glanced around the room again. Her panic on the rise, she made a break for the square of light and her way out of hell.

Brielle hurried up the rungs of the ladder. Planting her foot on the top rung, she launched herself onto the ground, rotating, landing on her back. Panting, she opened her eyes to the worried expression on Ronnie's face as he stood over her.

"Ye want me to go down and take measurements for ye? I'd be okay to do that. Ye just stay up here."

Sighing, she handed the flashlight to Ronnie, rolled over, stood, and made her way to her desk. Well, the "desk" was a plywood board over sawhorses, but it would do.

The work site was off to a good start on her first working day. The historical society sent all the archaeological equipment ahead of her, skimping on nothing. She had blueprints for the chapel, and she was creating a map of the crypt to add to the collection. Brielle couldn't believe she was the first to record it for all posterity.

She glanced up to see Mrs. Abernathy march through the door. "Och, look at ye. All dusty and covered in rubble. Poor dearie, gonna have to get that all cleaned up. The laird has asked to see ye right away, he has."

"The laird, as in the Laird MacDougall? He's here?" Brielle didn't know she'd have to meet him so soon, and when dust covered her—she was positively a mess.

Mrs. Abernathy huffed and replied, "Come on with ye, dust yerself off, and let's get up to the castle." Resigned to her fate, Brielle brushed at her clothing as she followed Mrs. Abernathy.

She slowed at the chapel doorway. Something had been off when she first entered, and now it made her feel like she was walking across her own grave. She laughed to herself. *I was standing over the crypt with a group of dead MacDougalls only a moment ago. Why would a doorway give me chills?* She jumped through the opening and made her way up the trail with Mrs. Abernathy.

This was the best time to ask about her dream. If anyone knew anything about the castle, it would be the housekeeper.

"Mrs. Abernathy, I want to ask about a dream I had

last night."

"Dream? The castle makes lots of people dream. It's old, has many ancient spirits, and carries many untold stories, happy and sad. Tell me what ye dreamed, and we'll see if a spirit came to speak to ye."

A chill shot up her spine, but she shook it off. "This lady, she stood at the foot of my bed. She wore a long, flowing dress, seemed to be seventeenth or eighteenth century, but it's hard to tell as she was transparent."

Mrs. Abernathy nodded as they strolled. "Oh aye, we got many female spirits here. Tell me more."

She tilted her head. "Well, she was kind of green."

Mrs. Abernathy gasped and grabbed her arm, stopping her on the trail. "Green, ye say?"

"Yes." She glanced at Mrs. Abernathy. Why would she get excited over a ghost?

Mrs. Abernathy huffed and grabbed Brielle by the shoulders. "Tell me, what was her expression?"

"Well, she was happy. The lady…was smiling." Brielle gazed out over the loch. "It's strange. An overwhelming sense overcame me. She likes me here. Like I'm a long-awaited guest. She wanted to welcome me. I felt a powerful emotion upon seeing her—this overwhelming sense of joy and happiness."

Mrs. Abernathy clapped her hands, glanced at the sky, and said, "Och, that's great news, my dear. Grand news, indeed! The Green Lady MacDougall has visited ye. Let me tell ye her story."

Mrs. Abernathy took Brielle's arm in hers and continued moving along the path, enjoying the lovely sunshine filtering through the trees.

"Why, this is a great blessing. The Green Lady

appears when either something very good or awful is about to happen to the MacDougall family. Why, before the laird and lady's accident, she came out on the wall walk in the bright of day, wailin' on as if ye thought someone died. John said she carried on until sunset, crying as if she was dying again. I couldn't handle it. Went home early, I did."

Ghosts, moving paintings, her dream must be her imagination or jet lag catching up with her. Or it was likely her mind's reaction to being immersed in Scottish lore, which was so different from that in the States.

When they arrived at the castle, Mrs. Abernathy showed her to the study. *Let's hope this is a good meeting*, Brielle thought. *I could use something going my way today.*

****

Colin peered out the window from his study. He didn't have time for the chapel-in-the-woods project, or for John's revelations about the Fae plus his duty to the stones and Dunstaffnage castle. He didn't need more pressing on his mind. His parents' sudden death weighed heavily upon him, an absence he felt every day. He could use his father's wise advice and his mother's comforting presence.

"So, have ye met her yet?" John said from behind him.

The chapel in the woods peeked through the trees, one of his parents' favorite places, and his ma's special project. He heard John huff. John had asked him a question.

Ahh, the wee builder.

"What has she done today?" Colin was curious about the American his ma picked to renovate the chapel. Why would his mother choose an American with her particular project and something so important to Historical Environment of Scotland? The structure remained one of the few private chapels with such architectural detail. The renovation would restore the chapel to its original glory, rivaling other churches across Scotland.

"This morning, they cleared all the overgrowth a day ahead of schedule. Brielle made sure we ordered from the quarry that your mother thought matched the original stones used to build the chapel. The shipment wasn't due for another day, so she was assessing the crypt's layout."

Colin was glad his ma did that, so they could honor her wishes after her death. He appreciated the *American* from the *Scottish* historical society saw the importance of it.

John interrupted his thoughts: "I was just down there—the lads tell me she's not fond of going into the crypt."

Colin glanced over his shoulder at John.

"Ronnie has asked if we can add lighting to the crypt. He thinks it will help her overcome her fears, and all the men agree," John continued. "They have taken a liking to her."

Colin turned back to the window. "It's good to know she's ahead of schedule, so I can get back to the law firm sooner."

****

Brielle walked gingerly toward the study. Why would the laird want to see her? Emily had laid out the plan for the renovation perfectly, and the historical society had already approved the project. What would the laird want to know—and would he find fault with her work? *Stop it, Brielle. He likely only wants to meet you.* It's a formality. It's custom.

Brielle came up short at the door, not realizing she had arrived. They'd left the door cracked, so she slipped into the study. John and another man were there. Neither realized she had entered, which gave her time to study the laird.

A tall man with jet-black hair stood in front of the window. John was right—he resembled the laird from the portrait, at least from what she could see. He stood easily over six feet, with broad, muscular shoulders. His jeans hugged his legs so well they molded the firm curve of his buttocks.

The laird didn't turn away from the window when he spoke. "Ye know, I spied on her from the wall walk today. I wanted to check on our guest, the anthropologist, and find out what the American was doing to *my ma's* chapel."

Brielle took a breath and spoke. "I'm not a hundred percent American. I'm half Scots."

As he shifted his weight, the reflection of Colin's face reflected clear to her. Their eyes made contact in the window's reflection.

She added quietly, "My mother was from Glasgow."

He turned from the window and regarded her. His eyes, cerulean blue, were the color of the ocean on a clear day. He grinned and tilted his head to the side, studying her.

Brielle took a deep breath, then let it out slowly as she rubbed her hands on her pants. *Why did I confront the laird? My emotions must be on overload, probably the jet lag.*

He raised an eyebrow. His fingers covered his mouth as he chuckled.

John stepped forward between them. "Brielle Elise DeVolt, may I introduce Colin Roderick MacDougall, thirty-first Laird to—"

"Clan MacDougall, yes, I know who he is. Thank you, John." She turned to Colin and nodded. "My laird."

Colin dropped his hand, smiled, and nodded at her formal address.

"Ah, probably the jet lag," Colin said as he leaned against the windowsill, folding his arms and crossing his feet at the ankle.

She peeked at him from under her lashes. He had a strong nose and jawline, and a rough growth of stubble framed his cheeks, making him strikingly handsome. His jet-black hair reflected purple in the bright sunlight shining from behind him. Her gaze traveled down. His tight light-blue button-down shirt bound his chiseled chest, and his jeans hugged his legs so well, the crease of his muscles showed through. Polished dress boots adorned his crossed feet, completing his sophisticated appearance. He radiated masculinity with an ease that made Brielle's knees weak. Under his stare, she had to shift her feet to find solid ground again.

She blushed. *I spoke my thoughts aloud. Will I ever learn?*

She fidgeted under his scrutiny; since her last relationship, she had a hard time being comfortable with men again. She glanced up. His gaze moved up her body, making her close her eyes and shiver. When she opened them, his eyes rested on her face. She studied him and saw genuine kindness there—a caring for those she didn't find in many people. An awareness, a sense of peace, washed over her.

John cleared his throat and said, "I'll just leave ye two to get acquainted."

She caught Colin grace John with an expression that promised he would consider revenge for leaving him alone with her. John chuckled and left the room.

****

Colin took a minute to study her. She was fair, with petite features and light-brown hair pulled into a loose bun, leaving golden tendrils desperately escaping, caressing her face. He wanted nothing more than to free the bun and run his fingers through the soft brown curls. Her cheekbones were high, with a spot of dirt on one side and a pert nose to match her tart personality. When she was angry a second ago, her eyes had flashed almost green. Now they were a light golden-brown, like a fine whisky.

His gaze traveled over her body. She wore twill pants and hiking boots with a button-down shirt that might have been tan if not for the light layer of gray dust. Under that sat a white tank top with a smudge of dirt on the front near her abundant cleavage. His gaze lingered, then continued to her petite features, set perfectly in her heart-shaped face. She wasn't what he expected, far from it. Wait, she said her mom *was* from Glasgow.

"Was?" Colin asked quietly.

Brielle blinked.

He stepped away from the window at her blank stare and approached her. "Was. You said your mother was from Glasgow."

She blinked again and rubbed the back of her neck, then gave two quick nods and replied, "Yes, she was. She died last year of cancer. My father passed the year before. I have a brother, but we aren't close."

He held out his hand, then glanced at it. Brielle stared at his hand, then tentatively placed her hand in his and peered at his face. He smiled as his other hand closed over hers and held it between his own.

Her hand was small and warm. It trembled so slightly he almost didn't notice. He could detect a callous on a finger. She didn't mind hard work. Strong yet vulnerable. *Brielle.*

He spoke honestly, for he understood her loss as much as his own. "I am sorry for their deaths and yer loss."

Brielle glanced at their hands, then back at him, and smiled, but her head nodded in a tic again. "I am truly sorry over your parents' loss as well. I wish I could have attended the funeral."

Colin stood there, holding her hand, the energy flowing through the connection. The earth took a breath and held it, waiting for them. He had never had this reaction to a woman upon first meeting her. His response piqued his curiosity. What else did his ma's special project have in store for him?

Brielle pulled her hand from his and squared her shoulders. "You called me for an update on the renovation. Shall we go over it?"

Colin traveled past her, sat in his desk chair, and waited as she stood there fidgeting. Ah, the wee builder was nervous. When he held her hand and spoke of her mother, he felt a connection, a loss they shared. She seemed like a bright, confident lass, and when she got angry...the spark in her eye, her sharp tongue. She was attractive in a way Colin found endearing. The businesslike builder covered her charm. He hmphed. Too bad she was an American who might ruin his ma's special project. He'd hate to ask the Historic Environment Scotland to replace her. She started to grow on him.

She watched him over her shoulder, and he smiled as he waved his hand, inviting her to the chair in front of his desk. He sat back in his chair, hoping to appear relaxed, wanting her to be comfortable.

Brielle cleared her throat as she crossed to the desk, sat upright in the chair, clasped her hands in her lap, and began her report.

"We've cleared away the rubble and overgrowth so we can start on the demo of the broken stonework..."

He watched her as she spoke. Her gaze traveled across the room, stopping at the fireplace and staying there momentarily. The couch in front of the fireplace was a favorite spot of his. Maybe she also enjoyed sitting in front of the fire on late nights?

Her gaze shifted back to him, then dropped to her hands. "As you know, your ancestors built the chapel around the thirteenth century as a private chapel for the family. We consider the stonework the most detailed from that era." He used to sit like this with his da, talk about life with a whisky in hand. He was always on the other side of the desk, nervous—like her. *A drink, that's what she needs, a smooth whisky.*

He rose and turned to the table. He didn't ask, just poured two glasses. The scent wafted to his nose, reminding him of his da. He walked to her. She still spoke, as she fidgeted with her hands. He stood directly in front of her and handed her a glass.

She put her hands up, and he wiggled the drink under her nose, knowing the scent would tease her and make her mouth water in anticipation of that first smooth sip with a nip in it.

"It's Scotland. We drink all the time, plus it's my da's best stock." He handed her the glass again. As she took it, their hands brushed, and awareness shot up his arm. He tried to appear unaffected as he leaned back against the desk with his arms and legs crossed.

"Slàinte," he said, leaning toward her and clinking her drink, "which is a toast to health."

"I know what slàinte means, thank you." She raised her glass and spoke. "Slàinte," she replied. She sipped it and smiled. He half expected her to choke, even though his da's whisky was the smoothest in Scotland. Still, she was an American unused to *uisge beatha*, or the "water of life." She relaxed more as she sipped her drink.

"He is well-informed in construction, being the owner of a historical castle. I guess he has to be."

"I own two castles, and I *am* well-informed." He laughed when her mouth fell open. "Ye always speak your thoughts out loud? Need to be careful about that, lass."

She sighed and took a larger sip from her glass.

Colin slid into the chair next to her and sipped his whisky, watching her over the rim. Brielle sparked his curiosity. She glowed from the inside out. Was she even aware of the effect she had on men, on him? He couldn't get over the fact that he felt such a powerful reaction to a woman upon first meeting her. Now he was curious about his wee builder. John had mentioned she seemed frightened of the crypt. Was that really the case?

"What's the plan with the crypt?" he asked.

Her gaze shot up at his question. Her hand rose to her throat, and a flush rose in her neck. He smiled into his glass as he sipped. He'd caught her off guard. Something he had perfected in law school.

She shivered and took a deep breath before she said tentatively, "W-well, it was your mother who discovered the crypt. There wasn't time to discuss it with your mother before the accident." She glanced into her glass, whispering, "I met your mom once."

That's right, she did. Colin wondered how much his ma had shared with her. Did she understand all his ma's hopes and dreams for the chapel? God, he missed his parents. He took a bigger sip this time and stared into his glass.

"Yea, John told me," he whispered.

"I wanted to collaborate with your mother. We talked so much about the chapel and the castle."

He glanced up as she spoke. She leaned back in her chair and crossed her legs, resting the glass on her knee. She tilted her head back, setting it against the chair's high back, and gazed at the ceiling. The whisky had worked its magic. She finally relaxed, and Colin knew he viewed his first glimpse of what she was like.

She hummed, a light, wistful sound. "Your family history is fascinating. Your ancestors descended from a twelfth-century prince, Somerled. They divided his lands in the Isles and Argyll on his death between his sons. Dugald, presumed to be the eldest, got Lorn, which was part of this land and the Isle of Mull. Dugald is the eponym of the MacDougalls." She glanced at him with her head resting against the chair's back.

She impressed him. She had done her homework. He could tell by the expression of awe and wonder that she enjoyed what she did—history.

Colin smiled. "Aye, and they thought either his son Duncan or his grandson Ewan might be the builder of the castle and chapel. Ye know the history well, lass."

Brielle blushed. "Ewan is such a nice name. I always liked that one." She sat forward as she spoke. "A charter of 1572 refers to a place on the property called *sen dun*, apparently an attempt at the Gaelic word *Sean Dùn*."

"Aye, 'Old Fort.' " She knew Gaelic. Intriguing. What other surprises did his wee builder have?

"The historic society identified it as Chapel Hill, a rocky ridge about one hundred and sixty meters southwest of the castle." She sighed. "Your mother wanted it to be the next project on the Historic Environment Scotland's list, to excavate the area for archeological artifacts. We discussed it at length."

As she spoke, Colin smiled and sat forward as well, bringing them face-to-face. "Did ye?"

She captivated him as she continued to describe the significance of retaining the historical accuracy of the chapel and how it related to his family history, something he had taken for granted for many years. Brielle's knowledge impressed him, and he now saw why his ma selected her over others with more experience. Her passion for the chapel matched his ma's. It made him happy, for he didn't want to have his wee builder replaced after all. Far from it: he wanted to see why his reaction to first meeting her was so strong and whether it would last if he spent more time in her company.

"Ye seem to have captured my ma's desires for the chapel well. I am certain she would have appreciated it. I appreciate it, lass. I trust ye to restore the chapel as my ma would have wanted it, possibly even better."

She sat back in the chair and blushed. "Thank you. I am thrilled about the work and plan to include everything your mother spoke to me about." She fidgeted with her glass. "I am certain you miss her, miss them."

He missed them, his ma especially. The chapel project was important to his ma, and here sat someone who'd spoken to his ma in depth about it and planned to carry out her every wish. Brielle was an enchanting lass and someone who reflected his ma in a way that endeared her to him.

They were both quiet, each left to their contemplation. Brielle's gaze scanned the room, resting on the *Fae Fable Book* in its glass case next to the window. She set her glass on the desk, got up, and crossed to the book casing set in the wall.

"Your mother granted me complete access to the family records, specifically the *Fae Fable Book*. Is this it?"

Colin reclined in his seat. He twirled the glass in his hand, letting the sunlight capture the golden brown of the whisky, which sparkled, making him think of his parents.

As Brielle studied the book, Colin spoke. "Ahh, the famed *Fae Fable Book*, presumed to be given to us by the fairies. One of my ma's favorite childhood bedtime stories is in that book. She told it almost nightly when we were children. She said the Fae always kept it open to a Corinthians quote." He quoted: " 'And now, these three remain faith, hope, and love. But the greatest of these is love.' "

She regarded him momentarily, then turned and examined the book as she spoke. "It is a beautiful book, likely from the eleventh century. The illustrations are extraordinary."

Her hands moved over the glass covering. "There's no seam, no lock."

He set his glass on the desk, rose, strode to the case by the window, and glanced over her shoulder. Taking advantage of his position, he stood close to her. Her scent came to him: light roses. He sensed the warmth of her body, and became aware of her life energy pulse near his. Earlier, she seemed nervous, but calmed once she spoke about her work and his family history. At first, he wasn't interested in the chapel renovation. Upon meeting her, he understood her passion for the renovation project, the same one his ma was so devoted to.

She turned toward him. "I am glad this is inside a case. You need to take care of it. Touch it, and the pages could melt to dust."

As she spoke, the pages flipped in the case behind her. Colin's gaze darted to the book. Did he see what he thought he saw? He bent closer to see the book on a completely different page. The book had changed on its own. He lifted his head and glanced at Brielle.

Brielle turned and bent over the bookcase. "You said it's always turned to a page that quotes Corinthians? Has someone opened the case?" She glanced back at him. "Because it's not on that page now."

He glared at the pages, still changed, and back at her. "It's been on the Corinthians quote my whole life, never changed." Was this the Fae at work? Brielle hadn't seen the pages flip. He ran his hand through his hair and glanced at the book again. He needed to figure out how he'd explain it to her. Hell, he wasn't sure how he'd explain it to himself.

"See, it's now open to a different page. It's changed." The sunlight shifted, and a ray of sunshine illuminated the page. "Do you see this?" Brielle asked. "The sunlight has just lit this part." She read, " 'Never fear in love, for perfect love casts out fear. The opposite of love is not hate, but fear.' " Brielle stared out the window. "What does that mean? The opposite of love is fear?"

The quote sparked a memory. Colin gazed into her eyes as his ma's voice came as clear in his mind as if she stood there today.

Colin had been young, clamoring to get into bed as his ma tucked him in. She promised to tell the story again, the one from the *Fae Fable Book*. Colin remembered the part that included the quote. The prince had been going to the stream to contemplate his lack of success in finding his true love. The Fae gifted him with the Stone of Love, which would glow when his true love was near. The Stone of Love would glow when he visited the stream alone, but no one was in sight.

Later, an evil Fae tricked the prince, and the stone glowed red for her, but he felt no love for that woman. Confused, he retreated to his favorite spot by the stream. Only on this trip, he spied a village girl. She had been secretly watching the prince on every trip and made the stone glow.

Colin heard his mom's voice continue: "As the prince sat there, a young village girl approached the stream to gather her water. The village girl did not see the prince sitting there, so he could observe her unaware. When the village girl moved, there was grace in her motions like swans sailing through the sky. The village girl's glowing, cream-colored skin and inner beauty captured him. There was an aura about her he had not seen in a woman before. Her light-brown hair glimmered in the sunlight as if to cast threads of a pure gold halo around her head. Her soul called to him. So caught up in his examination, he didn't notice the Stone of Love glowed red."

Brielle's voice broke into his thoughts. "Do you have the key?" She turned to him.

Colin blinked. She asked about the key, the key to the bookcase.

"Your mom mentioned access to the book," said Brielle. "There's a key somewhere." The light from the window shone brightly behind her head. The escaping wisps of her hair captured the sunlight, making a circle around her face like a golden halo. She shook her head as a thick curl came loose, caressing her face.

Colin spoke while staring at her. "The key. I've never seen a key. Never opened the case."

"Maybe John knows. Your mom thought it could offer insight to help with the chapel. What that might be, I am uncertain, my laird."

Colin brought his hand to her face but stopped. They had only just met. All he wanted to do was to lightly weave the curl around his finger and place it behind her ear. Then trail his finger down the side of her face. Would her face be as soft as it was in the sunlight from the window? Would that he could touch her as he desired. Brielle's vulnerability moved him, and he felt an overwhelming need to protect her. He stared at her lips and wondered whether they would taste as sweet as they looked. Temptation got the best of him, and he bent his head toward her. He paused, breathing in his nose. Roses again. She was hypnotic.

A cell phone rang. Jolted from his trace, Colin stepped back, breaking the spell. He took a deep breath and let it out. The phone rang again. It was his. He stepped away and strode toward the desk. The key. She had asked about the key. *Focus, Colin.*

"Yes, I'll ask John about the key and get back with ye on it." He answered his cell and told them to hold. He needed to leave. After drinking the last of his whisky, he went toward the door.

He paused and gazed at Brielle as she stood there staring at the *Fae Fable Book*, and damn, if she didn't appear like she was his dream girl from the Fae fable. The one woman he dreamed of his whole life as his soul mate.

The *Fae Fable Book* had changed pages. It revealed the story of the Stone of Love. John mentioned the Fae were active since his mother had opened the crypt and that the fables told the fate of the stones. Could this be the fable telling him his fate? Was this woman meant to be his soul mate?

He wasn't sure what it meant, and he wasn't sure what to do. He heard his assistant's voice from the cell, placed it to his ear, and left Brielle staring at the bookcase.

Chapter 3

The Fae Realm, Eleventh Century (human time)

Dagda sat in the throne room of the Tuatha Dé Danann castle of blue Fae crystal constructed at the beginning of time. His wife and queen, Tethra, sat at his side, holding his hand. From the ridge of Broemere, a spiritual location for the Fae, the sea glittered beyond the ridge in the distance. Next to them, imprisoned in a sphere of powerful Fae energy, Balor, king of the Fomoire Fae, stood with his arms folded. The arguing voices of the assembled Fae grew, each rising above the other, echoing in the large room.

Tethra squeezed his hand as he gazed at her, his true love. She leaned over and whispered, "Dagda, this cannot continue. The Fae kingdoms have tried to be together as one, but this is not working." Dagda grunted and squeezed her hand back. Damn, if the woman wasn't right. They had to do something, and it had to be now.

He took a deep breath and spoke in his booming voice, ensuring it resounded throughout the room. "Silence."

Everyone froze, then turned to stare at their king.

In the distance came the roar of a dragon, loud, piercing, and angry. Another answered its call, deeper in tone. Giant wings flapped, filling the room with their reverberating sound as the dragons flew near the castle. The whoosh of each beat carried an ominous threat to those who dared to cross a dragon's path. Outside the large balcony, the first dragon screamed again, shaking the castle with its sound.

The balcony curtains whipped out. The dragon flapped its wings as it hung suspended over the balcony, its square head rotating to glare at everyone in the throne room. Its body reflected the sun in a haze of crimson light. Each red scale had a glittering edge of black. Its body was full of muscle, its wingspan over one hundred feet. As it flew, its horn-ended tail flipped, demonstrating that it could do severe damage if swung at the right angle.

With a twist of its shoulders, the dragon shifted into a man, a well-bred warrior who easily stood over six feet, landing gracefully.

His jet-black hair absorbed the sun as he strode forward. He sported a beard trimmed in an intricate, distinctive pattern. He wore his kilt in the original highland fashion, bearing the Douglas clan pattern, and he had a broadsword strapped to his back. The dragon in him growled as he continued toward the sphere, stopping shy of it, his hands fisted at his sides, his breath raging in his chest.

Behind him, the second dragon roared as it flew low over the balcony and toward the sphere, skidding to a stop in the room. It screamed into Balor's face, who stood unaffected by the powerful display.

The same build as the first, the second dragon was blue with silver edges on its scales. When it roared, the scales flexed, and the horned tail whipped and hit the energy sphere that encased Balor. Upon each attack, the covering only blinked, staying firm, for it held the evilest of all Fae in existence.

Balor rolled his eyes, folded his arms across his chest, and spoke in a dull tone. "My sons. What a disappointment ye are to me."

The blue dragon shifted, and before Balor stood a tall warrior like the first with light-brown hair with edges dusted blond. He wore a kilt and broadsword like the man beside him. The brothers stood side by side, staring at their father with rage in their eyes and death in their hearts.

Dagda rose from this throne, approaching the men. "Dameon and Tiberius, I understand we owe ye for yer father's capture. The Tuatha Dé Danann are in yer debt." He glanced from one man to the other and asked, "Where is yer brother Magnus?"

Dameon, being the oldest, turned from his father, his dark hair reflecting in the light, and bowed to Dagda. "He wished to be here but could not. We pledge ourselves to the Tuatha Dé Danann and serve the good Fae in the wars our father started." He reached for his belt and held out a bag to Dagda. It clinked when Dagda took it. Balor roared from his prison, flying against the sphere, only to be thrust back to the ground by the energy's force. Tiberius rolled his shoulders, the tattoos along his arms shifting as his dragon growled.

Dagda gasped as he held the bag, for he knew what was inside. Their energy force pulsed in his hands. "The Stones of Iona. Ye have returned them."

Dameon nodded. "Aye, our father began this war to steal the Stones of Iona for the power they hold will control the Fae and human realms. We—Tiberius, Magnus, and I"—he glanced at his brother, who glared at their father—"our father cursed to seek the stones for his use."

Tiberius's dragon growled again as he watched his father rise from the floor in his cell. "Much good it did. All three of ye turned yer back upon me. Betrayed me, ye did, yer father."

Tiberius flew at the sphere, hitting it with his fists, the orb only blinking with each fierce contact of his hands. "Ye killed her, ye bastard. Ye killed yer own wife. Ye were supposed to love her, protect her." He cried with each punch of his fists.

"Ye— *wham!* — made — *wham!* — an oath — *wham!* — to love — *wham!* — and honor her —*wham!* — as her husband, — *wham! bam!*—and ye killed her."

The sphere's energy drained Tiberius with each contact. He fell to his knees, holding his head in his hands. "Ye killed our mother."

He glanced at his father with tears in his eyes. "How could ye?"

Balor roared from behind the sphere, "I did not kill her. Ye failed her, ye and yer brothers. With yer betrayal, she died, and her blood is now upon yer hands."

Dameon lowered his head and took a deep breath.

Dagda held the bag of stones to his chest and asked again, "Dameon, where is Magnus? Where is the third dragon, the one of green for the Stone of Hope?"

Dameon wiped his hand over his face, lifting his gaze to the ceiling as a lone tear ran down his cheek. "He found his soul mate, Mina, and pledged his eternal love to her."

Balor huffed at Dameon's admission.

Dameon snapped his head, glaring at his father.

"Someone tricked Mina into believing if she rejected his favors, his love for her would grow."

Balor held his arms out. "It was not as it seemed. Mina misunderstood. T'was her fault, I tell ye."

Tiberius rose and went to stand next to Dameon. "Magnus had already completed the steps for claiming his soul mate, so when she rejected his love, the curse took effect."

Balor stroked his beard as he finished. "And she encased Magnus in Fae crystal for all eternity." His gaze leveled with Dameon's. "Which is what I will see happen to the rest of my sons in due time."

Dagda waved at the Fae guard next to the sphere, who touched his sword to the globe, forcing Balor to freeze.

Dagda returned to his throne. He handed the Stones of Iona to his wife, and his gaze traveled around the throne room filled with his subjects and fellow Fae representatives from all the kingdoms. "I have heard enough. I am ready to render my decision. The Fae council ruled I should deliver a verdict over the Fomoires' crimes as they targeted war solely upon the Tuatha Dé Danann."

Balor's eyes twitched.

Dameon and Tiberius kneeled, awaiting the Fae King's ruling. Like their father, the Fae had charged them with crimes as well.

Dagda took a deep breath and let it out slowly. "For Dameon, Tiberius, and Magnus, I absolve them of all guilt for the theft of the Stones of Iona. Forced by their father to do evil, they have seen the good in the Fae and human realms. I free them from their charges."

Tiberius and Dameon spoke in unison as they

nodded and rose. "Thank ye, Dagda. Yer ruling is most generous."

The Fae guard released Balor from his frozen state.

Balor shifted his shoulders and glared at Dagda, who sat staring back at his enemy. "For you, Balor, the charges are grim. You are guilty of breaking many Fae laws. You have taken a human as a mate, married her, and bred children with her. Yer actions violate Fae's law and place both realms at risk."

Balor grinned and chuckled.

Dagda fisted his hands on the arms of his throne. "Ye have cursed yer sons to seek the sacred Stones of Iona, Love, Faith, and Hope, to fuel yer plan to overthrow all the Fae kingdoms and rule the Fae and human realms."

Balor yelled, "I would have succeeded if my *offspring* weren't such a disappointment!"

Both brothers shifted their shoulders. The tattoos moved along their arms as the dragons in them growled.

Dagda glanced at the two men, then back at Balor. The throne room sat in suspended silence for a moment, waiting for the term of punishment.

Dagda spoke in a heavy tone. "I shall sentence you to eternity in purgatory for yer crimes, Balor."

The Fae present gasped, but it didn't stop Dagda. "Ye will not exist in any realm and have no consciousness. Ye will be nothing." Tethra placed her hand on her husband's, and he squeezed it, taking comfort in her reassurance.

Dagda rose, and Tethra handed him the three stones. Red for love, blue for faith, and green for hope. He held them to his chest and chanted quietly.

I bathe thee in blood; I place fear in yer heart,

That the truest love, may ne'er depart!
Nor other women will go thy way,
Nor deal with ye, be it as it may.
But all these things together thrown,
his heart and soul that he be torn,
He may perish and forever be,
only not in my company.

A burst of light flew from the stones, piercing Balor in his chest.

Balor screamed, his body twisting unnaturally. His head turned one way, his body another, his form stretching like a bowstring. His body snapped loudly, making him jolt.

As he faded from view, he yelled, "This is not over! I will have my revenge upon my offspring."

He disappeared, and the guard touched his sword to the sphere, making it fade.

The Fae in the throne room stood still in silence.

Dagda sat down hard. The energy needed to unleash the power of the stones combined drained him. Tethra took the stones from him and placed them in the bag.

Dameon and Tiberius approached his throne.

Dagda leaned forward. "Dameon, I am truly sorry for Magnus. Is he at Tantallon Castle?"

Dameon nodded. "In the cliff caves, hidden from the humans."

Dameon took a deep breath and glanced at Tiberius, then back at Dadga. "We, Tiberius and I, come to serve you. We ask to live in the Fae realm. The human world is not a place for shapeshifting dragons." He glanced at Tiberius as he whispered to Dagda, "It is difficult to live among them, be like them, but not.

Because of our curse, we are now part Fae and immortal. The desire to shift into dragon form is difficult to hide among so many…humans."

He gazed back at Dagda. "We wish to live here hoping our lives might be easier and our talents put to use for the good of both realms."

Dagda sighed. "Dameon, yer intentions are honorable. Ye and yer brothers' hearts are pure. Which is surprising, as yer father cursed ye to serve evil." He waved his hand. "I cannot bring ye to live in our realm. Yer purpose is in the human world, being half human yerselfs. Yer soul mates are there for each of ye to find."

Dameon's cutting laugh filled the chamber. "Ye mean as Magnus did? No, we do not desire that end. We have returned the stones and seek to live our lives peacefully."

Dagda stood, crossed to Dameon, and placed his hand on his shoulder. "Yer duty is in the human realm. I need ye there."

He glanced at Tiberius and back at Dameon. "Both of ye. Yer destiny is not in the Fae realm, but in the human one."

He patted Dameon's face. "The humans need all three of ye, as ye have not served yer purpose yet."

Dagda dropped his hand as Dameon spoke. "But I—"

Dagda raised his hand, stopping Dameon. "I have seen yer fate. Yer duty is not here."

The brothers exchanged a glance, stood there a moment, then nodded. They strode to the balcony and, with a twist of their shoulders, shifted into their dragon forms and flew off with a roar exchanged between them.

Dagda returned to his throne and sat down heavily. The Fae people filtered out of the room, glancing behind them to ensure the dragons had left or if Balor might return for his revenge.

Tethra stared at the bag of gems in her lap and sighed. "Now, who can we entrust to keep the Stones of Iona safe for all mankind?" She glanced about the almost-empty throne room. "We have run out of Fae places the Fomoire do not know of."

Dagda tapped his fingers on the arm of the throne, staring at the setting sun. "Aye, the Fae realm has proven to be too accessible a place for the Fomoire. We need a new hiding place."

He sat quietly for a moment and then mumbled, "A place so obvious they won't think to search, a place that would be more difficult for them to reach but easy for us to get to quickly if a need arose."

Dagda shook his head. "No, it can't be so. It would be too risky."

He tapped his fingers and shifted in his seat. "But then, so close to the Stone of Destiny could prove dangerous."

Tethra patted his hand. "The energy of the Stone of Destiny would help keep the Stones of Iona masked. It would be easier for us to combine their energy."

Dagda stood and shook his head. "But to have them together. If the Fomoire ever gained them all at once, it would prove the end of our and the human realms. And can I trust mere mortals to keep their word? Can I trust the MacDougall clan? They would have to guard them for centuries. I doubt any human can keep a secret that long. They can't even keep one for a moment."

Tethra smiled at him. "You underestimate them. They are good, honorable people. And we can assign our best and most cunning to assist them."

Dagda's gaze shot to his wife, and she winked. "Yer daughters, my dear."

Dagda laughed loudly and returned to his seat. "'Tis settled then. The stones go to the MacDougall clan for safekeeping."

Tethra took Dagda's hand in hers and bent to kiss the back of it. "Is this the end of it?"

Dagda turned their clasped hands over and kissed the back of hers in return. "No, my sweet, this is only the beginning."

****

Colin shot up from his dream, panting. His hand reached for his chest as he glanced around the dim room, getting his breathing under control. He sat on the couch in the study. Earlier, he couldn't sleep. He hadn't stayed in the castle for years. The old place spoke at night—a creak here and a pop there. Buildings talked, and this one had kept Colin awake.

He had felt an energy flow through him he had no control over. Something that guided his soul where it needed to go. Lately, the nights felt too long, and the days too short. That's when he climbed out of bed, threw on jeans and a tee, and then went down to the study. He thought a dram and staring at the fire would chase the restlessness off.

He must have dozed off. Too much mulling over the Fae must have brought on the strange dream. He rubbed his hand over his face and rose to refill his glass with whisky.

He sat on the couch, took a long sip, and stared into the flames contemplating all John had told him about the stones, the Fae, the magic. How could they be responsible for his parents' death? Colin sighed, mulling over the issues with the Fae. The household and now guests, the people of Dunstaffnage. How could he keep them all safe? He took another sip of whisky, pulled the plaid from the back of the couch, and covered himself, settling back lazily into the corner.

The liquor's warmth with the flames' hypnotic dance lured him into that state between waking and sleep. Dreamlike but conscious, it was a very subdued sensation. His mind floated between the stones, the Fae book, the chapel, and his parents. It was a kind of mishmash in his head.

Almost asleep, a tinkling of light bells, childlike laughter, and a small voice filled his head.

"Hello, Colin," she said.

He responded in his dream. "Hello."

"I'm glad ye've come to talk. We need to get started."

"Started? On what?" Colin thought it was another weird dream.

"Not a dream. Open yer eyes, Colin."

He opened his eyes. "Am I in my dream, or is this reality?"

Did he say it aloud? The room seemed lighter, not totally in shadow but lit in warm, dusk-like light. On the mantel sat a small woman, maybe three feet tall. Her body flashed in and out of form, like flames of fire moving in a breath of air.

All this couldn't be real. It had to be a dream. The little woman was almost pure light, with long white-blonde hair that glowed with ethereal light and a beautiful soft face with pale, almost translucent skin. His gaze scanned her, and her light-blue eyes, glowing orbs, grew more hypnotic the longer he stared. Her translucent wings fluttered fast, and when she shifted, her hair fell aside, and the point of her ear showed.

Colin blinked as he tried to stop the trance, but it wouldn't go away. Her body was of a goddess in a sheer white dress that was curvaceous in a way that no red-blooded man could deny. He felt sinful to gaze upon her, almost heavenly to think of her.

This must be what happened when he allowed John to fill his head with fanciful Fae stories. Had he conjured up the most beautiful sexual dream? No wonder they claimed no mortal man could deny the attraction of the female Fae.

The little woman smiled knowingly, and her light dimmed, allowing Colin to focus on what she said instead of her undeniable appeal.

"We need to start on righting a wrong, Colin. Yer search for the stones must begin now. The sooner, the better, before we lose more lives. Like yer parents."

"What the hell do the stones have to do with my parents? Who are ye, and what the hell are ye doing in my dream?" Colin thought in his head.

"I am a Fae. Colin, I'm yer Fae. I am Brigid, daughter of Dagda, who is king of the Tuatha Dé Danann. The dream, Colin, I showed ye the beginning. We are the ones who placed the Stones of Iona into yer family's possession for protection against evil forces. But something has gone wrong. Our enemy Fae, the Fomoire, seek to overpower our kind again with a new plan."

She waved her hand, and a cloud of glittering dust flew around her. "A plan so ingenious I almost envy it. They are using human emotions to track the stones. This time, they have created three Stones of Evil to seek the Stones of Iona and gain their powers. The first of the evil stones, Fear, has locked upon the Stone of Love. Ye must stop the evil Fae from finding the Stone of Love."

She shimmered out for a bit, then returned. "It happened when they opened the crypt this time. That was when we realized something had gone wrong. In his haste, my father, Dagda, blindly scattered the Stones of Iona throughout space and time to hide them from the Fomoire. But he couldn't protect yer parents at the same time. The Fomoire, not finding what they wanted, the Stones of Iona, killed yer parents by creating the accident. It was how we knew the evil started here. Only after their accident did events change, when Roderick MacDougall went missing in 1720."

What is she talking about? This must be another dream.

The Fae grew taller and hopped down from her perch, flying toward Colin and floating just above him. A red light now burned bright around her as she grew, breathing heat into his face while yelling in his head, "*No*, Colin, this is no dream." She waved her hand in the air, and the lights flickered. "This is as true as yer parents' death, another wrong laid at our feet." Brigid's light flashed back to white.

She floated to the couch and sat next to him. "Yer parents' death was a mistake, a most costly one. Ye must right the wrong." She sighed. "But the wrong ye must right, it isn't here, not in this time."

In a flash of light, Brigid returned to her perch on the mantel. "The Stone of Fear began here when yer ma opened the crypt. Yer ancestors sealed the Stones of Iona in the crypt. The evil Fae, a *Fomoire*, armed with the Stone of Fear, tricked yer mother into opening the crypt. The Fae murdered yer parents when the Stone of Love wasn't there. Their accident happened so quickly—before we could react, yer parents were dead. In the same instant, Roderick MacDougall went missing in 1720." She bowed her head. "The evil from the Stone of Fear blocked our view, so now we can't see everything like we used to."

Colin jumped up and pointed his finger in her face, yelling, "Right the wrong, but not here? Ye right the wrong and bring my parents back to me, ye damn sprite! My parents' death was an accident. If ye are the all-powerful Fae as ye claim to be, then *ye* right that wrong."

He ran his hand through his hair, then paced in front of the fireplace. "I'm not doing anything for anyone until my parents are here where they belong. Go back in time? Hell no. I'll sacrifice myself for my parents to return before I do any time jumping. Trade me for them."

Fading into her small form again, Brigid lowered her light, responding in a whisper, "Ye will sacrifice more than yerself on this mission for the Fae."

She flickered in and out. "Colin, I wanted to bring yer parents back. I love them as ye love them, but the evil won't allow me to. Trust me; I tried and expelled almost all my energy. It practically cost me my existence. I spent months recovering. It has taken me this long to get to ye."

Colin sat heavily on the couch. Could this be real? The Fae caused his parents' death? John suspected it was so, but this?

Her light brightened as she spoke louder. "This evil is powerful and must not win. If it does, the evil Fae will overpower the realms and rule all. You must go back to 1720. Roderick shouldn't have disappeared, and his wife's murder should not have happened. Ye must pretend to be Roderick and uncover who the Evil Fae is. Ye must right the wrong."

Colin reached for his whisky and realized he had sat up, awake. It was not a dream, for she sat perched on the mantel. He sipped his drink—the sting too potent to deny it was not real. Colin gulped more, astonished that this wasn't a dream. His parents died because of some damn stones, and now he must find them. *Through time.*

Brigid fluttered like a flame about to be extinguished. "My time is close to its end. It drains my energy to appear before a human. Ye will gather what ye need and meet me at the chapel door at sunset, in ten days. John is your trusted ally with a Fae of his own. He will serve ye as his ancestors have done for centuries." She flickered out.

Colin stood with his hand out. "Wait. I need more time. How long will I be away?"

Brigid flickered back. "Ye have no more time." Then she disappeared. The light dimmed, and shadows appeared.

Colin shook himself and ran his hands through his hair again, trying to restore some normalcy. He sat back down on the couch, staring into the flames. More time had passed than he realized, as the room turned freezing cold. Colin gasped and saw his breath. Time seemed to slow. A light, icy breeze brushed his cheek. His ma's voice came to him. *Colin, this is the only way. We are all counting on ye. Ye must do this for me, yer father, and all mankind.*

He dropped his head into his hands at the sound of her sweet voice.

His eyes teared as he whispered, "God, Ma...Da— I wish ye were here."

Chapter 4

The following morning, the sound of metal hitting stones reverberated through the chapel. Ian and Conner cut down larger stones from the quarry to fix the broken stones they had removed recently. Some stones rang with a musical, higher-pitched sound. The larger stones made a louder clunk, like heavy boulders tumbling down a cliff.

The sounds stopped, leaving Brielle in blessed silence. A woman approached the chapel. She was short and had a skip to her step, making her sandy ponytail bounce with her. Brielle recognized her immediately from her picture on their email chain, preparing for the project. Dressed like Brielle, she wore khakis and a loose-fitting shirt, and was ready for a day at a construction site.

The woman put her hand out, and Brielle shook it as she spoke. "You must be Marie Murray. It's nice to meet you in person."

Marie took her hand, shaking it enthusiastically. "Aye, I'm happy to meet ye. Ye are well known in the academic world. Yer reputation precedes ye. The paper ye wrote on the Lord of Lorne and the start of Dunbeg village and the settlement that became Dunstaffnage castle was spot on."

Brielle blushed. Only people from Rice University had complimented her work. To have a Scot compliment it, that was truly an achievement.

Brielle glanced at the chapel. "You ready to work on the floor?"

Marie followed her look. "Aye, I am here to look at the ground, if it's a good time to do so."

Brielle waved her before her as they entered the chapel. Marie stepped around the flooring, examining the center section.

"I've been out before. John has shown me around." She glanced up and blushed, making Brielle smile. So, she liked John? Interesting.

Marie cleared her throat. "Emily was particular about the flooring and the window designs. We need to focus on those windows."

Brielle nodded in agreement. They had covered this in the emails leading up to the execution of the project.

Marie approached the altar as she spoke. "In some lore, they speculated that the floor design was magical. The first laird placed the mosaic flooring in the thirteenth century. The flooring depicted Christ on the cross with the sun as a halo around his head, spanning twelve feet."

Marie walked to the center of the chapel, waving her hands around in a circle. "They positioned the center of the cross precisely in the center of the chapel, pointing east and west, as all religious buildings have the altar facing east."

She stepped forward, showing east and west with her hands. "Emily believed the circular stained glass above the altar and door held magical properties, and it's sad the panes broke. We could find no drawings or depictions, and she hoped more research would guide us to what that design was." She sighed. "She believed that light from the west window at dusk hit the center of the chapel. The stained glass matched the flooring or, at a minimum, the cross. She thought the chapel held mystical power when the shadow crossed the pattern on the floor, but she couldn't figure out what or how. With her death, we won't know."

Brielle nodded. "Yes, we'll work on the window design once they finish breaking up the rocks." The banging picked up again as if on cue.

****

Later that day, after hours of banging, the sounds echoed in Brielle's head, making her almost dizzy. Marie approached her where she stood in the center of the chapel and yelled at her, but another bang from the rocks sounded, ringing in Brielle's ears and hurting her head. She waved at her ears, trying to tell Marie she couldn't hear her.

Marie yelled over it. "How about we get out of here? The pub at the marina serves a great lunch." Marie strode out the entrance, but Brielle stopped. Marie turned back and shrugged at Brielle, who jumped through the opening, rushing to catch up with Marie.

"I don't understand why ye have such an issue with that doorway," Marie commented as they strolled toward the parking lot.

"I know. There's nothing wrong with the doorway. But for me, it gives me chills," Brielle said as she got into Marie's car.

Marie joined her and buckled up. "Well, there's a lot of old things in Scotland that give many chills. For me it's Edinburgh Castle." She shivered as she started the car. "Every time I go near it. Chills."

Her blue sedan revved. The sound of gravel crunched against the wheels as she pulled out of the car park. Marie's little car navigated the winding road easily as they headed down the cliff. The tang of the sea air blew through the car windows, refreshing Brielle. From the cliff's point, the view of Loch Etive took her breath away. Farther beyond, the shadows of the mountainous landscape stretched for eons in the distance, resulting in layer upon layer of green highlands that fell into the loch, reflected like a mirror in the tranquil waters.

Brielle turned to Marie. "The village? Isn't that Dunbeg?"

Marie nodded as she turned off the castle road into the main street, taking them into town. "Ye'll love this little village. Parts are near as old as the castle."

On the drive into the town, Brielle saw the peppering of older-style crofts and houses where locals still lived. She gazed at the glen and realized it was almost untouched by modern man and provided a peek into Scotland's historical magic lands.

After a short drive, Marie made a left turn. "But today I've got a surprise for ye."

They pulled into a crowded parking lot of the loch's marina where a quaint old-fashioned pub sat. The building itself was Tudor style, with the brown wood framing against the stark white plaster.

Marie parked and jumped from the car, smiling at Brielle. She followed, and they approached the building as another group of people were entering. Seems lunch was a busy time.

Marie entered the crowded pub, and Brielle followed, elbowing the heavy door aside. A man called from behind the bar: "Marie, look at ye. Glad ye are back. Brought me a friend, have ye now?"

Marie pulled Brielle up to the bar. "Aye, Hamish, I have." She leaned over and cupped her mouth with her hand, whispering loudly so Brielle could hear. "A Sassenach!"

Brielle's gaze traveled over the Scotsman as she sat at the bar. Hamish was a tall, elderly Scotsman with a pleasant personality, reminding her of her professor back home, but Hamish was very thin, whereas Professor Mac was round. They both had booming Scottish voices. Were all Scotsmen loud?

While Marie settled on a stool beside her, Hamish poured them two beers. On the other side of Brielle was a floor-to-ceiling window. Outside sat Dunstaffnage Marina and a pretty view of sea vessels that docked on Loch Etive. Water that had a glassy sheen called for a gliding sailboat trip so one could admire the mountain range surrounding it.

She turned as he set a mug in front of her, saying, "On the house, for the pretty lassie."

Marie peeked back at Brielle and smiled. "Aye, Hamish, ye'll never guess who this is."

Brielle glanced from Marie to Hamish as he leaned on the bar. She had a feeling they were up to something, making her wonder what was in store.

"Ye the lassie who's come at Emily MacDougall's special request all the way from America? The Sassenach come to fix the chapel. Eh?"

Brielle turned her head toward Marie, who hid her smile in her beer.

"Yes, I am." Brielle sipped her beer—warm, heady ale. Nothing like American beer, but just like Professor

Mac preferred it, served at room temperature.

Hamish winked at her as he spoke. "Well, ye'll need a proper welcome"—he raised his voice so the entire pub could hear him—"a Scottish welcome." The patrons all clapped their hands or tapped the tables in approval.

Marie giggled. "Ye'll like this. Hamish begged me to bring ye by. The people of the town wanted to meet ye. I hope ye don't mind."

Hamish took a stone from his pocket, rubbed it, then handed it to her. "Hold this, dearie. Let Hamish tell ye the tale of the Iona Stone, the fisherman, and the fairies."

As she took the stone, she smiled. She loved it when her mom told her stories from Scotland. She always said, "Let Scotland's magic chase yer cares away." And it did every time.

Brielle held the white stone up so that the light reflected off it. One side was jagged, as if it had broken, making her curious about what had happened to the missing piece. Turning the rock in her hand, she let the sunlight from the pub window capture the color. It revealed a green vein running through it. It was unique, a type of stone she had never seen before.

She closed her hand around it, holding it in her palm for a moment. Brielle could sense the centuries of history, feel the people who had touched the stone thump in her heart like the blood pumping in her veins.

Hamish recited his story in his highland lilt, and she was excited to have another Scottish tale to add to her mom's collection.

"Many centuries ago, a man fell asleep fishing in the loch under a full moon. A solid yank on his fishing rod startled him awake." Hamish feigned pulling on a fishing rod. "The fisherman sat up and saw no one was there. He heard a soft, tinkling female voice say, 'Ask for news, and you will get news.' He realized 'twas a sea fairy trying to trick him as they long to do.

"Ye see, the fairies, or the Fae, they travel through portals between their realm and the world of man. The Fae like to play tricks on humans, as some people are easily fooled. But not all of us are taken into their trickies, like ye and me."

Brielle smiled as Hamish winked at her.

"So, the fisherman feared for himself and all the fishing village. He tried to banish her with a *rosad*. That's a Gaelic spell, dear. He did this by yelling, '*I put dia eadar dhuinn*,' which means 'I put God between us.' The fisherman yelled it repeatedly, hoping to banish this fairy and her evils."

Hamish threw his head back and yelled for her, "I put *dia eadar dhuinn*," and the bar patrons repeated the chant, the phrase ringing in her ears and echoing in the tavern.

Hamish rested his elbows on the bar, continuing his story in a quieter tone. "The fisherman's efforts were in vain, and he failed to expel the fairy from the human world. The fairy became so angered that she cast a spell that forced him to visit her each night. Over time, the fisherman tried to resist, but her power was too strong. The fisherman wanted a power strong enough to conquer her spell upon him. So, he carried a stone from Iona, a holy isle where to this day they consider its white stones magical and powerful."

He pulled another rock from his pocket and showed it to Brielle as she leaned over the bar to get a closer look. It was like the one she held in her hand, but round and smooth. "The fisherman, ye see, took this rock to his Fae, hoping that the stone's power would vanquish the fairy and her spell. He heard her tinkling call to him as he approached the shore. He held the rock to his chest and repeated the Gaelic spell, 'I put *dia eadar dhuinn.*' The water rose in a vast wall, taller than he was, and crashed down, hard." The pub owner's voice rose again.

"The wall of water continued crashing upon him, trying to drag him into the loch and out to sea." Hamish slammed his palm on the bar repeatedly, and the patrons at the bar all slammed their hands on the tables, Marie hitting the bar with them.

Brielle scanned the room, observing them all, laughing as they took part in the telling of his story. She glanced at Marie, who smiled at her.

Hamish had to raise his voice over the pounding to continue the story. "The fisherman fell to his knees, holding the stone from Iona to his heart and praying again and again. 'I put *dia eadar dhuinn,* I put *dia eadar dhuinn,* I put *dia eadar dhuinn.*' "

The pub patrons cheered, then suddenly fell silent.

Brielle turned to watch Hamish as he held the stone to his chest, bowed his head, and continued in a lower voice. "The crashing waves stopped after some time. The fisherman glanced up as the sun rose over the loch. The fairy's force to visit her, gone." He raised his head and held the white rock in the sunlight from the window. "And this, my dear, is why every boat captain on Loch Etive carries a Stone of Iona with him on every voyage."

The pub broke out in final cheers that quickly

faded as the patrons continued their everyday business.

Hearing a Scottish fable reminded Brielle of her mom, and her heart warmed.

Marie set her mug down and pulled a rock from her pocket. "I have one, ye know, an Iona stone. From my grandma."

Brielle handed Hamish back the stone, and he took it as he eyed her from behind the bar. "Wait, lass." He reached across the bar, taking her empty hand. He placed the stone in her palm and then curled his hand around hers as it held it. "You hang on to this one. It's a special one from a special friend." He winked at her. "I think ye'll need it, dear."

****

The women lingered after the patrons had cleared out from the lunch rush. Hamish was in the back, leaving them alone at the bar.

Marie turned to Brielle and asked, "Do ye miss it—home?"

Brielle rested her arms on the bar and frowned out the window at the loch. "Sometimes, yes, sometimes not." She glanced back at Marie. "I miss Professor Mac and his wife." She took a deep breath and blew it out. "I miss my mom. She died recently of cancer."

Marie patted her arm. "I am sorry to hear that. John had mentioned it, but I didn't want to intrude."

Brielle smiled. "It's not intruding. It's nice to talk about her. She was from Glasgow, like you." She stared at the loch through the floor-to-ceiling window. "Being here, it's like being close to her. She loved Scotland."

They sat silently for a moment, then Marie asked, "Don't ye miss yer friends?"

Brielle looked at Marie and then down. It took her

a minute to answer, thoughts of her ex, Tony, swirling through her mind. Flashes of memory flipping like an awful movie that would jump its frame as every memory changed, every one of them haunting her. She closed her eyes hard, then opened them to the sight of Loch Etive.

She took a breath, trying to sigh, but it came out as a hiccup. "I don't have any friends, not anymore."

Marie huffed. "Nonsense, ye are a nice person, great at yer work. Certainly, ye have friends back home?"

Brielle glanced at the loch and shrugged, not commenting. She watched Marie's reaction in her peripheral vision, hoping she'd drop it.

Marie turned fully, facing Brielle. "Brielle, what is it? Why not anymore?"

Brielle's eyes watered, and her nose ran. She sniffed, trying to make it sound like a breath, anything to keep the tears at bay. "You will think it's stupid. Probably selfish."

Marie took Brielle's free hand in hers and squeezed it once. "Never. Tell me." Marie smiled. "Unburdening yer problems will lighten yer load. I'm a friendly ear."

Brielle rubbed her nose and sniffed again. "Professor Mac, you know he and Emily MacDougall, Colin's mother, were childhood friends."

Marie released Brielle's hand. "Aye, John mentioned that's how Emily knew to put ye on her list of potentials for the renovation job."

Brielle glanced at Marie, then back at the loch. It was so pretty here. She loved Scotland. Professor Mac was right; coming here was the best choice. "Yes, Professor Mac had another goal in getting me this job.

He wanted me away from my boyfriend. He said it would do us some good. A separation."

Marie set her elbow on the bar to allow her head to rest in her hand. Brielle wished she could find comfort as easily.

Professor Mac's "consequence number three" popped into her head, the Scottish lilt rolling in her ear. He had a list of "consequences of staying in a terrible relationship," just as he had a checklist for "Is this man right for ye?" He said it was to help her stay grounded in herself. Consequence number three: "Ye be trapped with somebody who is just not right for ye."

"Why would separation be good? Was the boyfriend a *scabby bassa*?"

Brielle's face must have given away her confusion.

Marie smiled. "*Scabby bassa* is slang for 'dirty bastard.' And from the expression on yer face, he was, wasn't he?" She shook her head. "I hate those kinds of boyfriends."

Brielle looked at the loch, so many memories jumbled in her head, threatening to make it explode. She wanted so badly to tell someone who would help ease the pressure and pain.

She focused on Marie but didn't see her. No, she saw every moment Tony did something to her. The fists flying, the yelling in her face, the items flung at her. The sex. She hated thinking of the perverted games he liked to play, and he had been her first. Why the hell did she stay for so long, and how had she survived?

"He was more than a dirty bastard," she whispered. A tear escaped her eye and trailed down her cheek, and Marie gasped. "He had a hard time controlling his anger. It would spill out sometimes." She sniffed, and another tear escaped; this one she willingly let fall. "Sometimes, I got in the way. A fist here, a slap there. That was how it all started." She hiccupped a breath.

Marie patted her shoulder. "God, I am so sorry, Brielle."

Brielle blew out her breath. "Me too."

Professor Mac's consequence number two came to mind. It always did when she thought of the abuse: "You will know deep down that you deserve better."

Marie sighed. "Well, ye can talk to me anytime, Brielle. I'll be willing to listen."

Brielle wasn't there; she was here. She didn't have to do those things again. Or see him, ever. She took a deep breath and glanced at Marie. She had a friend, and it wasn't Tony's. Marie was *her* friend.

"Thanks, but all that's gone now, him, his friends." She smiled and dried her tears with her napkin. "I am here, in Scotland, my mother's home. A new place, a new job, and a new life."

Marie took her hands in hers. "Aye, and new friends."

Chapter 5

That afternoon, Colin sat at his desk, staring at his whisky glass as he held it up to the sunlight. The liquid reflecting the light reminded Colin of the day he met Brielle. That felt like weeks ago, but it had only been a day.

John spoke from his seat in front of the desk. "I had a similar dream as well. My Fae, Morrigan, appeared to me much as yours did to you." John took a sip of whisky. "She said they are sisters. Brigid serves your family, and Morrigan serves mine. Told me this is the way they have done it for centuries."

"Back in time. Brigid said I need to go back in time. How the hell does anyone do that?" Colin stood up and marched to the mantel, pacing before the fire. "Right the wrong. What the hell am I to right, and how the hell do I do it?" He paused, shook his head, and paced again. "Roderick, my ancestor, is in purgatory. Is that for real?"

John leaned over the back of his chair toward Colin. "Ye know yer father had a saying about the fables and purgatory. He said only the damned souls deserve to be there. If a good soul is sent there, he is automatically released in twelve moons."

Colin huffed. "I doubt one threat my da used to keep us in line as children rings true now, John."

"Well, it worked on us both, and yer sister Ainslie

as well. It seemed true when we were young." John chuckled. "It just seems true now that we face a reality that purgatory exists."

Colin rubbed his neck. "I donna know."

John sat forward as he spoke. "So, let's start with what we know. My grandma—she's still alive. Maybe she'll have some insight into this. I'll ask her about the key to the *Fae Fable Book* and what she knows about the Fae and the stones. Grandda was the captain of the castle for the longest. She must know something." John turned in his chair and set his elbows on his knees. "We need to think four dimensionally. Ye can't just think in this time. It would help if ye thought in all time, as it is simultaneous. Isn't that what yer Fae said? They can see all time at the same time. In theory, what happens in 1700 affects this time."

John shifted his hands one over the other, mimicking a folded paper. "It's like the folds of a piece of paper when the edges touch each other. If ye go back in time and do something different from our written history, it might change something that will have a butterfly effect here. Ye'll have to be careful in everything ye say and do." He lowered his hands and smiled. "Ye know I studied physics at the university. Time itself is the fourth dimension." Leaning back in his chair, he continued, "So, say ye were to stop Roderick from disappearing. That could change yer family history, because he may not remarry a Ross, as yer family history tells us. Or if ye were to save your great-grandma, Mary, from dying. Roderick wouldn't remarry, to a Ross, and there might be more descendants, as the MacDougall direct line would expand, and the Ross line would not exist."

Colin ran a hand through his hair. "Stop, John, ye're making me dizzy."

John sighed. "Well, another thing ye need to remember is that ye have my ancestor to help ye when ye arrive. He would know about the stones' duty and the Fae's existence. He's Archibald MacArthur. I will never forget that ancestor. My da always talked about him."

Colin glanced at John and nodded. "Yes, ye're right. I would need his help." He stopped his pacing. "It would be nice to communicate with ye while I'm there, but we can't."

Rising, John smiled as he crossed toward the fireplace. "Funny ye should mention it. My da showed this to me years ago." He reached down to a stone at the base of the fireplace and pulled it loose, mortar still attached.

"There is a box in a hole here for hiding valuables. My da told me when his da showed it to him. They had found old documents from the early 1900s in it." John put the stone back in place. "Ye could put documents in here for me, and I'll check it daily till ye return."

Colin frowned. "But if they opened the box hole in the 1900s, documents from the 1700s won't be there now."

John snorted a short laugh. "Ye are not thinking four-dimensionally. It will not happen until ye travel there. Anything ye, while in the past, put in the box isn't there now. Ye have to think simultaneously, what happens there happens here, at the same time."

He waved his hand to the side. "But they proved that theory wrong some years ago." John scratched his chin and shrugged. "Then again, none of those geeks have time traveled. The Fae, they do things their way."

Taking a moment, both men silently contemplated the entire situation.

"We've got ten days. Ten days to prepare, and then ye'll go. I'll keep an eye out for anything the Fae might do here," John said.

Colin stepped to the window. *If the Fae stories are true, anything the Fae might do here...* echoed in his mind. He glanced at the *Fae Fable Book*, and his ma's voice drifted into his consciousness, telling the Fae Fable story of the Stone of Love.

Upon arriving at the castle, he confronted the evil Fae. The Stone of Love burned in his clothes and chest when he approached her. Angry that they had discovered her, the evil Fae cast a spell upon the village girl and the prince, opening a portal to purgatory.

"True love or a lifetime in nothingness—choose yer fate," she yelled at the prince.

Confused, the prince asked, "Why do ye do this? Why do ye hate so much?"

The village girl answered for the evil Fae. "She does not hate, but is fearful. The opposite of love is not hate, but fear."

He offered the stone from his neck to his true love, the maiden from the stream. "I shall live forever in purgatory so ye may live a full life. Take the Stone of Love."

Her love for him was so strong she could not allow the great prince to sacrifice himself for her, the village girl. When he handed her the stone, she thrust it into his hands, jumped into the portal, and saved the prince.

So angered was the prince that he turned upon the

evil Fae and drove his sword through her heart, while holding the necklace with the Stone of Love in the same hand as the sword. The Evil Fae's blood dripped from the blade to the Stone of Love. Dropping his sword to the ground, the prince fell to his knees, gripping the Stone of Love to his heart. He concentrated on his wish that his true love would return to him.

Dagda, the king of the Tuatha Dé Danann, appeared. "I am sorry, prince, I cannot help ye. A spell cast by the evil Fae I cannot undo. But I can give you a chant, and ye may call the girl back if yer love is powerful enough. But I warn you, the chant will fail if she does not return your love."

Roaring in his pain, the prince focused his prayer on his one true love. He chanted:

I want to see love's highest power
Take me now, not to my past
Right now, at this hour,
Bring my true love back at last.

He focused on thinking, "Come to me," over and over. He closed his eyes and poured all his love into his one wish. The Stone of Love grew hot in his hand, so hot he had to let it go. It floated to the center of the room, hovering above everyone, glowing pure white. The prince kept his chant going, mentally saying it over and over.

The Stone of Love burst into a million points of light, blinding everyone for a moment. When everyone's eyes had adjusted, the village girl stood in the center of the room, where the Stone of Love had burst.

Overcome with emotion, the prince gathered her into his arms and kissed her. The sun shone through the glass window above them and cast them in a halo of light.

Dagda, the king of the Tuatha Dé Danann, said to all in the room: "The greatest power of all is true love."

Colin's head snapped up. "God, John, what about Brielle? What am I to do about her?"

John's gaze snapped to his. "What do ye mean? What will ye have to do about her? She's busy with the chapel."

"Aye, but yesterday as we stood by the *Fae Fable Book*. It changed pages."

John stood and crossed to the book next to Colin. "It what? The book hasn't changed pages ever." John bent over the book, reading.

"Aye, I know," said Colin, "but it did. It changed to the story my ma read me at bedtime. 'The Stone of Love.' And now the Fae tell me I must go on a mission to find that very stone. But here's what's got me concerned. The fable talks about a maiden sacrificing herself for her true love. She goes to purgatory for him."

John glanced at him. "Well, so? What does that have to do with Brielle?"

"When she stood here yesterday, by the window. I'll be damned, but she looked exactly like the description of the maiden in the fable, 'The Stone of Love' fable. At first, I thought it was the light playing tricks on me, but now with the visit from the Fae, I worry she's part of this. I worry about her."

She'd appeared as his dream girl since he was a child. Now that the Fae showed him they were real, that the duty and the stones were real, he feared for Brielle. If Colin pursued her as he desired, as a woman he might love, would he be placing her in harm's way? Would he endanger her life? He would find a way to see her and keep her safe.

Colin crossed to the mantel and paced back and forth. "Brielle is too bright. She would figure this out, the stones, the Fae. She would figure out a way to follow me. If what ye said about the *Fae Fable Book* telling the fate of the stones is true, she could not be near the rocks or the Fae."

John sighed. "We'll keep her busy with the chapel."

"When I go, I'll tell her I have to take a trip for work, a long one." Colin continued his pacing. *She must stay here, where she is safe.* He had lost his parents already. To lose anyone else would be too much.

"After all this is done, I'll make it up to her," Colin said, nodding to himself.

John sighed. "She will know ye're lying. She's not dumb. Brielle will see straight through this, through us."

Colin stopped pacing and moved to John, placing his hand on his shoulder. "Ye have to play along. Marie can't know either. It's too dangerous."

John shook his head. "Colin, I don't know if this will work."

"It has to work. We have no choice."

Chapter 6

A loud crack of thunder jolted Brielle awake to a pitch-black room. It was so loud it shook the castle. She never slept during any storm. Taking a breath, she thought, *I will not get scared.* Light. She needed light. John said the electricity might go out and mentioned keeping the candle by the bed. Where was it?

Lightning briefly lit up the room and the table in front of the fireplace with the candle and matches. She got out of bed, her feet recoiling when they hit the cold floor. She stumbled toward the fireplace, hit the chair, and fell. Lightning illuminated up the room again. Above her was the table. Brielle reached for the top of the table, placed her hand flat, and felt along it. Her hand found the roundness of the candle, and she snatched it to her chest. Thunder boomed again, making her jump. She felt around with her hand again. Lightning illuminated the room again as she grabbed the matchbox. Shaking, she opened the box, grabbed a stick, and struck. The light from the candle covered her small area, and relief washed over her.

Thunder rumbled, making her jump again. *God, I hate storms.* She held the candle upright so she wouldn't set the castle on fire. *Set the whole place on fire. Wouldn't that be the end of all that beat all?* She got up from the floor, grabbing a wrap. She put it on while holding the candle, trying not to blow it out.

Recalling the study couch before the fireplace, she descended the stairs. She hoped to curl up on the sofa, warmed by the fire, with a soothing book to take her mind off the storm.

At the study, the door was ajar. A low fire glowed around the room. *Good, someone already lit the fire.* Brielle slipped into the dim room, crossed to the fireplace, and set the candle on the mantel. A flash of lightning illuminated the room, drawing her gaze to the shelves beside the fireplace.

She perused the shelving, trying to find the perfect book. She realized the one she wanted was three shelves up, and she couldn't reach that high. Climbing to her knees on the lower cabinet, she stood and reached to the shelving above. Her fingertips barely touched the book she wanted. She stretched a bit more, and just as she was about to reach the spine marked *Love Poems and Sonnets*, a crack of thunder startled her, and she fell backward off the bookcase. Her cry was cut short when she hit something solid. A warm, muscular chest shifted along her back, and strong arms cradled her. Mortified, she kept her eyes shut. *How much worse could it get?*

Then the chest shook with a chuckle. The voice that belonged to it said, "Careful what ye seek, lassie. Ye might find something ye aren't looking for." In utter embarrassment, she kept her eyes shut. It was Colin.

"Ye can open your eyes, Brielle." She turned her head farther into his chest. That was a mistake. He was shirtless and smelled too damn good.

"Please put me down," she breathed. Colin moved to the couch and lowered her to the cushions. A plaid wrap lay on the sofa, still warm from a human body.

She was not the only one who hated storms. She peered up from the couch. Next to the bookcase, Colin bent and picked up the book from the floor. He glanced at the open book, then at her with a raised eyebrow, and read aloud:

Western wind, when wilt thou blow.
That the small rain down can rain?
Christ, that my love was in my arms
And I in my bed again.

"Some light reading for a storm?" Colin lifted an eyebrow.

"Something of the sort. I was hoping to pass the storm." Thunder boomed again. She jumped and squeaked.

"Storms scare ye?" He closed the book and went to the couch, handing it to her.

She went to take it from his hands, their touch causing sparks to fly up her arm. She glanced up at Colin's face. He stood there with his hand still outstretched. He gazed directly into her eyes. They paused a moment. She shook herself, put the book on the side table, then peeked from under her lashes at Colin.

He faced the fireplace, bending to turn up the gas. His back muscles rippled with the movement of his body. As he rose, his muscles undulated under the stretched material of his jeans. Sensual heat rose inside Brielle like a fiery flame. He twisted, gazing at her. His face had the same smoldering expression as the one in the portrait of his ancestor she'd seen the day she arrived.

Thunder surged again. She jumped, closing her eyes and keeping them shut. She took a deep breath, trying to calm her nerves. After a moment, a shuffling told her he had moved around the room. A clink of glasses and the sound of liquid pouring. The couch dipped, and his body shifted toward her. A familiar potent, tart smell filled her nostrils, making her mouth water, and she licked her lips. He had positioned the glass under her nose.

She opened her eyes and took the glass from him.

"Here, lass, we're in for a blow tonight. Ye'll need this. Power won't be back until morning, when the crews can get out this far." He reclined back on the cushions. "Have a wee nip, and we'll get ye back to yerself in no time."

She drew a sip, swallowing the liquor and welcoming the warming sensation. Colin took a sip of his. Another boom, and she jumped.

"Come lass, tuck in, and let me chase yer fears away." He settled her in the crook of his arm as they lay back on the couch. Colin wrapped them up in the red plaid with green and blue patterns, just like the one on her bed.

Another blast of thunder made her shudder. Colin stretched his arm farther around her shoulders and pulled her into his side, fitting her against him, and he hummed. She hadn't been this close to a man since her ex. Ever since their breakup, she'd been uncomfortable with men, being in their close company, but she was comfortable with Colin, wrapped in his body's warmth.

Another boom surprised her.

He squeezed her shoulder, concern evident in his voice. "Tell me, why do storms scare ye so much?"

Brielle took another sip of the whisky and sensed its warmth easing her nerves. Maybe telling someone would help. She'd told no one the entire story and never got the chance. Her ex—Tony—never bothered with anything that didn't revolve around him. He liked thunderstorms and always believed her fear was weak. Sometimes he would make fun of her fear, laughing and joking, taking pleasure in her discomfort.

Taking a deep breath Brielle pulled out the memory she had worked hard to bury over the years.

"I was eleven years old. My brother lured me into the shed, thinking he was joking around, and told me he had found something old. At a young age, I was always searching for old things. I enjoyed history and historical objects. They fascinated me." Thunder boomed again.

Colin rubbed her arm as he teased, "Oh, old things fascinate you? What a surprise."

Brielle laughed. "Yes, old things...they tell a story. Who owned them? What were they for? Were they valued and treasured?" She smiled. She loved talking about her work, loved the intrigue of those stories. Thunder boomed again, and she lurched. She took a sip of whisky, trying to convince herself that she could get through the memory.

"My brother told me he'd dug up something old. He claimed it was like an old pocket watch. Swore, he thought it was from the Old West. Knowing I couldn't resist, he told me it was just inside the shed."

Brielle took sip, and it rallied her confidence. "So, out I go to the old shed. He followed me, excited. I should have been wary, as he always played tricks on me." She took another sip of whisky. "I peered into the shed. He said, go in farther. So, I did. He slammed the door shut and locked it. Laughing, he yelled, 'Got ya,' and I heard him run."

Colin rubbed her shoulder.

"The rain had already started. It was dark, and the shed reeked of dirt mixed with old oil. I kept banging on the door and yelling, but nobody came. The storm worsened. Lightning, thunder." She was breathless when she finished. Thunder rumbled, and she jumped again. He squeezed her shoulder and stroked her arm again, soothing her.

She took a deep breath before she continued. "Time passed. The storm was still raging. I lost my voice. I curled up between the lawnmower and the wheelbarrow in the center of the shed, trying to find shelter from the noise. The thunder grew louder, boom after boom. I curled into a ball on the floor and prayed." She shivered in his arms.

Still running his fingers up her arm, Colin asked, "What happened?" Brielle blew out a breath she didn't realize she held, almost in a laugh.

Taking a sip of whisky, Brielle spoke as it warmed her. The next part seemed silly now that she'd told someone. "I finally fell asleep. I dreamed of storm gods stomping on me and crushing me in my sleep. Every time the thunder sounded, I jumped. Eventually, the storm died, and I slept in the shed. No one found me till morning." Brielle stared into the glass, not seeing the last bit of the light brown liquid.

Colin took another sip of whisky and asked, "Mm, what happened to your brother?"

Brielle shook herself. "Nothing. I never told my parents what he did. I said I was searching for something, and the door got stuck."

"Lass? I would have yelled it at the top of my lungs. Tattled on the brat good."

She shifted her gaze to his. "Well, he was the son who could never do wrong. But he always did terrible things and never got caught. I was the tomboy daughter, always into something." Brielle realized she had raised her voice. She rotated and sat back in his arms, staring at the flames in the fireplace. She inhaled his scent and relaxed into his embrace, his even breathing, the slow caresses of his fingers soothing her temper. He cared.

Professor Mac's rule number three floated into her head. *Does he treat you right?* She'd already answered that. Tonight, he treated her—well, better than just well.

Rule number five came to mind. *Do you know him?* She stared at the flames, turning the thought over in her mind. *He was angry at my parents for not noticing I was gone. He's a lawyer. He defends people and cares for them. But does he care for me? Yes.*

They sat silently, as the rain pattered on the stone and glass.

****

Brielle stirred in the quiet. Colin was still. The thunder was gone. Warm and toasty in Colin's arms, she was safe. It had been so long since she had felt this way. She did not want to let the mood go.

Colin turned and hummed. "'Tis a good way to pass the storm. A tot, a warm fire, and good company."

Blinking, Brielle thought Colin wanted this to end. "Yes, it is." She rose. "Well, I should get to bed."

He stopped her, grabbing her hand. "Brielle, let us bide our time here."

She nodded and sat back down, curling into his embrace, enjoying the sense of shelter in his arms. She closed her eyes and laid her head on his chest. His heartbeat thumped a steady rhythm, slow and comforting.

Colin's finger slid under her chin and tilted her chin up till she stared into his eyes. Colin leaned forward and paused so close to her lips that his breath mingled with hers.

His gaze shifted to her lips. "May I?" Then her eyes. "Kiss ye?"

Licking her lips in anticipation, she nodded as he lowered his for a fleeting, brief kiss. It tingled, sending a million sparks to her toes. He deepened the kiss and turned her body to fit alongside his. Those tingles that shot down to her feet rushed back up to her head, making her a little dizzy. Her breasts rubbed against his bare chest hair, sensing the springy tangle through her gown.

"Brielle, let me chase the storm away for ye," he whispered. Brielle sat on his lap, placed both hands on his face, and ran her hands through his hair. She practically climbed up his chest and gave in to the next kiss as a moan escaped.

His nostrils flared, and he growled softly. Colin tilted her head back, trailing kisses down her neck and back to her ear, sending jolts of need clear through her. Sparks of flames shot through her body. *This is the first time it has been like this with anyone...*

Colin turned her in his embrace, and she fell under his broad chest, lying on the couch. Need, as she had never felt before, rose inside her, nestled in the rapture of his embrace.

She sensed his growing response and wrapped her arms around his chest, molding her body to his. She rubbed against him, searching for the friction to arouse them both.

He shifted again, drawing her knee up so he could nestle himself between her legs, and rubbed against her heat. She moved her hand to his chest and slid it down, trailing her fingertips along the line of hair leading to the top of his jeans.

Colin growled deeper as he grasped her hand. "Careful, lass. I only intended to play. You go much further, and I cannot promise I will be able to stop."

He took her hand, drew it to his lips, and kissed the inside of her wrist. "Let's just relax and enjoy the rain."

Pulling her up to a sitting position, Colin settled himself behind her. She rested her ear against his chest, listening to the beat of his heart racing from their recent intimacy.

As his heartbeat slowed, the storm outside died down. The pitter-patter of rain against the window, combined with the rhythm of his heart, lulled Brielle into a protected place.

She must have drifted off for a while, for he roused her. "Listen. Can you hear it?" he whispered in her ear.

"Mmm, hear what? The only thing I hear is your heart beating," she whispered.

"The storm."

"What storm?" she whispered, gazing into his face.

"The storm's gone. No more thunder. Nothing to scare ye anymore," he whispered as he gazed into her eyes.

"No, I can't hear the thunder anymore, only your heart." Brielle laid her head on his chest and fell into a deep sleep.

****

Sun shone through the study window, waking Colin. He slid from their embrace, regretting the moment he left her arms. Brielle mumbled something in her sleep. Colin brushed his hand along her jawline, noting how perfect she looked, wrapped in his family plaid. He bent to gather her in his arms and spotted the book of poems on the floor. He grabbed it, carefully lifted Brielle still wrapped in his plaid, and carried her upstairs to her bedroom.

He was angry with her parents for not noticing she was gone all night. The fear her brother caused Brielle when she was young made him even more furious. All he wanted to do was chase her worries away. She was a strong woman whom he cared for. He hated that she seemed broken at that moment. Colin gazed at her in his arms and vowed that she would never know fear like that again.

He paused at her bedroom door, intent on putting her to bed and seeking rest. He could not bring himself to let her go. It had been a long night and promised to be an even longer day. He needed to take that bereavement leave Mr. Connell, his boss, had offered, so he could spend more time here fulfilling his duty to the Stones of Iona. More time with her. He shifted Brielle in his arms. She stirred and leaned her head on his shoulder, fitting perfectly. Resolved to the day, he elbowed the door aside and stepped into her room.

The sunrise lit the room in a warm haze. Colin carried Brielle to the bed, slid her into the mussed bedcovers, and admired her curves through her gown. As if sensing a chill, Brielle reached for the covers, and Colin covered her with the bedclothes. As he shifted the plaid wrap from under her, the poem book thudded to the floor. Colin picked it up and placed it on the bedside table.

"Rest easy, *mo chridhe*, my heart. I'll chase your storms away," he whispered as he leaned to her face and kissed her lips.

****

As he went about his routine, dressing for the day, he remembered her story, the shed, and the storm. As Colin ran the story through his mind again, understanding dawned on him. He stopped and almost kicked himself. That was why the workers did most of the work in the crypt. So, it was true; she was afraid of the chamber. Colin promised to consult with John to add a generator and lighting to the crypt so Brielle would be comfortable.

Thoughts of Brielle swirled in his mind—her eyes, her voice, her laugh, her vulnerabilities. He found himself in the hallway before her door without remembering how he had gotten there.

Colin opened the door and crossed to her bed. After seeing her in the growing dawn light, he realized she was more than growing on him. Colin sensed he was under a spell that drew him to her in a way no other woman could. If this was what a Fae spell was like, he wouldn't mind it one bit.

He caressed her cheek and leaned toward her, brushing his lips against hers, whispering, "*Codladh sámh, a thasgaidh*, sleep peacefully, my darling."

He smiled as he quietly closed her door and headed to the kitchen.

Up bright and early, Mrs. Abernathy had prepared breakfast. "I'll take it in the study," he informed her. "Need to talk to the law firm to clear my schedule for a few weeks."

"Ah, finally taking time off. You need it." She

turned to him and put her hands on her hips. She leveled him with a *you rascal* expression.

"Wouldn't have anything to do with our wee builder now, would it? I went up to check on her earlier, and she wasn't in her bed. You wouldn't have any idea where she might have put herself last night?" Mrs. Abernathy folded her arms and glared at him.

"Mm..." Colin ignored her raised eyebrow and replied, "She's in her bed now. Tell her I'll meet her at the chapel when she finally comes down. I want to go over progress there."

Mrs. Abernathy shook her head as he smiled and headed toward his office.

****

Brielle rolled toward the sun pouring through the windows. As she lay there for a minute, she tried to recall everything from last night. Everything seemed to be in a haze. Did Colin say *mo chridhe*? She didn't even recognize that Gaelic word. She tucked the covers under her chin, snuggling into the warmth. No man ever cared so well for her. There was something else, but she couldn't remember. She glanced at the blinking clock. Blinking meant loss of power, from the storm. The angle of the sunlight told her how late it was. Lord, she didn't have time for woolgathering. She jumped out of the bed to get ready for work.

Rushing through a quick wash and dressing, Brielle wanted to get to the chapel as soon as possible. She glanced at the bed and spied the book of poems on the nightstand. Colin had read a poem from the book, and she couldn't remember it. Brielle grabbed it and flipped it open. As she scanned it, she saw that every third or fourth page was blank. She couldn't find the poem about storms. There were love poems, one on enchantment, and a demon poem that gave her a chill. She slammed the book closed and stuffed it in her backpack.

The storm had stopped the electric clocks in the castle, and no one bothered to wake her or reset them. Late, she headed to the kitchen. Damn, she realized she must go right past the study. She went down the stairs. As she neared the study, she heard Colin on the phone. She tiptoed past the open door, peeking in. Relieved to see his back was to her as he stared out the window, Brielle continued to the kitchen.

****

As he entered the study, he pulled out his cell phone and dialed his assistant to clear his calendar for a couple of weeks. After confirming his updated schedule, he turned to the window. Colin caught sight of Brielle in the reflection as she tiptoed past, sneaking past the doorway unnoticed.

Enchanted by her behavior, he laughed, and cut his assistant off mid-sentence as he ended the call. He glimpsed out the door as Brielle entered the kitchen. He strode out the study door to reach the chapel before Brielle. Colin moved through the hall and wondered about her work on the ruin. Curious about her reaction to last night, he jogged up the trail. He smiled as he neared the chapel ahead of Brielle and hoped she enjoyed last night as much as he did.

****

Mrs. Abernathy had coffee and breakfast on a tray. Brielle ran in, glanced around, and tried to figure out what to do first. *Mrs. Abernathy must have one of those internal clocks that wakes her up every morning.*

Brielle didn't have one of those. She was constantly late.

"No, dear, my husband has the internal clock. He wakes me most delightful if ye ken what I mean." Mrs. Abernathy winked at her.

"God, I must have spoken my thoughts out loud." *Brielle, get control of your mouth.*

"Dearie, let me get ye something right for your breakfast. Ye sit down there, and I'll put you something together." Mrs. Abernathy said.

"I can't. I'm late as it is. Just coffee and a muffin." Brielle grabbed a muffin off the tray, stuffing some in her mouth. Blueberry, her favorite. She closed her eyes and moaned, wishing there was time to sit and savor the taste.

"Ye—sure, dear. Colin is up. He mentioned he would make his way to the chapel to see yer progress." Mrs. Abernathy handed her a tall Styrofoam cup of coffee.

"Spot of heavy cream, right? Just the way ye like it." Mrs. Abernathy winked as she gave it to her.

She choked on her muffin, nearly spitting it across the counter. "Colin, he is going to the chapel and wants to see me?" She grabbed a juice and washed down the muffin stuck in her throat. Mm, cranberry, another favorite of hers.

Brielle ran out the door thinking, *Oh, now he's interested in my business.* She would hate it if he started judging her work as not good enough. She tried to sip her coffee as she rushed through the woods toward the chapel. *Well, he has a right. I mean, I am rebuilding his chapel, his castle, his family's legacy.* She took a sip of coffee and swore as she burned her mouth, then stumbled as she rushed into the chapel clearing.

As the workers were arriving, she shoved the last of her muffin in her mouth and thought about the building. She was never comfortable going through the doorway. Sometimes she used the door behind the pulpit, where the crypt entrance sat. She had only been down in the crypt twice. It reminded her too much of the shed her brother had locked her in. Pushing that from her mind, she approached the chapel.

This time, she entered through the chapel door. She usually walked slowly through it but didn't have time for that today. She jumped over the threshold. A gust of wind blew in her face, icy cold against the warmth of the sunlight. The blast disappeared as quickly as it had appeared. When she passed through the doorway, a chill spread down her spine, and she shook herself to clear it away. It was time she faced Colin.

She turned toward the altar. Colin stood facing away from her. The rising sun shone through the small round window in the chapel's front, illuminating him in bright light. Purple flecks flashed as the sun struck his jet-black hair, making it seem like an obsidian mirror. Colin's feet stood apart, arms at his sides. He seemed like he was contemplating life. Brielle's chest felt light, as if some weight had lifted and carried her worries away. The emotion was so overwhelming it knocked the breath from her. She must have made a noise, because he turned.

He took a step toward her. "I have not been down here for years." He took another few steps, reaching her in the middle of the chapel.

Not taking his eyes off her, he said, "It's quite beautiful." He reached to tuck a stray strand of hair behind her ear, then trailed his thumb along her cheek.

Brielle's breath caught. She blinked, and then she remembered to breathe, breaking eye contact, her face heated. She glanced around and sipped her coffee. "Well, it was. It will be again, one day."

She took a deep breath and peered back at him. "Mrs. Abernathy said you wanted an update on the progress. Let's start with a tour." She moved away, leading him to the back of the chapel.

He reached out, touching her hand. "I lied to Mrs. Abernathy. I came here to see ye." He held her hand, rubbed his finger over the top, then gave it a light squeeze.

She glanced away and sipped her coffee. "Oh." She pulled her hand from his and spoke in a rush. "I suppose you want to talk about last night. I know it's not a common thing. I mean, it's not common for me to jump into anyone's bed. Well, technically, we weren't in bed." She sighed. Before she ruined this conversation, she should get on to another topic. She stepped away, letting her backpack slide off her shoulder and dumping it on the ground. She set her coffee cup down and leaned on her makeshift table.

Getting her best professional voice out, Brielle turned back to face Colin. "The review of work—yes, we need to cover that. The floor, you know, built in the thirteenth century was a stone mosaic with depictions of Christ on the cross with the sun halo around his head spanning twelve feet. We've been preparing for the restoration of the flooring. Marie will oversee it."

She walked to the closest window, the window for love. "The window enclosures are getting started today. The men will use the stones bought from the same quarry we suspect originally supplied them for the chapel. Under each window will be a stone box three by five inches. I have yet to figure out your mother's intention for them, but we will install them as she wanted." As she spoke, Brielle backed up to get a better view. She always got caught up when she discussed her work and rarely noticed where she stepped. The past always offered an escape for her.

"The boxes weren't in any original drawings we found, so I suspect your mother added them to the restoration plans." She pointed to the base of the window.

She didn't realize it until she turned, but Colin stood right behind her. He captured her in his arms and smiled. The sunrise filtered through the circular window above the back of the chapel, surrounding them in light, making it seem as if they stood in their own little world. He trailed his fingers down her arms to her hands and wrapped them around hers. She glanced down as goose bumps rose on her arms. Her gaze lifted slowly to meet his.

"Lass, do not be nervous about last night. I enjoyed every minute. It's the beginning of something, and I want to start it right. 'Tis why I held back. I want to do this at yer pace." He caressed Brielle's face. "I want to get to know ye better and see where this new beginning will take us."

Her heart melted a little, and she could almost believe him. She gazed into his eyes, as blue as the ocean on a calm day. She realized a girl could get lost there. It was all too good. She feared it would end before it had begun.

She placed her trust and her heart into his care and

replied, "I would enjoy that too."

Colin lowered his mouth to hers and brushed her lips with a kiss, light and feathery, making them tingle. They stood there, gazing at each other as the world faded. For her, there was no passage of time. There was no sound, only Colin.

She blinked and sensed she had woken from a trance. Colin watched her.

It seemed too good to be true. A good-looking, successful man was interested in her. *Fake love brought women down, making them believe they were ugly and worthless.*

Professor Mac's rule popped into her head. *Aye, this is the most important rule of all, dearie. Are ye settling? Are ye making concessions to make the relationship work, but at yer expense?* She honestly didn't know. It was too soon. She didn't know, but being here and having the magic of Scotland, she saw hope.

Colin spoke, interrupting her thoughts. "I must get to work. I am certain ye have work to do as well." He placed his hand on her lower back, his fingers barely touching her, but she didn't shy away as he escorted her to the doorway.

Holding his hand out to her, Colin raised an eyebrow when she didn't move. She placed her hand in his, and he smiled as he bent and kissed it. He whispered, "Until later."

She watched Colin stride away from the chapel, the sunlight reflecting off his black hair as he made his way back to the castle. Brielle turned to get to work as she realized she was watching as his retreat silhouetted in the window of love, and a chill ran up her spine.

Chapter 7

Brielle was sure another day of breaking rock for the chapel would smash her head open.

The guys from the wharf took off toward the loch for lunch. She saw a motorboat at the dock and watched them clamber into it, likely headed to the Marina Pub and a dram with Hamish. Marie was off to lunch with John. Brielle rubbed her neck and contemplated grabbing a sandwich from Mrs. Abernathy and hiding in her room.

She turned toward the door, and Colin stood there, smiling. "I thought ye might like a break." He swung a large basket from behind his legs. "And maybe lunch…with me?"

Brielle huffed. "Lunch would be nice. Aspirin would be a godsend."

Colin laughed as he approached her. "The banging of rock gettin' to ye, lass?" He brought his hand to her face, brushing the hair from her eyes. "Ye should not work so hard. I wouldn't want anything happenin' to ye."

She glanced away. "Yes, well then, where would you be? No one to oversee the renovation of your pile of rocks."

She sidestepped around him, but Colin's hand went to her shoulder, stopping her. "I mean what I said, and it has nothin' to do with the chapel, Brielle."

Staring at him, she noted his sky-blue eyes searched her face. He was trying to be nice. And he had brought her lunch, not asking for anything more than her company.

She sighed. "I am sorry. I get cranky when I'm ill."

Colin's hand slid down her arm to her hand. "Then let me make ye better. Come for a picnic."

She allowed him to take her hand and draw her toward the doorway. "Well, maybe for a little while. The guys are all gone, anyway." What would a little time in his company hurt? She was here to enjoy Scotland. Maybe she could enjoy the people, too. Enjoy new experiences and new friends.

Colin waved for her to proceed with him through the door. When she stepped into the doorway, the wind blew at her. A stone creaked, and Colin's arm wrapped around her waist, pulling her back into the chapel. A rock fell from the top of the doorway, landing with a thud where Brielle had stood.

She glanced at the stone, then at Colin, who took a deep breath.

"Brielle, lass, ye okay?"

She shook herself. "Yes, thank you. The stone must have been loose. It's an older one."

Colin glanced at it. "Make sure the guys check all the stones, Brielle; that one almost hit yer head."

She nodded, turning to the doorway. Now, more than ever, she feared the opening. Colin's hand brushed her back, and she shivered. He took her hand and led her through the door, steering her around the rock. She was glad he went first, for the chill disappeared when he cleared the arch. As she moved behind him, she took a deep, cleansing breath.

Colin stopped, rotated her hand in his, and kissed the back of it. "I want to show ye the picnic spot my parents always liked. Ye cannot see it from the castle, and it offers the most beautiful view of the loch and the mountains beyond."

Brielle thought of her view from her window. She loved sitting there and had thought about going there to escape, but spending time with Colin sounded more appealing.

She squeezed his hand once. "That sounds nice."

They strolled in silence, holding hands, allowing them to swing a little, making Brielle feel young and carefree. She hadn't done something so spontaneous in a long time—taking time to picnic. Come to think of it, she hadn't been on a picnic since she was a child.

She glanced at Colin, who kept his eye on where they stepped. His profile showed a relaxed, casual manner as he swung the basket and her hand in rhythm as they went.

He stopped short. "Now, close yer eyes, Brielle."

She watched him closely. "This isn't a trick, is it, Colin?"

He set down the basket, moving around her, covering her eyes with his hands as his arms encircled her.

He whispered, his breath tickling her ear, "Trust me, lass, ye will not regret this." He inhaled, then hummed deep in his throat. "Ye will never regret trusting me, Brielle, ever." Colin turned her to the left, took a step, then a few more. The breeze from the loch blew over her face, its salty tang tickling her nose. He stopped them and cut short his hum.

Colin's breath returned to her ear. "The sight of a

Scottish loch is one ye will never forget. The soft waters cast a mirror image of the vast mountain landscape, reflecting its beauty. Most fall in love at first sight."

His hands moved, trailing his fingers along her cheeks. She was almost afraid to open her eyes, but her anticipation got the best of her.

She opened them.

The loch spread out directly in front of her. At a lower angle, she had a clear view. She allowed her gaze to travel the landscape. She caught sight of the marina with all the boats docked and Hamish's pub beside it. Farther, and the mountains folded over one another, reminding her of her drive up the castle cliff. Colin placed his hands on her shoulders as he stood behind her, like an anchor keeping her from drifting away.

He slid his face next to hers, his breath on her cheek. "Some say it's love at first sight, the beauty of Scotland. But my ma always said it was…"

"Magic," she said beside him.

He squeezed her once, then turned her. "Aye. Magic."

She gazed into his face, wondering if he could read her mind. "My mother said the same."

Colin smiled. "Wise woman."

Her stomach rumbled, and he smirked. "And I have a hungry one in my arms."

He released her and bent to pick up the basket. He opened it and smiled as he handed her a plaid. They set up the picnic in silence, Colin situating them so their view was of the loch and mountain range while they lounged. He reclined close, and she wasn't uncomfortable—far from it.

He poured her some wine, handed her the glass, then picked up a plate. He glanced at her as his hand hovered over the finger sandwiches, and she nodded. After placing a couple on the dish, he hovered his hand over some fruit, and she smiled. He picked up some sliced apples and a few grapes, then handed her the plate with a wave of his hand. "For the lady."

She giggled, and he prepared his wine and plate. They sat and ate in comfortable silence, watching the loch. Every so often, a boat would come into view, then fade away in the distance.

He finished his third plate and set it aside. He lounged back with his wineglass, his free hand trailing up and down the arm she leaned on. "Yer headache gone now, Brielle?"

She turned to him. "Yes, thank you, Colin." He hid a smile in his wineglass as he took a sip.

She turned back to the loch, the sight ever changing in the afternoon light. A cloud would shift over the water, making the blue shimmer darker, then move away, creating sliver sparks on top like fireflies at night. Magic.

The sound of rock breaking reached them, making her sigh. "The guys must be back from lunch. I'll need to get back."

She shifted, and Colin's hand on her arm stilled her. "I told the guys ye wouldn't be back today. They said they knew what to do. Stay and relax. Spend time with me, please?"

She glanced into his face, warm and welcoming. Then she quirked a smile. "Well, you are kind of my boss."

He barked a laugh. "The Historical Society of

Scotland is yer boss, lass, but I'll take any excuse ye will give." She lounged back, and he shifted till they were side by side, their arms touching.

He reached behind him and brought around the bottle of wine, pouring more into each of their glasses as he spoke. "So, ye have come to Scotland on a grand summer adventure. What are yer plans after the renovation?"

Could she tell him the truth? Should she? She hadn't had a plan except to escape her ex. After the chapel project, there wasn't a plan. Which she knew sounded strange, but Professor Mac had encouraged it.

"Well, I started with only the plan of the renovation. I wanted to see what Scotland was like, then make my mind up after."

Colin snorted. "No plan? Ye head out halfway around the world for a project that might last only a few months? Then ye have no plan after?"

She huffed and sat up. "You didn't let me finish. I have a plan—well, somewhat of one." She nearly got up and walked away. He had criticized her. She knew this would happen. That he, a man, wouldn't be able to hold back.

Colin sat up. "My apologies, and ye are right. I cut ye off. Ye made me worry about what would happen to ye after the chapel project."

She had jumped to the conclusion he was criticizing her. Feared he might dictate to her what she should do, how she should act, how she should dress. *Stop it. He said he was worried. Trust him.*

She settled next to him, and he chuckled as he sat back. "Please tell me yer grand plan, that is no plan, so I will not worry about ye."

She sipped her wine, then spoke. "Tease all you want, Colin. There is a plan. I was waiting on the Historical Society's decision about the next project here."

He shifted. "There's another project? Here at the castle?"

She grinned, knowing she had surprised him. "Mmm, the ever-knowing *laird* doesn't know his property. The lowly worker must keep him informed."

Knowing more made her powerful. Funny, she had mentioned it when they first met. He must have forgotten. Strange. As a lawyer, he should be good with facts.

"I don't have to worry about this property. I have John." He took a sip of his wine, then spoke firmly. "Now, tell me about this next project."

She giggled, knowing he had just issued a command as the laird. She felt reckless and playful. She wanted to see where pushing Colin would go.

She set her wineglass down and sat up a bit, ready for the challenge. "Oh, so now it's the laird commanding his peasant. You said, 'I have John.' So let *him* fill you in." She spoke with authority, and when she got to "I have John," she dipped her voice, trying to duplicate his Scottish accent.

Colin set his wineglass down. "The *lassie* will not tell the *laird* what he wants to know." He tickled her, and she laughed out loud. "Ah, will I have to torture it out of her, then?" He tickled her more, and she squirmed in his arms. "What is the project, Brielle?"

She laughed and had to gasp for breath. "No."

Colin tickled her more. "Tell me."

She squealed and took in a large gulp of air.

"Mercy, mercy. I'll tell you!"

He laughed as his arms enveloped her. He lay there, watching her catch her breath. She heaved another gasp, then another, slowing her breathing.

His fingers brushed the hair away from her face. "Caught yer breath now, Brielle?" She nodded, and he leveled his eyes on hers. "The project, lass."

She sighed and spoke in her best Scottish accent. "*Sean Dùn*."

His head came back. "Old fort?" Then his eyes widened. "Chapel Hill. You mentioned it when we first met."

She grinned. He *did* remember.

"Yes, but there's no answer yet."

He huffed. "They will approve it. I'll see to it."

She pushed against his chest, trying to sit up, and he wouldn't release her. "You can't know if they will approve it."

He smiled as he held her tight. "Not only will it get approved, but I'll also see they assign my wee builder as the lead."

Now she knew he was pulling her leg. "Colin, you don't know who they will pick, and we won't know for some time."

He stopped her struggles with a squeeze. "I'm curious. If the project doesn't get approved, what is yer plan?" She froze. He'd asked directly. Should she tell him? Would it matter to him if she went back to the States? Would he want her to stay?

"Well, I wouldn't have anything keeping me here." She peeked at him, and he was glaring at her. "I mean, Texas is home, but it is nice here."

He squeezed her in his arms. "Do ye have plans to

stay, Brielle? If ye made friends here, like Marie, John, or even…me. Would ye want to stay?"

She grinned at him. "Truthfully, my college professor said if I got here and wanted to stay, I could use his place in Glasgow. Until I figured it all out."

He grinned widely at her. "Well, lass. My work is cut out for me, for I plan to convince ye to stay." He smiled at her. "Have dinner with me tonight?"

She was enjoying herself, simply appreciating his company.

She blushed and replied, "Yes, I'd like to have dinner tonight."

He made it seem so easy. When she first thought of coming to Scotland, the concept of staying seemed so complicated. The chapel project sounded so exciting, but to commit to staying? She had worried that it would be a harder choice, but now that she was here, it came easy.

He turned and caught her staring.

His mouth quirked a smile, and he winked at her. "Taking in the handsome sights, lass?"

He wiggled his eyebrows, and she couldn't help but laugh. "Colin, are you always so sure of yourself?"

His gaze moved out over the loch. His brows creased, then he glanced back at her. "Always, Brielle. I always know what I want and what I will do." He glanced over her face as if taking it into his memory.

He whispered, "And right now, all I want is to kiss ye."

He leaned over, brushing his lips against hers, then tilted his head, kissing her deeper. Colin caressed her face as she returned the kiss. He bent and swept her into a deep kiss soft on her lips, then built into a demanding dance. He shifted a bit as he laid her back. She gasped, and he took advantage of her open mouth, sliding his tongue in, sending sparks to her toes. He gave a light moan and ended the kiss.

He sat there momentarily and gazed into her eyes, making her feel wanted and cherished. "I think ye are a Fae, come to bewitch me with yer temptations. Every time I touch ye, I cannot help but want to kiss ye even more." He brushed his hand along her cheek. "Brielle, it's like magic. Ye are like magic."

Could she trust another man with her heart again? Professor Mac's last rule, number six, popped into her head. His voice was clear. "*Aye, this is the most important rule of all, dearie. Are ye settling? Are ye making concessions to make the relationship work, but at yer expense?*"

The other day in the chapel, she didn't have an answer. But today, in Colin's arms, in his company, the answer came easily. He allowed her to choose what she wanted. In this relationship, which was not at her expense, she was not settling.

****

Colin grabbed his water bottle and took a drink. He and John were jogging around the castle grounds, getting some much-needed exercise. They ended their run at the stone archway that was the ruins of the old stable. It had become a regular workout place for them in fair weather.

Colin took another gulp. "So, how are things going for Brielle, Marie, and the chapel?"

John rolled his shoulders as he answered Colin. "Things are good. The chapel is progressing well, and Marie will start her work soon. Brielle was so excited when they came across some artifacts on the chapel grounds. They've been busy cataloging them."

Colin smiled, knowing that Bree would find anything old invaluable. He needed to make sure everything went well for her—for them. Soon, he would have to go on the Fae mission to find the Stone of Love and return Roderick to his time, but he wanted to ensure Brielle had settled in. Colin smiled as he regarded the chapel. Brielle was becoming important to him.

John glanced off toward the chapel and sighed. "Marie and Brielle have been getting along well. They have become good friends."

Colin continued to drink from his water bottle. He, John, and now Marie, were all close to Brielle. She had made friends. She barely knew anyone in Scotland and remained a workaholic. She needed friends and people to support her. "That's good, aye?"

John nodded, took a breath, then blew it out slowly.

Colin glanced at John. "What is it?"

John glanced down and toed his shoe into the weeds by the stone wall. "Brielle's mentioned some events about her past to Marie, and it's gotten Marie concerned. They've talked about it the past few days."

Colin glimpsed at the chapel. What would there be with Brielle that would concern Marie? The renovation project has come along well. Bree was so happy. She took well to Scotland. The people in the castle and Dunbeg, the village near Dunstaffnage, liked her.

He glanced back at John. "How so?"

John sighed as he fidgeted with his water bottle. "Brielle had a boyfriend who wasn't nice to her." Colin turned and faced John. Was this why she was nervous with him?

"What had this ex done? Was he mean to her?"

John rubbed his neck and scowled at Colin. "He has been more than mean to her, Colin. The other day she said he locked her up for two days. He said it was for not meeting him after being at the university cataloging artifacts. She said it was innocent, that she had lost track of time. However, this ex thought she did it to embarrass him in front of their friends."

Colin glanced away at the castle. Locked her up; what the hell? How could anyone do something so evil to someone they professed they loved? It was an act Colin couldn't fathom. John took a breath, and Colin's head snapped back to him.

"Is there more?"

Nodding, John sighed. "Aye, he demeaned her over her studies for so long she almost quit. He made her think she was worthless."

Worthless? She was smart and intelligent, not to mention beautiful. *What kind of man does that to a woman, to anyone?*

John cleared his throat, making a sound as if he might speak, then glanced away.

Colin took a breath through his nose, and as he breathed out, he said, "Is that it?"

John stepped closer to Colin, lowering his voice. "No, Colin, the bastard got physical, violent. When she left for Scotland, he tore apart a classroom at the university after the professor refused to tell the arse where Brielle went. He became upset that Bree had cleared out completely. She rented her house, sold her car, and moved most of her belongings to storage. It seemed like she was leaving forever. After the jerk trashed the classroom, Professor MacGregor had him arrested."

Colin breathed deeply and unclenched his fist. A notion shot through his mind before he even considered the ramifications. The bastard might come after her. He didn't know what he would do if anyone did that. Colin sighed. *She's safe. She's here. Hopefully, the bastard's still in jail.*

"Colin, that's not all."

Colin turned his head. John's eyebrows drew together as his mouth frowned. Colin's heart dropped to his toes.

John glanced away and whispered, "He beat her. Bad." He stared at his feet. "One time, it sent her to the hospital for several days. Marie fears there might have been more than just the one beating. Bree's relieved the guy is in jail and can't come after her. She was worried he might."

Colin turned this over in his mind. How could anyone treat Brielle that way? The only reason a man mistreated a woman was to build himself up because he lacked confidence in himself. *No self-respecting man beats anyone smaller and weaker than he is.* The thought popped into his head so fast that Colin held his breath. Robert Kilpatrick, an old law school friend, was in the States. He could enlist his help.

"His name, John. What's the bastard's name?"

John shrugged.

"I need to know everything you can find out. Everything Marie can get." Colin stormed into the castle. What would he do if anyone came after Brielle?

Chapter 8

The sight from the window seat in Brielle's bedroom was spectacular at sunset. The place offered a quaint place to rest and reflect and was her favorite place to unwind from the day. The marina seemed remarkable, sitting against the background of Glen Etive, the scenery melting her troubles away. *I could get used to the view daily.* She pondered all that had happened since she arrived in Scotland.

The project she was working on had come along very well. She and Marie got along perfectly. In her, she had a new friend with whom she could spend hours discussing history. Then there was Colin. Upon first meeting him, she feared her self-consciousness with men after her ex would stand in the way of making another friend, but it didn't. She felt at ease with him.

Brielle glanced at her cell phone. It was close to dinnertime. She would need to clean up and get downstairs. She showered and changed into something presentable for this evening, nice but not too dressy. She stopped, examined herself in the mirror, and nodded. Now she was ready.

As she left the room, Mrs. Abernathy entered with more candles. "Got another set of candles for yer room, dearie. Colin said I had to make sure ye had something to light if the power went out again."

Colin worried over her—nice. She glanced at her

watch. Damn. She was late. "Thank you, but I'm late for dinner." She rushed out the door.

"Have a good evening." Mrs. Abernathy followed her out of the room. "Ye're not late, and the dining room is next to the kitchen, with big wooden doors. Ye can't miss it. Have a good time."

Brielle strode toward the dining room. She had yet to see this room and wondered about the restoration. Had they kept the original rooms' design or completely changed the space for modern uses? It must have been a storeroom converted to modern formal dining in the present. The grand wooden doors were slightly open, spilling light into the hall. She pushed them, and they opened to a view of the end of the long dining table. Seventeenth-century style oak chairs sat in wait for diners. Their finely carved backs had elaborate scrollwork, foliage, and indentations. They were heavily pierced and in superb condition, obviously from a first-class restoration workshop. The wood carving was crisp and attractive.

She stepped farther into the room, and her eyes caught two arched windows along the right wall overlooking the marina. Her room must be above the dining hall. Above her hung an ornamental vaulted ceiling with a seventeenth-century chandelier fitted with electrical replica candles that lit the space well. Moving alongside the dining table, she peered at the end, where a large decorative fireplace sat. This room hadn't been a storage room. The stonework was likely original and too ornate. In the past, the room was possibly a solar for the family.

Assembled before the fireplace sat a smaller table and two richly upholstered chairs. The table held an assortment of cheeses and fruit set over a decorative tablecloth. A door by the fireplace opened, and she turned as Colin entered.

"Good evening, Brielle. Can I get you some wine?" He strode to the table. He was good-looking in a white dress shirt, a tweed vest, and black dress slacks. "Chardonnay, right?" Colin picked up the opened bottle from an ice bucket, poured her a glass, and handed it to her. "Ye are very attractive tonight, Brielle."

She took the glass, his finger brushing hers.

He smiled at her, and her face warmed under his praise. "Yes, that is my favorite. Marie mentioned she and John were having dinner. They wanted to review the flooring plans again, even though they'd been working on this together for months. They aren't joining us?"

"Actually, no." Colin pulled her chair out and waved his hand. "John and Marie went into town for a night out and mentioned they were going to the pub. Mrs. Abernathy has already made our dinner. It's in the kitchen warmer when we are ready."

She startled. Alone with a man for dinner. Since she broke up with her ex, she hadn't had dinner with a man other than Professor Mac. She hadn't been comfortable enough, but after the picnic today, she found ease in Colin's company. Discussing his family history, the chapel project, and her plans after the renovation was something she enjoyed. She took a deep breath, telling herself dinner would also be enjoyable.

Colin cleared his throat. "Brielle, why don't you sit and enjoy the wine and the fire? Scotland is such a different climate than America. If ye need it, there's a throw for ye." She had been standing there staring at him, caught in her thoughts.

He smiled and waved to the chair again. As she sat in the offered chair, he spoke lowly. "I won't bite, Brielle. Please relax and enjoy yerself."

Moving to the other side of the table, Colin poured himself a glass of wine, then sat across from her, taking a sip.

They sat for a moment in silence. Just the two of them. Could she do this, dinner with a man, and have it go well? She waited. For what, she wasn't certain.

Colin sipped his wine, eyeing her over the rim. "Sip your wine, Brielle. It's a good year. I promise you'll enjoy it." The wine, the glass, was in her hand. She had forgotten she held it. She smiled and took a sip. The wine was excellent, probably the best she'd ever tasted. She took another sip and sat back in her chair, feeling more at ease.

Colin sat back, watching her for a moment. She set her glass down, then picked up a cracker and spread some soft cheese.

Colin tilted his head to the side, staring at her. "Brielle, tell me, has anyone ever called ye Bree for short?"

Brielle glared at the cheese on the cracker, brie, her favorite cheese but her least favorite word. Emotions swelled inside her, and she caught herself before crushing the cracker. She laughed at the irony, mad that her ex could invade such a lovely evening. Angry, she had allowed him to ruin her dinner with Colin. She sighed. She might as well get this over with, and when she thought about his nickname for her, it was kind of silly.

"Yes, someone has called me by the nickname

Brie. Brie is my favorite cheese." She took a bite of the cracker and closed her eyes, savoring the taste. He chuckled, and she opened her eyes.

He picked up a cracker, spread cheese on it, and held it up. As he gazed at her, he raised an eyebrow. "Cheese?" He popped it in his mouth and chewed, observing her.

She took a healthy sip of her wine, studying her half-eaten cracker. The familiar sensation of self-doubt returned, and then she chastised herself. It was foolish of her to allow it to bother her so much.

"Yes, my ex used to call me Brie. He used to joke that I was just an old, rotten cheese. 'You're Brie,' he used to say. 'You're old, rotten cheese.' " She warmed up to voicing her frustration, her tone sarcastic. "He thought it was funny, like some inside joke."

She ate the rest of the cracker, speaking softly after she swallowed. "I hate that name." She glanced at Colin and smiled. "But I still like the cheese."

Colin sat back in his chair. "Brie, the cheese?" He smirked and took a sip of wine, smiling at her over the rim. "What about Bree, lass?"

She huffed. "I just told you, Brie, the cheese."

Colin barked a laugh. "Lass, I thought you had the Gaelic in ye?"

She frowned, setting her glass down and folding her arms. "I have some words. Why do you ask?"

Colin smiled as he set his wineglass on the table and slid off his chair, kneeling before her. No man had kneeled before her, ever. She unfolded her arms, at a loss what to do.

He took her hands, caressing his thumb over the top as he spoke. "Oh, lass, Bree is Gaelic. It's spelled

B-R-E-E. It means disturbance or, for some, a storm. Not some old, rotten cheese."

He sighed as he spoke. "Bree." Then he chuckled lightly. "Your ex is an idiot and a complete arse." He gazed at her momentarily, and his expression shifted, making her heart lighter. "Ye...ye're a rare gem."

He brought her hands to his lips and gazed at her over them. As he whispered, his breath brushed her hands. "But there's a deeper meaning in the name. 'Tis different when a man calls a woman Bree."

He stared at her, his gaze traveling over her face, glancing over her hair in a caress she almost felt.

His gaze paused in her eyes, then he smiled. "From now on, when I call you Bree, I want ye to think of what the name means when a man calls a woman he's attracted to Bree." His breath tickled her hand, making goose bumps travel up her arm, causing her to shiver.

"It means strong." He kissed her left hand.

"Noble." He kissed her right hand.

"And most of all, powerful." He kissed both hands together.

Colin stared into her eyes, and her breath caught. He had just changed her most hated nickname to something special, revered, and treasured. Gazing at his handsome face, she suspected she could lose her heart to this man.

Colin lowered her hands into her lap and smiled as he rose. "Enough about cheese. I'm hungry. I'll get our main course, and we can visit a bit more."

Brielle rose. "I'll get it."

Half out the door, Colin turned. "No, lass, I'll get it."

Brielle picked up her wine and sipped as she

watched the flames. She knew in her heart this was what life was supposed to be like, sweet and serene. So different from what life was with...no matter. This entire night was a fresh experience, and she craved more.

Professor Mac's rule number three popped into her head. *Does he treat ye right?* For the longest time, she'd hated that nickname, and Colin changed the meaning of the word and what it meant to him when he called her Bree. But, more importantly, he changed what it meant to her. It meant his attraction drew him to her, and she felt drawn to him. She took a sip of wine. Yes, she was very attracted to him.

Colin returned with dinner and set the filled plates down, smiling at her as he sat. He picked up his wine and held it out. "To the new chapel and new beginnings."

She smiled as she clinked his glass. "Yes, to new beginnings."

After a couple of lobster bites, Colin spoke first. "So, yer studies in America, John mentioned anthropology. I have to ask, how does a woman studying human behavior end up gettin' a job renovating a building?"

She swallowed her bite of steak and took a sip of her wine before answering. "Well, it was Professor Mac who got me into historic buildings. My father was a contractor, so I've had a lot of experience building structures. Professor MacGregor felt it would be natural for me to combine my historical knowledge with my construction talents."

Colin froze, his glass midway to his mouth. "Professor MacGregor, ye mean old Graham

MacGregor?"

She nodded. "Yes, your mother's friend."

He tilted his head. "Aye, the one teaching in America, the…the food university."

She laughed loudly. "Rice University, in Houston, Texas."

He smiled. "Aye, well, if ye are a student of Graham's, then ye are practically a specialist in Scottish history and lore." He sat back and sipped his wine. "I'll be damned. Ye knew my ma *and* her best friend since childhood."

She blushed under his praise, and part two of rule three echoed. *Does he treat ye right, as in respect ye?* She smiled as she thought, *Yes.*

She forked her salad with raspberry vinaigrette and walnuts and asked, "So, you work at a law firm. What do you do there, besides *lord* around as a lawyer?"

He smirked and replied. "I work at the Connell Law Firm in Edinburgh. It's not lording around. I am a solicitor. We don't call ourselves *lawyers* in Scotland." She opened her mouth, and he continued, "I take care of legalities for people. Wills, property, personal affairs."

Brielle glanced into her lap. "Even divorce?"

Colin leaned forward and took her hand in his. "Aye, but I try to get them to reconcile first if I can."

Her gaze rose to meet his, and he smiled as he patted her hand. She understood a connection with him she hadn't experienced before with a man: friendship. Her heart melted through the evening, and her fear of being alone with him faded.

Rule number one popped into her head. *Does he have the same values as ye?*

And her mind answered. *Yes.*

She finished her wine and set her napkin on the table. "Colin, dinner was superb, but how did Mrs. Abernathy know what I like? Come to think of it, I've had all my favorites to eat since I arrived."

Colin smiled. "It's something she's very good at, always finding out about a guest's tastes so she can make ye feel at home."

Brielle grinned back.

"Well, Bree, are ye ready for dessert?" He got up and reached for the plates to clear them.

She stopped his hand and said, "You got dinner. I'll clean and get dessert."

Colin gazed at her. "How about we get it together?"

They picked up their plates and made their way into the kitchen. She had yet to see the kitchen, and a glance told her it was nothing like the original. This one was modern, sleek, and a professional chef's dream.

Colin set the dishes in the dishwasher, and she stopped, staring. It was the first time she had seen a man load a dishwasher in a long time. She chuckled at herself.

Colin glanced, then winked and waved to the oven. "Why don't you get the desserts from the oven? They are in those little white cups."

She opened the oven heater tray and turned to smile at him. "Is this what I think it is?"

Colin smiled teasingly. "Now, what would that be, Bree?" Laughing, she grabbed the oven mitts and picked up both ramekins. Colin retrieved two spoons from the drawer.

She turned toward the dining hall, but Colin stopped her with a hand on her shoulder. "Let's sit at the island bar in here."

She slid onto the stool next to Colin. "Okay." She passed him a ramekin, and Colin handed her a spoon.

Sitting in the dimly lit kitchen with Colin felt so domestic. Something she'd not done with a man she was attracted to yet that felt so natural with Colin.

Rule number two popped into her head. *How does he make ye feel?*

Her mind answered. *Comfortable.*

She spooned her first bite and dropped her head back, moaning in delight. "Melting chocolate lava cake. It's so warm and yummy."

She wanted to share with Colin, so she offered him a spoon from her dessert. "Here, try it." She said as Colin leaned toward her. She stuck her spoon into his mouth. Locking his lips around her spoon, he closed his eyes and growled.

Brielle smiled at him and removed the spoon. "Great, isn't it?"

He slid his stool closer to hers. Colin picked up his dessert and filled his spoon, offering it to her. She glanced at the spoon, then at him, and slowly wrapped her lips around it.

Colin slid the spoon from her mouth, his eyes never leaving hers. "Aye, it is."

He brought the spoon to his mouth. As his tongue dragged across the back of the spoon, his eyes held hers in a heated glare. He filled his spoon again and repeated feeding her his dessert, then licking the back of the spoon without taking his gaze from hers.

As he offered her a spoonful, she leaned in. Instead of filling her mouth, his lips brushed hers tentatively at first, but when she returned it, he deepened the kiss. He tasted like chocolate wrapped in sensual desire.

Rule number two popped into her head. *How does he make ye feel?*

And her mind answered. *Sexy.*

Dessert sat forgotten on the counter. Her heart raced, and a flush of heat flowed up her back. Overcome with desire, Brielle ran both hands up his chest to his collar, wrapping her hands around his neck. As he traced more kisses toward her ear, fiery sparks burst within Brielle. He sucked her earlobe, making Brielle gasp and drop her head back as tingles spread to her toes. She became light-headed. No man had ever made her feel this way, like a woman.

Colin slid his hands around her head and undid her twisted bun, causing her hair to tumble down her back. As he kissed her, he ran his fingers through her hair as a low hum rumbled from his throat.

He raised his head a little, and she opened her eyes to have his heated gaze return to hers. "I've wanted to do that since the moment I met ye, lass. Run my hands through yer thick waves of brown hair."

He drew her to him and kissed her again. Sparks continued to race through her body as Colin trailed kisses down her throat and back to her lips, kissing them lightly. As he slowed the kisses, she sighed.

Colin pulled back, resting his forehead against hers, a little out of breath. "Sorry, lass, I didn't mean to take advantage of ye. Ye seemed like ye would taste better than the dessert. I had to have a bite."

She was out of breath as well. "Oh, I didn't mind so much. I like the way you taste, too." Colin picked up his dessert, spooned another bite into her mouth, and kissed her again. Slow sensual kisses, tasting the chocolate on their lips, shot sparks of desire straight to her core.

He spooned her a bite of chocolate, then kissed her, repeating this until the bowls were empty. "Ye ate it all, Bree."

She giggled. "But you didn't get any."

Colin smiled and caressed her face. "Oh, Bree, I got the best part. I got ye." Colin kissed her once more, then picked up the dishes and placed them in the kitchen sink.

She sat and watched him. He had left her in a daze from the erotic dessert. No man had ever done anything quite like it.

She felt cherished, and a thought popped into her mind. *Four out of six. Not bad, Professor Mac.*

Colin returned to his barstool and took Brielle's hand in his. "I've enjoyed tonight."

The back door slammed open, startling them both. John and Marie entered, and laughter echoed in the room.

"Oh, sorry to interrupt," Marie said, raising her eyebrows.

Still holding her hands in his, Colin addressed the two. "Have a good time?"

John glanced at their clasped hands and smiled. "Yes, the pub was hopping, and the band sounded good."

Colin nodded toward the hall door as Marie stared a little moon-eyed at John, who nodded at Colin. Brielle hid a smile at the exchange.

"Yes, well, it's off to bed for us. Marie, I'll take ye to yer room." He waved her ahead, placing his hand on her lower back. He glanced back at them and winked.

"Have a nice evening, ye two."

Brielle stifled a yawn, and Colin smiled and patted her hand. "It's late, and we've both an early day. Let me escort ye to yer room."

Colin slipped off the barstool, and she followed. He draped her hand in the crook of his arm. Then they made their way through the hall, and Colin strutted like the laird escorting the lady of the castle. She giggled. Colin glanced at her and laughed.

They climbed the stairs together, turning the corner to her room. She was so comfortable with him. There it was again, *rule four. Does he treat ye well?* Yes, she felt safe in his company.

He stopped at her door, turned her in his arms, then swept her into a searing kiss that made her toes curl. She felt like a princess ending the evening. Sucking her bottom lip lightly, Colin ended the kiss.

He ran his thumb along her cheek. "Sweet dreams, my Wee Bree."

Chapter 9

John headed down to Dunbeg, the village near Dunstaffnage, which sat on the point that guarded the sea entrance to the lochs that led into the heart of Scotland. According to his grandma, it was also one of the most beautiful places on earth.

Driving past the marina, John headed into one of the housing estates filled with historical cottages. He hadn't been here in months, yet he remembered coming here as a child and having tea and cookies with his gran. After her husband died, she grew older, more content to sit in her cottage and watch the world go by. John remembered a lively older woman with a wicked sense of humor and a favored pastime of pranks on friends and loved ones. He really should visit her more often.

He was on her doorstep before he even knew it, so caught up in his memories he didn't realize that he had driven there, parked the car, and strolled down the short, cobbled path to the door. John raised his hand to knock, but the door opened before he could strike it.

"Och, son. About time ye visited yer granny. If yer da were alive, he'd skin yer rear for no' visiting." She shuffled back, waving him inside. "Got a pot of tea on, I do. Come on in, dear. Take a load off yer mind and tell ol' Granny what ye been up to."

John always felt at ease with Granny. It was like

time had never passed, and the conversation came easily. He sat at the kitchen table, covered with a cotton floral tablecloth with the newspaper set out. Granny shuffled around the kitchen, got her ceramic teapot, and reached for two teacups with saucers.

John stood to help, but Granny stopped him. "Och no, sonny, ye sit. The exercise will do me good." She reached over and squeezed his shoulder. "Ye seem like ye've been to the gym all day. Ye're all muscle, my brawny boy," she said, laughing.

John watched her for a bit. Though she shuffled as she walked, she was still full of energy. She set the cups on the table, then got the teapot and a tray of cookies.

Before he realized it, Granny had sat, poured tea, and looked at John with a twinkle in her eye. "Something's happened now, has it, my boy?"

John took a sip of his tea. "Now, why would ye ask something like that, Granny?"

Lightly laughing, she sipped her tea and glared over the rim at him as she swallowed. "I can see it in yer eyes, boy. I can sense it in the air. Yer heart is beating as if it's going to pop outta yer chest." Granny made a popping sound with her mouth and set her teacup down carefully. "The Fae—they are back, aren't they?"

John spat out his tea, choking on it. "Uh, um, aye."

Patting his knee, Granny said, "Tell me all about it, and we'll see what to make of the trickies the Fae are playing this time."

John's gaze shot to her face. "This time?"

Granny laughed. "Oh, John, ye don't think this be the only time the Fae be playing their games, do ye?" Granny leveled her eyes at John. "Many times, they play their games—some for good, some for bad." She smirked. "Some for life, and some for death. Ye got to have yer head on right to play with the Fae. Tell me, what are they up to now?"

John told Granny MacArthur about the Green Lady's first appearance, when she cried before the laird and lady's death.

Shaking her head, she said, "Och, that's a sad day, it was. I cried when I heard."

He explained that the wall facing the chapel crumbled, and the *Fae Fable Book* had changed the evening Colin arrived. He told her of the second time the Green Lady emerged when she smiled at Brielle, and Mrs. Abernathy called it a blessing.

Granny nodded as if it was a typical thing that happened at every castle in Scotland. "Brielle is a blessing to us all, my boy."

John wasn't sure how to broach the next topic, about how the Fae showed in his dream, so he bit the bullet and dove into the story. "Granny, the Fae, she came to me in a dream." John glanced at her, worried she would call him a lunatic.

She smiled widely, then gazed out the window. "Oh, Morrigan. I do miss her, ye know." She peered back at John. "I had many a good chat with her. How has she been? It's been near on twenty years since I've seen her."

John sat back. "What? Ye know her?"

Granny sipped from her cup and observed John. "Of course, John. She's the captain's Fae, the MacArthur Fae. It is her duty to inform us and keep us prepared for the duty of the castle. But, more importantly, the stones, John. Our duty to the Stones of

Iona." She smiled. "Ye know once, when yer grandda was very young, that Green Lady of MacDougall tried to take his pants right off when he was sleeping. Tricky thing that ghostie is. Ye got to watch out for her. It was before we met, but I tell ye, if I ever caught her trying that again, I'd blow some ash on her to get that ghost away from my man." Granny laughed loudly.

John shook his head. "Granny, how is it ye have never mentioned something so important as the stones and our duty to them and the Fae? Don't ye think I could have used some advice, some help on this before now?"

Granny took his hand in hers, patting it. "Och, son, ye can't just tell someone about something like that when ye want. The Fae must allow ye to tell it. I couldn't tell ye till ye knew and until the time is right. Then the Fae open ye mind and allow the thoughts to pass yer lips. It's like their riddles, it is."

Granny gazed out the window, letting go of his hand, and a faraway expression crossed her face.

She spoke in a hushed tone. "It's time. All I have lived for after my darling's death has led to this point. Morrigan said I would be needed. It wasn't my time to go when yer grandda went." She glanced back at John and patted his knee. "I so wanted to go with him. Loved him so deeply, I did."

Granny picked up her napkin and wiped a tear from her eye. She sighed and sat for a minute.

"Then yer da went missing. He did. Yer ma, she died years before that. I was told my duty was to outlive them all, all for the stones." She glanced at John and smiled. "Here ye be, and son, it has all been worth it."

John sighed and sat beside Granny awhile, just

gazing out the window. He saw nothing but realized everything—the duty to the castle and protecting the stones from the evil Fae. How important it was to do well in keeping the stones safe. His da said they had to. If the stones fell into the hands of evil, both realms would fall. When he was younger, he believed it was all myth, like Colin, but now, faced with meeting his Fae, the actions of the Fae around the castle, the reality of the duty became very real.

As he sat there in the peace and quiet beside his granny, everything came into focus. The stones, the chapel, the Fae, Colin, Brielle. He sighed deeply...*Marie*. He must keep them all safe. It was his duty.

John had almost forgotten the most important question he needed to ask. The key. "Granny, the *Fae Fable Book*...it changed. There's got to be a key somewhere. Colin said he had never seen one, but Emily told Brielle she would need access to it to help with the chapel renovation."

Granny focused on him and smiled. "The chapel renovation. I think that is the best project the laird of the castle has taken on in years. That chapel is special, John. Take extra care of it. Especially since after it's back to new, the Fae would see it for sure then. The chapel, ye must protect it."

John shook his head. Maybe Granny didn't catch the question. "Granny, the key to the book, where is it? The case, how does it work?"

Granny leveled her gaze at him with clarity in her eyes he hadn't seen for many years. "The key is not *a key* but is *the key*. The key can only be revealed when the heart is pure, and two true love's hands have joined.

The key will be shown to the one who needs it and when they need it most."

****

A sense of accomplishment overcame Bree as she stood admiring their work. This was what she had come here for, to restore this beautiful building to its original grandeur. She was here, really doing it.

Standing in the center of the chapel, Brielle and Marie went over the latest progress in the chapel. It had been almost four weeks since work had begun on the renovation, and the project proceeded well.

Brielle smiled at Marie. "You know, I could not be happier with all we've accomplished." The outer stonework was complete. The stained windows came in, six in total. On the north side of the chapel were windows depicting love, faith, and hope—the south side had more ominous designs of fear, lust, and doubt. They would be installed once the roof was completed.

She smiled as Marie said, "Aye, John stored the windows at the castle until the boys have completed the roof and can enclose the building."

Brielle glanced about again, and her eye caught the doorway to the chapel. Brielle still was not comfortable with the entrance. It gave her chills being near it, and her heart dropped when she moved through it. She couldn't understand why.

She looked over at Marie. "Well, at least today, the framework on the roof started. In our research, we still have not found the design for the round windows above the altar at the back of the chapel, as Emily had hoped." Brielle sighed. "The men from the wharf will install a plain glass window to cover it so natural sunlight might come into the space."

Above her, the ceiling was still open, her favorite. The wind tickled the branches in the trees, making them move a little. The blue sky beyond was almost the color of Colin's eyes. Some days she stood in the center of the space and took in the building's atmosphere and the nature surrounding it.

"I'll miss the open ceiling. I liked it when there was no roof and sunlight shone in the chapel through the trees, making designs on the floor." Her gaze traveled around the chapel. "Soon, they will install electrical work, leaving you time to mark up the floor with your design template for the mosaic flooring. The timing of projects seems to come together well." Brielle stood there for a moment, enjoying the sensation of accomplishment.

"So, how are things progressing between you and Colin?" Marie's question broke into Brielle's thoughts.

"Oh, well." Brielle blushed. "He took time off, and we've gotten to spend time together." Brielle raised her eyebrow and glanced at Marie. "And I notice you and John are spending an awful lot of time together. Care to spill the beans on that?"

Marie smiled. "Well, we seem to have a lot in common. Initially, I would only stay overnight on weekdays instead of commuting from Glasgow." She sighed. "I thought I wouldn't be comfortable staying out here full time, but I like it."

Marie picked up her backpack, slung it over her shoulder, and headed toward the church door. She asked, "It's been only a few days. Colin seems very interested in you. Is that going too fast for you?"

Brielle went to her work desk, the sawhorses with a plywood board that would soon need to move to make way for Marie's floor work. "Actually, no. And that's strange. I can't help it. This seems so right. From the moment we started spending time together, it's natural." *Rule number two, how do you feel?* She sighed. *Natural.*

Brielle picked up her backpack and followed Marie to the door. She stopped as Marie stepped through the doorway. The guys installed the door days ago, and she still had trouble moving through it.

Marie goes through the doorway without difficulty. Why me?

Marie responded, "It's in your head, Bree, and you're thinking aloud again."

Brielle laughed as she reached into her pocket for the stone Hamish gave her. She rubbed it and jumped through the doorway. It didn't banish the chill, but it brought some comfort to her. They strolled together on the trail to the castle.

****

Colin dropped his bag and stripped off his shirt, the breeze cooling his already sweaty chest. The warm-up jog helped clear his mind. Exercise always did that for him, helped him focus on tasks at hand.

John followed, dropped his bag, and drew his sword from the scabbard. "I went to see Granny to ask about the key. When I brought it up, she admitted she knew Morrigan. When she mentioned it, I spit out my tea. Granny hadn't told me about the Fae in all these years. She claimed the Fae won't let people talk about them until the time is right." John set down his sword and picked up a towel, wiping the sweat off his face. "She's known Morrigan all these years. She acted like they were the best of friends. It's baffled me, I tell ye."

Colin set his sword next to John's and picked up a water bottle. "So, you asked about the key to the *Fae Fable Book*. What did she say?"

John nodded. "That's when she got starry-eyed, like she was in a trance or something. I specifically remember what she said. Keyed it into my phone. It was so strange." John dropped his towel and picked up his cell phone.

He punched a few keys and nodded when he found the text. " 'The key is not *a key* but is *the key*. The key can only be revealed when the heart is pure, and two true love's hands have joined. The key will be shown to the one who needs it and when they need it most.' "

Colin shook his head. "What the hell does that mean?"

John shrugged. "I don't know."

"Where are we with the preparations for going back in time?" Colin took a sip of his water. It was bizarre to be talking so openly about jumping in time, the entire concept of the Fae and the stones still new to him. At times when he thought about the stones, it seemed the earth turned one way as he went the other, like he was out of place in the human realm.

Putting his phone back in his bag, John grabbed his water. "I have yer da's period clothing for ye from the reenactment event the castle holds every year. Glad it is the right time period—yers is too recent, being a modern kilt."

John took another sip of water and swallowed. "Did Brigid mention how ye were to get back?"

Colin shook his head. "No, and she wouldn't tell me how long I'll be away either. All she said was I must find the stones and return Roderick to his time.

Once I complete her task, I'll get sent back here."

John nodded. "Makes sense to me. Finish what she sent ye there to do, then ye get to come home. Simple."

Shaking his head, Colin put down the towel and bottle. "I don't think any of this will be simple."

Colin hadn't contemplated the thought of leaving for a long time. He hadn't considered that he would leave Bree for a while, possibly months. Hadn't told her about his sentiments for her.

I want to express how important she has become to me, to my life. I want to take the time to allow her to come to trust me, to trust our relationship.

Brigid had given him a limited amount of time before she worked the magic to send him back in time. He had to do something special for Bree, but mere days were all he had left.

The old hunting cabin wasn't far off, and John kept it in good condition. Colin recalled sailing to it with his da for a weekend hunting trip. It was a short sail to the cabin if he traveled the direct route. His grandda's sailboat was still moored at the marina. Come to think of it, he hadn't been out on the loch in years. Had Bree ever been sailing? He glanced at the castle, then back at John.

Decision made, Colin nodded and turned to John. "John, I need to go to the hunting cabin on Saturday."

John's gaze shot to him. "What? The day before ye leave, ye're going away?"

Colin turned and gazed over the loch. "I need to do something special for Bree. Something to show her how much she means to me. Take her to a special place to tell her I'm leaving, that everything will be okay." He glanced back at John. "Can ye get the cabin ready by

Saturday?"

John smiled. "Sure, today's Thursday. I'll make the cabin special for ye."

Colin picked up his sword and pulled the blade from the scabbard. The steel slid free and the high pitched ring triggered his anticipation for the workout. "At least Da insisted we learn to fight with medieval weapons, even if it was for the reenactment events. This will help me when I go back in time." He swung his sword once in practice. "Well, come on, John. Now that I'm heading to the eighteenth century, I've got to keep my sword arm up and running."

Colin swung again as John picked up his sword and eyed Colin. "Disarm only, no blood. I recall ye like to draw blood."

Colin smiled widely at John's recollection of their practices in their youth.

They took a ready stance, and soon the clang of metal rang loud in the yard.

Colin advanced on John—stepped left, parried right. After his block, John answered with a swing toward his left, forcing Colin to shift all his weight to the right to block his left side. The swords locked in forced tension, and Colin's gaze connected with John's. John smirked back at him.

The fight was on.

Colin broke free and started toward John, swinging an attack on each side, purposefully pushing him toward the old stable arch ruin, hoping to back him into the wall and take advantage of the lack of space John would have. He'd corner him, disarm him, and win this round.

Swing after swing, he worked side to side, moving

hard on John. He enjoyed working out. The exercise, a welcome escape for his mind to focus on something else. Today, he focused on the mission of the Fae, what he needed to concentrate on making the trip back in time go well and his return successful.

Swinging right again, then blocking another left advance from John, he thought of the duty to protect the stones. *In the mission to go back in time and assume my ancestor's identity, I'd have to embody the mask of an eighteenth-century man, conservative yet forceful.*

John rounded on him, striking from overhead, causing him to back step and block the blow. Colin blocked it and slid his sword to the side, forcing John's sword off his. He didn't pause, but struck again to continue his advance, backing John closer to the archway. *The Fae Fable. How did the fact that the Fae Fable foretold the fate of each stone figure into the mission? The story was about the Stone of Love and the Maiden.*

John swung for Colin's legs, forcing him to jump to avoid getting hit. *The Maiden. Brielle.*

As Colin continued his assault, bringing John closer to the wall, he thought he heard the faint voices of women. He shifted his attack so the opening archway ruin came into his peripheral vision.

Maire's voice came from the other side. "Is that metal?"

It was then Colin saw Bree stroll through the arched opening, crossing between him and John, and he was already in a full-force downward swing.

God, no! I have to pull back, but it's too late. I am going to hit her. I am going to strike Bree with my sword.

Colin threw all his weight to the side. With a roar, he twisted, throwing his blade out of line, and his momentum sent him stumbling into her. His blade missed her, but his body knocked into her. She hit the stone archway and cried out. Off balance, he stumbled into the wall too, scraping against it.

More than a mere sting burned his shoulder, but it was Bree he was worried about.

Marie ran into the yard, calling Bree's name.

Colin rounded on Bree, yelling at the top of his lungs. "Good God, woman, never walk into a sword fight! Ye damn near got yer head taken off!"

Bree crumpled into a ball on the ground, covering her head with her hands.

Everyone stood still.

She shook as she softly cried.

"Oh, God, Bree," Colin breathed. He stepped forward and touched her shoulder.

As his hand made contact, she screamed. "Please don't hit me, please don't hit me." She crawled farther down the wall on her hands and knees so fast that if he blinked, he would have missed it. She sat curled into herself, rocking back and forth, whimpering.

Colin stood frozen in place, surrounded by stunned silence. John had mentioned that her ex beat her, but he didn't know how bad or the toll it had taken. The idea that someone she trusted broke her turned his heart cold. Colin couldn't believe the same strong woman who took charge and managed roughened sailors and turned them into obedient puppies crouched before him, frightened out of her wits. *I must go easy with her. She's already broken. I can't risk hurting her more. That would kill me.*

Without taking his eyes off her, he spoke softly. "John, come take my sword. Take it away." Still not moving, Colin said, "Ye and Marie head into the castle. Go on. We'll be along soon."

John's arm grazed Colin's, the sword's weight shifted, then Colin released it. "Ye sure ye want us to go? Maybe we need to stay. Help or something," said John.

Colin shook his head. "No, I've got this." John gathered the bags, the clink of him collecting the swords, the swish as he sheathed each sword told Colin he'd heeded his request. Their steps and murmurs faded as John guided Marie toward the castle.

Colin took a deep breath and crouched down near Brielle and ensured he didn't touch her. If he spoke, would he hurt her more?

He spoke quietly yet firmly, so she'd hear his voice. "Bree, it's me. It's Colin. Can you hear me? Brielle…"

****

The man was going to do it. He was like the rest. He was going to hit her, and it would hurt again. She couldn't do this, not again. The last time it hurt too much. She couldn't go away as she had before, someplace else, till the pain went away. Last time she almost didn't come back. *Did someone say her name?*

"Brielle Elise, take a breath," he said. She did so and lifted her head to peek between her arms at the person speaking. It was Colin, not Tony. She blinked, and he didn't appear angry. He didn't come at her. Instead, he sat watching her. Blinking again, she saw him, and he didn't frighten her.

She took another deep breath as he spoke. "Bree,

will ye please come here? Ye have nothing to fear from me. I would do nothing to hurt ye. Please come to me."

Brielle fully uncovered her head to see Colin crouched next to her. His face was almost even with hers. She stared into his eyes. Kind and gentle, not flashing in anger and hate. She could breathe easier now that she saw his eyes. In them, she understood all his care and hope for her, and a calmness washed over her.

Colin glanced at his hand as he held it outstretched to her. "Bree, will ye take my hand in yers?" In a trance, Brielle reached out and took it. His hand was so large she had to use both hands to hold it.

It was soft, relaxed. She heard his breath hitch before he spoke. "Bree, my hand may be large, and my body may be strong, but I would do nothing to hurt ye, ever. Ye will have nothing to fear in me. I will always keep ye safe."

He gently squeezed her hand as his face tilted till his eyes locked with hers. "Ye have my word as a man. Whoever has hurt ye before, please know, I am not that man."

Brielle glanced at his hand in hers and then at his face. This man who could hurt her easily had shown her that he could be gentle and caring. Her gaze traveled to his shoulder, where beads of blood gathered from a long scrape where he'd hit the wall, trying to avoid her. Her eyes returned to his face, and he watched her calmly, waiting for her response.

He wasn't like Tony, not at all. She knew he respected her work. He told her he knew she would do well and trusted her. He said he would never hurt her. She had nothing to fear in him.

She cried and threw herself into his arms, knocking him back on his seat. "God, Colin, I am so sorry. Please think nothing bad about me. Th-the yelling. That's all."

Colin gathered her into his arms as she sat on his lap. "*Mo leannan, my sweetheart,* I am the one who is sorry—ye scared me."

He rubbed his hands up and down her back, soothing her. He was apologizing to her, yet she was the one who'd caused the commotion.

Colin sat back, holding her loosely. "I near cut yer head off with my sword. I barely shifted sideways to miss ye. But ye must tell me, what is this fear of being hit about?"

Bree shook her head and tucked it into his chest. He could never know, never find out the things done to her, the beatings, and the humiliation. If he ever found out, he'd toss her aside like damaged goods. She wasn't that woman anymore and wouldn't be ever again.

She spoke from his chest. "Nothing, it's nothing."

Colin squeezed her as he said, "That was not nothing."

He sat back, placed his finger under her chin, and lightly tilted her head till their eyes met. "Ye can talk to me, Bree. I want ye to trust me with your burdens. Share them with me so I can chase these fears away, as I did with the storm."

He caressed her cheek with his hand as he spoke. She sat frozen. Her heart nearly stopped as she stared into his eyes. She couldn't relive the past. Her breaths drew short. She couldn't go back there, even for Colin. She shook her head as a tear fell from her eye. For her, it was enough that he was a man who wouldn't hit first. It was enough that he would hurt himself before hurting her.

She could only say, "Hold me, Colin, please just hold me."

He held her in his arms. She shook as he rubbed his hands up and down her back. Her mind was a jumble. *I need the rules. Care? No, not right. One was* value. *Take a deep breath. Two, what was two,* feel…safe. *Next was three,* right…yes. *Four, God, what was four? Take a deep breath.* Treat him well was four. Settle*, six was settle. I am not settling. Five: five was* know, know him. *Do I know him, really know him?*

She knew he cared for her. She knew he wouldn't hurt her, not now and not ever. She took a deeper, calming breath. "Not hurt her ever" was enough.

They sat there for a long moment. She calmed down, and her breaths came evenly. The surrounding sounds returned to her, the wind in the trees and birds chirping in the distance. Colin's breath near her ear, his heartbeat steady and strong.

As he held her, he whispered, "God, if I ever come across the man who's done this to her, I will kill him."

Chapter 10

Colin led Brielle toward the dock at the marina. "What are we doing, Colin?"

He glanced over his shoulder and smiled at her. "It's a surprise—ye'll see soon enough." Ahead of them, Marie and John strode toward them.

"All's in order, my laird." John stepped off the dock and saluted Colin. He nodded in return. Marie winked at her and giggled as John led her off the pier.

At the entrance to the dock, Colin bowed and waved for her to go in front of him. "This way, my lady," he said. Brielle stepped up on the dock and walked down the narrow walkway with boats moored on either side. She glanced around as ships passed by…sailboats, fishing boats, and larger boats.

"What are you up to, Colin?" She tried to glance over her shoulder at him and stumbled.

Colin caught her in his arms. "Careful, we aren't going swimming today."

She turned in his arms, facing him. "What exactly *are* we doing today?"

Colin smiled at her and brushed aside a hair that had come loose from her ponytail, placing it behind her ear, taking his time as he gazed into her eyes. She stared back, and her heart swelled with emotion. He was a good man, and she was totally at ease with him.

"I have something special to show ye, *mo*

leannan." My sweetheart. Colin kissed her lips softly and took her hand. "This way, or we'll be late." Following, Brielle smiled.

They went farther down the dock, almost to the end, where a sizable ornate sailboat sat. It was old but well-kept, with a white hull, shiny black trim, and brown accents. The yacht looked more like a picture from a magazine than an actual vessel at this distance. Brielle wasn't an expert on boats, but this one appeared to be an antique.

As they got closer, Hamish came down the ramp. "All set for ye, my laird."

Brielle glanced at Hamish, then at Colin. "Colin, I've never sailed before. I'm not sure if I can do this."

Colin took her hands in his and kissed them. "Bree, ye can do anything. Never fear doing anything with me—I will always keep ye safe."

He winked at her. "Come on. I set us up for a fun day of sailing." He led her to the plank leading to the boat. As she walked on the narrow board, she peered at the ship's side. Painted on the side was *Mo Chridhe*.

"*Mo chridhe, chridhe?*" She had heard those words before, but she couldn't remember where.

Colin glanced over his shoulder. "Yer thinking out loud again. It means *My Heart*. My grandda dedicated it to my grandma." Colin jumped onto the deck, turned, and lifted her into his arms, swinging her into the boat.

He lowered her down the length of his body. She sensed every bump and crevice of his muscular torso. As he set her down on the deck, he swept her into a passionate and demanding kiss that shot tingles all the way to her feet. She raised herself on her toes to deepen the kiss, and Colin moaned lightly at her response.

"Ahoy, my laird, ready to push off?" Startled from the kiss, Brielle turned and saw Ronnie near the bow. She turned around, and Ian and Conner, the guys from the chapel renovation, were at the stern.

Colin leaned toward her and whispered, "I thought ye'd be more comfortable if the lads took us out today. I can't sail this thing alone, and when I mentioned taking them, they acted like boys who got a treat instead of working on the chapel. Sailors, all of them. They'd do anything to get out on the water."

The boat shifted as the guys pushed off from the dock. She was a little unsteady and must have moved, because Colin took her in his arms.

His breath brushed her cheek. "Ye'll enjoy this. There's nothing like seeing the glen from the loch. It's magical."

He took her hand and led her to the bow. "We'll motor out of the marina, and then the boys will let the rigging out and cut the engine. Then ye'll enjoy the smooth sensation of the boat gliding across the loch."

Wrapping her in his arms, Colin leaned his chin on her head. "Now, for yer brief sailing lesson. This boat is a yawl, a two-masted sailboat. It was my grandda's."

Colin lifted his chin and reached around her, pointing out each item as he explained what they did. "It's got a fore and aft rigged sailing with the mizzenmast positioned abaft. That's very close to the rudder. Connor is manning the large wheel that connects to the rudder, which steers the boat. Once we get out into the loch, Ronnie and Ian will loose the sails, and when we catch the wind, the boat will heel to the side."

He tightened his arms around her. "Don't be afraid.

This is how the boat gets its power without using a motor. At first, it may seem as if we will tip over, but we won't. We'll shift the sails into the wind to sail from one end of the loch to the next. When we are ready, we'll eat the packed lunch Mrs. Abernathy sent, and the guys will eat on their own and keep to themselves. We'll have a peaceful day on the loch."

Brielle turned in his arms, facing him. "Oh, Colin, this is so nice. No one has ever done anything so thoughtful for me, ever." She glanced at her hands and blinked away the threat of tears. "I'm looking forward to today."

Colin turned them to face the bow, keeping Brielle in his arms. The ship cleared the marina. The boys cut off the engine, and the boat drifted free. Brielle thought this must be what it was like to float in space. The fabric of the sails flapped in the wind, and the lads called orders to each other. The wind filled the sails, causing the boat to lean to the left as they headed toward the most gorgeous sight of the glen and mountains Brielle had ever seen.

Brielle saw stunning highland scenery as they sailed. The guys set out trolling lures behind the boat, hoping to catch fish, and much to their excitement, got a few.

As they sailed through the loch, Colin explained each landmark, holding Brielle wrapped in a MacDougall plaid. He said, low in her ear, "Loch Etive is a very special place."

She watched the breathtaking scenery as he continued. "Never more than a mile wide, it extends for nearly twenty miles between the base of Glen Etive and the open seas of the Firth of Lorn near the castle. There is no road access for most of the loch's length, except the road by the castle. It makes ye like a sea nymph because there are places only accessible via the water. The area is a U-shaped valley with a deep-water center section and a shallow 'cill' at the mouth with salt and freshwater sections beneath the surface. I will point it out when we get there because it is very exciting. The mountains that frame the loch are among Scotland's finest: Ben Cruachan, Ben Trilleachan, and Ben Starav." He pointed to each one, and she marveled at the view from the loch.

As they neared a large metal bridge, she glanced up, amazed. From the corner of her eye, she caught him watching her. He smiled and brushed his fingers along her cheek. She smiled back, taking joy that he not only admired her love for history, but supported it as well.

He smiled wider and his gaze lifted to the bridge. "This is Connel Bridge, a massive steel cantilever bridge. It first covered the Connel Sound in 1903, and they originally built it for rail transport, but now they use it as a road. When it became a road, ye could see horse-drawn carriages transporting people from one end to the other."

As she stared at the bridge, Brielle pictured the carriages in her mind and imagined the clatter of the wooden wheels on the old wooden structure. She found Colin intently watching her again. She smiled, and he bent and kissed her cheek. He reached around her and pointed ahead of them.

"It's what is lurking underneath that is far more important...the Falls of Lora. We must be careful when we approach the bridge. Loch Etive is hemmed in here, by the narrow gap and a shallow underwater cill I mentioned before."

The boys called to each other as they steered the boat away from the waves.

Colin continued. "Depending upon the tide, the level of the loch can vary by several feet from the sea level. As the ocean level outside the loch rises or falls, vast amounts of water spills into or out of the body of water. The resulting conditions range from a strong current that can stop a small boat or a strong rapid forming midstream. Kayakers gather at spring tides to surf the rapids. The falls are a law unto themselves."

Brielle glanced out over the falls. It must be low tide at this time of day. The falls were powerful. Fast, rushing water was almost deafening yet majestically beautiful. As they passed the falls, she saw a kayaker enjoying the challenge of the rushing waves. He went under, and she gasped. Colin held her close as she peered over the side of the boat, and the kayaker popped back up, shaking off the water with a huge smile.

The loch bent and widened to new views every mile or two around different headlands. They approached a series of ruins on the side of the boat, and the boys steered closer.

Colin pointed. "One landmark I'm sure ye'd find interesting on the north shore is Ardchattan Priory."

Brielle sat forward. "I know that place. That's where Robert the Bruce supposedly held Scotland's final Gaelic parliament."

Colin nodded, smiling. "Och, she knows her Scottish history."

"Can we stop and stroll around the grounds?"

Colin gathered her in his arms. "Another time. I

have some special plans for today."

As they continued to sail along the loch, Colin pointed out large, majestic Ben Cruachan, the mountain framing the view in the background.

"Did ye know Cruachan is the battle cry for highland clans Campbell and MacIntyre?" Colin asked.

She smiled and said in her best Scottish accent, "Aye, and I know the MacDougall battle cry is *Buaidh No Bas*, which means Victory or Death."

Colin laughed and kissed her. "Ye are a true Scottish lassie now."

They spent the entire day sailing across the loch, enjoying the sights. Brielle and Colin discussed their families, their lives, likes, dislikes. The ease of how they conversed surprised her. Brielle had never come to know a man so well before. She could tell him anything, and he would understand her, her emotions, her mind, and her heart. No man had ever done that this way, as if their souls were made for one another.

Do ye treat him well, lass? Professor Mac's voice drifted in her head. Rule four, she always had a hard time remembering rule four. Maybe it wasn't important, but now she knew it was very important. Did she treat him well? *Yes.*

Colin turned them a little so his face came even with hers. "Do ye recall when we first met? The first moment we laid eyes on each other?"

She giggled. "In the study? That first day?"

Colin smiled. "Aye, that was when I first fell for ye."

She smiled back. "Tell me about it."

Colin sat back and pulled her to his side, holding her close. "I didn't know ye was behind me when I questioned yer talents over the remodel. I was worried about my ma's special project."

Brielle tried to shift out of his arms, but he held her tight. "Oh God, that's when I snapped at you."

He spoke in an American accent that wasn't half bad. " 'I'm not a hundred percent American. I'm half Scots,' ye said."

She settled into his arms. "That's when you moved and I saw you, in the window. Did you see me?"

Colin nodded as he gazed into her eyes. "Aye, I saw ye in the reflection. That was when ye told me yer mother was from Glasgow." He trailed his finger down her cheek. "When I turned from the window, saw yer face for the first time, ye near took my breath away." He kissed her hand. "Even nervous ye were attractive."

Colin watched their hands as he rubbed his thumb over the back of hers. "That's when I first saw ye, up close. That was when I realized what a startling beauty ye really are."

His gaze shifted to her face. "Then ye spoke yer thoughts aloud. I wondered, 'Did she even realize how enchanting she is?' "

Bree's face warmed. "I am?" She sat up as a thought occurred to her. "When John left the room, you gave him a look. What was that?"

Colin chuckled. "I thought him a fleeing coward. But then I watched ye and realized ye said *was*, yer mom *was* from Glasgow. Ye had lost yer mom too."

She sighed, and Colin settled her in his arms. "That was the moment I first fell for ye."

They sat in silence for a moment, each left to their own thoughts. The moment felt natural—natural for her to sit with him, natural for her to talk to him, share herself. *Is this what life with love was like? Is this what she had missed before?* What she thought was love wasn't this. This was much more.

Colin spoke, the first to break the silence. "So, when was the first moment ye realized ye had fallen for me?"

She laughed out loud. "Who said I have fallen for ye?" She duplicated his Scottish accent, and he tickled her.

She squealed and cried out. "Mercy, mercy. I give up. I'll tell you."

She heaved a sigh, catching her breath, and settled back into the crook of his arm. He wrapped his arms around her and squeezed her once. She loved this moment as much as when she realized she had fallen for him, but that moment had been magical for her. Did he even realize what it had meant to her? How he had saved her from her own fear.

She took a deep breath and spoke lowly. "The first moment I realized I was falling for you...don't you know?"

Colin put his finger to his chin, tilted his head, and said, "Mmm, must have been when I asked ye about my handsome face at our picnic." She huffed as Colin laughed. "Oh, Bree, it had to be the night of the storm, right?"

She blushed. "Yes, it was after the storm, though I must have drifted off for a while. You roused me and whispered in my ear." She whispered, "Listen, can you hear it?"

Colin whispered back. "And ye replied, 'Mmm, hear what? The only thing I hear is your heart beating.' " They each repeated their part, whispering as they gazed into each other's eyes.

"The storm."

"What storm?"

"The storm's gone, no more thunder. Nothing to scare ye anymore."

"No, I can't hear the thunder anymore, only your heart."

Bree sighed. "That's when I fell asleep in your arms. I had never been so protected and safe."

Colin smiled as he caressed her face. "Bree, I will always chase yer storms away, always." He gazed into her eyes, then bent and kissed her mouth, soft and slow. Chasing her fear away was one moment. Giving her a new nickname was one more. This was yet another thing Colin had gifted her, and she wanted so many more moments with this man.

After a late lunch, they sailed toward the back of the loch. Brielle glanced around. It was getting late, and they were far away from Dunstaffnage.

Colin turned her in his arms. "Brielle, I have another surprise for ye."

Brielle smiled at him and kissed his nose. "I've already had my surprise—nothing can top this." Colin took her hands in his and then gazed into her eyes.

Her chest fluttered as he brushed her hair out of her face. "Before I reveal the surprise, I want ye to know, 'tis your choice of what we do. I don't want ye to be pressured. Ye'll have the power to decide what ye want, and I will gladly do as ye wish. I want ye to be safe with me, always."

Colin allowed her to decide their plans. It left her speechless. She had a hard time drawing her breath. She glanced at their hands, gathered herself, then stared into his eyes and nodded, waiting to see what he had planned.

He turned her in his arms to the bow, pointing over her shoulder at the shore. They had entered a small cove. Brielle was so caught up in what Colin had said, she hadn't noticed the boat had changed course. The motor hummed and vibrated. The boys had brought the sails in and put them away in canvas casings.

Brielle shifted her head as Colin whispered in her ear, "See the stone cabin on the hill, just ahead of us?" Brielle nodded as her gaze landed on a quaint stone cottage halfway up the hill.

Colin took her hand in his, lightly kissing the back. "That's the MacDougall hunting cabin. It's been here as long as the castle. I'd like to take ye there and spend this evening with ye, just ye and I." He turned her hand in his and kissed the palm. "But I want the choice to be yers, Bree. I'll not have ye afraid of anything we do together."

She twisted in his arms. "Colin, what about food, a change of clothes, soap for a bath?"

Colin laughed out loud. "*Mo chridhe*, I've seen to everything. Marie packed a bag for ye, and John prepared the cabin. All ye have to do is say, aye."

Professor Mac's rule five popped into her head. *Do you know him? Yes.* The rules ran through her mind. *One, value. Two, feel. Three, right. Four, well. Five, know. Six, settle.* Her mind had already said yes; her heart said it now, *yes.* She wanted to say yes to Colin, his way.

She giggled and spoke in her best Scottish accent. "Aye!" He gathered her in his arms and gave her a searing kiss that left no other questions in her mind.

The rules met. This man was right for her.

As the guys from the wharf pulled the boat to the dock and tied it off, she asked, "What about the boat, the men?"

Colin pulled her to stand, holding her in his arms. "The guys have a car waiting. They'll probably take their catch home and have a feast. The boat will dock here for the night, and we'll take it back in the morning."

Brielle furrowed her brow. "How are just the two of us going to sail this? I don't know how to sail."

Colin smiled, rubbing his thumb between her eyebrows. "Wipe that worried expression off yer face. We'll motor back. I'll keep ye safe."

She gazed into his eyes and spoke from her heart. "I am having a good time, Colin. Thank you."

Colin took her face between his hands and kissed her softly, "I know ye are, *mo chridhe*."

Chapter 11

Colin opened the door to the hunting cabin and waved Brielle in ahead of him. He dropped the luggage near the door, then took her by the hand and led them to the living area. He loved the hunting cabin and had forgotten the natural, comforting sense it gave him. The rustic decor with influences from nature reflected the place's original purpose, hunting for the winter stores. Now the family used it as a weekend getaway. Standing here made him recall some hunting trips with his da.

His gaze roamed the interior. John had outdone himself. A fire blazed in the stone fireplace. The coffee table had a wine bucket with a bottle of wine and ice. Two wineglasses and a tray of assorted cheese, meats, nuts, and berries sat next to it.

Colin took a long matchstick and went about the room, lighting candles that gave it a romantic setting. Now that he glanced around, he noticed more feminine touches, flowers on the side table, and the candles placed strategically around the room, offering the perfect candlelit glow—Mrs. Abernathy had been here as well. He smiled. Mrs. Abernathy would have the food already prepared and waiting for them. He needed to give that woman a raise.

Brielle sat on the couch. "John did all this?"

He smirked. "Well, I think John asked Mrs. Abernathy to do it, and I have a notion Marie helped in the planning as well." Colin tossed the matchstick in the fireplace and poured them both glasses of wine. Handing her one, he joined Brielle on the couch. He pulled the tray closer and took a slice of cheese from it, feeding it to her. She giggled and sipped her wine. He moved closer to her, wrapped his arm around her, and tucked her into the crook of his arm. He sipped his wine as Brielle nibbled the food, the candles flickering as they lulled them into a comfortable silence.

As Colin relaxed, he thought about his reasons for bringing Brielle here. He had a greater purpose this evening—he had to say good-bye but wanted to say it right, as they were only now building a new relationship. In his heart Colin knew how he felt about her and wanted to shout his love from the heights of Ben Cruachan, but he needed to ensure Brielle didn't seem pressured. He couldn't say good-bye now, and he didn't want to. This was only their beginning. Colin wanted tonight to go perfectly, and by the end, he hoped he could profess his love for her so that she would be clear on his emotions. He glanced at her and huffed a laugh. She was more than nibbling the food. Colin gathered her hands and pulled her off the couch.

"Let's get some dinner. Ye are about to eat that entire tray yerself."

Brielle covered her mouth with her palm. "Oh, I didn't mean to, but yes, I am hungry. The fresh air of the loch whets a girl's appetite."

Colin watched Brielle nibble on her bread as he sat back in his chair in the casual dining area. She picked the inner portions of the bread to eat first, then dipped the crust in the butter sauce and ate it in tiny bits, as if trying to savor every flavor. She was such an enchanting creature. The evening progressed as he planned, and it had come down to this moment. He had to tell her how much she meant to him. He had rehearsed it in his mind over and over, and it never came out the same way—always wrong. Colin wanted this moment to be perfect.

"Hello, Colin?"

He blinked. He had been gazing at her but not seeing her.

"You are a million miles away. I asked how your dinner was?"

"It was good, and yers?"

She sat back in her chair. "I'm stuffed, and yes, it was delicious."

He pulled his da's Iona stone from his pocket and held it in the candlelight. Now was when he needed to tell her how special she was, how magical she made his world.

He smiled as he started his tale. "An Iona stone, rumored to have magical powers."

Bree sat forward and gazed at the stone as Colin rotated it between his fingers. She looked closer at the rock, reached into her pocket, and withdrew another.

She held it up for him to see. "I have one too. Hamish gave me this one for luck. Said it had magic, so I've taken to carrying it everywhere now." Colin smiled as she set her stone on the table.

Colin sat back and stared. It couldn't be, yet there it sat: his ma's stone. The perfect half to his, his da's stone. His gaze shot to her face, which still focused on the stone. Did she even know? He blew out his breath. Hamish and his ma had been friends since childhood. Could she have planned this just as she pushed to have

Bree chosen for the renovation project?

He glanced at Bree, then back at the stone. "Ye said Hamish gave ye this stone?"

She nodded. "Yes, Marie took me there for lunch." She grinned. "She and Hamish planned it so the people from Dunbeg could welcome me. Hamish told me the story of why the boat captains carry an Iona stone with them every time they sail." She fingered the stone, then her eyes met his.

In his heart, he knew she was his soul mate, and he had picked the perfect way to express his love for her.

Colin held his stone between them. "Ye know there's a story about the MacDougalls and the Iona stones."

Bree laughed. "It's Scotland. There's a story about everything here."

Colin laughed. She was right. "Aye, but this one is special. Ye see, this story is about my parents and their love."

Bree set her elbows on the table, picked up her wineglass, and sipped it. "I love a good story."

Colin sat back in his chair, holding his stone, then closed his fist around it and took a deep breath. He hoped he could have their story end happily, for this story was still writing itself. He said a brief prayer to Brigid and the Fae. *Please let this go well.*

He opened his eyes and gazed at Bree, his heart.

This night, with her here, the right words came easily. "The Fae, ye see, gave Iona stones to the MacDougalls centuries ago for protection. Stones have become an important part of our lives. It's almost as if the MacDougalls have a lore of our own."

Bree set her glass on the table, sat back in her

chair, and tilted her head to the side. "Really, Iona stones from the Fae. Colin, are these more fables you spin like Hamish?" She giggled.

Colin held up his stone for her to see. "Aye, but this part of the story is true. Centuries ago, one of the first MacDougalls to settle the land where Dunstaffnage sits pledged undying devotion to his true love, his wife." Colin set his stone on the table halfway between them. "Ye see, he had an Iona stone made in the shape of a heart."

He picked up her half of the stone and placed it near his, but not touching. "To ensure his true love carried his affections with her no matter where they went, he had the one stone made into two halves." Colin pushed the two pieces together, so they touched, forming a heart. "Apart, they are two pieces, but together they make a heart. A representation of their true love."

Brielle sat forward and gasped. "How did you do that? Did you switch the stone?"

Her eyes met his as he spoke. "Bree, I did not switch the stones. Hamish gave ye my ma's stone, the other half of my da's, which I carry."

Brielle reached for her stone, but Colin caught her hand.

Her gaze snapped to his. "Colin, I cannot take your mother's stone."

He brought her hand to his lips kissing the back. As he gazed at her, Colin opened her hand, took her half of the stone, and placed it in her palm, closing his hands around hers.

He squeezed them lightly. "The chapel is very special, Bree. Ye have become even more special to me." She looked at their clasped hands, then back at Colin.

His heart nearly burst, for he saw her love for him in her gaze. "I wanted ye to know how special ye are to me, Bree. How much ye mean to me."

A tear slid down her cheek, and he wiped it away. "Carry the half of the stone, Bree. Carry my heart with ye always. So, no matter where we are, ye will know I love ye."

"Colin, you are special to me, too. I love it here in Scotland. I wish I never had to leave."

Colin leaned over and whispered, "Ye don't have to, ever," and kissed her.

She whispered between kisses. "I love you too."

****

Brielle stepped into the hallway as Colin returned from clearing the remnants of their dinner. "Can you show me our room? I'd like to freshen up a little, if that's okay."

Colin smiled at her. "Let me take the bags up and show ye about."

She blushed and allowed Colin to grab their bags as he led her to the cabin's upper level. As she followed Colin up the stairs, she had an eye-level picture of his rear in his jeans, and the view did not disappoint. Heat flushed up her neck, and her breathing hitched. She must have made a noise because Colin glanced over his shoulder and winked at her. Brielle followed Colin to the landing, stopping before the main bedroom.

The upper level was divided into two bedrooms, a master and a guest room, with a bath in the hallway.

Colin stopped in the hallway. "Brielle, why don't ye freshen up in the hall bath? I'll set yer bag here.

Later, if ye decide ye'd be more comfortable in the guest room, alone, that's fine. I'd like ye to have that choice. I'll not push ye."

She took a deep breath and let it out. Colin made her feel cherished. He was as careful with her emotions as if he held fine china. Yet, he understood her need to be swept into a fierce embrace when she wanted passion. Their souls seemed to speak to each other in their own language.

Brielle stepped closer to him. Did he not know he had already captured her heart? The fact that Colin allowed her the choice, the choice to be intimate with him. Did he not realize how important that was to her? He held her heart in his hand, and she was grateful that he cared.

She ran her fingers up his arm and clasped her hands around his neck. "Colin, I want to be with you. I will not change my mind. I want to freshen up in the master's and sleep with you." She kissed him deeply in what she hoped showed him all her passion.

Colin dropped the bags at his side, muttering, "Thank God," and took her in his arms, deepening the kiss. She pulled back and laughed lightly, bent down, picked up her bag, and strolled into the main bedroom.

Over her shoulder, she said, "Why don't you get dessert? You know how I like dessert."

Colin growled, "Don't worry. Ye'll get ye dessert."

A short while later, Brielle exited the master bath and walked to the master bedroom. The curtains were open, and the view of the loch was breathtaking, leaving the bedroom bathed in moonlight. She changed into a short gown with ribbon straps, that made her feel feminine and sexy. She wanted Colin to see her as a woman, a woman in love with the man of her dreams.

As she took in the room, she knew this was a moment she would remember for the rest of her life, a moment with no doubts. The bed was enormous, with a cushy down comforter beckoning her for a night filled with lovers' pursuits. Beyond the bed was a sitting area in front of a window that ran from floor to ceiling, giving her a most spectacular view of Loch Etive at night. The moon reflected off the loch, leaving the mountain range in a deep blue-purple haze that made the window seem more like living art. This was for her the most romantic place to share herself with Colin. It was perfect, this moment, in her heart. This was right.

Once her eyes adjusted to the dim light, she found Colin lounging on the settee in front of the window, sipping from a champagne glass. A bowl of strawberries coated with sugar sat next to another glass of champagne.

As she approached, her gaze settled on him. He had changed into lounging pants, was shirtless, and appeared completely relaxed. Brielle picked up the glass, sipped her champagne, and examined Colin from head to toe.

He looked younger, his hair messed from changing. He drew a deep breath, and as he released it, she marveled at his muscular, broad chest. A light dusting of hair covered the chiseled ridges, and her gaze followed the line of hair to his pants, where she could detect a distinctive bulge. Her chest grew light, and her head spun as she became aroused. The thought made her knees weak. It had been a while since she was with a man, and it filled her with nervous anticipation. Colin was a large man. Would all of him be the same?

Colin smiled. "Join me, please." Her gaze went to the strawberries, then back to him. She liked berries. Would he feed her, like the chocolate dessert? She wanted to be fed by him, in so many ways.

She tilted her head. "Will you give me my dessert now?"

Colin smiled and extended his hand without rising. She took it, and he guided her to straddle his lap. He set his glass down and picked up a sugar-covered strawberry. Colin lifted the strawberry to her lips.

She tried to bite it, but he pulled it away. "Open yer mouth for me," he murmured. He rubbed the strawberry around her lips, coating them with sugar. His other hand slid up her arm, holding the back of her head. He sat up and kissed the sugar from her lips, delving his tongue into her mouth, savoring her sweetness. He lay back against the settee and allowed her to bite the strawberry.

She took the second half of the berry, sipped her champagne, and rubbed the strawberry around his lips. He bit it and took the stem of the berry from her, setting it on the table. He took another berry and rubbed it on her lips, and when she tried to bite it, he took it away again.

She frowned as he smiled and placed the berry in his mouth and guided her to him.

When her mouth came close to his, her eyes met his, and she raised an eyebrow. "Want something, Colin?"

He opened his mouth, leaving the berry on his tongue, and kissed her before she closed her mouth. The berry burst into her mouth, the sweet taste blending with the taste of him as his tongue swirled in her mouth. When he pulled away, she had to chew and swallow the berry.

He sat back, watching her. "Do ye like yer dessert, Bree?"

She sipped her champaign and nodded.

Colin took a strawberry and bit into it. He set his glass on the table and reached for the ribbon on her shoulder and pulled the end, untying the bow. The corner slid down her breast, exposing it. Colin swirled the berry on her nipple, making it pucker, sending a bolt of heat through her. His hand shifted to her back as he leaned forward and laved the nipple. She moaned and arched into him, her free hand holding his head as he suckled her, the sensation making her want this man like no other. She wanted to please him and show him how much he meant to her.

He released her and sat back, then popped the berry into his mouth and chewed. Brielle drank the rest of her drink in one tilt, leaned over, and placed her glass on the table. Colin leaned with her, picking up another berry from the bowl. When she tried to lean toward him, his hand on her other shoulder stopped her.

He said with a wicked glint in his eye, "Want more dessert, Bree?"

She wanted more than dessert. She wanted to give herself to him—the man who made her life whole, the man who gave her joy and happiness. Colin.

She nodded, and he offered her the berry. She bit into it, and the juices dripped down her chin. Her hand reached for her face, but before it got there Colin sat forward kissing her hard. She moaned into his mouth, and he sat back. He pulled the ribbon on the other shoulder, and the top fell to her waist, exposing her to him.

He groaned as his gaze roamed her breasts. "The most perfect sight. God, ye are beautiful." He rubbed the berry on her other nipple, drawing a moan from her, for she knew he would lick it next. When he didn't lean forward, she peeked at him.

He sat back smiling, chewing on the berry. "Want something, Bree?"

She sat forward, running her hand over his chest, the hairs tickling her fingertips. She leaned toward him as he smiled. Her mouth close to his, she whispered, "Kiss me, Colin." He groaned and covered her mouth with his. His tongue danced with hers, sending hot jolts of heat to her core.

Colin built a fire in her, something she had not felt with a man before. Heat spread through her, igniting her flame of passion. Feeding off the fire, he consumed her in his kisses, making the two of them melt together.

He suckled her other nipple, and raw desire ripped through her, making her call out. She arched her back and pressed her core to his. He groaned deeply and moved to the other breast while massaging the previous one. Brielle mindlessly ran her hands through his hair.

She rocked on his lap against his rod, craving the friction they both needed. He kissed her and pressed against her core, and she moaned again. His hands traveled lower, guiding her in a rhythm that burned her soul. His hands clenched her hips; she rocked faster and cried out in a release she hadn't expected yet relished.

She tried to catch her breath as he sat back and pulled her gown swiftly over her head. He groaned again and drew her into his arms. He flipped her on the couch so that she fell under him.

She wiggled a little, and he sat back, whispering, "I wish to gaze upon yer beauty." She nodded, and he rested between her legs, his gaze roaming her body. She pulled her hair from under her head, letting her locks slide to the side of the settee.

His eyes returned to her face. "God, ye are gorgeous. Every damn bit of ye is perfect. And ye are mine. Mine to hold, mine to have."

Colin bent and kissed her neck, then massaged a breast. She arched into him while he trailed kisses down her cleavage. He shifted both hands to her panties and kissed farther down her belly. As she turned to allow him to move her leg, he looped a finger into her panties and pulled them off.

He took her left leg, kissing the thigh as he set it back next to him so that she became fully exposed to his view. He smiled as he bent and lightly kissed her from her knee to her thigh. The softness of his kisses sent chills over her body and tingles to her toes. Colin made her feel like a woman. Cherished. That's what he did, made her a cherished gift for him.

She gave her complete trust to him, for now she knew in his arms she would find the rapture of lovemaking that others enjoyed, and she had never experienced. When Colin neared her core, he smiled and blew on her curls. Brielle shivered. Colin reached for another sugarcoated strawberry. He slid the berry over her nexus and coated the nub with sugar and berry juice. He ate the berry, lowered his mouth, and slipped his tongue along her bud.

Brielle must have jolted, because he said, "Easy *m'eudail*, my dear, I only want to taste ye." She squirmed a little.

Colin slid up her body and kissed her lips. "Bree, I want to taste ye, but only if ye are comfortable with it. Just say the words, and I will stop."

Brielle blushed. "It's not that I don't want to. It's just—no one has kissed me there before." Smiling, Colin reached for another berry and fed it to her. The juice dripped down her chin, then he kissed her deeply.

He licked her chin and said, "Tell me what ye want, *mo chridhe*."

Her breath hitched. No man had ever kissed her there, and she wanted him to so badly. She wanted what others talked about, making love with the man of her heart, with a man who loved her, and she him.

She closed her eyes and spoke. "Please kiss me, Colin. Kiss me everywhere."·

He groaned and slid down her body, growling as he ran his tongue down her torso. As he opened her legs a little wider, he moved off the settee and positioned his head where she hovered on the seat edge. He licked her bud once. She jerked slightly.

He glanced up at her. "Watch me, Bree, watch me love ye with my mouth. Give ye pleasure." The glint in his eye told her he enjoyed this as much as she did. The smile he gave her as his tongue flicked against her nub again told her he likely loved it more than she.

Colin watched her as he licked her over and over, sliding over the nub repeatedly. Brielle moaned deeply and grabbed his hair as he clamped his mouth over her bud and suckled. He alternated between suckling and licking, over and over, as Brielle gripped the settee and moaned in delight.

He hummed, and the vibrations sent her into

shuddering pleasure. She sensed pressure building inside of her, centered at her core. His mouth was so warm, and her folds so wet. The sliding sensation of his tongue and lips rolling over her bud added to the pressure. Her mind reached for the sky—she had experienced nothing like this before.

The building of something vast inside of her centered on one pulsing point. Colin continued his assault on her core, pushing against a dam about to explode. He slid a finger into her folds, and she erupted in a scream, convulsing over and over. Colin continued his attack—his mouth, tongue, and finger glided together in sweet friction. She became aware that he had slowed his motions. Bree panted, trying to catch her breath. Her chest felt like she had run a marathon, yet her body still needed to run off excess energy. He licked from her core to the bud one last time, shifted up her torso, and kissed her passionately.

Colin rose, picked her up, and carried her to the bed. As he gently laid her down, his gaze traveled along her body, savoring her curves. "God, Bree, ye are so beautiful. My wee Bree, my little tempest." He climbed into the bed and gathered her into his arms.

She was beautiful. Colin called her beautiful. And he had called her his little tempest. She felt so sexy. "Colin, you have created a storm, and I'll not be able to stop tonight." Brielle ran her hands over his shoulders, down his back, and grabbed his rear. She didn't want him to stop. She wanted all this man had to offer and more. She wanted him to lose control as she had, and she wanted to watch him, see him vulnerable and excited as he had seen her.

Her hand caressed his face. "I don't want you to

stop. I want you. All of you. I'm not fearful of your storm. Please show me all of you, Colin." He kissed her, running his hands all over her body, making her hot and cold at once.

She grabbed at his pants and pulled them down.

He tore them off and tossed them into the air while he continued to kiss her, never breaking contact.

She ran her hand down his chest, wrapped it around his throbbing rod, and squeezed it, causing a drop to escape the tip. She rubbed her thumb over the moisture, brought it to her lips, and licked the dew off her thumb, making him groan.

Colin slid his hand down her flat stomach and wrapped his full hand over her nest. She bucked into his hand as he slipped a finger into her slit, sliding in and out, making Brielle moan. As Brielle stroked his member, he trailed kisses down her neck, then suckled a nipple.

She cried out, and he said, "Bree, I can't stop touching ye. I must have ye. Please tell me ye are ready." She nodded as she kissed him.

He slid his body over her and positioned himself gently atop her. Brielle panted—the tension built again. He slid into her a little, then stopped.

Under her hands, his muscles strained as he held back. "God, Bree, ye are so good. I want to go easy, but ye make me want to make mad love to ye now."

She stared into his eyes. "Colin, please take me. I want to be yours."

Breathing deeply, he slid in a bit more. He reached his thumb to her bud and rubbed it. Colin braced himself above her on his elbow, his other hand caressing her face. The man drove to the hilt and groaned. He did it again and again. He growled and slowed to an intoxicating rhythm while kissing his way to her breast. As he laved a nipple, he continued to slide in and out of her, the tension building again.

She ran her hands through his hair, panting, savoring the sensations as he switched nipples. His rhythm became stronger again and deeper with each thrust, touching her soul. He rose above her, leaning on his arms, and gazed in her eyes as he increased the rhythm. He watched her as he made love to her, and she watched him as his love flowed into her heart. She wanted to show him her love and her heart in return.

"Colin, make love to me, show me what love is"— she grabbed his shoulders to anchor herself as his thrusts became hard and demanding—"what our love is." She gazed into his eyes as she cried out at the sheer ecstasy of her release as a lightning bolt exploded through her. He rode the wave of her orgasm as it consumed her.

Colin drove into her over and over, growling deep in his chest and caressing her face. "God, woman, ye feel so good. Ye are driving me mad."

He buried himself repeatedly and took her soaring with him to new heights she had never experienced before. His entire body contracted. She sensed him reaching the summit, and he roared his release, crying out her name.

Panting, she pressed her head against his sweaty chest, still joined with him as he thrust a couple more times. Then, in a sigh, her body released him. Colin rolled to the side and gathered her into his arms, still trying to catch his breath. He trailed his finger along her shoulder.

"Brielle, that was wonderful, lass. Ye are beautiful." He kissed her forehead. "And sexy"—he kissed her cheek—"and making love to ye seems like coming home." Colin's thumb tilted her chin, and he kissed her softly on the lips. He paused and stared into her eyes, and she looked back into an abyss of emotion reflected there. "Bree, I love ye."

Brielle caught her breath, and tears gathered as she stared at him, her beloved. "Colin, I love you too."

He held her, lazily kissing her as they lay naked in silence for a time. He trailed his hand up and down her back, lightly caressing her as they calmed down from the storm of their lovemaking.

Bathed in the moonlight reflected off Loch Etive, the two drifted into sleep.

****

Deep in the night, a moan woke Colin. Brielle shifted restlessly. She moaned again. Colin put his arms around her as she whimpered.

"Bree, shh, I have you."

In a dreamlike state, Brielle said, "Colin, keep the storm away."

Squeezing her once, he replied, "Always, Bree, always." Brielle slipped back to sleep, leaving Colin awake. He kissed her lightly, then lay back and watched her rest.

Tomorrow, the storm would start. If the *Fae Fable Book's* stories were true, he must keep her away from the Fae and the stones. He remembered the Fae Fable story his mother told him of the Stone of Love. If Bree followed him back in time, based on the Fae Fable story where the maiden sacrificed herself for the prince, he might lose her forever. He couldn't lose her now; he had just found her.

Chapter 12

Brielle stood at the bow, watching the countryside glide past. She took in the loch's beauty, the calming waters, and the slow glide of the sailboat across the smooth water. Last night had been magical. She had opened her heart to Colin and he to her. Love—she had found love.

She turned, watching Colin steer the boat. His hair mussed in the wind as a relaxed smile sat on his face. Here out on the loch he was younger, carefree. Unencumbered from the role and responsibilities that came with being the laird of a clan. She hoped they'd have more moments like this, open and relaxed.

His gaze caught hers, and he waved her to him. She crossed the boat, sidestepping the main cabin, ducking under the ropes that held the sails secure. As she neared the back of the boat, Colin's grin went wide. Brielle went to stand beside him, wrapping her arm around his waist.

She rested her head against his shoulder as they sailed past the marina. "We aren't sailing to the marina?"

Smiling, he replied, "Nae, I have something to show ye first." Colin brought the sailboat along the shoreline, sailing past Dunstaffnage Castle.

The castle sat majestically upon a rock formation as if it reached for the heavens. As they approached the cliff's peak, the sun shone on the castle, forming a ray of sunlight surrounding the building, making it seem like angels touched it. She stood there a moment to take it all in, and it took her breath away.

Colin whispered in her ear, "Watch the shoreline as we come around the point."

Brielle shifted her focus, and as the boat came around the point, she saw a large group of seals lying on the rocks in the sun. Colin slowed the boat. Cutting the engine, he tied off the steering wheel, allowing the vessel to drift near the seals. Brielle watched the shoreline as the boat freely rode the water, as if floating in heaven. Time slowed for her, making her wish she could stay in this moment forever.

Colin took Brielle's hand and led her to the boat's bow. He wrapped her in his arms and held her as they watched the seals as they drifted slowly by.

Colin whispered in her ear, "The tale of the Dunstaffnage seals is one of love and sadness. Centuries ago, crofters brought their sheep to graze in Glen Etive. One summer, a man placed many sheep in the grazing area, taking more space than he needed. While on his way home to his true love, the man saw the seals on the point and killed one for food."

Brielle sighed, and Colin kissed her cheek.

"That night, a horrible rainstorm blew into Glen Etive, flooding parts of the glen, making it impossible for the grazing sheep to escape the high waters. The man who killed the seal, well, his sheep disappeared from the glen. The rest of the crofters didn't lose their sheep. They believed the seals on this point are the selkie Fae on land, and the man who killed the seal and lost his sheep was afraid he had upset them."

She blinked, rubbing his arms.

"The man took the sealskin to the seals as an offering to appease them, but his action angered the selkie Fae. As punishment, they wrapped him in the sealskin, casting a spell that turned him into a seal, thus launching him into purgatory. The selkie Fae left him forever separated from his true love."

Brielle took a deep breath. "How sad."

They stood there for a moment as the boat slowly passed the seals, which looked as if they floated on clouds.

Colin took a deep breath. "The man, now a seal, sat upon this very point—he could not leave because he wanted to be near his true love. Today, they say the seals are people who have done foul deeds. And the selkie Fae, as punishment, cast them into purgatory by turning them into seals, forever separating them from the ones they love. The seals stay up on the point so they can be near their one true love."

Colin turned her in his arms, and she gazed at him. He glanced over her face as he brought his hand to her cheek, caressing it softly. He whispered, "*Mo chridhe.*" His breath hitched, and tears gathered in his eyes. Brielle sucked in a breath as hers watered.

"Brielle, no matter where I go, no matter what separates us. Never fear that I will not come back." A tear traveled down her cheek, and Colin wiped it away with his thumb.

He took her face between his hands, giving her a kiss on her lips. He locked gazes with her, and Brielle nodded. They stood in the sunlight staring at each other as if they were lost souls as well.

****

Colin maneuvered the boat to the dock behind Dunstaffnage castle. Hamish and John stood there waiting for them. Brielle had mixed emotions, as that meant the ending of her special day with Colin, but also a start of a new day with their newfound love.

Hamish interrupted her thoughts by calling out, "I'll be takin' the boat back to the marina for ye, my laird." Hamish and John grabbed the lines. "We'll get her cleaned up and moored, ready for yer next trip."

The men docked the boat, tying it off. Colin and John grabbed the bags from the boat as Hamish helped her off the boat. Her first step was wobbly, and Hamish grabbed Brielle's hand as she stepped on the dock.

Patting her hand, Hamish asked, "So, did Colin take ye by the seal point and tell ye the story of the crofter?"

She turned and glanced at the seals on the point. "Yes, he did. It was so romantic but sad at the same time." She glimpsed back at the trail to the castle. Colin and John carried the luggage to the castle while she lingered with Hamish.

Hamish stood with her. "Ah, in another story, some say the seals are the souls of drowned people who get one night each year to return to their human form and dance upon the shore of the sea near their homes so they can be close to the ones they love. It doesn't matter which story ye tell. It's always the same. As punishment for doing a foul deed, the selkie Fae will send ye to purgatory by making ye a seal, and ye'll be sitting upon Dunstaffnage rocks to be near yer true love."

She sighed as she watched Colin and John moving up the trail to the castle.

Hamish untied the sailboat, jumped in, and waved as he motored the boat toward the marina.

Brielle stayed at the dock a little longer, sitting on a bench to take in the loch. She stared across the serene waters, which grew to a brighter lapis as the sun rose over them. She watched the clouds slowly move, their shade dropping the water into more of a navy blue.

Her gaze drifted to the seals sitting in the distance on the point. *Colin.* Last night was magical. She had never experienced something so intimate with a man before. When he shared the seal selkie story with her this morning, it moved her soul. But she couldn't shake the feeling his story was not told to say I love you but to say good-bye.

****

Colin glanced over his shoulder as he strode to the castle from the dock and saw Bree wave good-bye to Hamish as the sailboat launched from the pier. A sharp pain cut across his chest. He couldn't bring himself to tell her he must leave.

John broke into his thoughts. "I've got everything in order for today."

Colin tried to set Bree from his mind and focus on the journey ahead and the inevitable future awaiting him in the past.

He sighed audibly, and John's head snapped up. "Ye didn't tell her, did ye?" John cursed under his breath. "Her heart's gonna break into a thousand pieces, Colin. Ye can't do this to her, especially after spending a night together."

Colin knew he was being an ass. "I can't. There's something inside of me stopping me from saying good-bye. I don't want to tell her some lie about going to the law firm. I want to be truthful with her, but I can't tell her of the task the Fae have set upon me. How do I tell her I might be gone for a long time—or even forever?" They continued along the trail in silence.

Colin replayed the day before in his mind. He recalled her smile and excitement when they sailed. He remembered the burning passion she shared with him in his bed. He must leave her, and his heart felt raw, like an animal had torn through it and left it open, bleeding. Colin knew this was how Bree would suffer when she found out he had disappeared without telling her.

He couldn't do that to her. "I'll stop by the chapel later today. I'll tell her then. Just before we have to clear the area."

John shook his head. "Ye are taking the coward's way out, Colin."

****

Marie stepped out of the chapel doorway. "Are ye coming, Brielle?" Brielle stood at the chapel's altar, staring at the circular window, trying to envision what design it could have been in the past.

"Soon." She waved her hand, not glancing over her shoulder. The setting sun shone through the circular hole, spreading rays across her face. *Was it a cross, or would it have been a Bible?* She stepped closer to the altar and placed her hands on the stone slab, trying to sense the spirit of the chapel. She closed her eyes, stood still, and took a deep breath. A breeze blew through the building and raised the hairs on her neck.

Brielle closed her mind to the surrounding sounds and concentrated on the chapel. She imagined the way it might have been in the eighteenth century. In her mind, she saw a newly honed stone with transept supports across the ceiling, arching upward toward the heavens. The new wood roof cast a fresh scent, combined with the incense the priest had just used from a service.

The crunch of a footfall came from behind her. She whipped around, startled from her reverie. Colin stood in the center of the chapel.

"Colin, you startled me."

He stared at her, silent. She examined his face, trying to gauge his mood. She had never seen this expression on his face before. Brielle's heart raced, and her palms turned sweaty. It was only last night they had declared their love for one another. *What would make Colin act this way?*

"Colin, is everything okay?"

He smiled, but it quirked. "Everything is fine, Bree."

She searched his face again as she approached him, then pulled up short. He stayed so still, like a snake ready to strike. Like Tony before…Colin promised he wouldn't do anything to hurt her, and she need never fear him.

He took a deep breath and released it, stepping toward her, cradling her face in his hand. "Bree, I…" He breathed deeply. "I…I have to leave tonight. The law firm needs me."

Her breath caught.

Why so sudden and after last night? "But you'll come back for the weekends. I mean, come check on the renovation, right?"

He leaned forward, kissed her on the lips, and then rested his forehead against hers.

He didn't answer her. This was it. He would tell

her he didn't want her and, after giving herself to him, told him of her love. Consequence four rang loud in her mind. *You will live your life feeling unhappy and unfulfilled. No, this can't be true!*

Her breath caught on a sob she couldn't contain. As she peered into his eyes, a tear escaped. He caught it with his thumb, then bent and kissed her softly. He deepened the kiss, taking her in his arms. Her chest tightened, then her stomach dropped. He said he must leave and wouldn't visit, but his kiss was one of love. She followed as he continued the kiss, increasing their passion, igniting a fierce fire inside her.

Colin grunted and broke off the kiss, pushing her away. She stumbled backward as another tear trailed down her cheek.

Why is he acting this way?

"Colin, I…" Colin's face flashed in carved, harsh angles before he turned his back to her.

His words came hard and loud. "Head back to the castle, Bree. Head back there now, and don't come back down tonight."

Brielle stepped toward him. "But…"

Colin rounded on her and bellowed, "Dammit, Bree, I said leave, now!"

Shaking, she ran from the chapel and away from Colin.

****

Colin's hands shook. Instead of staring at them, he ran them through his hair. He went into the chapel and spied Brielle standing at the altar, sunlight from the circular window bathing her in a halo of light. Dust danced within the sunbeams around her head, making her seem ethereal. He had watched her for a moment, wanting to capture this moment and lock it away in his memory forever, for he knew now she *was* his soul mate. At that moment, he realized the maiden in the Fae Fable was Bree. *The Fae Fable tells the fate of the stone. I couldn't allow it to come true. If it does, that means I'll lose Bree.*

This morning, as she'd stood at the stern of the boat gazing at the view of the immense mountain landscape framing her modest body, she appeared so vulnerable. Would she be safe with him gone? As they approached the peak, he had turned to gaze at Dunstaffnage Castle, his home. *Would he ever see Glen Etive in this time again? Would he make it back to Brielle?*

He wished he could stay here—with her—stay and continue what they had begun. But the Fae did not care about his desires. There were more important duties to be dealt with before Colin could give his full attention to Bree. He had to right the wrong, to fix the past, to make the present right.

His wee Bree. He'd hurt her. But he knew it had to be this way. She would figure out the Fae, the portal, the duty. She would follow him, thinking she would help, and all she would do was get hurt. The evil Fae, they would only use her, use her against him. Colin feared in his heart they would spill her blood, and he would not let that happen, no matter the cost to him.

If the cost of her protection was a broken heart, so be it. She couldn't be the maiden. Failure was not an option. He must find the Stone of Love and restore Roderick to his time. With the Stone of Love, he'd return here. Their lives depended on it.

Colin dropped his head back and stared into the

sky. *God, please let me make it back to her, back to my wee Bree.*

Chapter 13

Colin changed into his father's plaid and shirt. He tucked his father's dirk into his belt, adjusting his sporran. In his father's clothing, he could conquer the world. He needed the extra confidence for the task he had to face.

John's gaze traveled over him. "Damn, Colin, if ye weren't moving, ye'd be that portrait of Roderick in the castle. Yer givin' me chills."

Colin slashed his hand to the side. "'Tis not a time to joke, John. We've gone over everything, and ye got yer instructions. Check the box hole daily and make sure ye keep the damn thing a secret." He gazed at the castle. Bree, he had hurt her earlier.

He turned to John. "Bree can't find out anything about me from the past. She'll figure out the assignment, get herself caught up in this, and get hurt. I want her kept safe."

John patted him on the shoulder. "I understand. Ye have my promise and my word. I won't let ye down."

Colin glanced one last time at John. Once, as children, when he visited the castle, they had been playmates. Over the years, time and responsibilities had separated them, his in Edinburgh and John's here at the castle. Now that Colin had returned and spent time here, John had become a good friend. He nodded to John, knowing he could count on him to keep things well while he was gone. It was time.

Colin slung his sword over his back and strapped it in place. "I appreciate that. Please take care of Bree while I'm gone. Promise me, John, see to her." He placed his hand on John's shoulder and squeezed it once.

John nodded. "I will."

Colin shook himself and glimpsed toward the altar. "I can't fail, John. I must find the stone, bring Roderick back from purgatory, and make it back home."

John picked up the discarded clothes, headed to the chapel door, stopped, and gazed back at Colin. "Ye have yer da's drive, his determination, Colin. I've got faith in ye—ye will succeed."

Colin nodded, rendered speechless by this declaration from someone who had worked closely with his father.

John smiled. "Plus, ye gotta make it back. The reenactment is coming soon. We need the laird to kick off the celebrations with the ceremonial toast." John winked as he left Colin alone in the chapel to face the challenge of his life.

Colin knelt before the altar, bowed his head. He stayed there in silence for a moment. Tinkling bells and light childlike laughter rang through the chapel. Colin glanced around. The sunset cast the chapel in shades of orange and red, making the building appear bathed in blood, chilling his heart.

"Ye are here." Brigid spoke from the altar.

Colin glanced up. "Aye, I'm here, ye wee sprite. Let's get this business over with."

Brigid laughed. "So eager to get started."

Colin stood. "I'll ask again, how long am I going to

be gone?"

Brigid flew to him and landed on his shoulder. "As long as it takes."

Colin swiped at her form, his hand passing through her as if she were air. He growled: "Ye damn nymph, how long?"

Brigid laughed again and hovered over the chapel doorway. "Ye must find the Stone of Love. Only through the Stone of Love can ye return Roderick from purgatory, back to his time. Then ye will use the stone to return to yer time." Brigid flitted in the light. "A warning, Colin, only the Stone of Love will return ye to the present, and only one stone per human can pass in the portal. Choices will need to be made. Ye need to remember."

Colin nodded and took a deep breath to gather his courage.

Brigid glowed brighter. "The time is now. Come to the door." Colin took a deep breath and moved to the doorway of the chapel.

"Raise your hand, Colin." '

He glared at her. "What for?"

Brigid smiled. "Yer blood, Colin. 'Tis the first time ye travel through the Fae portals. I need yer blood."

He raised his right hand, palm facing the door. A cut grew on his hand. He grimaced at the pain but held steady. Blood dripped from his hand to the stones. Brigid clapped her hands together, and lightning exploded over the chapel with a thunderous boom.

The winds swirled around the chapel, then whirled inside the building in increasing intensity as they churned around Colin. He clenched his hand over the doorway as the wind continued to build. He felt the blood drip from his hand. As if he were in a vortex, he heard the blood drip on the stone over the sound of the wind, drop by drop.

Brigid raised her arms to the skies, glowing lighter, and chanted:

Gatekeeper, open the portal,
Between the Fae and mortals,
As power freely flows,
And as our magic grows.
Send him back in time,
Send him to his own kind
Shield him from the evil one
To right the wrong which has been done

She clapped her hands over her head, the sound reverberating in the space. Light burst from the doorway, making the frame glow in brilliant white light.

He heard Brigid whisper under the wind. "'Tis time to step through the portal."

Colin took a deep breath, then took his first step.

As he stepped through the doorway, Brigid said, "Remember, the key is not a key, but is the key. The key can only be revealed when the heart is pure and true love's hands are joined. That which is the key will be shown to the one who needs it most, only when they need it most."

****

Brielle helped Ian set the last stone in the window enclosure.

She stepped back, admiring their work. "Finally! We have set the windows and can prepare them for the stained glass. Once we get the roof installed next week, we can put in the windows and close the building. Then

177

you can start on the flooring stones." Brielle turned to Marie and spied her staring at her like a mother hen.

Professor Mac's consequence number one ran through her mind: *You will always sense that something is missing.* She should have known better than to let go of her heart.

Marie turned to Ian. "Ye head on home."

Brielle turned away and stared out the window.

Marie sighed. "Ye've worked yerself to the bone, from sunup to sundown. Brielle, we are ahead of schedule. Ye don't have to work so hard."

Weeks had passed since Colin left. There had been no word. Not even John had heard from him, or at least that was what he claimed.

Consequence four: *You will live your life unhappy and unfulfilled.*

She shook her head, trying to shake the thought away. She suspected there was more to this sudden trip than met the eye, but who was she to question Colin? He had his own life. Hers was here, restoring the chapel, getting on as best she could. She would live without a relationship that complicated things—because they *always* complicated *her* life.

Brielle turned from the window toward Marie. "I'm fine."

She smiled, trying to convince herself she was fine, but it came as a grimace. Consequence two: *You will know deep down that you deserve better*. Did she really deserve better? She didn't think there was anyone better than Colin. If she could keep going every day, she could keep telling herself that his sudden disappearance had not affected her.

Ronnie approached her, holding something in his

hand. "Ms. Bree, the lads and I worry about ye. With ye sad and all since Colin left, I'd like ye to take one of my stone necklaces."

Ronnie held it out to her. It was a delicate gold chain. The end wasn't a pendant but a spring circle. "I know ye've taken to carrying the stone Hamish gave ye. I make these for the gift shop at the marina. It's to hold yer Iona stone so ye can keep it with ye all the time. If ye give me the stone, I'll put it in the spring for ye."

Brielle, touched by Ronnie's gift, sighed and handed him the stone from her pocket. He shifted the gold and popped the rock into the circle. The spring held it perfectly. He handed it back to her and patted her hand as she held it.

"Ronnie, thank you for thinking of me. You guys head on home for the day." Ronnie nodded once, stared at her for a moment, then turned to leave.

Brielle glanced at the necklace, remembering the day they went sailing and stayed at the hunting cabin. The day Colin showed her his father's stone and claimed she had his mother's. The day he told her he loved her.

Consequence three: *You'll be trapped with somebody who is just not right for you.* But he was right for her. She knew it in her heart, but she guessed he didn't. He told her she carried his heart, his love with her as she carried this half of the heart stone. Blinking back tears, she put on the necklace. She might not carry *his* love, but she carried hers for him.

She glanced toward the castle through the window, glimpsing only the wall walk. An ache came over her heart as she remembered Colin standing there and watching her work, as if he couldn't stay away from her for one moment. She rubbed the stone against her chest.

Marie placed her hand on Brielle's shoulder. "John and I are headed into town tonight. There's a band at the pub. Why don't ye get away from this place for a while? Ye haven't even left the castle."

Brielle shrugged the hand off her shoulder. "Maybe," she replied, knowing full well she wouldn't go. "You head on to the castle. I would like to sit here, enjoy the sunset and the quiet."

Marie patted her on the shoulder and then turned to head on the path back to the castle. She glanced back over her shoulder. "Okay, but if I don't see ye soon, I'm sending John back to get ye and convince ye to join us. While Colin is away, John's in charge of watching out for ye." Marie continued on, shaking her head.

Brielle said nothing; there was nothing left to say. A tear escaped, and she wiped it away, wishing to wipe away the ache in her heart.

She crossed the nave and grabbed her backpack but stopped short. An ominous sensation washed over her. Brielle turned her head to look at the doorway. Shadows shifted in the late-afternoon light, making it seem like spirits moved through the door. She reached to her chest and rubbed her stone on its chain. As she stepped out the door, a sudden gust of wind blew through the woods, a hard blast that cast her back, sending chills down her spine. The wind died down as soon as it passed.

Brielle turned from the chapel's doorway and sat on the ground amidst the stone rubble. She set her backpack on her lap and pulled out the book of poems she'd found in the library the night of the storm. God, she could not get that night out of her mind. It was the night she fell in love with Colin. She gazed at the sunset through the trees—it was peaceful and warm. She flipped through the book's pages, needing something to take her mind away, away from rules and consequences.

When she opened the book, the wind blew again, ruffling the pages. She glanced down, and the book had opened to a page she had not seen before. There were times she could open this book and see the same pages over and over; yet other times it was like she held a different book. She tried to read it, but it didn't seem clear. Her mind clouded, and she couldn't make out the words.

Say it out loud, she heard in her mind. Brielle turned her head but saw nothing. She heard it again. *Say it out loud.* Taking a deep breath, Brielle read:

Hear these words in my mind:
Heed my hope within my time
Send me back to where I'll find
The one I love, in their place and time

As she finished the last sentence, a crash inside the chapel startled her. Brielle shoved the book into her backpack and flung the sack on her back. She thought she was the only one left at the construction site.

She pushed up from a broken rock with her left hand. It had cut a large gash into her palm. "Damn, that hurts."

She held her hand and headed toward the chapel doorway. Blood dripped from her palm as she tried to put pressure on it. "Hello? Who's there?"

The wind blew harder, almost pushing her back. It was so strong she had to close her eyes as she went through the chapel door. On her next step, she tripped and fell on the floor, backpack, bloody hand, and all.

Stunned for a moment, she knelt, staring at her hand. Blood dripped onto the floor. In a daze, Brielle glanced up—the chapel was no longer a ruin. Damn, far from it. It looked like it had never been a ruin at all.

Her gaze traveled down to the beautiful stone floor. Grabbing her shirt hem, she used it to wipe up the blood. Close to the floor, she studied the intricacy and detail of the stone. It was a quality she had never seen before, a design and detail she'd only seen in history books.

Placing the shirt's hem on her cut, she stood on shaky legs and turned around, staring. The stained-glass windows were all intact. A completed roof was overhead. Could it be? Was the chapel complete? Would the mysterious round windows they couldn't find a record of be here?

She turned to gaze at the front and back of the chapel where the round windows near the roof were, and her mouth fell open. The stained glass was there, and it was gorgeous. The dusky light shone through, casting beautiful colors and shapes throughout the interior. Brielle turned in a circle, marveling at the beauty all around her.

She moved toward the altar, where a large man knelt. He seemed different—but she couldn't make out why. Brielle tilted her head to the side, trying to focus on what was different. He wore a white shirt and a Scottish plaid with the end draped over his shoulder. To her, he resembled one of those historical reenactments. She shook her head, then stared again. He was still there.

She must have made a noise because the man stood

and turned toward her. As he unfolded himself, she noticed he stood tall, very tall. Her gaze rose from his bare knees to his plaid, then his face, leaving her speechless. Him, it was him. Her breath whooshed out like a blow to her gut. His face held the strangest expression—like he had seen a ghost. Then his face shifted into carved, harsh angles, an expression she had only seen once.

"Colin?" she whispered. She dropped the backpack, the cut on her hand forgotten. He strode toward her. She sensed the anger radiating from him. She became dizzy and couldn't take in a breath. She blinked. He was still advancing, as he clenched his fists at his sides. She rocked back, jolted, catching herself from falling. As he got closer, he growled deep in his chest. She couldn't take her eyes off him.

"Colin?" The sides of her vision dimmed, and the last thought before everything went black was, *This can't be Colin.*

Chapter 14

Dunstaffnage Castle, 1720

Brielle awoke to a pounding headache. She didn't recall getting that drunk. Wait, she didn't remember drinking at all. She tried to lick her lips, but they were as dry as a bone. Turning her head, she glanced around and realized she was in her bedroom in the castle—the same, yet different.

A woman sat in a chair beside her, sleeping with her head dropped to the side, almost sliding off the chair. Brielle didn't recognize her, and her clothing was…outdated.

Her gaze roamed the room. So much was the same, but different. Her eyes went from the wall to the door, then to the bath. The bathroom doorway was there, but beyond was no bath inside, only clothes. There was no lighting, no electrical lamps, but an oil one on the table and candles around the room. The fireplace had a fire blazing, not gas, giving off a heavy scent of burning wood and something else. Brielle sniffed once more. *Dirty dry grass?* It was so much cooler in the room than before. As she sat up, she noticed she wore a long, rough gown.

The woman jolted awake, clapping her hands as she jumped up from the chair. "Glory be, ye're awake!"

The woman helped her sit up fully, then grabbed a

cup. "Here, dearie, sip this. I'm sure ye are thirsty." Brielle leaned against the bed's headboard and took a sip. She swirled it around her mouth—a honeyed flavor cooling on her throat. It reminded her of the sweet mead she once drank at a renaissance festival.

After taking a couple of sips, she asked, "Where am I?"

"Why, in the castle, Dunstaffnage castle. I'm Fiona. The laird said ye were visitin' so we must get ye up to see him. Ye've slept the afternoon away. It's near dinner now." Fiona crossed the room and opened the heavily draped window, illuminating the window seat and the entire room.

"Up with ye now. We'll get ye fed, bathed, and dressed. Then ye can have yer introduction to the laird. Fainting dead away at his feet isn't a formal introduction, now is it?"

As Brielle got up, a pain in her hand reminded her that she'd cut it. She glanced down. Someone had wrapped it in a rough cloth. She brought it to her nose and sniffed—*it smelled like whisky.* Her head spun, and she felt out of sorts. She touched her chest, searching for her stone necklace. It was there—she sighed.

Brielle slid out of bed, shivered in the cold room, and went to the window seat. At least the window enclosure was the same.

She stepped past the bench and stared out the window. Her breath blew out in an exhale at the sight before her. Nothing appeared the same. The road, the cars, and the pavement were all gone. People moved around dressed similar to Fiona. Some women carried baskets with produce. Some had laundry. A man wearing a kilt went by, leading a horse. A loud clanging

Margaret Izard

like an enormous hammer hitting metal reverberated throughout the bustling courtyard, which was right in the middle of the castle.

Brielle's thoughts raced as she gaped. She must have come through a portal of some sort. Because this wasn't the present time—she would guess she was somewhere in the seventeenth or eighteenth century. *Could that even be possible?*

"The laird?" Brielle asked, as she turned to peek at Fiona.

"Yes, Roderick MacDougall, laird of our clan. So sad his wife died. Oh, please don't tell anyone I mentioned it. We are all in mourning."

Roderick, the laird. Brielle took a deep breath and tried to piece her mind back together. She must be in the eighteenth century. That was why the chapel looked new. Roderick—not Colin—was the man in the chapel. He was the man from the portrait, the identical one.

Brielle recalled the story John had told when she arrived at the castle. Something about Roderick's wife, Mary, and how someone stabbed her on the chapel steps at their son's christening, a private family event. There was something about Roderick disappearing for a year and then returning, married to a Ross.

She sighed...so the year must be around 1720. Maybe she was wrong about her memory of the tale, but if not, that meant the man in the chapel was Roderick, yet shouldn't he be missing?

Brielle could have sworn he recognized her just before she passed out. He acted as if he thought she shouldn't be intruding. It all felt so much like Colin, but she knew it couldn't be.

She squared her shoulders and told herself, *Okay,*

186

Brielle. You can do this. It's possible to do 1720. You're a historian. Your area of expertise. How hard can this be?

She turned as Fiona dragged a tub from the dressing room. "Did ye say something, dear?"

More dismayed, Brielle shook her head. She faced a sizeable wooden tub that seemed like one she had seen in a drawing—like a hip bath. Fiona set it in front of the fireplace and glanced at Brielle.

A knock rapped the door. "Ah, the boys with yer water."

Boy after boy filed by, filling the tub with steaming water. Fiona poured some oil into the tub, and the fragrance of roses filled the room, reminding Brielle of home.

"Let's get ye bathed and dressed, dearie; the laird is waiting."

****

Brielle stepped from the tub, and Fiona wrapped her in a plain sheet that she'd heated by the fireplace. Another maid brought Fiona some clothing and stood by to help her dress. Fiona had already done her hair in a bun with a covering. Brielle typically tossed it in a messy bun, but Fiona insisted her hair be neat.

Fiona started with the same long shirt Brielle had on when she awoke. Then, there was a long skirt of white fabric. Next was another skirt over this last one. Brielle lifted the skirt—she had not worn many dresses, let alone long skirts. This would be interesting. It already felt so heavy. *Why can't I get my khaki pants back?*

Fiona put a bodice with boning on her. Brielle giggled because it reminded her of lingerie from one of those risqué lingerie shops. Fiona made fast work of the lacings and tightened the bodice. It forced Brielle to suck in her breath as Fiona continued to pull.

Brielle gasped. "Not so tight."

Fiona huffed. "We got to have ye laced in proper." Brielle rolled her eyes. Fiona finished with a wrap—in this time they called it an *arisaid*—in the MacDougall plaid. The familiar fabric was a welcome sight, and the shoulder wrap would help keep her warm.

Fiona presented her with woolen stockings and tied them above her knee. At least they were warm under the dress. Finally, Fiona tied shoes on her feet.

Fiona eyed Brielle up and down. "Well, that'll do ye, lass."

Brielle glanced around the room. There was not another piece of clothing.

She blushed and whispered, "What about underwear?"

Fiona blinked at her. "Why lass, ye got yer shift on. That's all ye need."

Brielle's blush deepened. "No, I mean the part that covers your privates."

Fiona nodded understandingly. "Do ye need something for yer courses, dearie?"

"No, I mean I wear bottoms all the time. Underwear that covers your bottom."

Fiona gasped. "No, dearie, ye don't wear that all the time, only during yer woman's time."

Brielle groaned. This was what she got for focusing her historical studies on buildings. She should have listened more in class when Professor Mac covered clothing. She thought the girls in class tittering about bodices and kilts silly. Now, she felt stupid for not paying attention.

Fiona took her arm. "Now that ye are ready, we'll get ye downstairs to meet the laird."

Brielle stopped. "Wait—my backpack—where's my backpack?"

Fiona glared at her, puzzled. "Backpack?"

She took a deep breath. "My bag. I arrived with a bag. It has my stuff and a book. My book of poems."

Fiona nodded. "It's on the chair, dearie, by the fire."

Brielle glanced and saw it on the chair, then sighed in relief.

Fiona led her out the door into the corridor. Brielle tripped on the skirt. Fiona glanced back and Brielle gathered her dress in her one good hand that wasn't cut. *Concentrate. You can do this.*

They headed down the corridor, passed the previous lairds' portraits, then went down the stairs. She was here, in the past. Could this be a dream? Still, Brielle was a bit excited. She would have time to study the chapel when it was new and complete, even if this was a dream. Brielle pinched her left arm hard to check. *Ouch.*

Fiona glanced back at Brielle like she had gone a little insane, and maybe she had. One step at a time. Follow along, and she would figure it out. Like—why the hell was she in the eighteenth century, and how the hell would she get back?

****

Colin paced in front of the study's fireplace, running his hand through his hair. *She was here, in the eighteenth century.* His plaid flared at each turn, a snifter of whisky clutched in his hand.

He took a generous gulp, leaning on the mantel, staring into the flames. "God, Archie. I nearly lost my mind. I heard something, and there she stood, blood dripping from her hand. Then she fainted. I almost didn't catch her." Colin ran his hand through his hair again. "I was right there, praying. Well, pretending to like we discussed. Ye sure ye didn't see anyone outside the chapel?"

Archibald shook his head.

This was part of their plan to draw out the evil Fae. Colin arrived back in time, just a few minutes past the stabbing of Roderick's wife, and got control of the situation. Upon his arrival, he saved Mary's life, and the attacker fled without finishing the murder.

He had been there for a few days already, and now Bree was here. "Ye sure she'll be all right? There are no hospitals here. How is she going to heal?"

"Hospital?" Archibald shook his head. "If ye mean hospice, no, we don't need to go to the priory. Agatha's the best healer in the glen been to see her. Agatha said it was only a wee cut in her hand, so she didn't have to sew her up. She just woke up, and Fiona is getting her ready to come to speak to ye."

Shaking his head again, Archibald continued, "*Chan urrainn dhomh seo a sheasamh, tha e gam ghluasad às mo chiall.*" I can't stand this; it's driving me crazy.

Colin glanced at Archibald. "I know ye hate it, but do this just for me until we get everything back to normal. Ye'll only have to keep the secret that Mary is still alive going for a little longer."

Colin thanked God for Archibald, John MacArthur's great-grandfather, Lord knew how many times removed. Initially, he didn't believe Colin was from the future, more than two hundred years. That is, not until Colin mentioned the Iona Stones. It was then Colin convinced Archibald that the Fae were at work. Archie helped Colin become Alexander Roderick MacDougall, twenty-third laird of clan MacDougall.

Now he needed to flush out the evil Fae behind Roderick's disappearance and find the Stone of Love. Now that Bree was here, it was too much to handle.

Archibald rubbed his face. "It happened just like when Roderick disappeared after the stabbing. She appeared out of thin air. I wouldn't have believed ye coming from the future if I hadn't seen Roderick vanish as I did. Then ye was right where he stood. It scared me something fierce. Thought ye were Roderick. The cloaked figure had stabbed Mary. Blood was everywhere, and yer bairn, I mean Roderick's bairn, was crying. Glad we put yer mother, Elizabeth, and Rose in charge of Mary's recovery, hidden away at the hunting lodge."

Three hard raps vibrated the door.

Archibald glanced at Colin. "She could not have gotten dressed this quickly. I wonder who this is."

Colin called out, "Come in."

Reverend O'Donnell stormed into the room.

The white preaching tabs on his collar flapped in his wake. "My laird, I need to speak with ye about yer wife's funeral. 'Tis highly inappropriate for ye not to have a Christian funeral with a reverend presiding. Why—I must pray over her soul and perform the rite of committal at her grave site."

Colin rubbed his neck and peered at Archibald.

The reverend puffed his breath. "Why, it's

191

blasphemous for ye to hold a private family burial. It's disrespectful to Lady MacDougall, your wife, to not allow the proper burial in the family cemetery here at the chapel. The clan women didn't even prepare the body. This is a sin, it is. God will have yer soul for this, my laird." His voice rose as he continued to speak.

Archibald intervened. "Reverend O'Donnell, now, there's nothing wrong with a private family service. Roderick wanted to honor his wife by burying her near the hunting cabin. No need to get angry."

Allowing Archibald to take the lead, Colin stepped back.

Archibald crossed to the clergy and tried to take his arm.

Reverend O'Donnell shook him off, turning to Colin. "Now, I hear ye are entertaining a guest, *a female guest*. Just mere weeks after ye buried yer wife. Why she's not even cold in the grave, and ye already have yer *whore* here serving ye. This is blasphemous, it is."

Colin's head snapped up. He stepped toward the clergyman, bellowing in his face, "She's not a whore, and ye will not call her that!"

Both men panted. The energy in the room was palpable.

Archibald stepped between them, placing his arm on the clergyman's shoulder. "Now, Reverend O'Donnell, I don't know what gossip ye have heard, but Brielle DeVolt is no whore. She's visiting my wife. A distant cousin that's come to help since Mary passed. Ye have it all wrong."

Colin stepped back, turning away from the reverend.

Archibald patted the reverend's shoulder, turning him toward the door. "Reverend, ye should know better than to listen to idle castle gossip. She's kin, a guest to help Rose when she returns."

The reverend shook his head. "If that's what ye say, then so be it. But mark me, if Mary doesn't get a Christian burial, ye both will burn in hell."

Reverend O'Donnell turned and stormed from the room.

Archibald closed the door behind him and turned to Colin. "You'll need to be careful with Brielle in the castle. If the gossip has already started, it will be hard to stop. Stay away from her. Give the appearance that she means nothing important to ye."

Colin could not stop thinking about Bree. He couldn't believe she was here, and the situation had just gotten worse.

"Archie, we'll have to come up with something to keep her busy. She is not the type of woman who can sit and do sewing all day, and I wouldn't call her docile. She's educated and used to long hours and hard work. I can't have her going to the chapel, even though she'll want to. She's a historian in our time, an expert. She won't be able to resist it. In our time, she was at the castle to restore the chapel. It's an obsession for her." Colin sighed, ran his hands through his hair, and glanced at Archibald.

Archibald tilted his head. "Historian, ye say. Well, we can have her record the family history in the family history book. Roderick's been meaning to add to the book for a while, but never gets around to it." He rubbed his chin. "I can have the elders come and talk her ears off on the clan history. She'll be in the great hall for weeks. We can say it's why she's here."

Colin smiled. "Aye, that would keep her busy."

Recording the family history would be good. God, it would be difficult. He wanted to be with her, touch her already. But he needed to be Roderick, a newly widowed man with a new bairn. He couldn't be yearning for another woman. He must stay focused and keep his mind on finding the Stone of Love.

Now that she was in the eighteenth century, he couldn't let the Fae Fable story come true. As long as she stayed away from the chapel, he could keep her safe. He would need to find the stone, return Roderick, and then get them back to their own time in one piece. *Easy as pie.* He sighed. The taps at the door interrupted his thoughts. *It's her.*

Colin stepped behind the desk, straightened his clothing, sat down, and folded his hands on the desk as he nodded to Archibald. "Come in."

****

As Fiona opened the door to the study, Brielle wasn't sure what to expect. She was in this same room just the other day in her time. She took a deep breath and walked into the room. Her eyes immediately sought Colin. No, it was Roderick, the man from the past. His eyes bore into her as he sat behind the desk. Brielle sensed an awareness wash over her, the same sensation she got when Colin settled his eyes on her. She internally shook herself, trying to shed the feeling.

Her gaze traveled over the room, noting the difference between the past to the twenty-first century. The mantel and shelf were the same, the desk as well, but the rest of the room appeared different. No oversized couch sat before the fire—only two chairs.

She shivered as there was no electricity to heat the room, making it colder, darker, more foreboding. The fire blazed, providing the only heat source. The *Fae Fable Book* sat open on its stone ledge next to the window.

At a glance, Brielle noted it was in much better shape. A clearing of a throat interrupted her inspection.

She turned to Roderick as he spoke. "Allow me to welcome ye to Dunstaffnage properly. I'm Alexander Roderick MacDougall, twenty-third laird of the clan MacDougall. Please, have a seat." He waved to the chair in front of the desk.

Brielle sat as she gaped at Roderick. *God, he looks and sounds exactly like Colin.*

Roderick raised an eyebrow at her. She hoped she hadn't said that out loud. She shook herself as a male chuckle came from beside her.

Roderick raised his hand, indicating the other man in the room. "I believe ye know my captain of the castle, Archibald MacArthur."

Brielle turned her head. The man standing by the fireplace had John's hair and stance, but parts of his face were different. She might see the familial resemblance, but it was not as apparent as Colin and Roderick. Roderick cleared his throat, and she shifted her attention back to him. It still amazed her every time she looked at him.

She took a moment to examine his face, trying to find something off—just one little mark, mole, or freckle. But Brielle got caught up in his eyes, blue like the sky on a crisp day.

Archibald cleared his throat. Roderick stared at his hands on the desk. Brielle glanced at Archibald. She did a double take back to Roderick. "Did you say I know him?"

Archibald stepped away from the fireplace and crossed to stand next to Roderick. "Yes, lass, ye are my wife's cousin. Ye've come for a visit from the lowlands. It's why yer accent is different. My wife, Rose"—he glanced at Roderick, then back to Brielle— "she's gone, caring for someone taken ill. 'Tis nice to see ye, lass."

Brielle stared, openmouthed, but recovered quickly. "Yes, I'm Brielle DeVolt." She started to stand and go toward him. But she stopped and folded her hands into her skirts, trying to avoid the urge to step up and offer a handshake. *A cousin? Okay, I can play a cousin.* Brielle didn't know what would happen when Rose showed up and noticed she wasn't her relation. But for now, this was an excellent cover. She could play along.

"Ah, good." Roderick sat back in his chair and tapped his finger on his chin. "I'm reminded now of a DeVolt. Some distant auntie married a French man, a scholar, which is how you became a scholar, like him. Yes, that's it. Well, seeing as Rose is away and ye'll be needing something to keep ye occupied till her return, I'll need ye to take on a task for me."

She spotted a glint in Roderick's eyes. Brielle glared at him. The uncanny resemblance caught her off guard, but the attraction sent tingles all over her body. She couldn't fathom the magnetism. This man was Colin's great-grandfather, many times removed. Her emotions were not proper. Regardless of the likeness, he was Colin's relative.

Roderick flattened his hands on the desk and stood

as he spoke. "I'll need ye to meet with the elders each day." He strode around the desk. "Ye'll record the family history as told by them. Archibald will get ye all set up. Ye'll work in the great hall daily."

He nodded, seeming very proud of himself. "Ye'll keep busy doing this *all day, every day.*" He leaned back against the desk, folding his arms and crossing his legs at the ankle. God, she couldn't stop staring. Brielle saw Colin do that same thing the other day in this same room. The other day, *in the future.*

"Yes," Archibald said, drawing her attention to him. "The laird has wanted this task done, and we can think of no one better."

He nodded to Brielle. Her mouth fell open. She couldn't believe it: tasked as a scribe. She wanted to spend her time studying the castle, the land, and, most important, the chapel. Since she was here, the past being her true passion, she hoped she would get a good look around. Brielle wanted to examine everything. To find a way to make a record of this time and take it back with her. She was going back. She would find a way.

Roderick interrupted her thoughts. "Oh, and stay away from the chapel. We've had some issues there. Ye are forbidden from the chapel."

Brielle's head snapped up. She resisted the urge to fold her arms over her chest by fisting her hands at her sides.

"Why? Weren't you just there, praying?" She had to see the chapel. She tried to come up with an excuse to go there. "Why would you deny *me* the right to pray? A girl's got to pray, right?" She was not the most devout. She hadn't been to church in ages, but there was no way in hell she would miss out on a chance to examine the chapel.

Roderick towered over her, raising his voice. "I'm the laird, and ye'll do as ye're told."

Brielle froze, staring at Roderick. A flash of an expression crossed his face but was gone before she could make it out. Yelling. She hated yelling.

Archibald approached Brielle, his voice gentle. "My lady, certainly ye understand the importance of such a task. Rose will be back soon. I am certain ye two can visit and spend some time together. But in the meantime, the laird has given ye a task, an honorable one. Best do as he says."

He took Bree's good hand, pulling her to stand. Archibald put her hand on his arm and escorted her toward the door.

"Well, all right, for a short while. Till Rose comes back," Brielle said. She would play along. But she would go to the chapel the first moment she could get away. Roderick "the laird" be damned—they could all be damned.

A final glance back at Roderick revealed him looking exactly like the portrait in the future. She could swear she heard him growl.

Chapter 15

Brielle walked to the great hall the following morning to break her fast. Last night the healer had advised her to rest, so Fiona sent a tray to her room. Brielle needed the respite. It had been a shock to come face-to-face with Roderick. She shouldn't have the affection for Colin's ancestor that she did for Colin, yet her attraction felt the same for both men.

She rubbed her forehead with her cut hand, forgetting the injury for the moment, then jerked her hand back at the sharp pain. *Damn.*

Regardless of her hand, Brielle felt ready to tackle this eighteenth-century project. Squaring her shoulders, she approached the great hall. The carved wooden double doors stood open in invitation to anyone wanting to join the morning meal. Walking through them gave her a sense of entering a new world.

Upon entering, she scanned the voluminous space. Scrapes of utensils against wooden plates and bowls combined with the low murmur of conversation filled the room. At one end, the enormous fireplace stood much as it has in the future, yet now black soot stained the opening from smoke. A large fire roared inside, providing the only source of heat to the chilled room. Tables lined the room as the villagers broke their fast. Perpendicular sat the head table on a raised platform. She knew there was a hierarchy to the seating arrangement, but she hadn't paid attention to historical social etiquette in class.

Roderick caught her eye as he rose from his seat and came to greet her. "I hope ye had a restful night. Please join me to break yer fast, Brielle."

He clasped her hand, notably avoiding the injured one, and placed it in the crook of his arm.

Roderick escorted her to the chair next to his, pulling it out for her. "How's yer hand today, Miss DeVolt?"

On her other side stood Archibald. Brielle sat between them, flinching slightly when the boning of her bodice poked her. Roderick's hand landed on her shoulder, holding her steady. It was hard to sit with this torture device on her body. She hated bras in the future and despised this straitjacket in the past.

She sighed and lied. "It's better. Thank you for asking, my laird." Roderick sat as she spoke, and the awareness of him near her was almost overwhelming. Her eyes said *Roderick*, but her body screamed *Colin*.

Archibald cleared his throat, glanced at Roderick, and then spoke through clenched teeth. "M'lady, call her M'lady, not Miss."

Brielle thought she saw Archibald make a face at Roderick, but she wasn't sure.

Roderick shrugged and bent to his meal.

Her gaze roamed the great hall as she watched the clan members casually eating. A servant brought her a bowl of oatmeal with a mug of ale. She stuck her nose near the bowl—mushy wet wheat with a bland smell greeted her. Brielle picked up a spoon and sighed, thinking this was probably the best thing they had to eat in the past. She still wished for a hot coffee, a muffin, and cranberry juice.

She huffed and dug into her meal as Roderick spoke. "I've asked Archie to arrange with the elders to begin yer book today."

Out of the corner of her eye, Brielle caught Roderick, spooning the pottage into his mouth, and could swear he grimaced. At least she was not the only one who hated gritty oatmeal that tasted like cardboard. She took a drink from her cup to wash it down and choked a little—she forgot it was ale and not water. Roderick stifled a laugh, and her gaze shot to him, but he stared into his bowl.

As they settled into quietly eating, a woman approached the table. She wore a satin gown of higher quality than anything she had seen since arriving. Her hair was in a bun, much like Brielle's, but appeared styled, with wisps artfully framing her face. Her *arisaid* was red and black, unlike the one given Brielle, in the MacDougall colors red, with blue and green patterns. This woman seemed more like an actor from a movie than a real person.

She swirled and gracefully sat on the other side of Archibald, who greeted her. "Good morning, Lady Constance. May I introduce ye to our guest? Lady Brielle DeVolt, this is Lady Constance Ross, a distant cousin to my kin."

Roderick peered at Archibald and raised an eyebrow. Archibald nodded to Roderick, making Brielle wonder what those two were up to.

Archibald spoke as if he were in a play, projecting it across the room. "Constance's come back for a visit. She journeyed home after the accident at the chapel but has returned."

Roderick nodded at Archibald.

Constance gazed at Roderick with a doe-eyed countenance. "I'm sorry for yer loss, Laird. I hope ye find peace."

Roderick nodded, his focus on his bowl.

Constance glared at Brielle and said quietly, "Good day to ye, Lady DeVolt."

A serving girl brought Constance a bowl and mug.

She scowled at it and screeched at the maid, "Where's my honey? I always have honey with my pottage!"

The maid jumped back and stood with her head bowed, then scurried off. Constance sighed audibly.

When the maid returned, Constance abruptly grabbed the honey from her. She dumped a generous portion in her bowl, cleared her throat, and spoke sweetly as she stirred it with her spoon. "Roderick, I want to paint yer portrait now that I have returned. Ye should have yer formal portrait." She sounded sweet-tempered, her voice almost fake in its tenor, reminding Brielle of one of her college classmates, a girl who often lied.

Roderick turned to Archibald and raised his eyebrows.

Archibald nodded and spoke. "Yes, Constance was to do yer painting, but the accident forestalled the plans. She's an artist, and a good one."

Surprised, Brielle thought most women in this time spent their days sewing or doing household chores.

She turned to Constance. "You're an artist?"

Constance eyed Brielle and said in her soft voice, "Aye, I lived in a convent during my youth, learning from the nuns."

Women learned to paint from the nuns. She didn't recall that fact from her classes, but the accounts weren't always accurate. Brielle didn't quite know what to think of her. As Constance spoke, an uncomfortable awareness came over her, but disappeared when the woman's gaze returned to Roderick. Now that she noticed it, Constance's gaze stayed on Roderick for the entire meal. Doting, she adored Roderick to the point her spoon missed her mouth several times. Sure, he was attractive, but seriously? Women of this age made no sense to her.

As Brielle returned to spooning her pottage, she sensed someone watching her. A chill ran down her spine as she tried to finish her breakfast. She felt as if a snake had slithered into the room, then stopped to glare at her.

She raised her head and took a sip from her mug as she looked around the room surreptitiously, seeking the source. She found the reverend staring at her from his seat in front of the dais. His red face and clenched jaw forced her to look down at her bowl. Heat crept up her neck. She peeked from under her lashes, and he was still staring, unmoving. He made her feel as if the world judged her.

That stare reminded her of her ex, Tony, making her stomach churn. It was the same expression he had when he was close to losing his temper—then everything would go to hell. A chill passed over her body, and her shoulders trembled. After she took another bite, her oatmeal got stuck in her throat. She gulped some ale and coughed. She closed her eyes and took a deep breath. *I wish Colin were here.*

Roderick whispered, close to her ear, "Don't

worry, he'll not bother ye, I promise. Ye are safe here."
Brielle's eyes snapped open. Again, he sounded exactly
like Colin. She glanced at him, and he stared at her with
his eyebrows drawn together, just like Colin. She
glanced down at her bowl. *I can't do this.*

After breakfast, Archibald set her up for her family
book sessions, or as he called them, yer *elder meetin's.*
"Here we are, Lady DeVolt, yer pile of paper."

He stacked the pages neatly for her on the table.
Brielle mentally noted she would have to be careful
using them and write no drafts. Paper was very costly in
this time.

A maid lit a candelabra as Archibald smiled at her.
"More light te help ye see better. And here's yer quill
and ink." Great, she'd never used a quill before.

Archibald patted her shoulder. "Conner is going to
be along soon to regale ye with the *MacDougall clan's
long* history."

He glanced up. "Here comes Agatha. I suspect
she'll want to check yer hand while ye wait."

Archibald left, heading to the study as a heavyset
woman she vaguely remembered from the day before
strode toward her. She carried a large basket and sat on
the bench next to Brielle.

"There ye are, dearie. I do not know if ye recall.
I'm Agatha MacDougall, the clan healer." She dug in
the basket, pulling out assorted items—rolled cloth, a
vial of some liquid, a pile of folded fabric. "We met
yesterday, but ye were out of sorts. I'm glad to see ye
up and about today—I knew ye'd be fine."

A serving girl brought Agatha a bowl of steaming
hot water, curtsied, then left. "Let's have a peek at that
hand."

Agatha wet her cloth, wrung the fabric, and cleaned the wound. Brielle winced as Agatha scrubbed but she endured the pain knowing it kept off infection. "There now. Let me get the ointment for ye, and we'll bandage that right up." She glanced about the room as she dug into her basket. "Wonder what is keeping Conner. Usually, he's ready to tell any tale about the family."

As Agatha worked, Constance approached and gracefully slid onto the bench on the other side of Brielle. A chill blew through the room, causing Brielle to shiver.

"Going to work on the family history book today?" she asked.

Brielle nodded. Agatha was still cleansing her wound, causing her to wince again.

Agatha raised her head. "Sorry, dear, I'm almost done."

Constance trailed her fingers along the paper's edge. "I heard ye were interested in the chapel."

Brielle turned her head to Constance. "Yes, I am." Someone would tell her about the chapel. This was great. Now she could learn more about the building to gain insight into the design elements.

Constance smiled and glared at Brielle for a moment before responding. "The chapel. Well, the history of the chapel I know well."

Brielle would do anything to get into the chapel, and if she could take notes to bring back, even better. "The only story I know of the chapel is about the laird's wife dying on the steps. What other stories are there?"

Agatha finished tying off the bandage and gathered the items in her basket. "Well, that's done for ye, lass.

Let me know if ye need anything else. I'll go find Conner. He should have been here by now."

She gathered her items, glared at Constance, then shook her head as she marched away.

Brielle grabbed the paper and quill. "Tell me about the chapel." She could hardly contain her excitement. She would finally get some information on the structure. She opened the ink well, dipped the quill in, and positioned herself ready to take some notes.

Constance settled into her seat more comfortably, preening under the attention. "Well, her husband, Ewan Alexander MacDougall, built the chapel hundreds of years ago, around 1200, for Lady Julianne MacDougall. He was the fourth laird and most powerful of them' all." She waited while Brielle wrote, then gazed off into the distance, starry-eyed. "It's a story of true love. His love was so strong that he gave his wife her chapel."

She spread her arms wide as she regaled Brielle with her story. "It was the grandest of all private chapels built." She clapped her hands together loudly. "Envied by many because it resembled the large churches and monasteries on the isle of Iona. They said he spared no expense in creating a holy place to honor their true love. He had expensive stained-glass windows made special for her to reflect their favorite quote from Corinthians.

" 'And now, these three remain: faith, hope, and love. But the greatest of these is love.' "

She took a deep breath, then continued with her tale. "The windows on one side of the chapel represent faith, hope, and love; the other side is fear, doubt, and lust. It was the window of love that was the lady's favorite." Constance sighed and stared off into the distance in a dreamlike state.

Brielle scratched wildly with the quill on the paper. She already had an ink stain on her finger from dipping the quill too quickly. She knew about the stained glass but needed more details about the floor and the other two stained-glass windows, the round ones at the front and back of the chapel.

She spoke as her gaze shot back to Constance. "The floor? What is the design? The other stained-glass windows, the ones at the front and back? What are their designs?"

Constance blinked out of her dreamlike state and waved her hand. "Yes, well, not as stunning as the mosaic stone floor depicting the Lord with a cross. Those stained-glass windows in the altar and the back of the church are merely crosses." She sighed again, and her dreamlike state returned. "But it is his love that's important. His love was so strong for her that he wanted it captured in the chapel for eternal memory."

"Ah, here we are now." Conner shuffled toward them and carefully eased himself down next to Brielle. "Such a sweet lass ye are to want to write all our family history. I'm sorry I'm late, but here I am."

Brielle glanced up from her notes and grinned at Conner. Many wrinkles creased his face making him look older than he likely was. His long gray hair blended with an even longer beard. He reminded her of Merlin from the King Arthur stories, but he wore a kilt.

She giggled as she glanced at him again, expecting him to draw out a large staff and wave it around the room, casting a spell upon them all. His smile was pleasant, making his eyes seem sweet. She had never met her grandfather but envisioned this might be what he would be like, a kind older man.

He gazed at her and smiled as she spoke. "It's okay. Constance told me about the chapel. It has a rich history, and I am glad I captured it on paper. I want to go down and draw out the floor plan one day too, if I may."

Constance beamed. "Oh, I'd love to take ye there. Maybe we should go now?" Constance grabbed her arm, and Brielle shifted at the force.

Conner frowned at her. "Lady Constance, Lady Brielle is here to record the family history. She cannot be going away. Why, I've just arrived."

Constance stilled, glared at Conner, then rose regally. "I'll be back later. Take ye on a stroll for a break. Ye'll need a break. Trust me, and I'll be here for ye." As she spoke, her voice dipped a bit. She patted Brielle on the shoulder. When her hand made contact, an icy chill swept through her chest. As Constance moved away, the chill faded.

She shook it off and turned to Conner. "Where do you want to begin?"

****

Colin headed out of the castle to a bright day. He did not want to do this, but he had to keep up appearances. He needed to sit for a painting, the painting of Roderick. The one that would hang in the castle. No wonder the damn thing looked so much like him. It *would* be him. And of all the people to paint it, Constance Ross. Archibald's cousin or not, she made his skin crawl.

He hated the Ross line in the future, and if Constance was an example of what they were like in the past, he despised them all. He rounded the corner and spied her sitting primly at the castle wall base. A picnic lunch set out on a plaid with her painting supplies fanned out beside it. It seemed like a perfect romantic setting, making Colin nearly throw up.

He groaned as he approached her.

She spied him striding toward her and waved excitedly. "My laird, I'm so happy we get to spend this time together. I am looking forward to capturing yer handsome face for all eternity."

Colin bowed. "Where would ye like me to sit?"

She twittered, "Why don't we have some food? I had the cook prepare something special just for us."

Colin shook his head. "I'm not hungry. Ye may eat if ye like. But ye need to paint soon. I want to get this over with quickly."

Constance frowned and lowered her head but gave a quick smile. "Of course, my laird." She rose gracefully and tripped, falling into Colin's arms. "Oh, my laird, thank you for catching me."

He set her on her feet, noting there was nothing she could have tripped over on the grass. He removed his hands from her waist, but she held on to his shoulders. He stepped back, forcing her to drop her hands.

He waved his hand at her supplies. "Let's get to that portrait."

Colin posed much like the painting in the future. His right leg rested on the rock of the castle foundation, with the castle behind him. Constance set her easel where she viewed him, but she'd still have to peer around the frame for a full view. She began drawing with coal, humming lightly.

It was not a familiar song to Colin and did not sound in tune.

She mumbled as she drew, and he thought she mumbled Roderick's name but wasn't sure.

She sighed. "*My* laird?"

Colin rolled his eyes. He saw her coming from a mile away. Archie warned him she might try a trick or two, as she once tried to get Roderick to marry her before he fell in love with Mary, his wife. Archie had mentioned that the MacArthurs did not like the Ross line, and Colin concurred. Since her return after the accident and then her abrupt departure after the stabbing, Archie had said that Constance was behaving strangely and that her return was out of character.

He realized he hadn't responded and preferred not to, but he didn't want to be rude. "Aye?"

She peered from around the portrait as her gaze traveled up his body. "Now that Mary is dead..." How she said *dead* sounded so final. She cleared her throat. "...I mean gone. Ye'll need someone to take care of yer son, Alex."

Colin grunted.

This would make for a sad dating scene if men in the eighteenth century fell for this old trick. "I have a house full of servants for that."

She huffed and continued to draw. "Well, ye might need someone to run the house for ye."

He tried hard not to look at her and stared into the distance. "Again, I have a house full of servants. I don't need anyone else."

A harder huff came from behind the canvas, and he smiled. She hummed again, and her tune changed. This one made the hairs on his arms rise. It sounded eerie and echoing.

She stopped, then said, "Why are ye so interested

in Brielle?"

Colin closed his face off from all expressions. He needed to hide his feelings for Bree.

"I'm not interested in her. She is in my care. She seems to fall into situations where she gets hurt. I have to make sure all in my care are safe."

She glanced from behind the picture again, glaring at him.

He looked past her off into the distance. She gave him the willies, and this painting project was an obvious excuse for her to trick Roderick into marriage. Well, he wasn't Roderick and sure as hell wasn't interested in anything she offered.

She stole a look from behind the canvas again. "Seems to me ye pay her more attention than ye do most. I would say ye have feelings for her. Do ye?"

Colin felt his anger building. He did not want to discuss Bree with anyone. "I don't, except for a laird concerned for someone in his care."

She nodded and retreated behind her canvas. Colin took a deep breath and released his hands, which had gripped into fists.

Constance burst into laughter. She continued to laugh, and it took on a tinkling sound like tiny bells. A chill spread fast down Colin's spine. He thought he had heard this sound before but could not place it.

Constance rounded the canvas, screeching at him. "I think she's bewitched ye. She has. She has cast some spell upon ye, taken ye away from me. I think ye had her. Fucked her well and good."

Waving her arms wildly, Constance continued her rant as she advanced on Colin. "She's a conjurer and nothing more than a *whore*."

The last, she yelled at such a volume it echoed off the cliff side of the castle, causing birds to fly from the trees. He figured everyone down in the village must have heard her.

Colin took her by the shoulders, stopping her advance on him. God, he never considered hurting a woman, but with this one, he might reconsider.

He growled low in his throat and shook her a little at each enunciation. "Ye fucking bitch, she's not a whore."

He tossed her down, making her fall on her backside. Colin stormed off, and over his shoulder, he growled, "Ye are done for the day."

The tinkling laughter followed him, haunting his thoughts.

Chapter 16

"And that, my dear, is the story of the fifth laird of MacDougall." Brielle was still scratching with the quill on the paper as Dougal, a clan elder, finished yet another long story of a laird of MacDougall. She dropped the quill, flexing her hand to cure the cramping. Writing with a quill was a lot harder than she figured. She doubted she would get the black stains off her fingers. It had been a week since she'd come through the portal, and the elders filled it with writing taking a toll on her.

Dougal stared at her, leaning close. "Why don't ye rest a bit? I've kept ye writing something fierce now."

Brielle nodded as he stood and shuffled away.

As she rolled her shoulders, Constance approached, her eyes scanning the room before she spoke. "Aye, ye need to stop writing. That's a fine idea. How about a stroll to the chapel?"

Brielle found fresh energy at this opportunity and gathered her paper, quill, and ink. "Oh, Constance, I'd love to."

Constance directed her toward the side exit that led to the bailey area near the kitchens. Brielle looked forward to some sun, since they'd kept her cooped up in the great hall most days. The chapel. Her stomach fluttered. She would finally see the inside of the chapel.

She stepped into the sunlight, squinting a bit. Even

with the multiple candles, it was still dim in the hall. The midafternoon sun warmed her face. She stopped, closed her eyes, and breathed deeply.

Constance grabbed her arm, pulling her along. As they strolled along the path, they passed the kitchens. The maids bustled about, preparing dinner for a castle filled with people. The smell of yeast from freshly baked bread and the tang of roasting meat filled the air, making her mouth water as her stomach growled. She glanced around as they continued toward the postern gate. Clan members rushed about—a maid carried laundry in a basket and another fetched water from the well. Something struck rock, and men yelled at one another in coordination.

Roderick had told her to stay away, but what harm could come from a short visit? As she and Constance strolled along, it amazed her that no one tried to stop them. The chapel—she would see the chapel when it wasn't a ruin. Brielle could hardly contain her excitement.

Constance spoke sweetly, breaking into her thoughts. "How has the family history book been coming along? The elders boring you much?"

She glanced at Constance, who smiled at her. "Not too bad. They are nice, even if wordy." It was strange that Constance was interested in the work she did. Since arriving, Brielle had barely seen her.

Constance opened the door to the chapel and strode in as if she owned the place. Brielle stopped. She still got that creepy feeling in the doorway, even in the past. Shifting her bodice, she touched her stone necklace and stepped through the door.

Coming to the center of the chapel, she took a full

turn, taking in the building's beauty.

Constance shifted behind the altar and stood examining the floor, then glanced at Brielle. "Ye've been here and seen it. Ready to leave?"

Brielle turned a full circle again. "It's amazing, and no, I am not ready to leave." Her gaze took in the stonework along the wall, then paused at each stained-glass window, noting the depictions of love, hope, and faith. Her gaze traveled to the other side of the chapel and the windows for fear, lust, and doubt. Stepping back, she studied the flooring more closely, stopping between the rows of pews to get the full picture. After turning another full circle, she stopped.

The two circular windows were complete. Her gaze shot up and took in the stained glass in red, green, blue, and purple, framing a clear glass cross in the middle of each one. Her gaze fell to the floor, noting that the sun cast a cross pattern on the mosaic stone. At sunrise and dusk, she imagined the crosses aligned. She would need to come back to make sure of her assumption.

She sat, setting her supplies on the pew next to her, grabbed a piece of paper, and drew the circle window design as accurately as possible.

Constance glowered at Brielle from behind the altar. Brielle shrugged and focused on her drawing. Constance sighed, moved to the front pew, and sat. She twirled a strand of hair while studying Brielle. "Why are ye so interested in this place?" Constance asked in a deeper voice than before.

The change in Constance's voice caught Brielle's attention, making her think that maybe Constance was a liar. She didn't glance up from her work, intent on capturing all she could while she had the chance.

Brielle almost replied, "It's historical," but caught herself. "It's a stunning building, a private family chapel. We should include it in the family history book."

Constance rolled her eyes, and her voice was sweet and high again when she spoke. "So, do ye like Roderick?"

Brielle started and made a scratch on her sheet. She kept her head down as she responded, "Me, no, not Roderick."

She didn't want to give away that she had conflicting emotions about Roderick only because of his resemblance to Colin. It was Colin she had feelings for.

Constance continued to twirl a strand of her hair as she stared off into the distance. When she spoke, her voice sounded ethereal, light like air. "His wife just died. He'll be needing a new wife soon. Whoever that is will become Lady MacDougall." She sighed. "I am certain he'll find true love. That's the strongest power of all, ye know."

Brielle nodded and turned to draw the altar on the back of her page, taking time to note the difference in the rock. Time must have worn away some details, so she wanted to record them. On a new page, she drew the ceiling vaults. She turned in the pew and captured the back of the chapel and the doorway farther down the page, trying to save the valuable paper.

After some time, Constance audibly sighed. "Are ye done yet?"

Brielle glanced up and noticed the sun had dipped lower, lighting the chapel in dusk's warm light. It was closer to sunset than she thought.

Surprised by how much time had passed, she hopped up, hoping she wouldn't get caught. "For today, yes. Let's go back to the castle before someone misses us."

Constance hummed lightly as the women approached the outer wall. She guided Brielle along the facade instead of heading directly for the postern gate. Brielle didn't comment on the extended route. She was happy to be out of the dusty, dim hall for once.

Constance stopped, looking around the grounds and then up at the wall walk. The bright sun was still above the edge. A creepy sensation traveled down Brielle's spine, as if someone watched her. She glanced around but saw no one.

Constance put her hands on her shoulders, and as she stepped Brielle backward, she said sweetly, "I'm certain ye will do grand work for the laird."

Brielle blinked as she stumbled on a rock. Constance glanced up at the wall. Curious, Brielle turned to see what the woman was staring at, but the sunlight blinded her.

Brielle glanced back at Constance as she let go of her and stepped back a few paces. She blinked, black spots from the sun dotting her vision. Brielle blinked again. Constance's eyes appeared all black. After she blinked, they appeared normal again.

Men yelling from the wall walk came from above her, but she couldn't make out the words. A sudden hard push hit her from behind, and a whoosh of air rushed down her back. As she fell, she flung her hands forward. A loud thud sounded as she fell headfirst into a cart. Then everything went black.

****

Voices came to Brielle, but nothing made sense. The words were all a jumble. She rolled her head to the side, and a piercing pain exploded through her skull. Bright lights danced behind her eyelids, making her dizzy. She tried to bring her hand to her face, but it caught on something. Maybe if she lay there and stayed still, things would seem better. She took a deep breath and released it, then winced. Everything hurt.

A voice broke through the fog. "Let me in. Let me by her." *Colin? Was that Colin?*

Another voice was closer, higher in pitch. "I struggled to save her. I tried to, but the boulder fell so close. Ye can let someone else care for her, Roderick— the rock almost hit *me*!" The plaintive whine brought on another wave of pain.

Was that Constance?

Someone lifted her left arm. She winced and cried out.

She felt a breath near her ear as a man whispered, "Bree, I am sorry to hurt ye. We must move ye." Someone raised her, cradling her against his broad chest. She breathed in and smelled a familiar warm, musky scent. *Colin.*

"Colin?" she whispered.

A whisper. "Hold on, lass, we have to get ye to your room."

Roderick yelled, "Make way! Send for Agatha. Archie, find out what the hell happened here."

Brielle winced again, whimpering at the loud voice. Constance's whining rang in her head. "Those men almost killed me! The rock aimed for me. They sought to kill me!"

Archie spoke quietly, "Ye can't sweep her up like

this. People will gossip. Hand her to me. I'll take her up. Ye stay and find out what's happened." Brielle cried out in pain as one man passed her into another's arms.

A low growl came from Colin. No, Roderick. "Let me know what Agatha has to say about her injuries as soon as she arrives."

Archie carried her away as the noise faded.

****

Colin stood numb as Archie took the woman he loved away. Bree was injured, and he couldn't help her. He couldn't even touch her, hold her, or comfort her.

"Roderick, ye need to take those men to task for trying to hurt me." Constance's whine pulled him out of his daze.

He glanced around, assessing the situation. Partially sunk in the ground from the power of the impact, the boulder sat where Bree stood earlier. If it had hit Bree, it could easily have killed her. He rubbed his neck and glanced up at the wall where the rock must have come from. Reverend O'Donnell stood glaring down from the top. What the hell was the reverend doing on the battlement?

He felt a hand on his arm. "Roderick, ye can look into this later. Stroll with me, please?"

He turned to Constance for the first time since his arrival and noticed she held Brielle's writing supplies. "What do ye have there, Constance?"

She hid it behind her back. "Nothing."

Colin folded his arms over his chest. "Are those Brielle's writing supplies? What were ye two doing out here?"

Constance gazed down and handed him the papers

as she tilted her head to the side and smiled at him. From her demeanor, he knew she intended to cause trouble. He hated this woman.

He examined the drawings. He turned them sideways and then flipped the paper over. When he realized what he was staring at, he yelled, "Ye were in the chapel? I gave that woman strict instructions to not go to the chapel."

Constance gazed at him and smiled as she placed her hand on his arm, then stepped closer. He broke the contact as he bent to take the quill and ink from her other hand. He stepped back and spoke to the guard standing by. "Ye, question everyone here. All the men on the wall walk as well. I want to know exactly how this happened. Report to Archibald or me when ye have finished."

The reverend still glared at him when he looked up at the wall. He rolled the papers into a scroll and marched away with a chill on his back. Throwing a glance behind him, he saw Constance standing alone, smiling sweetly at him.

Colin headed back to the hall to find out what Archie had learned. A boulder had almost hit Bree.

Running into Archie in the hall, he asked, "How is she?"

Archibald steered Colin to the study, lowering his voice. "Agatha is with her. Fiona stopped me in the hall. She said she doesn't think it's a grave injury, just a bump on the head."

Stopping at the door, he continued, "Fiona also said Brielle mentioned someone pushed her from behind, but Constance was in front of her. She could have sworn no one else was around. Fiona knows to

listen for details and report them. She's a good lass."
Colin nodded as Archie entered the study. "Fiona said
Brielle mentioned the bump could fill the great
canyon."

Colin sighed as he followed. Grand Canyon. She
must have said *Grand Canyon*. Her head must hurt
something awful. He set the drawing supplies on the
desk.

A guard signaled Archibald from the door and
pulled him aside. They exchanged words, whispering
for a while. Colin moved to the whisky decanter,
poured himself a large amount, and with a shaking
hand, took a generous swig. What would he have done
if Bree had become seriously wounded? No hospitals,
no surgery, no technology. He drank deeply again.

Archibald entered the study and closed the door.

Colin glanced up. "Well, what happened?"

Archie shrugged his shoulders. "Based upon what I
can find out, the men were repairing the wall, replacing
some stones that were worn down. I assigned it to a few
men a couple of days ago. They put the boulder into
place, and the sun blinded them for a moment. The rock
slipped." Archibald rubbed his neck. "An accident."

Colin nodded and ran the incident through his mind
again. He was missing something, something obvious.
He paced and replayed the events like a movie in his
head, picture by picture. There were people in the
crowd. He elbowed his way in, then found Bree on the
ground, hurt. He took another swig of whisky. *The
boulder. The wall walk.*

His head snapped to Archibald. "The reverend—
O'Donnell—he was on the battlement. When I handed
Bree to ye, I glanced up. He stood there. Did ye man

question him?"

Archibald shrugged. "I don't know. What would the reverend be doing up on the wall? He hates heights."

Colin nodded. "Ye need to question him. I can't. If I do it, he may figure out I am not Roderick. He's already acted suspiciously around me. Ye'll question him, and we'll see what he says."

Colin crossed to the mantel. "There's another thing." He shifted his head toward the documents on his desk. "Constance and Brielle went to the chapel."

Archibald shrugged in response. "Ye knew she might try this. Ye said she couldn't resist going there. Ye do have to allow her a break. She can't sit writing all day, every day."

Colin rolled his neck and leaned on the mantel. "I know, but to end up under the working area, were they even looking where they were going?"

Archie laughed. "What woman sees where she's going?"

Colin stared at the door. "I hope she'll be okay." He took another sip of whisky. "I might have called attention to my affection for Brielle when I went and picked her up. Glad ye caught me and stopped it. We can't have any more gossip."

Archie put a hand on his shoulder. "Don't worry about that. We have to make sure Brielle is well. Let Agatha do her healing, and she'll be down with a full report when she's finished. Fiona said it was just a bump on the head."

Colin gazed up at the ceiling and hoped Brielle was okay. It took all his willpower not to run up the stairs, burst into her room, and take her in his arms.

****

Later that night, Colin opened Bree's door. Moonlight from her window cast a blue glow in the room. Bree lay in her bed, sleeping. Colin closed the door with a soft click. He couldn't get caught here, but he couldn't stay away, either. Fiona told him Brielle would be okay, but he had to make sure for himself. Colin wanted to see her, touch her. He moved on light feet to the bed.

She lay half on her side. Her injured hand curled under her chin, the other stretched out. A cloth that had been on her head sat on the pillow beside her. Spread like birds' wings, her brown hair caught the moon's light. Colin bent his knee so his face came close to hers.

As he ran his finger down her cheek, he smelled roses. He wanted to take her in his arms so badly, but he couldn't risk waking her and the rest of the castle. She shifted in her sleep, moaning softly. He couldn't stand it.

Colin brushed his lips on hers and whispered, "*Mo chridhe, my heart,* it near killed me when I saw ye wounded."

She shifted again, whispering in her sleep, "Colin?"

He stepped back as he stood up, fearing he'd awakened her. All he wanted was to take her into his arms and away from here. Away, before things got worse. He had to figure out how to get Roderick back and find the Stone of Love fast.

He headed to the door, and as he slipped out, he whispered, "Everything will be all right, *mo chridhe.*"

Chapter 17

Colin strolled with Archie outside the castle walls under the pretense of examining the wall walk. Archie glanced around as Colin nodded. They were out of hearing range of anyone.

Archie clasped his hands as he spoke. "I questioned Reverend O'Donnell as ye asked. He wasn't pleased about being asked about the battlement."

Colin grunted. He did not give a damn what the reverend liked or not. "I need to hear his explanation about being on the wall when the boulder fell. I need to know why he was up there when he claims he fears heights."

Archie nodded. "Aye, he does. He admitted his fear outright. Said he was up there watching over the lasses."

Colin glanced at Archie. "The lasses? The reverend is admiring women?"

Archie rubbed his neck. "Aye, it surprised me, but I ken the man. He'd not besmirch his vow. So I pressured him, and it turns out he was watching Brielle. He's convinced there's something wrong with the lass."

Colin stopped Archie with his hand. "Well, did ye ask him about the rock, it going over?"

Archie turned to him. "Aye, he said he wasn't near it at the time. Only walked over after it happened. And I confirmed the fact with the men." They continued strolling as Archie sighed. "The reverend is mighty upset with ye—well, not ye but Roderick, after yer argument. Kept carrying on about Mary and how ye aren't grieving right."

Colin fisted his hands, not caring for the reverend either. "He's after Bree. I can feel it. He might claim he wasn't nearby, but I'm convinced he had something to do with the incident."

Archie nodded. "I asked the men about that. They claim the rock slipped as they set it into place on the wall. A couple of men said they tried to grab it, but it was too big. Said the weight carried itself over the side. We've since repaired that area and removed the boulder from the yard."

"Something like this happened in the future as well. A smaller boulder fell from above the chapel door, almost hitting Bree. It's so damned similar; I can't dismiss either incident. It must be the evil Fae."

Archie shrugged. "Both accidents? They happen all the time, Colin. Coincidence."

Colin stared at the loch in the distance. Boulders falling near the same person in two different periods wasn't coincidental. Colin knew the reverend was the evil Fae. He believed the evil Fae was behind the rock falling, possibly harming Bree. Colin had to ensure he kept her safe and that she didn't become involved in his mission.

"Ye got a guard on the reverend, as I asked? I want him watched closely. I wish to know if he pisses the wrong way. Ye ken?" Colin said firmly.

Archie nodded, then tilted his head to the side and smiled. "So, how did yer meeting with Brielle go? I hadn't heard what happened when ye confronted her about going to the chapel after ye forbade it."

Colin rubbed his neck, laughing lightly, recalling the day of the picnic from the future when the wharf lads were breaking boulders daily, and Bree had a headache. "Not well. She was in bed, still on the mend. I should have waited till she felt better. Her temper gets riled easily when she's not well."

Archie raised an eyebrow. "Really? So yer Bree had herself a wee storm, did she now?"

Colin grinned at the memory. "Ye could say that. Called me an arse, then pleaded a headache and kicked me out of the room."

Archie laughed out loud. That had been a week ago. She was up and back at work on the book again.

They kept moving in silence. Colin knew Bree would not intentionally put herself in danger. Still, he could not guarantee she hadn't become a target of the evil Fae trying to find the Stone of Love. He feared the same person who tried to kill Mary and put Roderick in purgatory was still here, but he could not figure out who it was. If it wasn't the reverend, then who else could it be?

Colin had requested Archie assign a guard to follow Brielle for her safety. She'd stormed into the study when she figured it out, interrupting a second sitting for Constance's painting. He grinned at the memory.

Brielle had burst through the study doors, causing them to bang against the wall. "What are you doing, *laird,* giving me an overgrown lug as a *babysitter?* I do not need a *nanny,* like some child." She glanced at Constance, who sat and huffed at her intrusion. "Not like some others around here." She turned and stormed out of the room.

Constance stood. "What is that woman doing interrupting our private moments? Roderick, ye must do something about that *whore*!" She had yelled the last so loud, servants came to peek into the study.

Colin sighed as he and Archie walked. Constance was growing bolder with her advances. He needed to get her to finish the painting soon, or he would need to find a task she could do so he would not have to be near her anymore. He needed to focus on finding the Stone of Love and end this.

As they approached the stables, Archie said, "All is ready for this afternoon. Are ye sure ye want to be doing this? Ye aren't supposed to be spending time with Brielle. It's bad enough the reverend's convinced ye are having an affair. We cannot have more gossip. It has finally died down, and most people accept Brielle for the sweet soul she is. It would be bad to stir things up again."

Colin stared into the distance and smiled. "She needs a break, and I want to show her around the land. In this age—when it's untouched and beautiful."

Archibald tilted his head. "I don't understand what ye mean by...untouched."

Colin sighed and gazed at the land before him, admiring its simple splendor. Loch Etive sat with no modern hindrance. The marina docks next to the small village were the only sign of something manmade; yet they still appeared natural, as if part of the landscape.

"It's hard to explain future civilization and what it does to nature. The land, its beauty—ye need to enjoy what ye have before it's gone."

They came upon a group of guards gathered

outside the stables. The group came to attention at the laird's appearance.

The stable master approached Colin. "My laird, all is ready for yer ride. I've sent my boy to fetch the lady."

Colin smiled and nodded. "Good. Ye got a gentle horse for her, as I asked?"

As he said this, Brielle strode into the group of men. "What's this? Someone told me the laird needed me."

Colin grinned, crossing his arms. She'd been bored, stuck in the hall day after day writing. Being from Texas, in the States, she loved to ride horses. She could not get mad at him for this. Just let her try.

"I've decided ye need a nice, long break. A ride around this magnificent countryside." He waved his hand at the scenery as he spoke.

She turned, blinked, and then gathered herself. "A ride? I have not ridden in years. I love to ride."

Her smile was wide. He knew she would love this. All he wanted was to make her happy.

Colin bowed as he said, "Yer wish is my command, my lady." She giggled as he bent toward her and escorted her to the mounting block.

The stable master led a brown mare to the block. Brielle whispered to him, "He asked you to get me a soft mount. Stupid man, I've ridden for years."

As she placed her foot in the stirrup, hands grabbed her waist, lifted her from behind, and set her on the horse.

When the laird's hand rested on her thigh, she glanced down as he stared at her. She looked at Roderick's hand, so much like Colin's. She glanced up and realized the stone entrance to the stable was the archway from the future—the archway where Colin and John had practiced with their swords.

His words came back to her, his voice clear in her head:

"Bree, my hand may be large, and my body may be strong, but I would do nothing to hurt ye, ever. Ye will have nothing to fear in me, and I will always keep ye safe." He had gently squeezed her hand as his face tilted and his eyes locked with hers. *"Ye have my word as a man. Please know whoever has hurt ye before, I am not that man."*

Her eyes teared up at the memory. She shook her head, blinking the tears away.

Roderick watched her silently, then said for her ears only, "Do not fash, lass. I will always keep ye safe." He smiled, patted her thigh, then went to mount his horse. *He sounded just like...* The head guard's call for everyone to ride out broke her concentration.

Roderick guided his horse close to hers and signaled the guards to encircle them for protection. They rode in comfortable silence side by side as the group moved out of the castle courtyard. Her mind drifted as they rode two by two, an extra guard positioned on either side of her mount.

Her gaze roamed the countryside. The tall ships that passed on the loch were magnificent and serene. The old-style vessels seemed so new they appeared as if they were out of a historical movie.

The group made their way through the small village named Dunbeg in the future. As the party made their way through the town, many people stopped and greeted the laird warmly. Roderick stopped and spoke in a friendly manner to each one, giving Brielle time to examine the village. Brielle saw the small lane of cottages, all newer than in the future. The pub was much smaller. Bree smiled as she touched her stone necklace, thinking of Hamish.

When they approached Connell Sound, the giant steel bridge of the future was not there. The group rode past where the Falls of Lora should be, but the waterfalls were not there on this trip.

She must have made a noise because Roderick leaned close to her. "The falls only appear during tide changes. It's low tide right now." She nodded and stared ahead.

She caught a glimpse of the past, at living history right before her eyes. Seeing the glen in the past, she felt as if she peered through a spyhole into a different world. She took it all in and still craved more.

She glanced at Colin and smiled. *Wait.* She shook her head. *That's Roderick.* Her emotions betrayed her, kept pulling her toward him. She tried to shut them off—she could not have feelings for Roderick.

The group circled back, came up to the castle's rear, and stopped. Brielle spotted the point and the seals from her mount. It reminded her of when Colin had taken her sailing, finishing the day with the romantic night in the hunting cabin.

Colin's voice came clear in her mind:

"Brielle, no matter where I go, no matter what separates us. Never fear that I will not come back." *Brielle stared into his eyes, and a tear traveled down her cheek. Colin wiped it away with his thumb.*

He took her face between his hands and gave her a light kiss on her lips.

She touched her lips as if he had kissed her.

Roderick broke into her thoughts. "Did ye enjoy yer outing today?" He had been next to her while she watched the seals. She sensed his gaze upon her, making her crave him like Colin. She wasn't entirely certain what to make of it. When she observed him, she sensed Colin but saw Roderick.

Every night since she'd arrived, she'd dreamed of Colin visiting her. The dreams were almost identical. He appeared to her, caressed her cheek, called her *mo chridhe, my heart*, and told her everything would be all right. Colin haunted her every moment, and Brielle worried she would go crazy.

She shook her head, peering at the seals, whispering, "Yes, I did."

Roderick turned to look at the seals. His expression shifted from wonder to something more. Did he pine for someone as she did? He had lost Mary. Was she his true love, as Colin was hers? He turned his horse away, and hers followed without cue.

Roderick led the group through the woods toward the chapel. She allowed the horse to meander, hoping to prolong the ride. The horses had to weave in and out of the trees, and Roderick stayed close to her. They brushed legs a few times, and Brielle glanced at Roderick, caught his eye, and blushed.

Whoosh! Thunk! She gasped as her head snapped to the tree beside her. An arrow vibrated near her shoulder. Before she could turn her head back, Roderick grabbed her from her horse, pulling her onto his lap. He bent over her, covering her. *Whoosh! Thunk!* This one faster. Men shouted at the same time. She became dizzy being bent over his legs. He turned his horse, and she grabbed onto his leg to hold on to something, anything.

Roderick shouted over the men, "Find him, search the area. He cannot be far if he is using arrows. I want him found and brought to me for questioning." He galloped away as he held her on the horse, covering her with his body.

Roderick stopped at the first building he came to, dismounted, and whisked her off the horse. The chapel. That's right, they were close to the chapel. He opened the chapel door, marched in, then slammed the door with his foot. He sat on the first pew he came to, gathering her in his arms.

"Bree, are ye okay? Did an arrow hit ye?" Roderick's hands roamed over her body.

Her stomach turned as the ringing in her ears faded. "No, I'm fine."

She tried to slide out of his lap, but he held her tighter. He stared into her eyes, and she halted—he looked so much like Colin. She pushed against his chest, but he would not let go.

"Roderick, please let me go." She pushed against him again, but he still held her tight.

A throat-clearing came loud from the altar. "I believe the lady asked to be let go, my laird." She startled, then froze as they both turned their heads to see who was there. Reverend O'Donnell stood there, holding a Bible.

Roderick slid her off his lap, stood, and shielded her with his body. "Reverend, I did not realize ye were in the chapel."

The clergy stared coolly at Brielle, then at Roderick. "I am preparing for my sermon. I usually do so here, away from the castle, so I can find solitude and peace in the Lord's presence."

The reverend looked again at her. "Are ye well, my lady?"

She nodded and opened her mouth to say something, but Roderick interrupted her. "Actually, no." Roderick stood with his feet apart and folded his arms over his massive chest. "I have a few questions for ye."

Roderick marched toward the altar. "Where have ye been for the last thirty minutes?"

The reverend folded his hands around his Bible. "Why I just told ye, preparing for my sermon here at the chapel."

Roderick stopped. "Here in the chapel?"

The reverend nodded.

Roderick asked his next question with more force. "Did ye at any point leave the chapel today?"

The reverend shook his head. Roderick crossed his arms and watched him for a minute, then uncrossed his arms, placing his hands on his hips.

The reverend glanced around Roderick and glared at Brielle. "I see ye have not taken my advice, my laird. Ye will do well to focus on yer clan, yer family, and yer duties. Not some...woman." Why did the reverend hate her so much? What did she do?

Roderick growled softly. "Watch yerself, Reverend." He took a deep breath. "Do ye own a bow and arrow?"

The reverend's mouth fell open and then shut with a click of his teeth before he spoke. "Why, no, my laird. Before I became a reverend, I used to. I have taken an oath against all weaponry. I'll leave it to the warriors to make war, my laird."

Roderick nodded once, then paced.

Brielle watched this exchange from the back of the chapel. A strange sensation overcame her. She'd seen this back and forth before but could not pinpoint exactly where that was.

Roderick paced. "Do ye know how to use a bow and arrow?"

Reverend O'Donnell sighed. "Of course I do, and a sword as well. I was a soldier before my calling to the Lord's work."

Roderick stopped and glared at the reverend. "Have ye killed?" he asked in a hushed tone.

Reverend O'Donnell straightened his collar. "Aye, I have. All soldiers have had to at some time. I have asked the Lord to absolve me of my sins. 'Tis why I took an oath against all weaponry."

Roderick studied the reverend, who drew his brows together, tilting his head. "My laird, ye already know all this—why are ye asking me?"

Brielle stared, trying to place where she had seen this. The aisle down the middle of the chapel led to a large table, behind which the reverend stood in black robes.

As she was about to put the pieces together to form an answer, the door banged open, and a guard burst into the chapel. "My laird, I saw ye come in. Is everything all right? Do ye need anything?"

Roderick looked up, then back to the clergyman, who glared at him.

"Not for now, but I'll have a word with ye outside." He started for the door. "Brielle, come with me."

As Roderick strode by, she rose from her seat. She glanced back at the Reverend O'Donnell, who glared daggers at her as she followed Roderick out of the chapel.

He spoke privately with the guard and returned to her side, huffing. "Come, we've had enough excitement today."

Chapter 18

Sitting in the great hall, Brielle waited for the next elder to arrive to regale her with more tales of the great MacDougall family history. Agatha sat beside her with the ointment and bandages ready to treat her hand. She sighed, then yawned as she held out her hand.

Agatha kept up a rolling commentary as she worked. "Aye, healed well, ye have. And worked hard on the book too." She reached into her bag for more supplies. "It will be good ta have the history written. We get fewer stories these days from the elders over drink as they get older—think it's their memory fadin'." She laughed.

Brielle was almost in a snooze when a young boy approached her, handing her a mug. "Here's your drink, my lady."

Brielle glanced at the cup and then at the boy as he hurried away. *Well, that was nice. I am thirsty.* She peered down into the cup and noticed flakes floating on the top. Sniffing it, she reeled back at the odd smell. She put her finger into the ale, swirled it around, and stuck it in her mouth. Not odd tasting, so she took a generous gulp. First, it numbed her lips, then it moved to her throat.

When she spoke, her voice came out a little slurred. "Thab's odb. Itb does tases fubby."

Agatha looked at Brielle and gasped, grabbing the

236

mug. She examined it, smelled the contents, then flung the liquid into the rushes on the floor. She grabbed Brielle's uninjured hand, pulled her closer, and stared into her eyes.

"Did ye taste any, my lady?"

Brielle tried to see her, but she couldn't seem to focus. Her head swirled, and she blinked twice. Agatha faded out of focus, and Brielle felt dizzy, hot. Her stomach threatened to heave. The world tilted, and then everything went black.

****

"Good God, not poison," Colin groaned. He sat beside the bed with an unconscious Brielle, her hand held between his. Agatha sat on the other side, wiping a wet cloth over her forehead.

He kept running those last moments over in his mind, trying to figure out where the poison had come from. By the time he'd gotten to Bree, she couldn't seem to hold her head up and couldn't focus her eyes. He scooped her into his lap and brushed her hair away from her face, trying to get her to wake.

Agatha spoke from across the bed. "I think I got most of it when I made her vomit. She took in a little, though. I think she took a sip before I noticed what was in the mug. The amount of poison in the cup had to be deadly for one sip to act so fast."

She wet the cloth, wrung it out, and wiped Brielle's forehead again. "She's going to sleep most of it away, but someone will have to sit and wake her every couple of hours to ensure she doesn't get the sleeping death."

Colin stared at Archie and shook his head, then dropped it to rest his forehead on Bree's hands. First the boulder, then the arrows, and now poison. It became too much. The evil Fae had targeted Bree, and he needed to do something different. But first, she had to heal. He couldn't imagine what he would do if he lost her.

Archie shifted closer to Colin, his voice commanding. "Start from the beginning, Agatha. Tell me what happened."

Colin raised his head. Agatha watched him intently.

He glared at her. "Explain, woman."

Agatha frowned back at him, then glanced at Archie and cleared her throat. "I was getting my healing things ready to care for her hand. I didn't see the boy until he moved away. When she said it tasted funny was when I noticed the mug. Herbs floated in it, more than any normal drink. I grabbed it from her, but she had already started turning green. That's when I called her name, then yelled for you, mi laird."

Archie pinched his nose. "That's when ye made her vomit." Agatha nodded. Her gaze was still intent on Colin. Let her stare. He didn't care. All he cared about was getting Bree better.

Archie was quiet yet firm. "Agatha, where did the ale come from?"

She glowered at him. "A boy, a servant. One I've not seen before."

She glanced from one man to the other, then blew out a heavy breath. "Mi laird, when ye came upon us, ye asked what belladonna was. Ye know damn good and well what belladonna is."

She rounded on Archie, pointing her finger at him. "Then, Archie, ye told mi laird to take her to her room. Said we need to deal with this in private. Ye were holding her in yer arms and drawing attention." She heaved again. "Then I saw Constance, who stood with her arms crossed and was ready to start a fight. Servants were whispering to each other, and some pointed at ye." She dropped the cloth and stood facing Archie with her hands on her hips.

"Archibald, I've put up with enough of your *geamannan* and *cleasan* ways these past weeks and not asked one question."

Archibald held up his hands. "Now, Agatha, there're no games and tricks here. This is serious."

She huffed. "Nothing's making sense. Mary got stabbed, then you hide her away with yer mother Elizabeth, Rose, and the bairn. Ye lie to the entire clan claiming her dead, for God knows why." She waved her hand at Bree. "This new guest arrived, hurt. And you, mi laird—" She turned, pointing her finger at him. "I've known you my whole life, since you were a ween on your ma's teat. You're not acting right—like you are not right in the head. Why are ye paying so much attention to this guest? 'Tis Mary ye love! Who is this woman, and why does she hold yer affections? It's strange. Ye look like ye, but ye aren't ye." She glanced back and forth between the men and stamped her foot. "What's going on, boys? Tell me now!"

Colin sighed, placed Bree's hands on her chest, and nodded to Archie as he spoke. "Archie, it will probably be best coming from ye. Ye'll have to tell her. We'll need more of her help in the days to come."

Archie stepped to Agatha and patted her shoulders until she sat back down in her chair. He paced for a moment, rubbing his neck.

Colin moved to the window, looked out at the marina, then glanced back, hoping Archie would explain it well.

Archie stood at the end of Brielle's bed and regaled Agatha with the story of how a cloaked figure stabbed Mary, how Roderick had disappeared in the chapel's doorway, and how Colin had appeared shortly after.

He explained how the Fae sent Colin to bring Roderick back from purgatory and set the MacDougalls right in the past and in the future. Archie told Agatha everything he could without going into the parts about the Stones of Iona, impressing Colin, for they had already revealed too much to too many people. This had gotten out of control and needed to end soon.

Colin turned away from the window to find Agatha staring at him as she spoke. "I know the Fae are at work here, but he looks so much like Roderick."

Colin snorted. "I do. I am his great-grandson, Laird Colin Roderick MacDougall, thirty-first laird, from the future." He bowed to Agatha, who raised an eyebrow.

Archibald continued. "We need not only your help, but your confidence. You cannot speak a word of this. Someone stabbed Mary and is after something the family has protected for generations. For the sake of all, you must keep this a secret."

Agatha nodded once. "You have my word, Archibald." Waving toward Bree, she said, "Now, what's her story? She's no normal guest. Her clothes the day she arrived were not what a lady wears, and her bag seems like a gypsy bag."

Colin moved to Bree's bedside and ran his finger down her cheek. "She's from my time, a scholar sent to renovate the chapel that's fallen into ruin in the future. I don't know how or why she came back in time, but she's here, and I'll do everything in my power to protect her. To get her—us—back to our time." Colin took her hand in his.

They spoke in low tones, Archie addressing Agatha. "Agatha, ye'll have to keep the poisoning silent. Say she drank bad ale. We don't want the person doing these things to know we are aware someone is behind these acts."

Archie glanced back at Colin, then at Agatha. "Also, ease everyone's concern at the attention Roderick is paying to Brielle—say it's simply concern for a guest. Colin and I will require more time to figure out who is behind this to capture them."

Agatha nodded. "Anything for the laird. I've been sending my assistant to the hunting cabin as ye asked. Everything's good there. Mary is recovering well under yer mother's care, and Rose and the bairn are safe."

Archibald turned to Colin. "We'll need to go down and address the clan and ease some of the tension."

Agatha gathered her things and went to the door. She stopped, turned, and spoke to Colin. "Roderick— er, Colin—she'll be fine. A night of rest and she'll be healthy. I'm sure of it."

Agatha opened the door but turned back again. "I'll send a maid to see after her till she sleeps this off. We will care for her well, mi laird."

Colin only nodded. What else could he do? Bree needed time to heal, and he needed a plan to end this quickly.

After Agatha left, Archie paused at the doorway and closed the door.

Colin didn't want to leave her. He wanted to be the one to sit with her and ensure she healed. Every moment she didn't wake was agony. Every breath she took told him she was alive and healing. He had tried so hard to keep her safe, and nothing worked.

He spoke without taking his gaze off Bree's face. "I need some time alone with her. I can't leave her here suffering, but I know the clan cannot see me paying this much attention to her."

Archie opened the door. "I can only give you a few moments alone. The clan is likely already talking. I'll guard the door till the maid comes. We'll address the clan together, ease any concerns, then head to the study and figure out our plan."

Colin rested his head on Brielle's hands.

Archie opened the door and slipped out of the room. The latch clicked, announcing that Colin was finally alone with Bree.

He glanced up at Bree's face, holding back tears. *Brielle, his wee Bree.* She'd almost died right before him, and Colin couldn't do anything. The evil Fae were everywhere all at once, closing in on them. No mortal weapon could fight the power of the Fae.

A tear trailed down his cheek as he gazed at her, pale from the brush with death. He'd almost lost his true love for the Fae's task. If the *Fae Fable Book's* prophecy came true, each act pushed them closer to an end he could not accept, an ending where he would lose Bree forever.

If the evil Fae took Bree... Colin wouldn't accept it. He had to figure a way through this to catch the evil Fae, return Roderick from purgatory, and see that he and Bree went to the future together. Colin would win. He only needed a plan.

Chapter 19

"Colin, ye are not seeing this the right way. It's someone close to the family. The evil is coming from someone here at the castle." Archie sat in front of his desk while Colin paced before of the fireplace. Someone was close. He knew it had to be the reverend. He had enough evidence against the reverend that, if in the future he had to press charges, he would have already had the magistrate arrest him.

"I agree, but I am convinced it's the reverend. His behavior toward Bree is too telling for me to ignore," Colin said as Archie snorted. "Listen, let's consider the facts." Colin counted on his fingers. "First, there's the reaction to the funeral for Mary, or lack thereof, combined with his reaction to Bree's arrival."

Archie shook his head. "That was just the wrong time. I don't think the reverend's hatred toward Bree is anything more than alarm over your attraction to her and the proximity to Mary's supposed death."

Colin ticked off his second finger. "The boulder. I know he was part of the boulder falling."

Archie shook his head in disagreement. "Reverend O'Donnell had nothing to do with why she was at the wall. I am convinced the boulder incident was an accident."

He paced in front of the fireplace, ticking off his third finger. "Ye cannot discredit the proximity of the chapel to the attack on Bree with the arrow."

Archie nodded. "Agreed. However, ye are not considering yerself as a target. The arrow was close to both of ye, and ye may still be a target—or Roderick, that is."

Colin grunted. "I am convinced they meant the arrow for Bree. I was right there; they'd aimed for her heart, not mine." He could not forget that incident and had nightmares of an arrow piercing her chest over and over. He had been mere inches from her and could do nothing to stop it.

Archie scratched his chin. "I questioned the kitchen staff. The reverend was in the kitchens when the lad brought Bree that ale."

Colin pointed at Archie. "See, I told ye, it's the reverend." He knew it. This was the last piece of evidence he needed to prove the reverend was the evil Fae. Archie had to agree now.

Archie held his hands up. "Wait, Colin, he was there, but the drink didn't come from the kitchens. The head cook swears by it. Her family has served the MacDougalls for generations. I'd take her word over anyone's."

Colin shook his head again. "I'm telling ye, Archie, ye weren't there when I questioned the reverend. He's hiding something. His religious dedication is his undoing. It's more than an obsession. It's fanatical."

He ran the poisoning incident through his mind again. Had run it over and over till it near drove him mad. He needed to focus. There was something he was missing, and he had to find it. He should be able to see the clues, but his worry for Bree clouded his mind. The cup came from the boy, the cup filled with poison.

Colin glanced at Archie. "What about the boy who brought her the drink?"

Archie shrugged. "Nothing. No one knows him. No one saw him come or go. He appeared and then vanished."

Vanished. Damn the Fae and their tricks. They always seemed a step ahead of Colin, as if they knew what he would do next and planned ahead.

Colin strode to the window and gazed out. Bree would be healthy and back to normal in a couple of days. *How could I have been so blind?* She was the target all along. He should have seen it, should have protected her better. Each attack grew bolder. He couldn't allow another attack to occur—Bree might not survive it. "I'm still convinced Bree is the target of the evil Fae."

Archie cleared his throat. "Well, I am convinced Roderick was the target initially, and possibly Mary. But I believe that changed when ye and then Bree came through the portal."

Colin ran the events over in his mind. First, an attack on Mary, the stabbing. Then Roderick disappeared, and the good Fae claimed he went to purgatory. Then the good Fae contacted him in the future and sent him back to the eighteenth century.

Everyone in the future thought Roderick had disappeared except those at the chapel when Colin came through. That would be only him, Archibald, Mary, Rose, Elizabeth, Roderick's mother, and Alex, Roderick's son. *But why attack Bree?* Why, when she appeared in the past, would the evil Fae attack her? It didn't make any sense.

The evil Fae needed to be exposed soon. He had to

change the outcome to favor him and Bree. If he kept Bree close, he could keep her safe and prevent further attacks. He needed a plan, one that purposefully kept Bree near him. Something the entire clan would accept without question. He needed to push the reverend into admitting he was the evil Fae. Then Colin could get him to expose the Stone of Love by using the Stone of Fear.

Colin tapped his finger on his chin as an idea formed in his mind. The more he thought about it, the better his plan sounded. He could change the outcome and expose the evil Fae so he could find the stone, return Roderick, and get back to the twenty-first century.

He turned and faced Archie with a smile on his face. "If it's as ye say, if both Bree and I are the targets, the only way to draw out the evil Fae is to trick them into exposing themselves. We need to push a few buttons."

Archie glanced at him. "What does buttoning clothing have to do with this?"

Colin laughed. "It's a modern term from the future." Colin waved Archie off. "It means we need to push the evil Fae to make a mistake."

"I don't understand what pushing a button through a hole will achieve." Archie shrugged. "What's yer plan, then?"

He crossed his arms, smiling. "I have the perfect plan to push the reverend right where we want him. He'll go nuts over this."

Archie scrunched his face. Archie's expression made Colin laugh. "And I'll be protecting Bree the entire time. I'll be by her side. It can't fail."

Colin crossed to the desk, rubbed his hands together, placed them flat on the desk, and leveled his eyes on Archie.

"We'll get married."

Archie sat back as his eyebrows went into his hairline. "Ye'll what?"

Colin nodded. "Aye, we'll get married."

"But ye're already married. I mean, Roderick is married to Mary. Ye can't marry two women at once."

Colin raised an eyebrow and crossed his hands. "In the future, in some areas of the world, ye can." He waved Archie off. "But let's not go into that now."

Archie peered sideways at him, folding his arms. "I don't think I want to know what the future has to say about marrying more than one woman at a time. One wife is enough trouble for any man."

Colin laughed again. "Agreed. But here's the plan." He took a deep breath. "We'll hold a wedding ceremony and ask the reverend to preside. We'll need a week to plan and prepare for the event. In the meantime, Bree could take time to heal." He smiled. "If we tell the reverend now, it'll allow him a week to stew, and the preparations will enrage him even more. By the time the wedding ceremony occurs, he will be beside himself and explode."

Archie shook his head as Colin continued. "We'll hold him until he produces the Stone of Fear or take it from him to locate the Stone of Love."

"I'm still not convinced it's the reverend. And yer plan has weaknesses. Ye have not thought about the solicitor. Who's going to draw up the wedding contract?"

Colin shrugged and smiled. "That's the best part. I

will—I'm a solicitor by trade. The laws haven't changed much. I can make the contract for us."

Archie made an *O* with his mouth.

Colin smiled widely. "It's the perfect plan."

"Colin, aren't ye forgetting the most important part?"

"What?"

Archie rolled his eyes. "For a man from the future, ye are dumb, ye *eejit*. Ye haven't asked the lassie yet. What if she says no?"

Colin grinned. "We'll tell her it's a farce to draw out the person who has been attacking her. It'll be perfect."

Archie sighed. "Colin, she may be from the future, but I'll bet my best dagger all women are the same. She will not like a fake wedding. They all want real ones, a wedding that means something. Flowers, a dress, rings. Ye're going to hurt her this way."

Colin shook his head. "No, it will work. It has to work. The reverend will lose his mind and emotionally crumble before the wedding. He will expose who and what he is. We'll find the stone, get Roderick back, and Bree and I will go back to the twenty-first century. It will work."

****

Later that day, three raps sounded on the study door.

"Enter." Colin stood at the window, while Archie stood by the fireplace on the opposite side of the room.

Reverend O'Donnell entered the study and stood by the door. "My laird, ye wished to see me."

Colin smiled. "Aye, I did. Please have a seat. It's Patrick, right?"

The clergyman glared at Archie, who didn't move.

Colin moved to the table, poured three glasses of whisky. As he strode past Archie, he passed the first to Archie, who raised an eyebrow. Colin smiled and winked.

He turned, offering the second to the reverend, who didn't accept it. "What is it ye boys are celebrating so early in the day?"

Colin smiled. "Take it, Patrick. We have cause to celebrate."

Reverend O'Donnell took the glass but didn't sip from it.

Refusal. This is a good start. Colin had to hide his smile. He didn't want to give the plan away.

"What will we toast to, my laird?" the reverend asked.

Colin went back to the window as he kept his back to the reverend. "My wedding! Congratulations are in order. I'm taking a wife." He turned to face Archie, and they raised their glasses in unison.

"Slàinte!" they said together and drank.

The reverend stood there, fuming. Colin waited. The moment would come soon. Maybe this could end here. God, he hoped so.

"Ye blasphemous bastard," the reverend roared, slamming his glass on the desk and spilling whisky. "I'll not be drinking to some wedding for ye. Why yer wife is barely in the grave, and ye're taking another so fast?"

As he took another sip, Colin smiled over the rim of his glass. This was going perfectly. The reverend reacted as he suspected he would. Now, to push those buttons.

"Why, Reverend, it's love at first sight. I can't help myself. It's true love, the strongest of all loves. My *heart* is *glowing* with *true love*."

The reverend paced between the two men. Archie stayed still and silent, watching. Colin waited. He had hoped that using some words from the Fae Fable story—*heart*, *true love*, and *glowing*—would enrage the evil Fae.

But the reverend didn't react to the words, only to the marriage. "True love is the most powerful of all, but ye had that with yer wife, Mary. I renewed yer vows in a special ceremony for ye. Ye cannot be in love so fast." He stopped and pointed his finger at Colin. "It's a lie."

Colin shrugged and sipped his whisky. The reverend continued to pace, ranting. "Why ye are blind, I tell ye, my laird. What of yer son, Alex? Have ye just cast him away as ye did Mary?"

"No. He's due back as soon as Rose finishes with her healing task that I, her laird, sent her on," Colin replied coolly.

Reverend O'Donnell stopped pacing and ran his hands through his hair. "Who is this woman, this *Brielle*? She shows up from nowhere, and ye decide in mere weeks ye have to marry her? Bewitched ye are. 'Tis the devil's work I see here—it's her! She's done this to ye."

The reverend pointed at Colin repeatedly. He took a step toward Colin, and his voice grew in volume. He yelled each word. "She's yer whore. She's bewitched ye, and ye are now one with the devil."

Colin didn't budge as he quietly replied, "True love is the greatest of all loves and one ye cannot deny."

Spittle flew from the seething reverend's lips. He marched straight to Colin and pointed his finger in his face as he yelled, "I won't agree to it! I won't marry my laird to this whore."

Colin stared directly into the reverend's eyes for a moment, searching for the evil Fae. He could not see the fairy, but he knew it was there, lurking.

The reverend glared back, searching Colin's gaze. For what, Colin wasn't sure, but they were at a crossroads.

Colin whispered, "Ye'll do as yer laird commands."

The clergyman blinked. He glanced from side to side, backed away, turned, and glanced at Archie, who stood still by the fireplace.

"I won't marry ye to that whore," he said firmly.

"She's about to become yer lady. Ye will give her the respect and honor her position demands. Ye'll *never* call her a whore again and live to see another day." All three men paused in silence.

The reverend straightened his coat, fixed his collar, and then glanced back and forth between Archie and Colin. He swung his head as he turned, storming from the room.

Colin sighed and gulped the rest of his whisky. "Ye got the guard still on him?"

Archie drank al! his in one tilt of his glass. "Aye, my laird."

"Good, now all I have to work out is convincing Bree this is a good idea."

Archie laughed. "Ye'll not be getting any of my help with that, Colin. But ye may be right about Reverend O'Donnell."

Colin nodded. "Now, only time will tell."

Chapter 20

Colin stood at the window, staring out for some time. He had retreated to the study instead of lying awake in his bed, gawking at the canopy of bed hangings. His mind, going over the wedding plan. He was missing something but could not put his finger on it. When he ran through each scenario, he could only see the same end: himself, with Bree at the altar.

Damn, he still hadn't spoken with Bree about the wedding plan. Agatha wouldn't let him close to her, saying she was still on the mend but should be up and about tomorrow. At least that gave him more time to mull over what he would say to her. He had to figure out how to keep her safe. His plan must succeed.

Thunder boomed in the distance. His gaze focused on the rain pouring outside the window. He'd been so wrapped up in his thoughts that he hadn't noticed the storm's approach. Another crack of lightning reverberated off the castle, making him worry over Bree.

Colin figured she would appear soon. He should leave his study and return to bed, but he could not bring himself to. She would surely retreat to the study during a storm, and he wanted to be there. Moving away from the window into the room's shadows, he wasn't certain how long the storm had been going on or how long he needed to wait.

Finally, the door creaked open, and Brielle peered around it, staring at the fireplace. He smiled in the shadows. He hadn't had to wait that long after all.

She went to the fireplace, set her candle on the mantel, and pulled her wrap closer. On silent feet, Colin stepped out of the shadows and approached her. She held a volume between her palms as she stared into the flames. He noted it was her poem book from the future.

Thunder sounded again. She jolted and squeaked.

He could not stop himself from speaking. "Careful what ye seek, lass. Ye might find something ye aren't looking for."

Brielle whipped around, dropping the poem book. She glanced down, then tried to cover herself better with the plaid. She wore only her shift, and the light from the fire made the fabric transparent.

The fire's glow accentuated the outline of her legs, and as his gaze traveled up to the juncture of her thighs, he could make out the darker shadow of her nest of curls through the material.

Colin nearly groaned out loud as she spoke. "Roderick, I'm sorry—I didn't see you standing there. I didn't mean to intrude. I-I'll be going."

She started for the door, but Colin moved around the chairs, heading toward her. "Lass, ye do not need to leave on my account."

He offered his hand. She stared at it for a moment. Bree unfolded hers and placed it in his. Her palm felt ice cold, and he caressed the top with his thumb. She shivered.

Thunder boomed, jolting her again.

Colin squeezed her hand once. "Come sit by the fire, lass."

He led her to a chair in front of the fireplace. As she sat, Colin crossed to the table, poured two glasses of whisky. Returning, he handed her one as he sat in the chair beside her. This was the first time Colin had spoken to her since her brush with death. He had so much he wanted to say, but as Roderick, he couldn't.

Colin examined his glass and spoke softly. "I'm happy to see ye better. Ye gave us all a fright."

Bree replied quietly, "I didn't mean to cause any trouble. My apologies. Please forgive me." Next to him, she sat staring into the flames of the fire.

He'd forgive her anything; she only had to ask. Colin studied her for a moment. Her hair glowed soft in the firelight, her shoulders curved almost in defeat, and the corners of her mouth creased. God, he hated seeing her this way. He only wanted to see her happy, smiling at him with love in her eyes. Seeing her now, he did not know how much longer he could keep up the charade of being Roderick. Her ill, near death, had nearly done him in.

Thunder rumbled, and she jolted again.

The words came out of his mouth before he thought them through. "Storms scare ye, lass?"

She nodded once and sipped her whisky.

Colin spied the book on the floor, and he could not stop himself. He needed to hold her, to keep her safe. All he wanted was to take Bree in his arms and make love to her.

He set his glass down, rose, and picked up the volume. It was on the same page it had been in the future, the last time they hid out from a storm in this very room.

Colin glanced at Bree as she stared into the flames.

He couldn't resist. Fate had spoken, and he could only follow through. Damn the consequences. He'd sort that out tomorrow.

"Some light reading?" he asked. Bree blinked. He read from the book:

Western wind, when wilt thou blow
That the small rain down can rain?
Christ, that my love was in my arms
And I in my bed again.

Bree sucked in her breath and her eyes went wide. He smiled. Soon she would smile and gaze upon him with the love in her heart.

"Ye know, this poem has another verse..."

Eye of Heaven, pray gently, smile,
And though the cold wind blow,
Soft, may you warm and mind my love
That I love her so

Bree smiled, then her gaze fell to the floor. "That's beautiful, Roderick."

He closed the book, got out of his chair, and knelt in front of her. She set her glass on the table and placed her hands in her lap, folding them over one another as he had seen her do when she was nervous. He picked up her hands, set the book between them, and wrapped his hands around hers.

As he spoke, he squeezed her palms for emphasis. "It is a beautiful addition, but they added it in *2014*, Bree."

Her gaze snapped to his. He smiled and watched her mind turn over what he had said.

She stared at their hands and cocked her head to the side. "Roderick, did you just say 2014?"

He laughed lightly. "Aye, lass, it's me, Colin, not

Roderick." She sucked in a deep breath, released it in a whoosh, then turned as white as a sheet. She dropped the book, swayed a little, and he feared she might faint. He captured her in his arms, switching their positions, so she sat on his lap.

He caressed her face as he gazed into her eyes. "Bree, are ye okay, lass?"

She sighed and stared into his. "Okay? I am more than okay. Colin, is it really you?"

He chuckled, "Aye, lass." He wrapped her in his arms and held her for a moment, savoring the sensation of her again. Brielle closed her eyes and took a deep breath. He knew she would ask questions and try to make sense of her confusion.

Brielle cupped her hand on his cheek. "Has it been you the whole time?"

Colin knew she was clever and would piece this together, but he could not allow her to figure out the complete puzzle. He had to keep her safe. He knew what he wanted, had been craving since she came through the portal. It would be the perfect diversion for her quick mind.

"Aye, lass. Questions are for later. I have something else in mind." She gazed into his eyes as he spoke. "I've held back for weeks not being able to touch ye. It damn near killed me. I want to touch all of ye, Bree."

She'd once asked him to kiss all of her, and he had. Now that she knew it was him, that's all he wanted. He wanted to kiss all of her, and she all of him.

He kissed her deeply, and she moaned between kisses. "Colin, it's been torture. I've always sensed you were Colin, not Roderick, but it's been…confusing."

God, he missed holding her, touching her. And now he wouldn't have to hold back. She would be his again.

Colin lifted her in his arms. "No confusion now."

He slipped from the study with Bree in his arms—exactly where she belonged. As he carried her up the stairs, Bree rested her head on his chest and sighed, fitting perfectly. He carried her down the hall toward the laird's room, elbowed his way in, and closed the door.

Colin lowered Bree down his body, sliding her over every curve. The friction sent tingles over his whole body. He kissed her deeply, and she moaned lightly.

"Bree, God, it's good to have ye back in my arms. I have wanted to kiss ye for an eternity, but I couldn't."

He drew Bree into his embrace and ran his hands through her hair, pulling the mass over his arm as he watched the golden highlights reflected in the firelight.

Bree ran her hands up his arms and around his neck, kissing him deeply. "I have missed you so much. I often think of our night in the cabin, and I miss you all over again," she whispered.

Colin smiled at the memory. "Bree, do ye still have the stone, the Iona Stone?"

Bree reached into her gown and pulled out the chain with the stone in its setting. "Ronnie made a chain and holder for it so I could carry it always, and I have."

Colin reached into his sporran as Bree slid the rock from the spring. They held them together, forming the perfect heart. She slipped the stone back into the spring on the necklace, and Colin placed his stone in his sporran as she nestled in his arms.

He remembered the night at the hunting cabin, how he'd introduced her to so much. He growled softly. "Bree, I know ye enjoyed my loving of ye with my mouth. Ye know ye can always return the favor?"

Bree stiffened in his arms. "Y-You want me to?"

Colin nodded. "Very much so."

****

Brielle wasn't sure what to do. She knew she'd have to face this. Tony always liked oral sex but only her giving to him. It had become an obsession for him, something he demanded, regardless of her objections. Demanded while she often went mentally to someplace else. She had dated no one since their breakup, and she hadn't faced the issues from Tony's sex games. She should have known this would creep up on her, and now was the worst time.

She took a deep breath. She could do this. Colin was nothing like Tony. He loved her, and she wanted to do this for him as he had her.

She knelt before him, his kilt rising. Her hands traveled up his legs, the hair tickling her fingers a little. They touched his rear, and it flexed. She grasped it, liking the fact it differed from Tony's flat one. Maybe she could do this if she focused on the differences in their bodies, the things that reminded her that this man was Colin. Her palms roamed his rear, firm and strong. The muscles flexed again, reminding her of his attractive body.

He shifted, so he leaned against the bedpost. Brielle refused to glance up at him, so she stared at the plaid. She knew that's what Tony always demanded. She closed her eyes. His gravelly voice echoed in her mind. *"Brielle, look at me, bitch. There you are. My perfect whore in her place. On the floor, kneeling at my cock. You'll suck it, Brielle. Suck it like a good whore."*

She shook her head. She couldn't be thinking of Tony now. Her eyes snapped open to see the MacDougall plaid in front of her. *I'm in Scotland. This is Colin.*

She brought her hands to his front. Colin groaned as she wrapped her hand around him. She rubbed up and down, her other hand braced against his hip. Tony's voice echoed in her mind again.

"That's how you do it. Start slow. Warm your favorite toy up. Make it hard. Pump it harder, bitch. Get it ready for me to shove in your mouth." Tony slapped her, hard. *"Tell me you like it."*

Her hand stopped. Tony did the same thing every time, hurting her to gain his pleasure.

"Be good, Brielle, and bow before your master. Now, stay on your knees where you belong, beneath me. Open that mouth, whore." He gripped her hair in his hand, holding her in place. He slid his cock into her mouth, going to the back of her throat and then back again. He slapped her.

Colin's hand came to the back of her head. "Bree, that was nice. But ye promised to love me as I ye." He lifted his plaid. His hand gripped her neck. She had to do it Tony's way, or he'd hit her. Her mind clicked, then she was back…with Tony.

"You mean service you?" The tone of her voice had changed, almost robotic in her ears.

She reached to unbuckle his belt, methodical in her actions. "Yes, sir, I'll service you."

He let his plaid drop and caught her shoulders.

"Bree, what are ye doing?"

She heard a voice, but Tony was still in her head. *"Now, stay on your knees where you belong, beneath me."*

He drew her up so she stood before him.

She stared at him, seeing Tony. "You said I had to serve you—that's what I'm doing."

A hand caressed her face. "Bree, look at me."

Tony's voice echoed. *"Brielle, look at me, bitch. There you are, my perfect whore, in her place."*

He joggled her. "See into my eyes, Bree."

She blinked, then focused on the man before her. Colin.

His voice came quiet yet firm. "I don't know what ye've done in the past, but that is not what I want."

He cupped her face in his hands, large but soft, and looked closely into her eyes. She blinked once, then closed them.

His voice came to her, melodic and dreamy, not hard and demanding. "What we do together is special and sacred only to us." His palms were soft on her cheeks. It was Colin, and he wasn't hurting her. She was listening now.

He kissed her cheek gently as his lips brushed her skin.

She opened her eyes and saw Colin before her.

"I made love to you that way because it gave me joy to see ye appreciate my loving. I did not do it to *service ye*. Ye only need to do this type of loving if it brings ye bliss. Not just an act that brings only me pleasure," he said.

She stood there a moment, staring at him. He told her she only had to do what she wanted and what brought her joy.

Colin kissed her other cheek, tenderly, not hard.

As his head came away from her face, his gaze met hers. "What we share is something beautiful that we enjoy *together*."

A tear ran down her cheek, and Colin kissed her lips lightly. "I will never ask this of ye again. When ye are ready to do this type of loving, and it brings *ye* joy, then ye may do so."

He caught her tear on his thumb as she whimpered. He wasn't Tony. This was Colin, and her heart nearly burst. He was telling her what had happened to her was in the past. Told her what they did together was what mattered. He was telling her—her desires mattered.

She took a deep breath. "Oh, Colin. I love you."

He sighed. "I love you, *mo chridhe*."

Colin lifted her to his bed. Laying her down, he covered her with his body, kissing her hard, then he trailed his lips to her neck and returned to her lips. She returned his kisses with vigor, running her hands over his shoulders, then down his back. She loved that sensation, her hands caressing his muscular form. The power he possessed and wielded with such care made her love him more.

His head came up, and his gaze roamed her face. "God, Bree, ye get more beautiful each day."

She sighed. "Colin, I have missed you." He kissed her again as his hands wandered her body, sending tingles along her spine. Their tongues danced in a hypnotic rhythm that took her to a place where only the two of them existed.

Colin rose a little, his eyes connected with hers, and he stilled. "We only do what brings us joy, *mo chridhe*."

She caressed his face with her hand. "Please, Colin, please touch me. Show me what love is."

He shifted to her side, then inched her gown up her legs. He bent his head and kissed her again. His fingers trailed up and down her thigh, sending shivers up and down her legs.

She shivered, and Collin chuckled into the kiss. "Being around ye for weeks and unable to touch ye has driven me mad, mad with desire. I want to see all of ye, all of yer beauty, in one glance."

Colin growled low as he pulled her torso up. He reached for the bottom of her gown and removed it in one motion. She lay back, and he lounged, gazing at her for a moment, his expression one of wonder. His eyes roamed her naked body, taking a moment here and there to stop and stare.

His gaze stopped at her breasts, then his wonder turned into a smile. He reached out, molding his hand around her breast. His palm fit around the globe, making the peak tingle. He bent and suckled the nipple, turning the tingle into fire, making her arch with a moan.

He smiled as he settled one leg between hers and suckled her nipples while each hand massaged a breast. She moaned as she ran her fingers through his hair. His mouth, soft then firm, sent jolts of heat to her core, and her legs clenched in response to his attentions.

He kissed her lips, rose, stripped off his shirt, and slid his chest over her breasts. The friction sent a shock wave to Brielle's core. She wanted to see him, his magnificent body, firm and muscular. Her hands trailed their way to his belt. As she kissed his shoulder, she unbuckled the strap, letting it fall aside. He rose, gripped his kilt, pulled the fabric away, tossing it behind him. He grinned as he stood there. Her gaze shifted from his hard staff to his broad chest. His muscles lifted as he inhaled, then exhaled. Her eyes moved to his handsome face as he stood smiling at her, and she sensed love flowing from him. She locked the picture in her mind to keep forever.

He went to her, growling deep in his throat as he trailed kisses up the middle of her chest. They met in a searing kiss with tongues that mated in a fierce dance.

Colin shifted to the side while still cradling her in his arms. His palm slipped down the middle of her torso as he watched its path to her nest of curls.

He smiled, kissed her deeply, and cupped her core with his hand. He lifted his head, watching her.

He whispered, "Want to fly, Bree?" Then he kissed her hard and lifted his head, waiting for her answer.

She whispered back, pleading, "Please, Colin, please make me soar."

His fingers flicked her apex of curls.

She hitched a gasp, and their eyes met. "Here, Bree? Is this where ye wanted me to touch ye?"

She nodded as she spread her legs wider for him. He kissed her then, hard and demanding, making her moan as he slipped his finger along her slit.

He glided it in as he spoke. "God, woman, ye are so hot and wet."

He kissed her hard as he stroked her, bringing her more pleasure. Colin lifted his head and watched her as his finger found her nub, and he rubbed it. Her head fell back, a low gasp escaping. She was putty in his hands, something he could mold and form.

She heard him whisper, "Ye like that?"

Between gasps, she groaned her reply. "Yes."

Colin's thumb pressed on her jewel, making her head snap up, and she kissed him hard. He smiled into the kiss, then increased the rhythm. Her pants came harder between kisses, nearly driving her over the edge.

Colin slid a finger inside, and she cried out as her hips bucked against his hand. He took a nipple in his mouth as she arched, pressing her chest toward him, and he answered her request, sucking deeply.

Her hands dug into his hair, and she pulled lightly, making him growl as he began a driving pace. Colin sucked hard on her other nipple, making her moan loudly.

Without stopping, he slid a second finger inside her, maintaining his rhythmic pace with the movement of her hips. Still panting, she tried to catch her breath. Colin kissed her as he increased the pressure and speed. He lifted his head to watch her. She writhed in his arms, the pressure building inside her. He gazed into her eyes and kissed her hard.

Never had she made love so connected with a man. His love poured from him into her, feeding her soul, making her one with him. Her passage closed in on his fingers, and he whispered, "Ye are the most beautiful creature I have ever seen. I want to see my love come undone in my arms." She couldn't think, only experience his love for her, the sheer joy he took watching her pleasure.

She moaned louder, and he quickened the pace until her walls gripped him tighter. She was close. His thumb flicked her bud, making her hips buck as she cried out his name. He continued his attack, giving her more, more to savor. She cried out again as her legs closed, gripping his hand. Colin watched her as she cried out his name and then froze in a tense moment, tiny gasps of air coming from her.

She dropped her head back, closing her eyes; then lights exploded behind her eyelids. Her walls spasmed around his fingers, heat flooding her body. She relaxed in one long sigh, totally spent, as he withdrew his hand and settled her into his arms.

He held her tight. "God, Bree, ye are beautiful." Bree stared into his eyes as he smiled and kissed her. "Did ye fly, *mo chridhe*?"

She returned his smile with a devilish one. "Oh yes, but now I want to see you fly."

Bree rolled him onto his back and climbed upon him. He growled softly. She rubbed her bud against his rod and spread her wetness along his shaft. He smiled, and she winked at him. He huffed a laugh, but it came out as a brief sigh as his hands traveled to her waist.

With his guided help, she rose and slid down his shaft, wrapping herself around him and filling herself with his hardness. She buried him to his hilt, moaning as she rocked a little, making her walls tighten. Colin's head dropped back, and his hands tightened on her hips. His rod jumped inside her, making her gasp. He took a deep breath, rolling his hips a little. She sighed, and his hands traveled up her body, cupping both breasts. She wanted to give him what he had for her, raw pleasure. A heart-stopping act of love that he would enjoy as much as she had earlier.

As she began her assault, she smiled. She brought her hands behind her and rested them on his thighs, starting at a slow pace. She glided herself entirely from the tip to the hilt with each stroke. The rise of his staff pulsed against her, and it gave her power to affect him this way. She had a good grip on his thighs to steady herself, and her head fell back as she rocked, enjoying the friction. Colin's hands cradled her lower back, supporting her weight, helping her move her body. She was in for a ride, was in control, and she loved every moment.

Bree quickened her pace, gliding along his rod. She felt him plant his heels into the mattress and shift his hips. He moved faster, harder, making the pressure build inside her. Heat flooded her body. Her core clenched and then burst, making her see stars. She cried out, arching fully with the motion as he pounded into her, making her spasm again. She allowed him to take the lead, molding herself to his body and giving in to her release. She rocked forward, resting on his sweaty chest. She gasped as he panted. She caressed his face as she lifted hers, then kissed him with all her heart. He had given her pleasure first, and his gift humbled her.

As she moaned, he whispered, "Bree, I need ye."

Colin rose to his knees as she wrapped her legs around his back. He rocked his hips while holding her waist, her arms wrapped around his neck, poised in perfect balance. Their eyes connected as they made love slowly.

They watched each other, the erotic, emotional high of each reflected in the other. Still overcome with desire, she wanted to be with this man, share herself with him; and she wanted him to cherish her.

As Colin rocked faster, as his dam was about to burst. He held her hips and pumped into her over and over. The heat built again, consuming her body, reaching her soul. As she cried out in release, Colin arched his back as he continued his assault. He drove in to his hilt, holding her still as he shouted his release. He thrust again, and they cried out together as they soared on the waves of pleasure. He wrapped her in his arms. Their foreheads rested together while still joined.

"*Mo chridhe*, you have my heart," Colin whispered.

Bree sighed. "Colin, you have mine."

****

Bree lay snug in his arms, where he wanted her to stay for all time. He ran his hand up and down her arm.

Bree stirred from her slumber. "Colin, how is it possible we are here in the past? What does all this mean?"

Colin knew the questions would come. He had sat up most of the night planning how he would explain their situation, time travel. She was intelligent, and he would have to make sure she got a good enough explanation without learning about all of it.

He spoke finally. "It's the *Fae Fable Book*."

Bree glanced up into his face. "The book in the study?"

"Aye."

Bree crossed her brow. "The book sent us back in time?"

He chuckled. "Not exactly." He took a deep breath, pressed his lips together, and blew it out with a long sigh. He stared off into the fire, watching the flames dance, hoping what he shared with Bree would be enough—enough to keep her safe.

"The Fae made the book to hold the fables. Stories about the stones. They gave it to my family centuries ago."

Bree's gaze shot to his. "You mean like the stone Hamish gave me? The stone we share—its magic sent us here?"

Colin nodded. "Aye and no. Let me finish."

Bree settled into the crook of his arm, her head on his shoulder next to his heart. He wrapped her in his embrace and took a deep breath. He would need to be careful with what he revealed.

"The stories are about the Stones of Iona, three stones entrusted to my family for protection: hope, faith, and love."

Bree gasped. "The three windows of the chapel."

Colin nodded. "For my entire childhood, my ma told these stories to my sister, Ainslie, and me as bedtime fables. And for a long time, that is all I thought they were, stories. It wasn't until recently that we found out the stories are true."

Bree lifted her head. "We?"

Colin glanced at her, then back at the flames. *Colin, don't reveal too much. Remember, she's smart.*

"John MacArthur as well. He knew the truth of the stories before I did. It's why he called me to the castle."

Bree sucked in a breath. "That's why you came, not because of the chapel renovation."

Colin tilted her chin till she was staring into his eyes. "Aye, but I am pleased I came to the castle when I did. I met ye."

He kissed her lips, then caressed her cheek. "The good Fae have cast the stones through time to hide them from the evil Fae. If they fall into the hands of evil, both realms will fall. The good Fae sent me to this time to find the Stone of Love and return it to the twenty-first century. My resemblance to Roderick made me a natural fit for the mission."

Bree frowned. "How do we find this stone?" Damn, he knew she couldn't resist getting involved. He'd have to keep her close, yet far from the stones, from the Fae. This would be near impossible, but he had to do it. Her life depended on it, and his relied on finding the stone and finishing this mission.

He glared at Bree, pointing his finger between himself and her. "*We*...aren't doing anything. *I* will find the stone, and *I* will return Roderick to this time."

Bree frowned at him. "I want to help, and what's this about returning Roderick to this time? Where is he?"

Colin hated lying to her, but she was smart. He needed her safe, not wise. "I don't know, but I need yer help with one task."

Bree smiled, and her eyes went bright. "Okay, what do you need?"

Colin smiled. "I need ye to marry me."

Bree sat up, half turning to face him. "You what?"

The sheet slid off her shoulder, baring her to the waist. Colin's gaze traveled over her body. He raised an eyebrow. She glanced down, grabbing the sheet to cover herself, but Colin beat her to it, gathering her in his arms and pressing their naked chests together.

As they lay down, he covered them both with the sheet. "Ye do not need to panic, and it won't be real."

Bree huffed. "You ask me to marry you, and then you tell me it won't be real. This is what's wrong with men these days."

Colin chuckled. "Men in the eighteenth or men in the twenty-first century?"

Bree hit him in the chest. "Both!"

Colin chuckled. They lay silent for a moment. "Bree, this is no joking matter. I need yer help to find the evil Fae."

Bree stared into the fire. "The things happening to me—the boulder, the arrow, and the poison. Those aren't accidents, are they?"

Colin squeezed her closer. He knew she would figure it out quickly. "Aye," he said.

Her voice shook when she spoke. "Colin, am I the bait or the target?"

He growled, grabbed her by the shoulders, and sat them both up. "Neither. I will protect ye at all times. Until we know who it is, ye will stay guarded the whole day and night. Ye *will* be safe," he said as he gently shook her.

She shivered and glanced down. "I don't understand."

Colin glimpsed away. He had already shared more than he had planned to. *I must focus.*

He peered at her. "Let me tell ye the Fae story, and maybe it will make better sense."

Bree nodded, and Colin took her in his arms as they lay down.

He took a moment to collect his thoughts. He needed to craft the story so that he did not reveal the end to Bree. That the maiden sacrificed herself for the prince. He needed their ending to be different, so they both would go back to the twenty-first century, together.

He took a deep breath and began his version of the fable. "The story is more fable than truth, but I always liked this one. There was a prince who lived in the castle. The Fae gifted him with the Stone of Love. The stone was very powerful, and the Fae charged him with guarding it. He made a necklace with a heart-shaped stone and always wore it so that he would know when his true love was near, because then, he was told, the stone would glow red. Many maidens came from far and wide to see if the stone would glow for them, but it never did. The prince became depressed, thinking he'd never find his true love. He would sneak away to the village and sit at his favorite spot by the stream to contemplate the issue with the stone. It would glow every time he went there, but he was always alone."

Bree sighed. "That's so sad."

Colin cleared his throat.

"I'm sorry, continue," Bree said.

"One day, a beautiful woman came to the castle. Gorgeous and sensual, she went near him and made the stone glow. While the prince was physically attracted to her, he did not know love for this woman. Confused, he snuck off and went to his spot by the stream. As he sat, he saw a maiden approach the stream."

He tilted Bree's chin till their eyes were level. "She had glowing cream-colored skin and an inner beauty he had not seen in a woman before."

Colin picked up a strand of Bree's hair and held it out in the firelight. "Her light-brown hair glimmered in the sunlight, seeming as if to cast the threads of a pure gold halo around her head." Colin wrapped the strand around his finger and placed it behind her ear. "Her soul called to him in a way he had never felt before."

Colin kissed her. "So caught up in his examination, he had not noticed that the Stone of Love glowed red."

Bree smiled as she gazed into his eyes. "You made

that last part up. You just described me."

Colin stared directly into his love's eyes. "I swear on my mother's grave—that is how the story appears."

He touched her hair and ran his finger down her cheek. "When I saw ye in the study for the first time as ye stood by the window, the light shining in yer hair. I felt the Fae had delivered my soul mate. The woman of my childhood dreams." He kissed her deeply.

After a moment, Bree tilted her head and huffed. "Well, so how did the story end?"

Colin looked at the fire. He couldn't tell her the rest of the story. If she knew the maiden sacrificed herself to save the prince, he feared that was precisely what Bree would do. He couldn't let that happen—he had to keep her safe. Even though he hated lying, he had to.

His stilted voice filled the room. "They fell in love and lived happily ever after, like all fables."

Bree shifted her head back to meet his eyes. "That's it? 'The End'?"

Colin nodded without glancing at her. "Aye, that's all."

Chapter 21

Brielle launched herself across the room, barely making it to the chamber pot in time, waking him with her movement and the sound of her retching.

"Bree, what's the matter?"

She heaved and panted. "Nothing, Colin, I'll be fine soon."

He bounded out of bed, not noticing his nudity, threw open the door, and bellowed, "Archie, find me Agatha, now!"

Leaving the door cracked, he strode to Bree as she came out from behind the privacy screen. He snatched a sheet, wrapped her in it, and settled her in a chair before the fireplace. Colin grabbed his plaid, shook it out, and laid it on the floor. He was quick as he folded the pleats and lay on the floor to pull the fabric around his body.

Bree watched him. "I always wondered how you got all that fabric to do that." He pulled the sides of the fabric around to the front, wrapped his belt around him, securing the long piece of material.

He glanced up. "Aren't ye the anthropologist?"

Bree shook her head and moaned, then put her hand to her head.

He jumped up from the floor and knelt beside her. "*Mo chridhe*, are ye still ill? I thought the poison was all out by now."

Agatha elbowed her way through the doorway with

a tray. "Och now, here we are, dearie." She set the tray on the table and handed Brielle a mug and a piece of bread. "This will cure ye right up."

Colin stood frowning at Agatha. "I thought ye said she was well. That she would be okay."

Agatha placed her hands on her hips and glared at him. "Look at ye, kept her up all night. Now it's morning, and she's naked in yer bedchamber. What's the clan going to say about this?" Agatha waved her hand toward Brielle as she said *this*. He huffed at her accusation.

At the perfect moment, Archie strolled into the room. "Nothing, Agatha. They are engaged."

Colin folded his arms over his chest. "Aye, we are, and ye need to keep her well. I don't want her overdoing it."

Agatha raised a brow. Colin had the impression she knew what they had been doing all night, and overdoing it was exactly what he had been doing with Bree. He relaxed his features, trying to seem innocent.

Agatha shook her head at him. "Is that so? Well, come on, dear, let's get ye back to yer room and tend to ye."

Colin put his hand out, stopping Agatha from reaching for Bree. "She stays here with me. She's to be guarded the whole while, day and night." He stood firm, glaring at the healer, doing his best intimidation stare he had practiced for the law firm.

Agatha straightened, then nodded. "Aye, mi laird. I understand the way it is now."

She turned to Archie, bent her head to the door, and then said, with her voice carrying over the room, "We'll be leaving ye as ye wish, mi laird. Bree dear, I'll send up a bath."

Bree nodded as Colin bent by her side.

****

Outside the door, Archibald stopped Agatha. "How did ye know to be at the castle this morning with a tray ready for Bree? I didn't even have to summon ye when he bellowed. Is she still suffering from the poison?"

Agatha smiled and patted Archibald's cheek. "Men…ye aren't the smartest of them all, are ye?"

Archie opened his mouth, only to be interrupted by Agatha. "She's ill only in the morning, Archibald."

Archibald shifted his head back. His eyebrows went up as she laughed. "If ye take a woman to yer bed, as I suspect Colin has before they traveled through the portal, then what're the results of yer actions?"

Archibald gasped. "Oh."

He glanced at the closed door, then back at Agatha. "Well, aren't ye going to tell them?"

Agatha shook her head. "No, and ye will not either. They will return to their own time soon, and then they can deal with it in their own way." She smiled. "Ye should deal with yer own business instead of the laird's."

Archibald narrowed his eyes on Agatha. "What do ye mean by that, Agatha?"

Agatha rolled her eyes. "Ye haven't seen yer Rose in weeks, Archibald. Roderick disappeared only a few weeks past yer own wedding."

Archibald pointed his finger in her face. "I've been busy with Roderick's disappearance and Colin's appearance. Then there's the Fae targeting Bree. Yer task is with seeing after Rose, Mary, Elizabeth, and Alex so that I can be here working on this Fae problem."

Archibald suddenly paused in his tirade and took a deep breath. "What's happened? Is Rose ill?"

Agatha winked. "Ye need to sneak away and go see yer Rose, Archibald. She's been ill every morning for up on two weeks now."

Archibald grabbed her shoulders. "Why didn't ye tell me she was ill?"

Agatha rolled her eyes. "I just did...but she's not ill."

Archibald glanced at the door, then back at Agatha. "Ye mean, my Rose?"

Agatha smiled. "I'll make excuses for ye. Sneak away and see yer wife, congratulate her on yer bairn."

****

The following day, Colin stood fuming in the doorway to Bree's bedroom as she hid behind the door. "What do ye mean, I cannot come in? She's going to be my wife." Fiona rolled her eyes.

"That may be true, but ye cannot see her in the wedding dress before the ceremony. 'Tis bad luck, it is." Brielle peeked at him through the door crack. Colin seemed ready to explode.

She sighed. "*Roderick*, it will be okay. I'm only here in my bedroom." She spoke irritably from behind the door. "I'll be fine." Colin glared at Fiona and then at the door and nodded once.

He turned and stormed down the hallway, calling over his shoulder, "I'll be in the study. I'll send up a guard."

Fiona giggled, closing the door. "He's so taken with ye. Must be true love."

Brielle smiled, but it didn't reach her cheeks.

"Mmm, *aye*."

Fiona shook the dress out—it was the prettiest color of blue Bree had ever seen. It reminded her of Colin's eyes, cerulean, like the sky.

Fiona spread it out on the bed. "It's Rose's wedding dress. We spent weeks making the dress alone, then another month on the embroidery. I'm sure she won't mind ye borrowing it. I wish she was here for this wedding."

Bree moved closer as Fiona held out the sleeve. There were green vines and roses embroidered all along the hem in pink, red, yellow, all in different sizes and stages of bloom. She reached out her hand to touch it and ran her fingers along the threads.

"It's beautiful," she whispered. Fiona shifted the dress on the bed, and Brielle saw the same embroidery on the hem and the entire bodice. It was the most beautiful dress she had ever seen. Twenty-first-century wedding dresses may have a lot of tulle and lace, but this was so simple and elegant. Tears formed in her eyes. It was the perfect wedding dress, if only this were for real.

Fiona patted Bree's arm. "Ye are so lucky."

****

She sat on the window seat, staring at the marina. Fiona had just left to alter the wedding dress, and she was alone for the first time in days. She spied her backpack, the edges of paper sticking out. She pulled those out to examine them—her drawings of the chapel. It was months ago when she'd arrived at Dunstaffnage to oversee the remodeling of the chapel in the woods.

As she examined her drawings, not complete but representing the entire chapel in this time, an idea popped into her head. The chapel wasn't far, and no one would be down there at this time of day. What would it hurt to do more drawings? Brielle snatched up her supplies, shoved them in the backpack, and peeked out her door.

Fiona stood speaking to the guard in the hallway. They had both backs turned, and Fiona tossed her head and giggled. The guard kissed her on the cheek. This was her chance. She slipped past them, unnoticed.

Casually going down the stairs and through the main hall, Bree tried to seem nonchalant. Servants were about, but no one commented on her presence. As she neared the study, she saw that the door was ajar, so she peeked inside. Colin sat at his desk, bent over papers with a quill in his hand, intently working on something. She hurried past without his noticing. She made it out the door and headed to the trail that led to the chapel.

****

Bree stayed at the chapel all afternoon. She hadn't been able to resist the opportunity to draw the chapel so she and Marie could make sure the future renovation was as accurate as possible.

Her hand cramped, again, and she rubbed it harder. When she glanced up, the sunbeams that shone through the window were a warm hue. Damn, it was closer to dinner than she thought. She would need to get back before Colin noticed she went missing.

Brielle gathered her items, packed them away in her backpack, and picked it up. When she turned to the doorway, the reverend blocked her way as he watched her. "Hello, Reverend O'Donnell. I wasn't aware you were here."

He glared at her, red-faced, his hands gripping his

Bible as he breathed deeply. "I see that."

Bree tried to move past him, but he grabbed her arm. "What are ye doing here?"

"Nothing, I only drew the chapel."

She tried to pull her arm away.

Dropping his Bible, he tightened his grip, dragging her toward the altar with both hands.

"You are hurting me. Stop it. I wasn't doing anything wrong."

He stopped at the altar, twisted his hands on her arms, and forced her to her knees, making her cry out in pain. "Ye are a witch, ye are. Why would a woman be drawing the chapel unless she was in line with the devil?"

The reverend shifted his grip to her hand and jerked her arm behind her back, forced her to bend over as he shoved her face to the floor.

"I'm not," she said. "I'm faithful. I'm only interested in recording the design for history. Someday, someone will want to see the beauty of this place before it falls to ruin."

The reverend bellowed, "Liar!" and twisted her arm tighter.

Bree cried out in pain as she tried to look back at the reverend.

A sword sang as someone removed it from a sheath, and the blade appeared under the clergyman's chin. "I would advise you to let the lass go, Reverend."

Her gaze followed the sword to who held it. Colin. So caught up in the attack on Brielle, the reverend hadn't noticed Colin enter the chapel or the guard behind him.

The reverend backed away and leaned against the

altar, panting.

Keeping the sword pointed at him, Colin stepped between them. "The stone, ye will give me the stone now, ye evil sprite."

The reverend leveled his gaze at Colin, seething between clenched teeth. "This woman bewitches ye. I don't know of any stone and don't know what ye refer to." The reverend straightened his robes, never taking his eye off Colin. "Ye are not the Roderick I know."

Colin leveled his eye down his sword at the reverend. "I am Roderick. Ye will apologize to the lady, and ye will marry us on the morrow."

Bree huddled on the floor, sniffling.

The reverend glanced at Colin, then Bree. He jerked as if another presence that had been occupying his body had left, and a familiar, more friendly expression returned to his face. Colin put his sword to the reverend's chest as he tried to step around him.

He blinked at Colin and gasped, "Lord, what have I become? My lady, I am so sorry. Please forgive me." He turned and knelt before the altar, his whispered prayers echoing in the chapel.

Colin sheathed his sword and strode past Bree. "Bree, you will come with me *now*."

She glanced at Colin. His back was to her as he faced the doorway. "Now, Bree," he bellowed.

She rose unsteadily to her feet and gathered her bag. Rubbing the arm that the clergyman had twisted, she shakily moved out of the chapel, with Colin following. He exchanged nods with the guard.

She took the trail to the castle, with Colin following close behind. Bree turned to him as she walked. "I only wanted to draw the chapel."

She tripped, and Colin caught her.

She cried out in pain when he grabbed her around the arms. "Damn it! Bree, ye hurt yerself again." He picked her up and carried her the rest of the way.

Colin elbowed his way into the study, slammed the door with his foot, and carefully placed her in one of the chairs before the desk. She dropped her backpack, rubbing her arm.

Colin leaned against the desk, crossed his arms and feet in his usual manner as he sighed. "Do I need to send for Agatha?"

Bree shook her head and sniffled.

"Do ye want a dram of whisky?"

She shook her head again as her shoulders drew in, the attack reminding her of her ex. All she wanted to do was curl into a ball.

Colin rubbed the bridge of his nose. "Bree, do ye understand why I ordered ye to stay away from the chapel?"

She took a deep breath and let it go with a shaky exhale. She nodded in one jerky motion. Why did the reverend hate her so?

Colin bent down till their faces were even, forcing her to gaze into his face. "Will ye be okay?"

She nodded.

He stood and looked out the window as she frowned at her hands. They both remained in silence, lost in their thoughts.

After some time, Colin knelt, took her hand, and kissed it. "I have something to show ye—if ye are up to it?"

Bree glanced into his eyes, saw their edges crinkled in concern, and nodded. After the confrontation with the reverend, she felt haggard, but she allowed Colin to escort her around his desk.

He pulled out his chair and waved his hand, inviting her to sit. In front of her were two large sheets of thick vellum. The writing appeared swirly, and there were small areas where the ink on the page was wider than the rest, where he must have dipped the quill just before writing. It seemed like she stared at a historical document, but these were new. She glanced from one to the other—they were identical.

The top of each said, "Contract of Marriage."

Bree gazed up at Colin as he rested his hand on the back of her chair. He leaned over from behind with a smile and a deep sigh.

"Colin, why would we need a contract of marriage if the wedding is fake?"

Colin smiled, his eyes twinkling as he spoke. "We have to make it convincing. In this time, if we got married without these, the clan wouldn't believe it. I need everything to appear real."

Bree, too tired to argue, nodded. "Okay, Colin," she said, and picked up the quill. She tried to read parts of the contract, but the curly lettering was hard to read, and she was too tired to care.

When she dipped the quill, Colin stilled her hand with his. "Wait, ye have to wait for the witnesses before ye sign."

Witnesses? She sighed. *Colin must know what he's doing.*

Colin strode to the door and waved in Archie and Agatha, who must have waited close by.

Archie, Agatha, and Colin gathered around the desk. Brielle glanced at each person—all three were smiling. Colin sighed deeply. Brielle rubbed her forehead as a headache came over her.

Colin spoke from behind her. "Now, ye may sign the documents." He leaned over, whispering in her ear, "Ye have to use yer formal name and sign both, please, Bree."

She glimpsed at Colin again, his face even with hers, so close the silver flecks in the deep azure of his eyes shimmered. Her gaze traveled over his face, and he smiled at her with such warmth. The documents wouldn't matter if the two of them weren't staying in the past. If this made him happy, she'd sign them.

She dipped the quill and signed *Brielle Elise DeVolt* on both. She handed the quill to Colin, who grinned when his hand brushed hers.

He slid the papers toward himself and scribbled on both. Archie and Agatha repeated the process, with their names beneath Colin and Bree's.

Agatha sighed, and her hand went to her chest. Archie sniffled but smiled. Colin slid both documents in front of Brielle, picked up a fistful of sand from a container, and sanded the signatures, sealing them for all time.

When Colin dusted off the sand, Brielle glanced at his signature and saw *Roderick MacDougall*. Bree stared up at him as he gazed at the papers, still smiling.

Brielle rose from her chair, crossed to the window, and gazed out as she hiccupped a sigh. A tear slid down her face, and she wiped it away. She had contracted to marry Roderick.

****

Colin stepped outside the study to confer with Archie as Agatha left. Through the cracked door, he saw Bree by the window—she seemed so tired and worn.

He whispered, "Archie, he attacked her, had her on her knees with her arm twisted behind her back, and screamed at her."

Archie rubbed his neck. "The guard following the reverend explained it when he came to alert me she was down there. After alerting ye, I grabbed Agatha and came as soon as possible. Is she all right?"

Colin peeked through the cracked door. "Aye, just tired."

When she signed the marriage contracts, tears stained her cheeks, but she looked to have gathered herself. He didn't like it. She still appeared sick, and it worried Colin. He had hoped the contracts would lift her spirits, but they seemed to only drive her deeper into despair. The reverend—he needed to ask about the reverend—his behavior was beyond strange.

He shook his head. "I don't know, Archie. I confronted the reverend about the stone. He was honestly surprised. Said he did not know what I was talking about and accused me of not being Roderick."

Archie glanced away. "I told ye I didn't think it was him."

Colin sighed. "What if I've made a mistake? What if it costs me the woman I love?"

Archie glanced back at Colin. "We stick to the plan, see who reacts, and then adjust. Whoever the evil Fae is, the guards are ready to take them."

Colin nodded. "Aye, I am not ready to absolve the reverend of guilt just yet."

Colin shifted back into the study. Bree stood by the window. He stopped and studied her a moment, praying he hadn't made the mistake of his lifetime by involving her in his plan. He vowed to change the ending of the fable so that it would be one they both could live with, one that saw them together.

He went to stand beside Bree and ran his finger down her cheek. "One more day, Bree. Please give me one more day, and all this will be over."

Another tear ran down her face. "I don't know, Colin…it's becoming too much to bear. I don't know if I can do this."

He hugged her close. "Not much longer, *mo chridhe,* I promise."

As he kissed her gently, the *Fae Fable Book* thumped once in its case. The pages flipped, then halted.

They both stared at the book, Bree reading aloud the words in red lettering in the center of the page:

Let Love never leave you;
Bind it around your neck.
Keep it in the core of your heart.

Bree gasped. "Colin, is this from the Fae story you told me the other night? It's referring to the prince's necklace, right?"

She glanced at Colin, but he kept his face downcast. The damn Fae. He had to finish this his way. He gathered himself so that she wouldn't see his worry when he looked at her.

After a deep breath, he glanced at her and smiled, then ran his hand over her hair. "Don't worry, *mo chridhe*, everything will be all right."

Chapter 22

Today, of all days, she should be happy. It was her wedding day. As she watched the sunrise over Loch Etive, Brielle sat in her favorite spot, the window seat with the view of the marina and mountain range. Still in her shift, she nibbled on bread and sipped water. Thankfully, Fiona figured out that Brielle hated ale and preferred fresh water.

She set her mug and bread down and reached for her necklace that held the Iona stone, gripping it in both hands. With all her heart, she wished today was her real wedding to Colin. Closing her eyes, she held the stone for a moment, praying. A moment passed, then another. The sun shifted across her closed eyes, and she opened them. Nothing had changed.

A soft knock tapped at her door, and Fiona peeked in. "Och, good, ye are up."

She opened the door wider to allow a boy to drag a tub inside her bedroom. Two guards stood outside her door. One had his back turned, and the other leaned against the wall across from the door. When she looked at him, he smiled and saluted her. *Oh, that Colin, so high-handed. Always must have it his way. Let him—I don't care—he can post one hundred guards. This ends today.*

Later that day, in a day gown, she sat waiting for the approaching hour of the wedding. She shook off her wedding jitters, still wishing it wasn't fake but an actual ceremony with Colin.

Fiona sat with her, working on some sewing. A knock rapped hard at her door, and Fiona answered it.

A guard entered with Reverend O'Donnell and another guard following. Both guards bowed to Bree. Upon seeing the clergyman, she felt her heart leap to her throat as her hand went there. The urge to jump up and run to the other side of the room came so strong that she stood and backed into the bench, causing her knees to give, and she plopped back down. She released the breath she held and took another deep one to gain her bearings.

His voice drew her gaze to him. "My lady. I offer my sincere apology for yesterday. I hope I have not caused ye grief."

His apology struck her speechless. Only yesterday, this man had convinced himself she was a witch. Attacked her for simply drawing the interior of the chapel. All she wanted to do was capture the design to restore it in the future. It was a fact he didn't know, but no matter. The man was demented. Yet, here he stood, offering an apology.

She gathered her courage, squared her shoulders, and replied, "I forgive you."

The reverend smiled. "The laird has tasked me with giving ye some instructions for today."

Bree blinked and held her hands together in front of her to still their shaking. The clergyman opened his book and approached her. One guard stopped him with his hand. The reverend glanced at the guard and then at Bree, nodded once, and handed a folded paper to the guard.

As the guard gave it to her, the reverend said, "The laird has asked for a special ceremony today—while it's an old Gaelic custom and rather unorthodox, if ye ask me."

The guard admonished him quietly, "No one was askin' ye."

The reverend closed his eyes and took a deep breath. "He has asked for a stone vow ceremony."

Bree opened the paper. "A stone vow ceremony?"

The guard smiled as Fiona sighed. "Oh, my lady, it's an old and romantic tradition."

The reverend cleared his throat. "I am to ask ye to memorize those vows and bring yer stone to the ceremony. My laird has assured me you know which stone he refers to."

Her hand rose to her necklace. As she grabbed the stone, the night in the hunting cabin flashed in her mind—Colin speaking of his ancestors and the broken heart stone. Colin's voice came to her. *"Carry the half of the stone, Bree, carry my heart with ye always. So, no matter where we are, ye will know I love you."*

She blinked, and the reverend's expectant expression was before her. She nodded.

The reverend bowed. "Good, till later."

He left, with the guards following. At the doorway, one guard turned to her and winked.

The day passed in a blur, and though Fiona delivered a tray with food, Brielle could not eat it. Agatha stopped by to check on her, but she felt fine. She dressed in a daze. *What does all the fuss matter?* It was not real.

Before she knew it, the elder, Conner MacDougall, stood next to her, and she faced the door to the chapel.

****

Colin took his place next to the reverend and gave him a side glance, checking the man who stood staring at the back of the chapel. He and Archie had set everything up for their plan. Archie was next to him, secretly armed.

He cast his gaze around the sanctuary again and noted that a guard stood beside each pew. They'd disarmed the guests as they entered.

He must finish this now. He sensed the evil Fae was among them. Colin was ready.

He stared at Bree as she entered the chapel. When she raised her head, their gazes locked. She appeared radiant in her blue gown, simple in design, yet elegant. The sun shone behind her, creating a halo with her golden-brown hair, reminding him of the maiden from the Stone of Love fable. His soul mate.

From the front of the sanctuary, he sensed her heart as it pulsed with his. Colin would do anything in this world or the next to keep her safe. As he stood before her, ready to be her groom, he gazed at her and willed her to see his love. In the end, he would give Bree all her hopes and dreams. For now, he would do anything to keep her safe. He hoped she would forgive him for what he was about to put her through.

****

Brielle entered the chapel, then stopped and stared at the floor. She ran the vows through her mind like an actor might run lines before a show, trying to still her nerves. It was a wedding, her wedding. A fake one, but one that seemed so real to her. A hush descended over the room. She glanced up. Colin stood next to the reverend, who wore a dour expression on his face.

The setting sun shone through the rear stained-glass window, illuminating Colin in the warm light of the cross in its design. Bree's heart skipped a beat. He smiled, and his face held an expression of warmth and welcome. The day could begin and end with him, and Bree would never want for anything. She reached for her stone, closed her eyes, and wished this were real, that she wed Colin.

Conner handed her a bouquet—roses—her favorite. She gazed at Colin's face and wished again that this was real. Not taking her eyes off him, she walked down the aisle. He wore a formal highland plaid and coat. The colors of this plaid were brighter than his other one. The brooch fastening on his shoulder was an intricate swirling pattern, and his coat was deep blue, reflecting the deep blue of his eyes.

Gazing into Colin's eyes, she did not realize Conner had handed her off to Colin until he touched her hands. A jolt of awareness shot through her. This was the only man for her, the only man for her heart.

Brielle took his hand, and he tucked hers into his arm's crook as he spoke. "*Mo chridhe*, everything will be all right." She sighed, and they turned to face the reverend together.

The wedding service started, and Brielle spent most of the time staring at the altar or the stained glass behind it. Anywhere but at the reverend. Too soon, it came time to face Colin and recite their vows. Her hands turned sweaty, and her breathing picked up. She turned toward Colin but stared at her hands as the reverend said for all to hear.

"Family and friends, Roderick and Brielle will now make their vows using stones." The reverend glanced at

Colin and Bree. "Can I please ask you each to hold your stone in the right hand and place your left hand over the other, holding the stone, joining ye both in a circle as one?"

To the congregation, he said, "They shall put their hands together on a stone as they repeat their wedding vows, as an oath given on a stone will pledge their love for eternity."

Brielle passed her flowers to Fiona in the front pew and took her stone necklace off to hold in her palm. Colin took his rock from his sporran. They clutched their stones in their right hands.

Colin whispered, "Bree, please take the rock out of the pendant."

She glanced at him, then her stone, and flipped the rock from the spring, handing Fiona the necklace. He smiled as they held the stones out and joined his hands with hers. Once joined, she could not take her eyes from his.

Colin gazed into her eyes as he spoke. "I," Colin paused, closing his eyes. He whispered something under his breath and stood there for a moment.

She thought she heard his name but wasn't sure.

He opened his eyes and stared into hers as he continued in a loud voice so all could hear. "Roderick MacDougall, in the name of the spirit of God that resides within us all, by the life that courses within my blood, and the love that resides within my heart, take thee, Brielle Elise DeVolt, to my hand, my heart, and my spirit, to be my chosen one. To desire thee and be desired by thee, to possess thee, and be possessed by thee, without sin or shame, for naught can exist in the purity of my love for thee."

He paused and squeezed her right hand, that held the Iona stone. "I promise to love thee wholly and completely without restraint, in sickness and in health, in plenty and in poverty, in life *and beyond*, where we shall meet, *remember*, and love again. I shall not seek to change thee in any way. I shall respect thee, thy beliefs, thy people, and thy ways as I respect myself."

Brielle gazed at Colin, listening to him say the marriage vows as if this were a real wedding. Her heart felt like breaking, for when he spoke the words, she deeply felt that he meant them. When he emphasized *beyond* and *remember*, she thought he was trying to convey something, but she was too caught up in the moment to try to figure out exactly what he meant.

The chapel fell silent. He had finished. It was her turn.

She closed her eyes, swallowed, and said a prayer to herself. *Please let this be real. I love Colin with all my heart. Please, God, if you are listening and have any mercy, make this real.*

She opened her eyes, took a deep breath, and met Colin's gaze. "I, Brielle Elise DeVolt, in the name of the spirit of God that resides within us all, by the life that courses within my blood, and the love that resides within my heart, take thee…"

She paused and took a deep breath. Colin whispered, "Whisper my name, Bree, whisper *Colin*, please."

Her gaze shot to the reverend. He hadn't heard.

She blinked at Colin and whispered, "Colin."

His eyes closed as he squeezed her hands, then opened as she recited the rest of her vows:

"…Roderick MacDougall, to my hand, my heart,

and my spirit to be my chosen one. To desire and be desired by thee, to possess thee, and be possessed by thee, without sin or shame, for naught can exist in the purity of my love for thee."

She gazed into his eyes, wishing beyond all hope that this was a real wedding and that she truly married Colin. "I promise to love thee wholly and completely without restraint; in sickness and in health, in plenty and in poverty, in life and beyond, where we shall meet, remember…"

Her eyes watered, her throat closed, making it hard to speak. She took a shaky breath. "…and love again. I shall not seek to change thee in any way. I shall respect thee, thy beliefs, thy people, and thy ways as I respect myself."

Reverend O'Donnell cleared his throat. Colin jolted and pulled on her hands but stood still.

"Listen to the words of a special Stone Blessing for the bride and groom."

Above ye are the stars, below ye are the stones.
As time passes, remember:
Like a star, yer love will be constant,
Like the stone, yer love will be firm.
Let the power of desire make ye happy,
and faith in yer dedication make ye inseparable.
Possess one another yet be understanding.
Have patience, for storms will come, and they will go,
forced to dissipate in the light of yer love.
Be free in giving of affection and of warmth.
Have no fear and let not the ways
or words of the unenlightened give ye doubt.
For yer love is with ye,

Now and always.

Reverend O'Donnell finished and paused. Colin glared at him with a raised eyebrow. The clergyman glanced at his hands and shifted the Bible. Colin tensed, and Archie moved closer as Reverend O'Donnell said in a flat, rough voice, "Now ye may put away those stones and exchange yer rings."

Colin released a breath. Brielle thought she had missed something. He put his stone in his sporran as Brielle handed hers to Fiona.

Colin took her right hand in his as he held a ring poised, ready to slide on her finger. He stood staring at her for a moment. His gaze traveled over her face, then her hair, and his eyes crinkled at the edges. His gaze returned to hers, and he drew a deep breath as he pushed her ring to the first knuckle and stopped.

He spoke in a raspy voice. "With this ring, I thee wed." As he slid the ring on her finger, he held it there for a moment, squeezed her hand, then released it.

She glanced down. The heavy gold band held heart-shaped rubies interspersed with delicate Celtic scrolls. The ring was beautiful and perfect. She glanced at Colin. He smiled as he gazed at her.

Archie handed him something, then he turned and gave her his ring. It was heavy and oversized, made for his larger finger. He held out his right hand. As she stared at his hand, she remembered the day he talked about how his hand may be large, but it would never hurt her.

Tears gathered in her eyes as she wished this was real. She examined the ring she placed on his finger, a circle that was supposed to represent their bond of matrimony. The pattern appeared identical to hers, a perfect match. As she held his hand, it blurred with her tears.

Her breath hitched when she spoke as a tear escaped. "With this ring, I thee wed."

The reverend spoke. "Ye may kiss yer bride, my laird."

Colin clung to their joined hands and kissed Bree deeply. He wrapped her in his embrace and shifted until his back was to the reverend as he finished the kiss. They stood close for a moment, their breath mingling as one, and gazed into each other's eyes.

His thumb caressed her cheek as he whispered, "I love ye, Bree."

A tear slid down her cheek. "I love you too."

Chapter 23

Constance linked her arm with Brielle's as the wedding party entered the great hall for the wedding feast. "Oh, that was so romantic! Come, let's go refresh ourselves."

Colin gripped her hand, pulling her back to him. "No, she'll stay with me."

Constance fluttered her lashes. "We'll only be upstairs, Roderick. We'll be right back."

He nodded and released her hand but squeezed it once before fully letting go. "I'll be here. Don't be gone long, Bree."

The two women headed toward the stairway. But as they neared, Constance changed direction toward the kitchens.

Bree pulled on her arm. "Where are you going? My bedroom is upstairs."

Constance stopped smiled sweetly as she spoke in a high-pitched voice, "I thought ye and I could have a friendship stone vow in the chapel."

She wasn't certain what Constance was getting at, wanting to return to the chapel. A friendship ceremony. She doubted this woman had one ounce of friendship in her body.

She smiled. "Constance, that really isn't necessary. We are already friends."

Constance dragged her out the kitchen door into

the bailey. "I insist. It will only take a moment, and then ye can be by yer lover again."

Constance was adamant about it. Maybe she was genuinely trying to be a friend.

Brielle glanced over her shoulder as they strode away from the castle. "Well, only a moment."

Constance dragged her into the dark chapel. When everyone left, they had extinguished the candles, but she could still smell the heated wax lingering in the chapel. In the distance, thunder rumbled, and a shiver rolled down her spine.

Brielle tried to pull her hand from Constance's. "Constance, maybe we should do this tomorrow. It's getting late, and they will miss us at the feast."

"Nonsense." Constance dragged Brielle behind the altar. "Here, here is where we will make our vow."

Shadows creeped all around them, as if the spirits of the dead were closing in. Constance pulled a gem from her pouch and held the stone palm up, offering it to Brielle. She glanced at Constance, then at the stone. The rock appeared oval, in a purple so dark it was almost black. She picked up the gem and held it in her palm. The stone was very cold.

As she stared at the stone, it glowed, lighting up the chapel with its deep purple hue. Thunder boomed, causing her to jump.

Constance took hold of both her hands, wrapping them around the gem, and held her tight. She softly whispered words Brielle could not understand, then released her hands as she stepped back. Brielle stood there a moment, staring at Constance. A peculiar sensation washed over her, as if someone walked over her grave.

Constance clapped her hands above her head just as lightning lit the chapel. The wind swirled around the inside. Brielle looked around the chapel, then turned to Constance and gasped. Constance's eyes were black, her face an ashen gray. Her hair had come undone and flew about her. The woman lifted her face to the ceiling as the wind whipped harder around them. Brielle held on to the stone, trying to find an anchor in the surrounding whirlwind.

Constance chanted into the wind:

Wind blow and trouble turn
bring forth the might and shed a tear,
Let not the lover's heart yearn
for her, bring forth her greatest fear

As a deep purple light radiated between her fingers, the rock turned to ice. Brielle tried to drop it but couldn't. Why wouldn't her hands move? And they were so cold, she feared they had frozen to the stone.

Constance cackled and said in a deep tone, "Tell me, *whore*, what's yer greatest fear?"

Brielle panicked as the stone held her frozen and the wind whirling around them sped up. *No, this cannot be happening. My fear. I cannot tell her. The dark place, all alone, the storm raging.* She sucked in a breath when the memory came at her, fast. It was so vivid that she cried out, and a tear escaped. The storm—the shed—the thunder. *No!* She fought against her mind.

Brielle yelled over the wind: "No, I will not tell you."

Constance cackled again, then leveled her black glare at her. "Too late. I already know."

Constance clapped her hands above her head.

Thunder cracked again, and the lightning's glare filled the nave. The stone flashed a bright white light, once.

The floor gave way beneath Brielle, causing her to fall into the crypt and land on her side as she cried out in pain.

Constance glared down from the opening above her. "Whore, ye had to get in the way. In the way of our plan. It was so easy. Kill Mary, cast a love spell on Roderick, and he would lead me to the Stone of Love."

Brielle tried to sit up, but everything hurt. Her arm slipped, and her body fell back to the floor. *Why, why is Constance doing this, and for what plan? Whose plan? Wait, the Stone of Love, she said, Stone of Love, the Fae stone.*

That's when it hit her—Constance was the evil Fae.

Constance laughed again, then pointed her finger at her. "When ye appeared at the portal, I knew they sent ye, the good Fae. Brigid thinks she's got the best of me, but she won't win. She won't find the Stone of Love."

Brigid? Who is Brigid, and why would she send me? She squinted up at Constance. "Who is Brigid?"

Constance screeched at her, spittle flying from her mouth. "Ye whore, ye know who she is!" Then she stilled and spoke calmly. "But it won't matter. Nothing will matter for ye anymore."

Constance waved her hand, and the purple stone flew into her palm. Brielle glanced at her own hand, empty, then back up at Constance. What was she doing with the stone?

Constance held the gem above the opening. "Good-bye, Brielle."

The stone glowed. The opening to the crypt closed.

She'd left Brielle alone in total darkness.

She tried to breathe but couldn't draw in air. As she shifted, she became dizzy. Her body hurt all over. Blackness closed in around her, seeming to squeeze her body. In the distance, thunder rumbled, and her heart nearly stopped.

****

Colin glanced at the stairs for the hundredth time. *What's taking that woman so long?*

He sat on the dais overlooking the hall of people as he took in the room. The reverend sat chatting with some people from the village. Colin eyed the guard, who casually leaned against the wall, and nodded once. The guard nodded back. Colin wouldn't allow the reverend out of his sight until this task was done. He glanced toward the stairs. Tonight would prove to be a long night.

He sensed someone slide into the seat beside him, Bree's seat. Thank God, Bree was back. He turned to face her, but it was Constance who glared back at him. He glanced around for Bree.

Constance picked up Bree's chalice, reserved for the wedding toast. "Roderick, I wish to toast ye."

What the hell was this woman about? She'd just witnessed his wedding to Bree.

His nostrils flared, and he bared his teeth as he spoke. "Where's Bree?"

Constance's deep laugh sent a chill down his back. "I toast my love for ye, Roderick." She drank the entire contents of the chalice and slammed it on the table.

His gaze slid to Archie, who shifted in his seat, turning toward them. Colin turned and spied the reverend standing across the hall, glaring his way.

"What have ye done, Constance?" he growled.

She filled the chalice again and drank it. He grabbed her hand, spilling the wine. A crimson stain spread on the white tablecloth. A chill slithered down Colin's spine. Constance scowled into his eyes. He stared back and saw that her eyeballs were entirely black.

Dread knifed through Colin when she spoke again. Her voice was deep and raspy, nothing like what Constance sounded like before.

"Yer whore, she is not here, Roderick. She's gone forever."

Colin's heart nearly stopped. Rage like nothing he had ever known spread through him when Constance said those words—*She's gone forever*. He yelled as he grabbed her, dragging her toward the study.

Bree couldn't be gone. He refused to accept it. He'd grill Constance for information, and then he'd find his wee Bree.

He bellowed behind him, "Archie, have the guards secure all entries and exits to the castle. No one comes in, and no one leaves without my permission. Have them search for Bree. Begin upstairs."

Constance cackled as he dragged her to the study, sending another set of chills down his spine. The wedding guests gasped as the spectacle unfolded.

Archie paused at the study door, whispering to two guards, who nodded as he closed the door after Colin and Constance. "The guards are searching the castle as we speak, my laird."

Colin threw Constance into a chair, placed his fists on both armrests, and glared into her face. She leaned forward, trying to kiss him.

He bucked back. "Ye bitch, what are ye about?"

Constance cackled again, then sounded like a toddler who had her toy taken away, her eyes still black. "I tried every spell on ye, Roderick. Every love spell I had. Ye needed to fall in love with me so we could find the Stone of Love and be all powerful."

The Stone of Love, she said, the Stone of Love. Good God, what had he done? It wasn't the reverend. He had made a mistake. No matter how hard he had tried, he had failed. He chose the wrong person. Good God, the Fae Fable—he had failed to keep Bree safe.

Constance spoke again in a high-pitched whine. "I needed the Stone of Love. The evil Fae will gather the Stones of Iona and control both realms."

Colin stepped back from her, pulling his hands as far away as possible. "It's ye. Ye are the evil Fae." He fisted his hands by his sides. "Love spells? Ye cast love spells on me for Roderick?" He threw his head back and laughed. "Yer foolish goblin, ye damn spells won't work."

He bent so his face was close until his nose almost touched hers. He wanted to make sure the evil Fae got his message. "Try all ye want, because I am not Roderick. I am Colin, his great-grandson from the future."

Constance switched to the low, raspy voice, which sounded like nails scraping on a chalkboard. "Ye are all fools. All of ye! Ye do not know the power we wield."

Colin stood back and stared at Constance as his mind reeled—the Fae had Bree. The maiden in the fable. Bree was the sacrifice. The Fae story had come true.

****

It was so dark she couldn't see anything. Not able to sense the surrounding space, she felt as if she hung in empty air. Thunder rumbled in the distance repeatedly, growing louder with each boom. She huddled in a ball, shaking. Everything hurt. Breathing hurt; thinking hurt. She lay there for a minute, then another and another. Her mind seemed to drift along with the black clouds of her mind, as if she floated out into the vast unknown. She feared she lost her sanity and curled deeper into herself, allowing her mind to shut down.

After some time, she remembered seeing the chapel for the first time through the woods, the setting sunlight flashed the building in crimson making it appear bathed in blood. She shivered. She then remembered meeting Colin for the first time in the study. Her breathing eased. She recalled the lads working in the chapel and her friendship with Marie.

After releasing some tension in her body, she took a deep breath. She no longer saw the dark but her fondest memories. The images flipped through her mind like a movie. She saw Colin and herself having dinner, sharing dessert and chocolate kisses. She took a deep breath and sighed.

She recalled coming to the castle for the first time; John and Mrs. Abernathy smiled at her. She remembered the stone Hamish gave her and the story of how the fisherman wished the Fae spell away. The pub joining in on the telling of the tale, making her feel welcome.

She reached for the necklace and gripped the Iona stone. Willing to try anything, she breathed deeply and chanted in her head, *I put dia eadar dhuinn, I put God between us*. She repeated it. *I put God between us*. Her mind's voice gathered strength as thunder reverberated louder, coming closer to the chapel.

She came up on her knees and gripped the gem to her chest. Her body curled over the stone, and she continued to chant aloud. "I put God between us. I put God between us."

She grasped the stone tighter as the thunder vibrated the crypt. She cried out and closed her eyes tighter. In her mind, she saw Colin as he held her through the storm in the study. Heard his heart beating against her ear. She focused all her energy on her love and passion for Colin at each beat of his heart: *bump bump, bump bump*. She felt her heart: *bump bump, bump bump.*

The Fae story Colin had told her came to her. Colin's voice came clear in her head. *"He made a necklace with a heart-shaped stone and always wore it so that he would know when his true love was near, because then the stone would glow."*

The quote from the *Fae Fable Book* where it had fallen open after their signing of the marriage contracts came to her. *Let love never leave ye; / Bind it around yer neck. / Keep it in the core of yer heart.*

The image of the sarcophagus lid of Lady Katherine MacDougall flashed into her mind. She recalled approaching the lady's casket and shining her flashlight on the top stone. The design was so beautiful. Her face was so serene. The Lady's arms lay folded across her chest, holding a heart. Brielle gasped. Lady Katherine was Roderick's ancestor. The casket was here in this time, here in the crypt.

"I know where the Stone of Love is," she whispered.

Brielle opened her eyes to a bright crimson light that glowed in the crypt. She turned to the sarcophagus of Lady Katherine MacDougall. The light came from the top. Brielle tried to get up but fell. She cried out and tried again, lumbering to a standing position.

Holding her Iona stone to her heart, she limped up to the coffin and peeked over the top, never taking her eyes from the flaming light. A heart-shaped stone glowed bright red on the top of the casket. Brielle reached for the gem. But when she tried to pick it up, her hand passed through it.

****

Colin stood over Constance, the evil Fae, as she spewed her venom. "Our power is greater than you could ever know. Ye are just as much a fool as yer mother was. The Stone of Love was there. I knew it. The Stone of Fear glowed and told me so."

His mother. Why was Constance speaking of his mother?

Constance glanced down, then back at Colin. "But when we opened the crypt, the damn stone was gone," she said, panting. "Yer mother claimed she knew nothing of the stone, but I knew she lied, and they both died for it. True love, *bah*! Ye are a fool like yer parents."

Colin's heart stopped. He wasn't certain he'd heard her right. "My parents?" She spoke of his mother, the crypt, and the Stone of Love.

Then it clicked in his mind, and he gasped. "It was ye—ye were there. Ye possessed Sarah Ross in the future, just as ye have possessed Constance now in the past."

He growled deep in his chest. She had robbed him

of his da, his ma. "You were the one, the evil Fae. You did it." He heaved a deep breath. "You killed my parents."

Where was his wee Bree? Constance knew, and he had to get it out of her. Colin had to find her before they killed her, too. He had to get to Bree.

Constance screamed and grabbed a stone from her pouch. "Ye will now know the worst fear ye have ever known."

Archie lunged, grabbing the rock from Constance. "No, ye won't be using that."

Colin took Constance by the shoulders, lifting her from the chair, her feet dangling off the floor.

She smiled into his face as he roared into hers. "What have ye done to her?"

Constance smiled as she whispered in the deep, raspy voice of the evil Fae. "Her greatest fear will be her doom. She will die tonight and rot in her grave for eternity."

Colin dropped her. Her head hit the desk, knocking her out.

He stood panting in panic. *Her greatest fear?* He ran the words through his mind. *Rot in her grave for eternity. Where could she be?* Rot in her grave. A grave. Thunder boomed in the distance. *Bree's afraid of...*

His gaze snapped to Archie. "The crypt, the chapel."

Archie handed him the purple stone. "Ye'll need this. I suspect it's the Stone of Fear the evil Fae have been using."

Colin nodded to the unconscious Constance lying on the floor. "Bind her. Don't let her loose. I've got to save Bree."

Colin ran along the path to the chapel. He knew roughly where the opening to the crypt was and hoped he had arrived in time. Lightning sparked and thunder surged. His heart shuddered with each flash and boom. *Bree. He had to get to her.*

He crossed to the altar, stepped behind it, and glanced around. *Open it.* There had to be a blade, a hammer, or something. All he had was the Stone of Fear. There was nothing he could do to break the stone flooring.

The Fae stones are powered by human will and emotion, echoed in his head. A line from the Fae Fable story. A Fae stone. He stared at the purple stone in his hand. It was up to him. He must make this work. This was his only chance to save Bree.

Gripping the Stone of Fear, his fear grew deeper in his heart. He focused his energy on the stone, and it glowed purple in his hands. His fear leaped. The thought snapped into his head so fast it was dizzying. He controlled the stone's power. All he must do was concentrate on wielding it. *Bree, I'm coming.*

He concentrated on his fear for Bree. Lightning lit the chapel as thunder exploded closer. He concentrated harder, thinking of his love for Bree, pouring all his emotions from his heart through his arms, to his hands, and into the stone. It glowed brighter as his love for her flowed from his heart. He closed his eyes, concentrating on his fear that he wouldn't be able to keep her safe.

The stone warmed and glowed brighter. He needed more, more power. Colin opened his heart to his emotions for Bree. The rock grew hot. He opened his eyes, and red glowed from the hole in the floor before him.

He dropped to his knees, leaning in. "Bree?" he yelled.

Only silence answered his call. His heart skipped a beat, and he listened, but still nothing. He sucked in a breath and shouted again, but stopped when a shuffling sound came from the crypt.

God, let her be alive.

He listened, and the shuffling came to him again. Then came the best sound he had heard in his entire life.

"Colin?"

He dropped into the crypt and spotted Bree immediately, lying on the ground. Scrambling to her, he gathered her into his arms, kissing her deeply. Tears streamed down her cheeks. He cupped her face in his hands and stared into her eyes as she gazed back with love flowing from her heart.

The red light pulsed. "Colin, you will not believe what I found."

He released a breath he did not realize he was holding. "Ye found something old that ye liked, did ye?"

She smiled. "Better. I found the Stone of Love."

Colin blinked. The crypt was lit in a red light. *She said the Stone of Love was here.* His love was before him, and the stone glowed.

She grabbed his hand, trying to stand, and he helped her up. "See, the glowing red stone? It is the Stone of Love. It was inside her necklace like the Fae Fable story. But when I went to pick it up, my hand passed through it."

Colin continued to hold her in his arms. He had

her, had saved her, and would not let her go. He glanced at the stone. As he held her, he sensed her heartbeat. The stone pulsed, and he felt his heart pulse in response. He stared into her eyes and saw his love, his wee Bree. He knew then the greatest power of all, the power of true love.

Brigid's voice echoed in his head. *"Remember, the key is not a key, but is the key. The key can only be revealed when the heart is pure, and both true love's hands are joined. That which is the key will be shown to the one who needs it most, only when they need it most."*

They were the key. "It must be both of us, Bree. Apart, our love is strong, but together, combined, our love is powerful. We are the key together."

He took her hand in his, and they approached the sarcophagus. Linked, their hands formed the shape of a heart. Sliding their hands beneath the stone, Colin felt the weight.

Together, they picked up the Stone of Love and held it between them. The red glow pulsed to the beat of their hearts.

****

Colin pulled Bree out of the crypt and held her in his arms. "God, I'll never let ye go again."

He slid his arms around her, supporting her as she limped with him toward the chapel entrance. A whoosh filled the nave, and he glanced back. The opening to the crypt had disappeared. The stone floor was the same as before, as if nothing had disturbed it.

Bree shifted in his embrace and gripped both stones in her hands. Colin's arms supported her as she limped with him. Everything would be okay now. They could travel back to the twenty-first century and return Roderick to his time.

Colin had found the Stone of Fear and the Stone of Love. He had captured the evil Fae. Bree was safe with him. He had changed the course of the Fae Fable story. He drew a deep breath and released it.

They made their way to the door of the chapel. Colin prayed this would be the end of his task and that they would go back together.

He opened the chapel door. A dark figure rushed them, wielding a knife aimed at Bree's heart. Colin reacted without thinking. As he shifted Bree behind him, he grabbed the knife, twisted, and stabbed the cloaked figure in the chest. Colin caught the person, and they both slid to the ground. He flipped the figure over to see who it was.

Constance Ross lay panting, a grimace of pain on her face. In her normal voice, she whispered, "Why? Why couldn't ye love me?" Blood flowed from her mouth and down the side of her face as she coughed. She took a gurgling breath, and another, then froze, never breathing again.

Colin rose and stepped backward. Constance's blood spread out under her, covering the chapel entryway. He glanced at Bree, who stood holding the stones to her chest. Colin covered her hands with his, and they stood there in the chapel doorway. This must be the end of their journey. He could now get them both back to the twenty-first century.

The doorway glowed in bright white light. Colin felt the stones warm his hands. He saw Bree glance at their hands, which glowed brightly.

Brigid materialized over the door. "Ye must make

a choice."

Colin roared. "No, I choose us both!" He pulled Bree close to him, gripping the stones.

Bree glanced up. "Colin, is that a Fae?"

Brigid shook her head. "This cannot be undone. Colin, the evil Fae have cast their spell. One of you must take the Stone of Love forward in time. The other will go with the Stone of Fear to purgatory. It is an evil Fae spell. It cannot be undone."

Colin roared again. "No, I will not do it this way. True love...the story said true love would conquer all." He panted as he held their hands close to his chest, trying to bring her closer to his heart.

He yelled louder. "I love her. It will not end this way, ye damn sprite. I refuse to accept this."

Brigid sighed. "Choose, Colin, or the Fae will make the choice for ye."

He held Bree tighter, trying to shut Brigid out. Brielle glanced at the stones held between them, then stepped out of his embrace. He didn't know why, but he let her. She gathered his hands in hers, both stones held together between them. All he saw was her, his wee Bree.

Tears streamed down her face. "Colin, I love you. I'll go...I'll be the one." She handed him the Stone of Love, holding on to the Stone of Fear.

Colin shook his head as tears built up in his eyes. *No, she would not do this!* He wouldn't allow it. He wanted to keep her safe, safe from evil, and he had failed. He failed her, and he failed the Fae. It was him. He had to go. She needed to remember. He had to tell her, so she'd know he'd come back.

He took her hands in his, a stone in each hand. "Ye

remember the day I took ye to the cabin?"

Bree nodded, tears flowing down her cheeks.

"Do ye remember the seals at the point? The seal story I told ye the morning we sailed back?"

Bree nodded and whimpered. He took a deep breath. He had to make sure she knew he loved her with all his heart.

"Brielle, no matter where I go, no matter what separates us, ye will always and forever be my true love."

Bree shook her head as tears freely streamed down her cheeks.

He drew a shaky breath and whispered in a broken voice, "Never fear I will not come back."

He gave Brielle a kiss on her lips, took the Stone of Fear from her hands and stepped back through the doorway while shoving the Stone of Love into hers, pushing her backward into the chapel and into the future.

****

When Archibald arrived at the doorway, Roderick tripped out the chapel door and fell over the cloaked body on the ground, flipping it over.

Archibald ran to his side and helped him up. "Colin, I got here as soon as I could. The damn bitch got away from me."

As Archibald helped the man from the ground, he stared directly into Roderick's eyes. "Archibald, who the hell is Colin?"

Archibald glanced at the body on the ground.

Roderick followed his gaze. "God no, Mary! Someone stabbed Mary." He bent over the body and turned it over. It was Constance.

Roderick glanced from Constance to him. "Why is Constance dead at me chapel door, and where is Mary?" He turned around. "Where are Rose and Alex? My mother?"

Archibald smiled, grabbing Roderick in a tight hug, clapping him on the back. "God, it's good to have ye back, Roderick. Ye will not believe what I've been through these past weeks."

Archibald released him from the embrace, and the heavens broke open into a downpour.

Covering their heads with his plaid, Archibald grabbed Roderick's arm. "Come on, let's get back to the castle and out of this rain. I'll tell ye all about it inside."

Roderick stopped. "What about her?"

Archibald waved his hand. "I'll send the guard after her body."

As they hurried back to the castle, Archibald chuckled. "I tucked Mary, Alex, and Rose away in the hunting cabin, safe with yer ma. Ye will not believe what we've been through. Oh, and I have news. I'm to be a father."

Roderick stopped and clapped Archibald on the back. "Archibald, that's great news."

Archibald replied, "Aye, it is. But call me Archie. The nickname has grown on me."

****

Dunstaffnage Castle, Present Day

Brielle tripped and fell on the floor, still holding the Stone of Love as she cried out in pain. She scrambled to stand and turned to the chapel door. It was closed. She whipped around, looking throughout the chapel. It was in a state of disarray from the construction. The scent of dust hung heavy in the air.

She ran to the door and banged on it, crying. "No, no, no, Colin, no." She hit it again with her hands and cried out in pain.

She slid down the door, curling into a ball, and yelled as loud and as long as her breath allowed. "*No!*"

Chapter 24

"Is she at the dock again, staring at the seals?" Marie nodded at John's question. Marie sat on John's bed and couldn't stop her hands from fidgeting. He paced before the fire and ran his hand through his hair.

"Ye need to tell her, John. She can't keep going on this way." John stopped and stared out the window. A month had gone by since they found Brielle in the chapel. She was inconsolable since she had come back from the past. He and Marie had tried different tactics to bring her out of her deep melancholy. Mrs. A. had tried plying her with food—made her molten lava cake, her favorite, which only made her burst into tears. Even the chapel renovation project couldn't lift her spirits. And now that it was almost complete, she had sunk deeper into depression.

Marie sighed. "I saw her yesterday staring at the portrait again, the one of Roderick that seems like Colin." Marie took a deep breath. "John, she says it moves. But when I stare at it, it's the same painting I've seen repeatedly. There's no movement. I'm worried."

John nodded. He was worried as well.

Her pregnancy did not help the situation either. John rubbed his neck. She had talked about returning to the States, convinced Colin would never return. John had hoped he would have returned by now. Brielle constantly mentioned that she feared the spell would last forever.

He blew a laugh. He even resorted to standing in the chapel one night, yelling at the top of his lungs for Morrigan, his Fae. When she didn't appear, he yelled for Colin's Fae, Brigid. When she didn't appear, he left the chapel. To this day, he'd heard nothing from them.

He was so desperate he paid a visit to his grandma.

Granny only shrugged and said, "If it's how the Fae want it, then that's the way it will be."

John glanced at Marie, who sat waiting for his response. "I've asked Ainslie to visit with her. Maybe that will help."

Marie shook her head. "Having Colin's sister visit Brielle won't help her if you don't tell her all ye know. I know ye are waiting for Colin, but I don't think he's coming back. She has a right to know what he has done and what it means for her and the baby."

John shrugged. "All right, I'll agree with ye and Ainslie. Let's call a meeting."

****

The following day, Brielle made her way to the study. John had asked for a meeting, saying he had some things to discuss with her. She avoided the room since her return, not sure if she could set foot in there without Colin.

John insisted she stay in Scotland to have the baby, but she knew she couldn't stay here without Colin. She was not his wife. She didn't belong in his family home. Even though John told her that was not an issue, it still didn't seem right to stay there.

Brielle was more worried after her recent checkup at the doctor.

She sighed, thinking of a dream she'd had last

night. In it, the Green Lady, the ghost of Dunstaffnage castle, stood at the end of her bed, smiling while tears streamed down her face. Smiling meant good for the MacDougall family, while crying meant bad—*but both?*

Brielle stood at the study door, staring at it. They had left it cracked open, but she didn't want to go in.

She must have made a noise because Marie opened the door and smiled at her. "You are here."

She took Brielle's hand and escorted her to the couch. Colin, the storm, the couch. Her mind flooded with the memories of when she first fell in love with him, and tears gathered in her eyes. Marie sat on the sofa and pulled her down next to her.

She glanced up to see a tall woman with jet-black hair standing at the fireplace, watching her. She was very regal but with a sweet smile. Brielle examined her. There was something familiar about her, but she couldn't quite pinpoint what it was.

Her face must have shown her thoughts, because the woman spoke in a heavy Scottish accent. "I know. The resemblance is uncanny, eh? But at least I don't look exactly like some old portrait."

Brielle scrunched her nose, and the woman laughed. She moved gracefully, fluidly, like a cat, and sat next to her on the couch.

John spoke from his spot near the fireplace. "Bree, this is Ainslie, Colin's sister. I asked her to come today, to represent the clan. She knows about the stones, the Fae, and who Brigid is. About Colin's true location."

Ainslie patted Brielle's hands. "Ye are Brielle, my brother's true love."

She stared at this woman, seeing Colin in her

features, and a tear escaped. "I miss him so much," she whispered.

Ainslie gathered her in a hug. "I know ye do. I do too."

Ainslie rocked her as she softly cried, then released her. Marie offered Brielle a tissue.

"I'm sorry. I'm a mess these days," said Brielle.

Marie hugged her. "It's okay. We are all here for ye." Marie glanced at John, making a face.

Brielle wished, more than ever, that Colin was here.

John cleared his throat. "I had hoped to wait for Colin's return."

Brielle tried not to cry, but a soft sob escaped.

Marie patted her hand as John continued, "Marie and Ainslie insisted I go against Colin's instructions and tell ye now."

Instructions? What instructions would Colin leave? How could he have known anything before he left? So much has happened in the time since he went back in time. What would he have her do, now that she was here, and he was gone?

"Colin's instructions?" She sat forward.

John nodded. "Ye see, Colin and I developed a way for him to send me documents from the past so I can get them in the future. I'd gotten documents from him until the wedding day."

He'd piqued her curiosity. Brielle dried her tears and sniffled, wiping her face with the tissue. He sent documents. What would he say? What would he have her do? Was he sending her away now that he was not returning?

"W-What has he said?"

John smiled. "Well, the day ye went back in time, he told me a storm blew through the chapel door. So, I knew ye had gotten there safe. I was anxious when ye disappeared without a word."

A storm blew through the chapel door, his wee Bree. Her heart lifted, hearing his nickname for her, his endearment. At that moment, she fell in love with him all over again.

She smiled and took a breath. "What else did he say?"

John glanced at Ainslie, who rose and joined him at the fireplace. His gaze went to Marie, then her. "Well, the day before yer wedding, he sent a scroll of documents. One had orders on what I was to do with them here, in our time."

Brielle tilted her head as John spoke.

"He instructed me to send one document to Edinburgh, to his law firm, for filing with the courts. It also contained orders about what to do if he didn't come back through the portal with ye."

A document filed with the courts. What would he want filed here in the present while they were in the past? Had she done something wrong?

Brielle stared at her hands, held in Marie's, and spoke with a hitch in her voice. "What was the document he wanted filed in Edinburgh?" Marie briefly squeezed her hand, and the couch dipped as John sat next to her.

He patted their hands. "It was the marriage contract ye both signed in the past." Brielle's head came up, and she blinked at John.

He nodded. "Ye are married to Colin, Brielle." Married? Did John say married? But he said it was a lie, a trick to oust the evil Fae. The whole thing was a ruse.

She shook her head. "That can't be true." She glanced at Marie, then Ainslie, and back at John. "I watched him sign it. I saw the signatures. He signed *Roderick MacDougall*. The contract was for me to marry Roderick, not Colin."

John chuckled. "Ye don't know Colin as well as ye think."

Ainslie laughed. "She knows him. He's just never played his tricks on her until now."

Brielle stared at them all. Had she gone nuts? They all believed she was married to Colin, but she saw the signature.

John got up from the couch and retrieved a document from the desk. Returning, he held it in front of her. She took it, the paper shaking as her hands trembled.

John stood before her, smiling. "This is a copy of what we filed for ye and Colin."

She held the document, the modern paper at odds with the curvy script written with a quill. The copy seemed the same as the one she had signed in the past, confusing her more. At the top, it said, "Contract of Marriage." Her gaze dropped to the signatures at the bottom, Roderick MacDougall and Brielle Elise DeVolt. She grasped the stone around her neck, the memory of their wedding so clear in her mind. She choked on a sob. The signature was the same. It was not Colin's name.

"It says *Roderick MacDougall*."

John grinned. "Ye aren't looking close enough, Bree... It's before the *R* of *Roderick*." Brielle squinted at the signature, loopy and decorative. Not typical for a man as masculine as Colin. She blinked and then saw it, a *C*.

She scrunched her nose and glanced at John. "There's a *C* before *Roderick*, but that doesn't make it Colin, and I doubt this document is legal in our time." She tried handing the document back to John, but he stood there with his hands folded, smiling at her.

Ainslie laughed. "He's got ye good this time, Bree. I couldn't have come up with this one."

Brielle glanced at Ainslie, thinking she had gone crazy.

Marie patted her back and gave John a stern glance. "John, explain it to her before she falls into another fit of tears."

John took a deep breath. "Bree, Colin's middle name is Roderick. His formal name is Colin Roderick MacDougall. Ye are legally and truly wed to Colin in the past and in this time. He explained to me he had ye sign two documents. One dated in the past, and one dated in the future."

She let her breath out in a whoosh and must have wavered sideways, because Marie held her upright. At the wedding ceremony he had paused before saying "Roderick." She thought it strange at the time to stop before saying his name, but now she realized why he had her whisper his name before her vows. He had her whisper "Colin," so she'd say his full name.

She looked at John. "Wait, he told me the wedding was fake. He claimed it wouldn't be real."

John shrugged. "This is what he sent me, Bree. This is real as they come, and ye are legally his wife."

Brielle rubbed her forehead. If she thought things were complicated before, they were genuinely difficult now. Instructions. John had talked about "instructions." What would Colin expect of her, now that she was his wife? "You mentioned instructions if he should not return. What are those?"

John nodded and took a deep breath. "Well, what I can tell ye is he thought ye both would return together, but if he didn't, I was to wait for him to come back. It's been some time, but he left separate instructions for me if he didn't return." Didn't return. He knew he might not return to the present. How had he known, and how long had he known? What would he want from her now, have her do?

"What were his directions?" Her breath hitched as she spoke.

John rose from the couch and crossed to stand next to Ainslie by the fireplace. "I haven't opened them until today and only at their insistence." John gestured with his chin toward Ainslie and Marie. "And I am glad I did. I hoped he would make it back by now. He had intentions of telling ye about the wedding on his own. He has given ye the full support of his family. Ye have the clan of MacDougall as yer family now. And now that you carry the heir, be it the future laird or lady, ye will have the clan's full benefits to support ye."

Have the clan support her? What does that mean? Did she want any of this without the one man who had made it all worthwhile? Did she want any of this without Colin?

She glanced from John to Ainslie. "What does that mean?"

John stepped forward and knelt before her. "Well, ye can live in Colin's flat in Edinburgh."

Ainslie picked up the conversation. "Or Dunollie

Castle, where we were raised."

Marie took her hand. "Or here at Dunstaffnage, where you fell in love."

Brielle sobbed, new tears streaming down her face. Here is where she fell in love, in love with Colin. Here without him, alone. She couldn't do it. She didn't have the strength to do any of this alone.

John smiled widely. "Ye will want for nothing. Ye will raise Colin's child here with his family, yer family."

Brielle put her head in her hands. *Here without Colin*. It was too much. She could not have his children without him—she simply could not live without him.

She jumped up from the couch and paced before the desk. "I can't live here without him. I can't live *anywhere* without him." She stopped and stared at the three people desperately trying to help and not seeing the one person who could. "He's not coming back."

Her throat closed up, and fresh tears flowed down her face. "I won't live in his home without being with him—us, together. It would tear my heart out, and it would kill my soul." She hit her chest with her fist as a new sob escaped. "He's not coming back. I want to go away. I want to go home, but I don't know where home is without him."

Brielle crumpled to her knees, and Marie came and put her arms around her.

She sobbed on her friend's shoulder. "I can't have his children without him."

Marie sucked in a breath and looked at John.

"Children?" he said.

Brielle lifted her face. "Yes, I just found out I'm having twins."

They all gaped at her in stunned silence, and all she could do was double over and cry.

Marie was the first to respond. "Bree, that's great news."

Her statement made her cry harder. "No. If I go back to the States, I'll have to do so soon, or I won't be able to travel until after they are born."

John grunted. "Ye will not be leaving. Colin would not want that, and I won't allow it." She raised her head and looked at him through her tears. He almost sounded like Colin.

Ainslie chimed in. "This is great news. We get two for the price of one."

Brielle stared at them. They'd all gone nuts, and she feared she'd gone crazy as well.

Marie patted her back again and made a face at John, then looked back at Brielle.

Now what did they have in store for her? This was the end of her rope, the last thread of her sanity, and it was almost gone.

"Ye need to give her the letter," Marie pleaded as John nodded. Marie helped her up, settling her in a chair before the desk.

John picked up a sealed scroll and held it out to her. She sat staring at it, fearful of touching it, for it seemed old. But John said Colin had written it and left it for her. Something of his to her.

If she touched it, would she sense him? Would she feel Colin?

John spoke softly. "I have not opened it, on his instructions. I was to give it to you if he could not make it back within a year, but the women felt differently, considering the pregnancy."

She sniffled. "A year? Why a year?"

John huffed a laugh as Ainslie spoke from the fireplace. "It will sound silly, but da always insisted that only the damned deserve to be in purgatory. If they sent a good soul, it would release them in twelve months. My ma said it was the passing of the moon cycle. They argued over it constantly."

John nodded. "Colin believed that since he was a good soul, he would only serve a year in purgatory and not forever. He always thought he would come back."

As she took the scroll from John, Colin's voice echoed in her mind. *"Never fear I will not come back."* The thick, old vellum crinkled as she took hold of it.

John glanced at Ainslie, then Marie, and nodded at the door with his chin. "We'll leave ye to open it alone. Just call if ye need anything." They filed out, leaving her holding the last proof of Colin's existence on earth.

She went to the window, holding the scroll to her chest, close to her heart. Knowing Colin had touched it was enough to sense his soul touching hers. She stared at it and couldn't help but get excited to read the words, words from him to her. She broke the seal and carefully opened the scroll.

1720, 15 April

My Dearest Bree,

If John has given you this letter, it has been a year since I've held you in my arms. Too long to be apart. I hope ye never see this letter and that I followed ye through the portal. If I have not made it back by this time, we have only one hope.

I pray that your will and love are strong enough for the trial you will face.

Ye must read the entire story of the Fae Fable

Book, the Stone of Love. There ye will find the way to bring me to your arms.

Please remember the seals. Bree, no matter where I go, no matter if something separates us. Ye will always and forever be my true love. Never fear that I will not come back.

Your true love,

Colin

Brielle wept. The Fae locked the *Fae Fable Book* in a case with no key. How was she supposed to read the story and find the answer?

She pulled the Stone of Love from her pocket. Bree had not let it out of her possession since she and Colin found it. She carried it everywhere, hoping it would glow, telling her Colin was nearby. She even slept with it, believing Colin was with her.

She held it against her Iona stone—his mother's stone. The same rock on which she had pledged her love to Colin. A stone with which she would never part. The MacDougall love stone, for Colin held the other half, and together it made a heart.

Brielle sobbed again, held both stones in her hand, and prayed for Colin's return.

The *Fae Fable Book* thumped in its case. Her gaze shot to it. The glass case was gone, and the book sat open so she could touch it, hold it, and read it. She approached the book, not sure of what she would find. She reached out to touch it, not believing that the glass cover was gone.

Bree touched the page. It was warm, like a warm body breathing hope into her soul. She sensed Colin's presence, felt his arms embrace her. She closed her eyes, afraid it would go away. She took a deep breath, opened her eyes. The book lay open to the Stone of Love fable, and her pulse quickened.

She read the first page, then turned it and read some more. When she got about three-quarters into the story, the version Colin told her wasn't this version. She came upon the end of the fable and gasped. Here was what Colin wanted her to see—here was the answer to her prayers. She read on…

Upon arriving at the castle, he confronted the evil Fae. The Stone of Love burned his clothes and chest when he approached her. Angry that she had been discovered, the evil Fae cast a spell upon the village girl and the prince, opening a portal to purgatory.

"True love or a lifetime in purgatory—choose yer fate," she yelled at the prince.

Confused, the prince asked, "Why do you do this? Why do you hate so much?"

The village girl answered for the evil Fae. "She does not hate; she is fearful. The opposite of love is not hate, but fear."

Taking the stone from his neck, the prince offered it to his true love, the maiden from the stream.

"I shall live forever in purgatory so ye may live a full life. Take the Stone of Love." But her love for him was so strong that she could not allow the prince to sacrifice himself for her, the village girl. When he handed her the stone, she thrust it into his hands and jumped into the portal, casting herself into purgatory, saving the prince.

Brielle gasped—this was what Brigid meant at the chapel doorway in the past.

Colin roared, "No, I choose us both," as he gripped her close.

Brigid shook her head. "This cannot be undone. Colin, the evil Fae have cast their spell. One of ye must take the Stone of Love forward in time. The other will go with the Stone of Fear to purgatory. It is an evil Fae spell. It cannot be undone."

Colin roared again. "No, I will not do it this way. True love...the story said true love would conquer all." He panted as he held their hands close to his chest. "I love her. It will not end this way, ye damn sprite. I refuse to accept this."

Brigid sighed. "Choose, Colin, or the Fae will make the choice for ye."

Colin had chosen her life over his. A tear trailed down her face as she read on.

So angered by this, the prince turned upon the evil Fae and drove his sword through her heart while holding the necklace with the Stone of Love in the same hand as the sword. The evil Fae's blood dripped from the blade to the Stone of Love. Dropping his sword to the ground, the prince fell to his knees, gripping the Stone of Love to his heart. He prayed to the Fae that his true love would return to him.

Dagda, the king of the Tuath Dé, appeared. "I am sorry, Prince, I cannot help ye. A spell cast by the evil Fae I cannot undo. But I can give ye a chant, and ye may call her back if yer love is powerful enough. But I warn ye: the chant will fail if she does not return yer love."

Roaring in his pain, the prince focused his prayer on his one true love. He chanted:

I want to see love's highest power
Take me now, not to my past
Right now, at this hour,

Bring my true love back at last

He prayed over and over. He closed his eyes and poured all his love into his one wish. The Stone of Love grew hot in his hand, so hot he had to let it go. It floated to the center of the room, hovering above everyone, and glowed pure white. The prince kept repeating his chant. The Stone of Love burst into a million points of light, blinding everyone for a moment. When their eyes adjusted, they saw the village girl standing in the center of the room.

Overcome with emotion, the prince threw his arms around her and kissed her. The sun shone through the glass window above them and cast them in a halo of light.

Dagda said to all in the room, "The greatest power of all is true love."

Colin's voice echoed in her head once more. *"Remember, the key is not a key but is the key. The key can only be revealed when the heart is pure, and both true love's hands have joined. The key will be shown to the one who needs it most, and only when they need it most."*

Brielle gazed at the Stone of Love in her hand. She gasped and looked out the window through the trees to the chapel in the woods. Then she recalled the rest of what he said, the night in the crypt when they'd found the Stone of Love:

"It must be both of us, Bree. Our love is the greatest power. Apart, our love is strong, but together, combined, our love is powerful. We are the key together."

Colin's mother, Emily, believed the chapel held power. Hamish's story flashed through her mind. The fisherman prayed over the Iona stone, and the spell vanished. The Fae Fable came true. One had gone to purgatory. It also said the prince prayed over the stone and brought the maiden back *from purgatory*. She held an Iona Stone, a magic Fae stone.

She knew what she must do. She now knew how to bring Colin back to her.

Chapter 25

John, Marie, and Ainslie sat on the couch in the great hall before the fireplace. Marie kept glancing over her shoulder at the study door.

She glanced back at John. "It's been a while. Ye think we should check on her?"

John shrugged. "This was both yer ideas. I went against Colin's wishes, hoping ye women would know what was best."

Ainslie laughed. "John, ye're such a typical man. Ye went along with this because ye knew it was the right thing to do. Sometimes, Colin can be such a blockhead—he needs a good kick in the—"

The study door burst open.

Bree ran into the great hall. "I'm coming, Colin. I'm coming."

The three by the fireplace stared at each other. There was a moment of stunned silence.

Marie was the first to speak. "Did she just say, 'I'm coming, Colin'?"

Ainslie smiled. "Aye, she did."

****

Brielle was out of breath by the time she reached the chapel. No longer afraid of the doorway, she burst through the double doors and glanced up at the circular stained-glass window. It was exactly like the one in the past. She thanked her pictorial memory. She'd reproduced almost all the drawings from the past so Marie could finish the chapel renovations.

This was the first time she had seen the new windows, and she was thankful she had waited for Colin. It was nearing dusk, so the cross-shaped light from the window should soon align with the cross on the mosaic flooring. Colin's mother had suspected there was mystical power when the window and flooring pattern aligned. Well, Bree was ready to put that theory to the test. Anything to bring Colin back—*anything.*

She faced the altar and lowered herself to her knees in the chapel center. *Please make this work.*

Holding the Stone of Love with both palms, she pressed the gem against her skin over her heart. Recalling the chant from the Fae Fable, she took a deep breath and closed her eyes. She thought it over once, then chanted it out loud repeatedly:

I want to see love's highest power
Take me now, not to my past
Right now, at this hour,
Bring my true love back at last

Brielle poured all her emotions into the chant. She thought of her love for Colin. When she peeked from beneath her lashes, nothing happened. She concentrated harder, demanding the stone's magic to work. *This must bring back Colin.*

She thought of when she first met him, speaking of his mother's loss and hers. She thought of the picnic he took her on, wanting to help her headache go away. The dinner they shared, chocolate kisses. She continued to chant, but nothing happened.

She recalled the sailboat trip, all the conversations they shared, their hopes and dreams. The hunting cabin, the storm in the present and the past. The past and how he healed her soul, chased away her fears like he had with the storm. She peeked again at the stone. It hadn't glowed. She cried out, desperate to get her true love back.

Time had passed, and she grew weary. Her knees hurt from the stone flooring, but she continued. She remembered the moment at the portal and how he took the Stone of Fear, going to purgatory to save her. Colin needed to come back. She lowered her head to the floor and kept chanting. So tired, she curled up in a ball. Her chanting came out like a whisper now, as she had almost lost her voice. Still, nothing happened.

The sun's rays through the stained glass crept along the floor. The cross shadow slipped over her aligning with her body and the cross on the floor. The Stone of Love warmed in her hand. Brielle gasped and peeked down. The gem glowed, but only in the center and not bright as in the past.

She sat up, gripped the stone with both hands, and placed it in the stream of sunlight from the stained glass. As the rock became hot, it glowed a vivid red. So hot and bright that Brielle had to release it. The stone lifted from her hands, floating in the chapel, rising to the center. Bree got up and stood directly under it as it pulsed with the beat of her heart. Her Iona stone warmed on her chest. She wrapped her hand around it.

She closed her eyes and concentrated, focused on her love for Colin. She pictured his face smiling at her, his charm, his humor, his love. *Colin.* She sensed his spirit nearby and opened her eyes. A flash of light from the stained-glass window shot through the gem to the altar, momentarily blinding Bree. She covered her face with her arm, still holding her stone necklace, not wanting to let go of anything that felt like Colin. The light faded, and she lowered her arm. The Stone of Love was in one hand, and her Iona stone was in the other.

Her name whispered in the wind, so light she wasn't certain if she had imagined it or not. She turned toward the altar and gasped. Colin stood in his wedding clothes from the past. She blinked, thinking it might be a dream, a shift in time, for they stood in the same places they had when she had traveled back in time. Only this time, Colin smiled and chuckled. A tear escaped her eye and rolled down her cheek as he approached her. She swayed as he reached her and swept her up in his arms, spinning her around. He lowered her along his body. His brow knitted, and he gave a slight jolt that disappeared as he set her on her feet and kissed her.

He tightened his arms around her, making it seem like the kiss would go on forever. A forever kiss. Bree didn't care. Colin was back in her arms. As he ended the kiss, more tears fell.

He wiped the tears with his thumbs as his gaze roamed her face, making it seem like a caress. "Don't cry, *mo chridhe*. I'm here. I said I would always come back to ye, and I have."

She sobbed. "Oh Colin, I've missed you so. These are happy tears, happy tears for you."

He smiled and kissed her again. "I knew ye'd figure it out. Ye are smart, my wee Bree. Ye brought me back."

She nodded and sniffled, trying to stop the flow of tears.

Colin held her with their foreheads pressed together. He drew back to glance into her eyes. "I think there's something ye need to be telling me, Bree."

Her head shifted back as she huffed and tried to pull out of his arms, but he held her tight.

"You told me the wedding was fake, but you had John make it real. Why didn't you tell me?"

Colin grinned. "It was my surprise for ye. I knew ye wanted it to be real. My plan was to oust the evil Fae, recover the stone, and travel back that night. The marriage was my wedding gift to ye, Bree." Colin tilted her chin and kissed her. "There's something else ye need to tell me."

What would he be referring to?

Colin stood back from her, keeping her in his arms.

His hand slid from her back to her lower belly, which made a slight bulge. "I hope ye will tell me that John opened the rest of my instructions before a full year, or there's something in here that doesn't belong to me. And if that is so, I will become a very angry man."

She gasped. "How did you know?"

Colin smiled. "I've memorized yer body, dreamt of ye over and over again. A little bulge won't get past me. Ye've had the flattest belly until now." Colin took her in his arms again and kissed her deeply. "I don't think I'll ever get tired of kissing ye."

"Me neither."

Colin took her hands in his and found the Stone of Love. He held it between their hands. It was warm but no longer glowing.

"How long, how long has it been?"

Bree's breath hitched, and her eyes teared. "About a month."

Colin grinned. "So, will I have a son or a daughter?"

Which one would he want? A strapping son, the image of his father, or a beautiful girl with her mom's whisky-brown hair and her father's sky-blue eyes? What would he say when he learned the truth? Would he be happy?

She glanced down and said softly, "Will it make a difference to you, one or the other?"

He tilted her chin until her eyes met his. "Whatever we have created will be of our love, and only that will matter to me."

Bree smiled and tilted her head to the side. "What if I told you one of each?"

Colin gasped, grabbed her around the waist, and spun her in a circle. She had to grab his arm. His spin nearly brought up lunch.

"Colin, you will make me dizzy if you keep doing that."

He gently set her down, and his hand shifted to her belly. "Och, I'm sorry, *mo chridhe*. I didn't hurt them, did I?"

She laughed. "No, you didn't. But do that again, and I might puke."

Colin held her as he laughed, the sound so welcome to her. Having him close again, holding her, she nearly burst into tears again.

Colin's hand found hers, and he brought it up, both holding the Stone of Love.

Bree glanced at it. "We have the Stone of Love. Where is the Stone of Fear?"

Colin took a deep breath and huffed. "It vanished when I went through the portal. It's gone."

Her gaze shifted to his. "The Stone of Fear disappeared? What about the Fae?"

Colin grinned. "Dinna fash. I completed my mission. We have the Stone of Love."

Bree glanced at him. "What now?"

Colin stood still and stared into her eyes. As his hand caressed her face, reflected in his stare was their love.

His gaze traveled the chapel interior, hers following, shifting from one window to the next until they stopped at the window holding the stained-glass depiction of love. The boxes his mother insisted on being added to each window to the chapel renovation sat under them.

He sighed, then nodded. "I know what to do. I know what we need to do with the Stone of Love."

Colin took her hand in his and moved to the stained-glass window bearing the depiction of love. Colin knelt, and when she didn't follow, he helped her kneel with him in front of the stone box.

"I wondered why your mother had these added under each window. Is this the reason?"

Colin nodded. "It is our love together that powers the Stone of Love. The strength of our love captured it. The power of our true love will protect the stone for all of mankind." She smiled as she gazed into Colin's eyes, so happy he was back.

He held the stone out, and she wrapped her hands around his.

They gazed into each other's eyes as they held the stone between them, love pouring from their hearts.

The lid on the box vanished, and together they placed the stone inside. As they sat gripping each other's hands, the lid appeared, and all the stone boxes in the chapel vanished.

Colin rose, helped her to stand, and stepped toward the chapel door. Colin stopped in the center of the chapel. Bree's hand went to her stone necklace, and she gripped it.

Colin turned to her. "What is it, *mo chridhe*?"

"I'm afraid."

Colin gathered her in his arms. "Of what?"

She hugged him and placed her ear near his heart so she felt its solid beat. Could she hold him forever?

"Of losing you again."

Colin smiled and took her face in his hands. "I'll always chase yer fears away, my wee Bree, always." He kissed her on the lips. "Brielle, no matter where I go, no matter if something separates us, ye will always and forever be my true love."

As she gazed into his eyes, a tear traveled down her cheek.

Colin wiped it away with his thumb. "Never fear that I will not come back."

Epilogue

Dunstaffnage Castle, Present Day

Bree stood at the castle's doorway, ready to join Colin for the first time as Lady MacDougall so they could officially kick off the reenactment festivities. "I'm fat. The fattest lady that ever existed is me. I am like a huge blueberry."

Professor Mac laughed. "Ye are beautiful. Ye are ripe with babies. Ye are supposed to be a blossoming flower."

She sighed.

Professor Mac leaned down and whispered, "He will only see the woman he loves and the woman who will give him children born of yer love for one another."

Bree sniffled. She could not start crying now, because she wouldn't be able to stop.

She had Mary's wedding dress from the past duplicated so she could wear it now, in the future, for the historical events. The embroidery was just as exquisite, the material handwoven to be more authentic.

The doors to the castle opened, and Professor Mac escorted her toward Colin, who stood at the entry landing overlooking the castle grounds. Her gaze went around the castle yard. People from the castle, the village, and a few old friends from her college had made the trip. They packed the grounds full of people waiting in anticipation for the first celebration from the new laird and lady.

Mrs. MacGregor, Professor Mac's wife, was there, smiling. Mrs. Abernathy dotted her eyes with a tissue. Ian, Conner, and Ronnie beamed at her. Granny MacArthur was there too, smiling as she held the arm of an elderly gentleman. Some of Colin's friends from law school and the firm were there.

Brielle's brother Dominic had even made the trip over the pond. Upon his arrival, he greeted her warmly and promised to be more involved in her life.

She glanced to her side. Marie and Ainslie were there, dressed in historical gowns. Both teared up behind their smiles. John and Hamish were next to Colin, proud and dapper. She stared at Colin. His love for her radiated from him like the sunbeam that shot through the stone.

They arrived at the edge of the landing, and Professor Mac handed her off to her husband. Professor Mac whispered, "Treat her well, or I'll tan yer hide." Colin nodded, and Bree laughed.

They had agreed to make a promise over the MacDougall stones to begin the reenactment ceremony, since this was their first year hosting as laird and lady. She'd known this moment would come, and still she teared up, knowing what it meant to Colin, her, and to the clan. She had her stone in her hand. Colin pulled his from his pocket and held it out. They clicked the gems together, making a perfect heart, just as Colin did in the hunting cabin.

He leaned down and whispered, "The MacDougalls' Iona stones, a heart stone. Representing a love for all time."

She sighed. "Our time has only begun."

"Aye, our beginning." Colin bent and kissed her, taking his time to caress her lips with his. As he finished kissing Bree, the cheers of the people echoed across the land. Colin stood holding their stones together, gazing into her eyes. She saw her love reflected in his, making her smile through her tears.

John leaned in and whispered, "Can we continue?" They pocketed their stones. John handed Colin an ornate golden chalice, and Ainslie passed Bree a matching one, the set used for centuries to begin celebrations, a tradition they planned to continue.

John said softly to them, "'Tis a good omen. The laird toasting the beginning of the reenactment celebration."

Colin agreed. "Aye, the laird has never missed one." He glanced at Bree and winked. "And he won't be missing one from now on."

They clicked chalices, and Colin announced to the crowd, "Let the celebration begin." They both drank from the cups and passed them back as the crowd cheered.

Colin placed her hand on his arm; they turned and strode back toward the doorway to the castle.

As they crossed the threshold, Bree cried out and grabbed her belly as water gushed out from under her gown. "Colin, I think our kids want to join the celebration."

Colin's eyes grew wide. "N-N-Now, Bree?"

She cried out again, and Colin swept her into his arms.

****

Stone of Love

Dunollie Castle, a few months later

Bree and Colin were on a brief holiday from work and prepared to take the twins, Evie and Ewan, for a stroll. Bree was happiest in Scotland. Each day was better and better with her new family.

Connell Law Firm had made Colin a partner. Bree was hard at work cataloging the artifacts from the chapel renovation, preparing them for the debut of the museum display. She would never have believed it, but Professor Mac was right. The Historical Society wanted the artifacts on a museum tour. They'd contracted for the next project at Dunstaffnage, the excavation of Chapel Hill, the original village area. The Historical Society selected Marie to oversee that project which started this week, and an elated John beamed that she was staying on longer at the castle. Everything had turned out well for all.

Bree held up Evie, who smiled a toothless grin complete with drool dripping from her chin. She had jet-black hair like her father, but Bree's sweet smile.

"You get cuter every day." Colin smiled as he gazed at his daughter. Brielle watched him, her heart warm with contentment.

His cell phone rang, and he checked the caller ID. He stepped into the hallway to answer it.

Bree fussed over Ewan, who wouldn't let her put his coat on. She had a mini arm-wrestling match with her husband's mini-me. "You braw wee man. Put your coat on." He waved his arm with a tiny, tight fist at the end, making her laugh. "Just like your father."

Colin stepped back into the room and sighed as he tapped his phone. Bree looked up at him. His face was downcast, and a frown sat on his mouth.

"What is it?" she said.

"It was John. The *Fae Fable Book* has changed pages."

Bree gasped. "To what story?"

Colin sighed. "The Stone of Fear. But that's not the bad news." He rubbed his neck, and Bree stood and wrapped her arms around his waist. He gathered her to him and kissed her head.

"A priest from Iona came to see the chapel and interview Marie. He has taken her. Someone kidnapped Marie."

A word about the author…

Margaret Izard, raised in the suburbs of Houston, Texas, spent her early years through college into adulthood dedicated to dance, theater, and performing. From this, she developed a love for great storytelling in different mediums. Be it movement, the spoken word, or the written word; she does not waste a good tale. She discovered romance novels in middle school, which combined her passion for romance and drama, and she has been hooked ever since. She writes exciting plotlines, steamy love scenes and always falls for a strong male with a soft heart. She lives in the Houston area with her husband and adult triplets and spends her free time crafting, dancing, and traveling. She loves to hear from her readers.

www.margaretizardauthor.com